For all my readers.

Without you there really would be no point at all.

We are the very definition of a co-dependent
relationship – but a great one!

Special shout out to readers Nia Oldall and Sophie Howard.

# *Dora*

No little girl grows up dreaming of becoming an escort. A sex worker. A whore.

Keep that in mind.

It's a job, right. A lot of people do difficult work, and many don't like their jobs. That's a fact about being an adult. We suck it up for a myriad of reasons. Maybe because we can't think of anything else to do. Or we don't believe there is anything else we *could* do, as we don't have qualifications, or opportunities, or simply the energy to draft a new CV. We do however have rent or mortgages to pay, electricity, gas, and the lure of the local pub that sells a really average Chardonnay. So, we need to make money. From time to time, miners, couriers, sous chefs, debt collectors, refuge collectors, HGV drivers, labourers on building sites, care workers (list not finite) must all complain about the way they earn money. And they are entitled to. All those roles incorporate high-pressure deadlines and have low income-growth potential. I'm just saying, none of us lives in Disneyland.

OK, PR girls, the ones in marketing and events management,

you might very well be all wide-eyed and incredulous at this moment; you might be insisting, 'But I love my job.' Good for you. You will also be thinking it is not paid well enough; you will be planning on marrying someone rich if money matters to you, or living in rented accommodation all your life if it doesn't. If you are thinking of marrying someone rich to supplement your lifestyle, to allow you to continue to pursue your dream job, then you need to pause on that thought before judging me. Look, don't take offence. I'm not saying you are like me exactly. I'm just saying maybe we're not a million miles apart. Telling it as it is, is a core skill of mine. If I ever had to write a CV, I'd include it.

Being rich doesn't really matter to me. That might surprise you.

Being valued does, and that might surprise you more, because people assume women who are prepared to accept money for sex have self-esteem issues.

Side note: being rich – obscenely so – matters to many, many of the people I am surrounded by, so I know money is power and I play the game. I know what money can and does buy. Anything. Everything. When we get to know one another a little more, I will elaborate on all of that. Let you in. Maybe even tell you how I started out. But not yet. I don't think the best relationships begin with retrospection. It's indulgent. I'm all about the moment we're in; I nod to a future when I dare. Looking back isn't my thing.

I think most sex workers would agree with me.

And that issue I mentioned, that no little girl grows up wanting to be an escort, well that's true, but they – we – had dreams. Plans. I know I did.

Today is perfect. The sun is shining just enough. The job I've just finished was perfectly fine.

Fine. He didn't want to insult me, humiliate me, urinate on me. He didn't smell. I have a good nose. Well, I say good; in fact it's a mixed blessing in my line of work. I probably should retrain as a perfumer or something. You can imagine the drawbacks of having that heightened sense in my job. The smell of a good cologne is usually guaranteed, thankfully. Men who can afford me can afford decent aftershave. But other smells come into it. His balls, neck, feet, crack. There are a lot of ways a man can become unappealing. I've learnt to breathe through my mouth. I just have to deal with it. If they do smell very badly, sometimes I suggest we shower together, take a bath. It is what it is. But today I wasn't presented with any of those issues. I actually quite like him. Or I could if I met him somewhere else. If I was someone else.

Both things are impossible. I mean, where else might we meet? It's not like I'd ever turn up at his local Neighbourhood Watch, or the monthly executive board meeting at his enormous blue-chip company, or any of the annual charitable trust meetings that he patrons, chairs or fundraises for. Cancer, modern slavery, national ballet are his causes. These are the places he hangs out when he's not with me. Being respectable. Being brilliant and philanthropic. With me, he's filthier.

I've been looking after him for about five months, and we get together every couple of weeks in a small boutique hotel in Richmond. I assume he must live or work nearby. He hasn't said, and I never probe; clients find it unnerving. I prefer hotels over private homes. My regulars are always easier jobs. I guess I enjoy them the most; or more accurately, I fear and dislike them the least. I know what I'm walking into. I can gauge their moods, their needs. It doesn't absolutely remove the risk, because people are unpredictable, but it certainly reduces it. Today we had sex in an efficient, satisfactory way. The way a couple who have been together a decent period of time and know their way around one another's bodies might. After the sex, he still had thirty-eight minutes on the clock. He'd paid up front for two forty-five-minute sessions. As he's a regular, I might have allowed him to carry over the second session, but he didn't want to. He wanted to talk.

Some of them are talkers. They think they want sex, but in fact they want company, so they pay for sex hoping that when it's all over, they can have a chat. With those clients, I see my role as something similar to that of a therapist. Therapists will hate that analogy; they will be rushing to post outraged (although carefully phrased passive-aggressive) tweets refuting any parallel. They'll be frustrated to discover I don't have any social media accounts, so they can't cancel me. I'm not trying to offend therapists. I apologise if I have. I do appreciate that very few people like their profession being put on a par with mine. I'm simply saying that if I look hard enough, I can find the similarities, and I have looked. But it's just my opinion; you don't have to get worked up. Both my clients and the clients who lie on a therapist's couch undergo a stripping-back; they are laid bare, either physically or mentally. Is it so different? Frankly, I think it's easier to take your clothes off than allow access to your deepest and darkest thoughts. Take my deepest and darkest orifices over that any time. Sorry. I crack jokes when I'm nervous. I realise that I can come across as inappropriate. I guess I am the epitome of inappropriate; it's

4

a professional hazard. I did briefly consider being a therapist, but I figured it would be exhausting. All those feelings.

All that feeling.

Obviously, I don't really do a lot of feeling in my line of work. It's a golden rule of survival.

Anyway, all he wanted to do was talk. My client – Daniel – is almost forty. He is unmarried; he tells me most of his friends assume he's gay. I don't get that vibe. Paying for heterosexual sex must be pretty low down on a gay man's list of prioritisations, even if he were still in the closet. It's quite obvious that he is in love with his best friend's wife. He talks about her all the time. When I mooted the idea, he looked horrified. Maybe horrified that I'd found him so transparent, maybe horrified because it was the first time the thought had occurred to him. I don't know. However, in the moment the thought did occur to him, he must have known his love was doomed. Sisi (the object of his adoration and idolisation) doesn't know he is in love with her, because he's a shy, nice guy who has never dared make his feelings known, not in the time before she married his bestie and certainly not since. He has placed her firmly on a high up, out-of-reach pedestal, and no other real woman can come close.

The majority of his relationships have not stumbled past the three months anniversary. He tells me that the women he's dated are too ambitious, not ambitious enough, self-centred, overly clingy, boring, exhausting … and so on and so on. It's a shame. Daniel, I admit, is no looker. He has a face only a mother could love, but he is decent, clever and very wealthy. I think he could be the answer to many women's needs, if not dreams. He has told me that he's stopped investing emotionally in relationships now. He's happy paying me twice a month (to have the sort of sex a girlfriend might tire of) and then to chat about Sisi (something I think even the most understanding girlfriend would find irritating). He is one of my favourite clients. I feel so comfortable with him that I shower before I leave. I dress in the bathroom, so he doesn't see that I've shoved my lacy knickers in my handbag and have put on a pair of sensible cotton briefs. I wear my heels until I'm outside, back on the street, and then swap into trainers. I have to maintain standards, no matter how easy-going the client is.

It's a warm late-May day; I sniff the air and can almost smell summer. I love spring, not in its own right, but because it's the predecessor to summer, my actual favourite season. I have learnt that anticipation is genuinely a gift. Hot days slow my blood and heal my bones. They take me back to being young. Younger. I'm thirty-one, so some people, like the wives, would think I am young now. But others – the daughters – would think I am old. My clients don't know I'm thirty-one. I am whatever they want me to be within a range of eighteen to twenty-six. My manager, Elspeth, and I never speak of the age issue. I earn enough to indulge in all the high-end beauty treatments I want. I use filler and Botox to build up collagen and tighten jowls; lasers to vanquish spots and redness; fat-dissolving acids to lose the extra bit under my chin and radio frequency treatment for my neck. This, combined with a strict diet and lots of sleep, means I look like the angel I most certainly am not.

I am young, old, ageless; it depends on your viewpoint. I am all things. Sometimes it feels like I'm nothing at all.

And yes, I have a manager. You might think of her as

my madam or my pimp, if you are the sort of person who thinks of your PA as a secretary. I text her to let her know I've exited the job safely. Even though he is a regular client, we always follow procedure. She texts me back instructing me to drink lots of water and reiterating the importance of keeping hydrated for beautiful skin. After most jobs, she gifts me a little beauty tip. I think it's her way of showing she cares. Texts swapped, we can both let out a sigh of relief, although we never acknowledge that we exist in a state of perpetual anxiety.

Elspeth is well worth her thirty per cent. Some girls baulk at paying the commission; they try to get clients to call them directly. A route that always leads to trouble. I think it is money well spent, because everyone knows you can't put a price on your health. Health and safety has a totally different meaning in my job. Nothing to do with donning a high-vis jacket or being given an orthopaedic chair to counter the strain of long hours at a desk. Avoiding a beating or a STD is so much more immediate, don't you think? Besides, she introduced me to an accountant who was prepared to manage my VAT and tax returns. Officially I'm registered as a self-employed clairvoyant; an extremely popular one. Without him, I'd never have got a mortgage.

Our system, if you are interested – and I find most people *are* curious – is that Elspeth's telephone number is on my business cards and the agency's website, as are those of about twenty other sex workers. She is the filter. The barrier. She vets all my potential clients. She establishes that they have funds and ideally no criminal record. She does allow some white-collar convicts, but never a perpetrator of a violent crime. My game, like every game in a capitalist society, is a matter of supply and demand. Elspeth maintains that with the sort of girls she supplies, we can afford to be choosy about our clients. She finds out what they are looking for and tells them which of her girls can accommodate their tastes. She does call us 'my girls', which annoys people who are devoted to politically correct nomenclature. We are in fact women, all above the legal age. However, all sex workers have been called much worse than 'girls'; few of us lose sleep over this matter. Elspeth sets up the rendezvous. She alerts and bribes hotel staff so they can also be invested in our well-being. There have been two occasions during my career when hotel staff have reported a 'funny feeling' about the client and the assignment has been cancelled. On another occasion, hotel staff called the ambulance.

When I arrive at an assignment, I text Elspeth to say so. She contacts the client, he transfers the funds, I receive a text from Elspeth to say she has the fee. I can then proceed. If I don't get her text confirming the deposit of the money, I leave. This administration is done in front of me, but I never discuss it with the client; I remain silent throughout the transaction. It helps create the illusion that I'd be there irrespective of the money that is changing hands. Elspeth also sets up checks at sexual health clinics, and gives advice on a range of subjects from underwear to clients with halitosis or unusual sexual proclivities (and they really do have to be unusual if they can't be catered for by one of the girls in Elspeth's portfolio). She has done her time as a sex worker and so is vigilant, practical and unsentimental. I appreciate all three things about her. She is just eight years older than I am. I suppose she embodies some sort of career path trajectory. I too might work up to the dizzy heights of managing my own girls one day. I don't have an older sister, but if I had, I imagine our relationship would be something like the one I have with Elspeth. She makes me feel a little less alone.

# 2

# *Dora*

It's not late, so I decide to catch the Tube home rather than take a cab or an Uber. I usually take cabs to jobs so I can arrive looking my glamorous best, not windswept by the elements or flustered by train delays, but I like to save money where I can and so opt for public transport when leaving, if possible. I like stations. I enjoy the sense of purpose and energy that people who have to get somewhere inevitably have. I don't mind if they selfishly push to the front of queues or jostle for space on platforms; I can forgive that human frailty of assuming their journey is more important than mine if I experience the vitality and assurance in return. Sometimes after a job, even an easy one like Daniel's, both things seep away from me and I feel a need to be recharged.

The platform isn't especially busy this evening. There are a few very tired-looking commuters, who really ought to have escaped the office a few hours ago; a couple dressed up, ready to embark on a date night – I notice that the tag is still attached to the woman's dress, and I wish I could pull it off for her before her date spots it. I can't, so I can only hope that the label scratches her slightly and she gets the opportunity to discreetly remove it herself. My eyes drift to a gaggle of students who have yet to learn how to handle their booze and have clearly peaked too early but seem unperturbed about the fact. Some of them are sitting on the platform bench, two deep, as girlfriends sit on their boyfriends' laps. Those who can't squeeze onto the bench at all loll on the tiled floor. I used to sit on platform floors. Not in abandon or despair like a homeless person might. The opposite. When I was a student, I'd sit like I was king of the world. Not queen. King. Even then I knew being a queen was still second place to being king. I wanted to be top of the world, cream of the crop, number one. I was going places from A to B, C to D, on to E … it was limitless. Endless. I thought.

I notice that one or two of the students are surreptitiously checking me out whilst continuing their rowdy, cliquey, attention-grabbing conversations. The boys are wondering whether they'll ever lay a woman like me (answer: you should probably hope not). The girls are wondering whether they'll ever afford the Burberry trench coat I'm sporting (answer: it depends on what you are prepared to pay). The station is towards the end of the line and therefore above ground. There is a waft of hash in the air and an occasional breath of cigarette smoke, despite the constant stream of public address that blares out reminding us that all forms of smoking are illegal on stations. I glance about and notice a man in his fifties furtively flick a butt to the ground. He grinds his heel to stub it out.

I turn back to the students; I marvel at their verve, their carelessness. It's beautiful and painful to watch the very young people. Like looking at a photo of your favourite place and knowing you'll never visit there again. My clients are often older than I am. Quite a bit older. Sometimes more than twice my age. There's no point in my getting hung up about that. Fastidiousness about age or attractiveness is not something I can nurture. Everyone looks for something different in their career: I benefit from job security, rising wages, flexible hours and excellent working environments. I must be accepting visually, and I am. By contrast, the men who pay what I cost get to be extremely specific about the sort of woman they want to have sex with. They can, and do, tell us what clothes, nail gel and scent to wear. They can specify black, white, Asian; blue, brown, green eyes; curly, straight, long, short, blonde, brown or red hair; tall, tiny, full-breasted, small tits, voluptuous bum, androgynous limbs; freckles, long legs, dimpled thighs, big bush or no hair down there. The list goes on. We are laid out like chocolates in a box, waiting to be devoured.

There have been a lot of men. That's possibly the thing people find most difficult to accept about me. It's not just that I'm paid to have sex; it's the fact that I've had sex with very many men. I'm often asked how many exactly. I don't know the answer. Most women have been sold the la-la, soulmate, fidelity thing, and even if their search for the elusive One means there are several along the way, that is palatable. Romantic even. I, and everything I embody, debunk the world's most comforting illusion. No one wants to hear that we're mammals, led by instinct; that sex is one of the most powerful impulses, just after hunger. Even my clients shy away from that.

I pull out my phone and tap in some notes about Daniel. Details about the day he first met Sisi, which he revealed during our post-coital conflab. Naturally I keep notes. It's nothing sinister; it's simply a level of professionalism, organisation.

I haven't always kept my files up to date, which is why I can't say how many men I've had sex with. As my career progressed, I realised that laissez-faire attitude towards my clients was unacceptable. Even a one-off encounter is now recorded. I keep notes on who they say they are and their profession; if they talk about a wife, or family, or friends; bosses or competitors often feature. It's all part of the service. They like me to remember things about them. They expect that. They are wealthy men, often important in their own field, in their own way – even those who I consider a bit sad – so they expect to be remembered. They are more alike than they imagine; than they'd *like* to imagine.

I want to count the cash tip Daniel gave me. He handed me an envelope as I left. He usually does. Some men tip. The fee goes directly to Elspeth, electronic transfer. Strictly speaking, I should declare the tips. I don't, and I don't know a single working girl who does. I don't declare them to Elspeth or the taxman. There is a certain type of man whose tips rarely have anything to do with my sexual prowess; more often than not, they are to do with his. If he thinks he's really pleased me, that he's done really well, he tips heavily. I'm a confidence boost. That's why I always behave as though I'm having the time of my life.

My phone buzzes in my hand. It's Elspeth. 'Darling, where are you?' she asks without any preamble.

'Richmond station.'

'Good, you are heading back into town?' I live in north London, as does Elspeth; neither of us really accepts Richmond is London, even if it is on a Tube line. It's Surrey. Practically provincial.

'Yes.'

'Would you like to take another job?'

'Tonight?' I'm surprised. Elspeth rarely books back-to-back appointments. She knows the importance of down time.

'I wouldn't ask, but the gentleman requested you particularly. You've been referred by a friend of his.' Neither of us is convinced the sort of men I deal with deserve the term 'gentleman'. It's a laughable euphemism, but, as such, useful. I try to limit the number of clients I take on to sixteen a month. Tops. My hourly rate is at the highest end of the sex-worker scale, so sixteen clients offers me the financial security I need. I do four a week, or some months I like to do five in a week and then take a week off when I have my period. Two to four hours, four times a week doesn't sound like a full-time job, but it can be exhausting. They grab at me, needy and greedy; expectant, entitled, like badly behaved toddlers. Besides, there are extras. Shopping for underwear and, if requested, specific outfits, visiting the beautician and hairdresser, health checks, that sort of thing. Believe me, it feels like a full-time job. However, since the pandemic, maintaining sixteen clients a month isn't always achievable. This month has been lean; I shouldn't turn away work. On the other hand, I am tired. I've just smiled for one and a half hours straight, breaking only to pout or suck.

'I don't have fresh underwear with me,' I point out, buying time to weigh it up.

'I don't think that will be a deal-breaker.' Probably not, but I have my own standards. In an ideal world I wear fresh, straight-out-of-the-expensive-packet lingerie for every liaison. Afterwards, I wash them and take them to Bravissimo, as they have bins for unwanted bras in their stores. For every kilogram they receive, they donate to charity. All the bras are apparently recycled. The usable ones go directly to women in developing countries across the world. Although I'm not sure my sheer, skimpy, peekaboo numbers make that cut; most likely they are broken down into recyclable parts. Still, at least I'm not adding to landfill. 'From my conversation with him, I think his needs are very straightforward,' Elspeth says encouragingly. 'It shouldn't be especially arduous.'

Elspeth knows my limits. She jokes that I'm the most conservative whore on her books, but she never tries to wrench me out of my comfort zone. She knows we can both make a living because many of the clients like the fact that I have a strict 'no' list. They see me as almost wholesome – well, if that's a stretch, then at least I'm not too intimidating. I enthusiastically partake in all the sex acts that cheerful girlfriends offer on special birthdays, but I don't entertain the suggestion of anything that might be demeaning, painful or cruel. There's no place for it in the fantasies I invent. The men who come to me have to be made aware of that. I might agree to be tied up. Ribbons, yes. Ropes, maybe. Handcuffs, no. There are men who like to think of me as classy and unattainable. Setting limits creates that illusion. It's amazing what people tell themselves.

'It's just with him being recommended by one of your regulars …' She leaves the thought hanging. Sometimes this is how regulars move on. They pass us on. You can't let it worry you. They are paying for sex, not a relationship. Men bore of sex they are paying for just as easily as they bore of the sex they are not paying for. It's not jealousy I feel when they move on, it's irritation. A gap opening up on my calendar is a pain. The more thoughtful regulars are perhaps aware of this and so try to suggest a replacement. It's still irritating. I guess this is how a schoolteacher must feel if a child leaves her class mid-term and a newbie arrives, all keen but anxious, needing to be shown the way of things.

'He wants to meet at …' Elspeth names a luxurious hotel in Mayfair that I know well. Some of the hotel rooms I'm invited to are bigger than my apartment, certainly markedly more sumptuous. This is one such place. The reception is enormous, and easy access – a quick in and out – seems appealing. If I agree, Elspeth will be pleased with me. Our working relationship is good. She likes it that I'm clean, sober, prompt, reliable. Not traits that can be attributed to every sex worker, but important if you are charging what we do. It's a profession. The oldest profession, we all agree on that, right? As Elspeth is ultimately responsible for my cash flow, it's important to keep her respect and goodwill.

So I say, 'I can be there by eight thirty.'

# 3

# *Dora*

The loos in the hotel lobby are dimly lit, but I make do. I rummage in my handbag and see what I have to manage with. My lenses feel gritty, so I take them out. I'm long-sighted, so his features might be a bit fuzzy, but that might be a bonus. With the tip of my finger, I dab a little lipstick on my cheeks and then on my lips. I apply lip gloss. Glad I slipped it into my bag at the last minute. Men like lip gloss. Wet lips. Obvious. I pull my hair into a messy updo because Daniel has mussed up my blow-dry. It's fine. Men like my hair off my face. They want to see what they are paying for. I fish out my lacy pants and change back into them, although doing so feels grim. I swap back into my heels. I'm not a fan of keeping heels on in bed, although I'll do it if asked. It takes some careful choreography not to tear sheets or puncture a shin with stilettos and yet still deliver the sort of service I'm famed for.

I regret accepting the job the moment I enter the room. When I was growing up my mother liked to bake. I remember she sliced vents in pies to let out steam. His eyes look like those dark slits. It's his eyes I focus on, because he's wearing a face mask that covers his chin, mouth, nose. This is not necessarily a kinky thing; it's just as likely to be a hygiene thing nowadays. I'm vaccinated and very regularly tested; he will have been given those assurances from Elspeth, as it's part of what they pay for. So the mask suggests he is particularly paranoid or considers me particularly dirty. Both things potentially lead to complications I could do without. He might be mistrustful; he might be cruel.

On the other hand, he's not expecting to be kissed on the mouth. No slobbering, no acrid breath. That's a bonus.

He is already wearing the cream towelling robe that the hotel supplies when he opens the door to me. A sign that he's keen to get down to business. My phone buzzes. Elspeth confirms he has deposited the fee for three hours of my time. Undoubtedly good money, but I'd have been happy with committing to just half of that. As my lack of eagerness is the last thing I want him to be aware of, I pull my face into an expression of virtual ecstasy; I've yet to meet a man who can read my mind. Being in the mood is not a luxury afforded to sex workers. The clue is in the name. It's work. Some girls drink champagne or do drugs to help them get there. I never do drugs but will drink the champagne if that's what the client wants. When they ask me to eat with them, I follow their lead. Some working girls limit themselves to salads when they eat with clients. I don't know why: maybe to keep a flat stomach, maybe to perpetuate the myth that women – attractive women – don't need anything as base as food to sustain them. I do not sign up to this bullshit. Firstly, I have twice almost choked on a peppery rocket leaf, and secondly, because women do eat and besides men like women with appetites. Appetites for life and sex and food.

Most important of all, I eat well when they are paying *because* they are paying – basic maths. If they order a rich, buttery dish, I do too. I'm a fan of thick, carb-rich pasta dishes, so dense and glutinous that I have to bite at the spoon. I know this one won't be wanting to dine.

He pours himself a glass of champagne, comically edges his mask to the side, knocks it back, pours another, sips that, and only then does he turn to me. He holds the bottle up. I take it from him and drink from the neck, never breaking eye contact, letting the frothing alcohol spill down my chin. The liquid singes the back of my throat. He takes off his robe, pushes me to my knees and we take it from there.

# 4

# *Dora*

'Fuck, what the hell happened?'

'I walked into a door,' I offer. When Evan called me this morning, I was in two minds about letting him see me this way. I knew he'd be distraught. I didn't want to traumatise him. I sometimes think it's almost unfair of me to be in Evan's life at all. Without me, his life is shiny perfection, but my existence smears and stains that perfection; today, I'm more likely to out-and-out shit on it. However, I'm only human, and I needed the comfort, so when he rang and said he wanted to pop over with some freshly baked sourdough bagels, bought from the new artisan bakery that has just opened near his apartment, I didn't have the strength to push him away. Which may be a bit selfish of me, but you have to understand my life is the reverse of his. Sometimes I think he is my glimmer of perfection in a big fat turd of a life. Today is one of those days.

Evan looks like he is about to cry. A sweet response from a twenty-seven-year-old heterosexual male. He is a trust-fund baby, set to inherit millions; he works for Daddy in a huge international property and land management company. I don't think anything truly awful has ever happened to Evan in his life, but instead of that fact making him annoying or condescending, he is the most sympathetic, humane being I've ever had the good fortune to encounter. Honestly? I don't think I've come across anyone quite so lovely even in a book. You couldn't make him up. He hesitates in my doorway. Normally we hug when we see one another, but he doesn't know where he can touch without causing me pain. He tenderly kisses my forehead. He is my best friend and he hates what I do, but he loves me. So, it is what it is. He plays with the cuff of his jacket. A habit of his when he is nervous. He sighs. 'Shall I put the kettle on?'

I met Evan through work, four years ago. Don't worry, he isn't one of my clients. We haven't had sex. It's that fact that makes him so special to me. Not all my work involves sex. Theoretically, legally, none of it should. You see, it's not illegal to hire an escort; if that's all I do – escort, accompany – then I'm within the bounds of the law. Men – or women if they want – can pay me to attend parties, make conversation with them and their clients: flatter, fawn, laugh at their jokes. I met Evan at one of those parties. It was fairly adorable really, looking back on it. He had just turned twenty-three, out of his depth but thrilled to be playing with the big boys even though it transpired he had no idea what the game was, let alone the rules. The investment bank that was throwing the glamorous Christmas party has a lot of cash tied up in Evan's father's company, apparently. Evan and his father had been invited along, although only Evan had accepted the invite. When I say glamorous, I mean dozens of four-metre-high Christmas trees sparkling with decorations custom-made by Tiffany's. I'm talking dancers from the Royal Ballet and singers from the Royal

Opera House offering entertainment, and waiters dressed in Paul Smith offering unlimited vintage champagne and Russian caviar. No one attending wanted subtlety.

No party is complete without pretty girls, and whilst there were a few female employees and clients in attendance, they were definitely in the minority. Besides, as I heard a senior-looking employer comment on the night, 'You can't shit on your own doorstep nowadays. HR are all over it. Fucking hashtag MeToo. Death knell to fun.'

'Would you want to, though? Hardly any of them are worth a second glance,' responded his colleague. 'Bring in the clowns, I say.'

We were the clowns. The escorts. Girls discreetly sprinkled throughout the party, there to be noticed, but we had to go under the radar of HR. It was fixed up at a high yet untraceable level. We were all dressed in our black-tie best: beautiful, nubile, consequence-free women, ready to divert and decorate. A job like that one isn't particularly hard work. Accepting obvious compliments, laughing at not especially funny jokes, chewing on your bottom lip when you listen to an explanation about a company's fiscal policy doesn't really stretch a RADA-trained actress. Even a part-trained one. However, I knew that the job would get increasingly tiresome as the night wore on. Some of the guests would not be satisfied with flirtation. Inevitably the question of whether I provided extras would be broached. I wasn't above that. Indeed, by that point in my career, I was a fully fledged, no-holds-barred call girl, but I'd had a busy week and wanted an easy night. Plus, I'd borrowed my dress and didn't want to return it damaged, so it was best if I avoided ending up on my knees. Rebuffs always had to be delivered carefully so not to cause affront; a drunk, offended man is never a pleasant prospect. I knew it was important to find someone who wouldn't embarrass either of us by asking for extras in the first place.

It was about two thirds of the way into the evening when I spotted Evan, standing alone in the corner of the room, near a vodka ice luge. By the look of him he had indulged in his share of free alcohol. He was glassy-eyed and swaying a little. I noted his youth and felt almost sorry for him. I made a beeline in his direction and started chatting, the way we are instructed to.

'Wow, this party is amazing,' I commented, all astonished and awestruck, even though I'd attended several similar parties that season in London as well as Dubai, New York and Milan. I thought he might be finding the set-up rather extraordinary and therefore would appreciate someone else appearing amazed and excited. I hadn't factored in his extreme wealth, which meant he'd attended sumptuous events such as these since he was a child. He wasn't particularly impressed. Later, I understood he had drunk too much because he was bored rather than overawed.

He smiled good-naturedly and nodded. 'The women are extraordinarily hot.' The way he said this wasn't a come-on. In fact, he blushed the moment the words were out of his mouth as he clearly recognised it could be taken as such. He rushed to clarify. 'I mean, the canapés and champagne are great, of course, but there seems to be an especially high count of beautiful women here tonight. Are all the women who work in banking totally stunning? If so, I'm definitely in the wrong field.' He grinned. Still a boy, but even then, I could see the man he would become; it was clear he'd never have to worry about attracting beautiful women.

'These women don't work in banking.'

'Oh, then they are the girlfriends of the guys who do,' he asserted, nodding.

'You think? Look closely. Are any girlfriends ever that adoring, that obliging, that fascinated?' I asked. He looked confused, possibly at my cynicism. I realised it was entirely possible, since he was young and rich and handsome, that he had only ever experienced entirely adoring girlfriends. 'They are escorts. They are hired to tart the party up. Literally,' I explained.

'No way?' And it was a lovely reaction, because he didn't judge; he seemed amused rather than disgusted or lechy, which are more standard responses.

His reaction inspired me to push on. 'I know because I'm one of them. I'm an escort. I'm being paid to be here.'

'Really, and how do you go about getting into that sort of work?' he asked seriously, without skipping a beat. He tried to pull his face into a more sober, attentive expression. Exactly the sort of expression a drunk might aim for if he was asking someone how they became a brain surgeon or a circus ringmaster or a librarian. He was curious about my unusual career choice and wanted to take me seriously, which was novel and kind. Most men ask what my hourly rate is.

'I was a drama student. I view this sort of work as decent role-play practice. Not quite qualifying for points towards the Equity card, but arguably more dignified than being a Legoland entertainer.' He smiled. I had dropped the breathy, astonished voice and was being straight. 'It offers flexible hours and decent enough cash. More than I could earn as a barista.' I threw out a big grin. The explanation I gave him as to how I got into this work wasn't the truth, the whole truth and nothing but the truth. There was more to it than that, nuance, but in a nutshell, those were the advantages as I saw them.

'*Was* a drama student?' Evan asked. 'Have you graduated now? Will I have seen any of your work?'

'No. I never graduated.' I was grateful that he didn't ask why. I didn't want to have to lie to him.

'I'm in property.' He said it as though he was trying out the phrase. 'Not as glamorous as your line of work.'

'It's not all parties.'

'Oh.' The tips of his ears turned pink as he gathered my meaning.

'Escorting earns a few hundred quid for a couple of hours' work. Easy money. Good money, I think you'll agree.' I cast my eye over his suit. It cost way more than a few hundred quid by the look of it; maybe he'd think an escort's salary was loose change, so I qualified, 'Well, most people would class it as good money. But once you take off the cost of a blow-dry, a manicure, dress hire, taxis and a manager's commission – all necessary costs – I earn less than half that. At some point – and it's hard to pinpoint exactly when, as these things sneak up insidiously – it is no longer good money. It's not even just enough money.' I shrugged, paused, took a sip of my drink and then clarified, 'So, you know, needs must.'

'Right.'

I think I was testing him. Could I scare him off? Did I want to? My conversation was unguarded, potentially incendiary, certainly challenging. I wanted to catch and hold his interest. That was vitally important to me from the get-go. I didn't have many friends. I still don't. There was a connection, straight away; I felt that.

I didn't want him to pity me, so I added, 'Keeping trim is crucial in my business, but even I can't live on fresh air alone.' I hoped my beam would take him far away from the reality of the poverty I'd fought and lost. Of course, it did, because he couldn't envisage my life. He did not know what it was like for your stomach to rumble embarrassingly, painfully, as you sat in an interview trying to persuade someone to give you a job that paid the basic minimum. I didn't suppose he'd ever come home to a freezing-cold flat that had had the electricity cut off, or worse still, returned to find his possessions piled outside and the lock changed because he'd failed to meet the rent. Food, rent, electricity, gas, council tax. Living in London is expensive. So yes, the plan was to simply escort, to smile, nod and laugh, but when the bills stacked up, earning a bit extra for a hand job, more again for a blow job, seemed like the only solution. By the time a client suggested he'd just like to put his tongue between my legs, how much for that exactly?, the lines were so blurred it seemed squeamish to say no. Churlish. Foolish.

'Let's just say my career has been more snakes than ladders,' I commented wryly. Evan laughed out loud, and I found I liked making him laugh. I still do. More than anything.

# 5

# *Dora*

Evan has never tried it on. Not that night we first met, nor in the weeks that followed when our friendship blossomed, or indeed since. Naturally, I wondered whether he was gay. Look, I'm not so arrogant that I think every man on the planet *has* to fancy me, but most twenty-something men do have a crack at their female best friends sooner rather than later, usually when they are going through a bit of a dry patch romantically. And since Evan and I spend an inordinate amount of time talking about sex, you'd think that curiosity alone would be enough of a motivator for a drunken miscalculated grope. It has never happened.

For the record, I've never made a move on him either.

Some working girls do manage to have boyfriends and sustain their careers, but it's never appealed to me. Too confusing. I deal with enough emotional situations without coming home to a jealous boyfriend. It's easier to keep things platonic. Cleaner. Keeping sex separate from love keeps the mind focused; avoids any unnecessary, debilitating fog. I realise that makes me sound damaged or callous. Go figure. Look, I'm not a man-hater, which, when you think of the sort of men I meet on a daily basis, basically demonstrates a level of hope in humanity that puts me on a par with, I don't know, the Pope or something. I mean, if I wanted to be a man-hater, I have evidence enough to write them off as dumb, selfish, cruel. So yay me, right?

But yeah, Evan and I do a lot of talking about sex. Mostly we talk about his sex life/romantic life/love life, call it what you will, and my work. He says my honesty on the matter is refreshing and helpful in relation to understanding women. I've tried to warn him that understanding a hooker's point of view on sex is unlikely to be relatable when dealing with the trust-fund girls he dates. The conversations we have about sex run along the lines of him asking me things such as 'But isn't it, like, gross? Touching all that old-man flesh?'

'Sometimes. Not always.'

'How do you get off on it?'

'I don't get off on it. I never come at work.'

'But you don't have sex outside work,' he pointed out.

'Correct,' I admitted. He knows far too much about my life.

He paused, ruminated. 'God, that sucks.'

'You get used to it.' You never get to like it.

'Do you ever do women?'

'Occasionally.'

'But you're straight?'

'Yes.'

'Then how?' This showed more insight than most men generally muster. The majority of men simply enjoy the thought of a bit of woman-on-woman action; few reflect on what it must be like to have this sort of sex if your proclivities are not aligned.

I tried to explain. 'It's not a million miles away from the work of a beautician who waxes, a nurse who carries out smears, midwives who have ringside seats. It's just a body part.'

'I don't think you are comparing like-for-like.'

'My point is, for many different professionals, handling flesh is just part of the job. I think being a chiropodist might be worse. Feet are hideous.'

'Or a dentist,' suggested Evan, understanding me. 'That weird smell on floss is disgusting.'

'Exactly.'

'What's it like to be, you know, you?'

'A sex worker?'

'To be *you*.' I think this is one of the best questions he's ever asked me. I'm not sure it really falls under the banner of 'conversations I have with Evan about sex'. At least, that's not how I interpreted it.

'It's like being everyone else, I guess. In some ways. I mean, I feel the things everyone else does. I get excited, scared, happy, fed up. People don't think that. I mean, it's obvious if you think about it for, I don't know, maybe a nanosecond, but people don't think about us for that long. Not the people who use our services, or even those who don't.'

Evan shook his head. 'You are not like everyone else, Dora.'

'That's rude.'

He smiled. 'No, it's not meant to be. I say you're not the same, because you are more. You are your own person. You're wild.'

Another time he asked, 'What's the funniest thing you've ever been asked to do?' I liked this question. It showed he wasn't hung up on the weirdest, the most demeaning. Men who ask you to retell shameful moments are not that far apart from the men who create them in the first place. Evan's question showed compassion and a sense of humour.

'One man once wanted me to wear nothing other than an apron he'd brought along. Then he wanted me to spank his bare bottom with a wooden spoon. He strained to watch in the mirror as his wobbling arse turned slightly pink. The apron smelt of chocolate cake. As he left, he told me it was his mother's and he that he'd never washed it since she died. The spoon was hers too. I really don't want to unpick that fantasy.' Evan laughed out loud. I did too. We both laughed until it hurt. Until we couldn't catch our breath.

He's not laughing now as his eyes roam over my bloody lip, my black eye.

'Have you been to the hospital?'

'Yeah, I went last night. I needed them to glue my eye. I thought my ribs were broken.'

'Are they?'

'Luckily not.'

I hobble through to the kitchen, trying not to wince too obviously. I clearly fail, as Evan insists that I sit down; he makes tea, sets the bagels on a plate, tries to behave normally. I can see from the way he is holding his shoulders – high around his ears – that he is furious, scared. 'Have you been to the police?'

'No.' Evan asks a lot of good questions; this is a stupid one.

'Won't the hospital report it?'

I shrug. 'Maybe, but I said I fell down the stairs.'

'And they believed you?'

'Probably not. They'll think my boyfriend did it to me. Not

much can be done about a domestic if the victim won't call it out.'

'Oh well, that's all right then,' Evan says sarcastically as he slams down the just-boiled kettle onto the kitchen counter. I see drops of water jump out of the spout and splash on his hand.

'Careful,' I mumble.

He doesn't seem to have noticed the scald and looks confused. 'It's you who has to be careful, Theodora.'

'Oh, my full name, you really are serious about this.' I try to smile, but it hurts my cut lip. Laughing is out of the question.

'Don't joke, how can you joke? Look at you.'

Actually, I haven't been able to bring myself to check my reflection in the mirror. I don't need to. The severity of my beating was reflected in the faces of the taxi drivers I encountered last night – the one who refused to take me to the hospital – 'Nah, love, you'll get blood on my seats' – and the one who tenderly helped me into the car and refused to accept any money for the fare. I saw my injuries on the face of the receptionist, the nurse who glued me, the one who X-rayed me, and now, most tragically, on Evan's face.

'Who did this to you? I can go after him.' I roll my eyes. 'I can send people after him. You know I have the resources.' He does. He doesn't talk about it directly, but over the years, I've come to understand that he is spectacularly wealthy, or at least his family is. He has the sort of reserves available to him that most of us can't even conceive of. I suppose he'll inherit shedloads in the future.

'He said his name was Jonathan, but I don't imagine it is. Elspeth can't reach him on his numbers or trace him through his transaction. I've described him as best I can to her so that he doesn't find his way to any of the other girls, but he was wearing a mask throughout. There's nothing more to be done.' I shrug.

Evan carries two strong, hot mugs of tea to the small kitchen table where I am sitting. He spoons three sugars into one and stirs it vigorously, I don't take sugar, he knows that. He pushes the mug my way and then stirs vast amounts of sugar into his mug too. We both need help with the shock.

'Why do you do this?' he asks. His upset and frustration make him sound impatient and defeated in one sentence. 'There are other ways to make a living, you know.'

This is the question he returns to most frequently. He's right, I should get out of this. I know that, but I haven't got the energy to pore over websites advertising poorly paid positions; I dread the thought of writing the necessary sycophantic covering-letter emails. How would I explain what I've been doing with myself this last decade? I've painted myself into a corner.

'A job for life,' I reply.

'However long or short that might be,' he adds sardonically.

I try to strike a note of cheerful nonchalance. 'I'm attracted to the sense of tradition. Women have been doing this forever. Jesus's best friend found gainful employment this way.'

'Stop it, Dora.'

I bounce on, hating the compressed intensity that is clouding the room. I always try to make a joke when I hurt the most. It means I sometimes come across as a bit weirdly dismissive, but better that than appearing vulnerable. 'Hey, at least there are always job opportunities. Whores and funeral directors, can't do without them.'

'Don't you like yourself?'

I pretend not to hear him. I'm not up to going deep on this right now. 'Who am I harming?'

'No one other than yourself,' he mutters. He drops his head into his hands, takes a deep breath, then straightens to look me in the eye. He knows not to be overly judgy with me, because no bestie relationship can withstand an excessively robust examination of behaviour; humans are too imperfect for that. The point of a bestie is to offer support, understanding, make tea, pour vodka. He tries to make it clear that I don't disappoint him, but the world does. 'I could get you a job,' he offers, not for the first time. He sees me behind the reception desk in the impressive lobby of his father's London office. Lots of glass and chrome. No doubt I'm wearing a pencil skirt and killer heels in his imaginings.

I don't know anything much about Evan's daddy's industry – property – but I do know, for certain, I don't want to work there, even if his father would agree to the idea. I don't want to owe Evan. I can't think of a polite way to say as much, so I just keep quiet. The silence gnaws.

'Do you want to talk about it?'

'Not really.'

He sighs again, frustrated, sad. I match his sigh with one of my own, hating that I'm taking on his pain too. He should keep it to himself. I have enough of my own to handle. I agreed to him coming here because I thought he would comfort me, cheer me up. My mind flings itself back to the hotel room last night, even though it's the last place I want to be.

'It's all a bit of a blur. One minute I was on my back, eyes closed, giving a good impression of being in the throes. It seemed, as Elspeth had promised, straightforward. The cuffs

33

came from nowhere. *Click*, and my arms were pinioned to the headboard. The blow was a surprise too.'

Evan winces.

It's been my experience that life is full of surprises, few of them good.

I take a sip of my tea. It's not enough. 'Do you have a cigarette?' I ask.

'I thought you'd given them up.'

I roll my eyes and he concedes the point. It isn't the moment to point out I might die a slow, horrible death, since we are both scared shitless that I might die a sudden, horrible one. He fishes around in his jacket pockets and pulls out a packet of Lucky Strikes. The only brand he ever smokes. He once told me that in the 1920s, Lucky Strikes were marketed as a symbol of female liberation. Young women were encouraged to light up their 'Torches of Freedom'. Cigarettes were an emblem of women's aspirations for equality and a better life. Ha ha, the irony. He lights one, hands it to me. As I inhale deeply, he lights another for himself.

'He had big hands and the first punch landed on my ear and jaw.' I make a little motion to point to the injury. Silly really. Evan knows where my ear is. 'I screamed, as much from shock as pain, sucked at the air. My eyes sprang open instinctively, but I wished they hadn't, because he was staring right back at me, and I could see he was enjoying my fear.'

'Fuck's sake.' Evan slaps his hand down on the table, causing it to jolt. The tea judders in the mugs, the haphazardly piled magazines slip a fraction. I swallow and stare at him.

'Please don't.'

'Sorry.'

34

'I won't tell you any more if you are going to act like this.'

'No, really, I'm sorry.'

'And you can't pity me.'

'For fuck's sake, Dora. Look at you. How could I not? Everyone pities someone. It's a good thing. It keeps us humane. It propels us towards empathy and charity.'

'Or superciliousness and arrogance.'

'Why do you always have to make everything so complex?'

'Because everything is,' I mutter. I stay silent. I'm scared. He thinks I'm sulking.

'Look, I'll try and muster a response that you think is appropriate,' he says, biting back his frustration, 'Just go on. Please.'

The please is painfully authentic. 'I kicked and struggled, but he easily overpowered me. I mean, he was twice my size and my hands were tied. Hardly a fair fight, I think you'll agree. He cuffed my ankles together so I could do little else than squirm away from him. But not far enough away from him.' I take a drag on the cigarette, hold the smoke in my lungs until it hurts; one pain distracting me from another. A life philosophy?

'Did you call out for help? Did anyone help?'

I glare at him. I don't like the implication that I could have helped myself more, avoided this. He reads my expression correctly.

'Sorry, sorry.'

'Yes, I called out, but he clamped his hand over my mouth as soon as I did. I tried to bite him, but he said he'd kill me if I made any noise. I believed him.'

Evan reaches for my hand as I tap the ash into a discarded Diet Coke can. He squeezes it, carefully. 'Of course, who wouldn't believe him. This is not your fault.'

I pull away from him, irritated. I don't think this is my fault, I haven't thought so for a moment. 'Anyway, then he gagged me. A gag and two set of cuffs makes me think that this was a thought-through attack. Even something that he's done before, maybe several times.'

There are men out there who hate women who do what I do, or who don't value us at all – not even enough to hate us. Quite a lot of men think that way; some think they have the right to hurt us, even kill us.

'And then he lost control?' Evan asks.

I shake my head. 'It wasn't a frenzied attack. That was what was most scary. I don't know how long it lasted. The blows were spaced out, a minute between each. Less? More? Enough time to register the pain, and most cruelly, believe it might stop, only to feel another punch.'

The pain of each stike was excruciating. I remembered falling from a swing as a child, landing on my knees, hurt and shock invading my body, leaving me breathless. It was like that, over and over again. I became conscious of every individual cell and blood vessel bruising or bursting, each nerve ending anticipating, then taking, a blow. I could hear and feel my heart thumping thunderously in my ears.

'I scrambled about as much as the restraints would permit, trying to avoid the blows. I tucked my head into my chest to create a protective ball, but he just punched my ribs and spine.' Evan's hand is quivering. I get the sense he wants to rain down punches of his own. 'I closed my eyes and kept them squeezed shut throughout, so he was at least denied the pleasure of seeing my fear.' I don't tell Evan that at one point I took myself outside my body. It's a trick I employ sometimes when I'm on the job. I imagine looking down on myself, as though whatever is happening is happening to someone else. It helped. I was able to tell her – the woman it was happening to – that it was going to be OK, that she'd get through it. But I couldn't maintain the illusion for long. With each additional hefty punch, I violently re-entered my body. The pain was searing. Outrageous. 'Have you ever been in a fight Evan? Ever been punched?'

'No. Only accidentally on the rugby pitch.' He looks embarrassed, but I'm glad. 'Did he speak to you?'

'No,' I lie. 'Just when I thought it was never going to stop, it did. He got dressed and then unlocked the cuffs. Left.'

'Just like that?' Evan is incredulous.

'There's no accounting.' I trust Evan, like him better than every other being on the planet, but I can't tell him the scariest part of all. I just can't. If I repeat what my attacker said, the words will gather more power. I want to silence him. I want to ignore him. Deny him. Forget him. Only I can't. His words keep going around and around my head. *You disgust me. Stop what you are doing. Stop it now. Or next time will be worse. Next time will be the last time.* I shudder. 'Can we talk about something else now?' I ask.

Evan eyes me carefully. 'Yes, actually I do have something totally different to talk to you about. Are you up for a gentle walk?'

# 6

# *Dora*

It feels surprisingly good to be out of the flat. To have fresh air brush my face. Well, as fresh as the air ever is in London. I spend a lot of time indoors. In hotel rooms, exerting myself. In my flat, preparing for that exertion or recuperating from it. In bars, restaurants, at parties. It surprises people to discover that I grew up on a farm in the north of England. I don't miss it. I like being behind closed doors. My flat is above a dry cleaner's, which means all the rooms are constantly infused with a particular, peculiar chemical smell. Most people don't like the smell, but I am OK with it. I like any smells associated with cleaning: Pledge, Cif, Flash, Ariel, they lift me the way Jo Malone Lime and Basil might bring joy to another woman. Besides, because the flat is over a dry cleaner's, it fell within my budget.

It has original features – beautiful high ceilings, wooden floorboards and elegant fireplaces – but the bathroom and kitchen are modern. Perfect. I own it. To be exact, I own about seven per cent of it and the rest is covered by an enormous mortgage, but it is mine in name and that's important to me.

Vital. I'm someone a lot of people think they own. They are all wrong. I'm my own boss, and the flat reminds me as much. I never take clients there; even Elspeth doesn't have this address. It's my sanctuary, and I don't use that word lightly, especially on a day like today. I've painted it in dark Farrow & Ball shades and maxed out on velvet curtains, cushions, sofas, chairs in dark blue, jade and plum. My inspirational Pinterest board is basically Moulin Rouge meets Folies Bergère. I live near King's Cross, and whilst the area has undergone extensive redevelopment in recent years, to purge it of its less salubrious connotations, sometimes it crosses my mind that I couldn't really be more of a cliché unless I chose to live in Soho.

Evan and I head for Granary Square. Don't think green and leafy; it's a series of concrete steps flowing onto a concrete square, but its super-stylish and there's a brilliant coffee shop nestled amongst the bars and restaurants that Evan swears sells the best coffee in London. I buy the coffees. We take turns, because I'm always having to remind Evan that he shouldn't pay for other people's stuff. It can ruin a friendship. When I say as much, he laughs and says he wouldn't have friends if he didn't pay for other people's stuff. He would, though, he'd have me. 'What can I say?' he jokes. 'I like being liked, it's my modus operandi. Without external approval, I'd have to depend on self-worth; it's exhausting always having to come up with that.'

We settle down with our coffees and watch kids duck and dive in and out of the jets of water that come up from underground. The children seem to love the element of surprise, and the fact that they often get caught out by the sequencing of the flow and end up soaked; personally, I like my fountains to work with gravity and flow downwards.

'Shouldn't you be at work today?' I ask. Evan has a very loose relationship with his contractual working hours. It's a perk of being the boss's son.

'They can call me if anything urgent crops up.'

They won't, though. If there's a problem, his underlings, or even his (nominal) boss, will sort it without bothering him. Evan doesn't have a clue how much he is protected. It's not his fault. It's just the way it is. He was born into extreme wealth, privilege, but he had no more control over that than I had over being born to a poor family in a country that no longer exists. My family owned a newspaper kiosk and made a living selling comics and newspapers in Yugoslavia until around my first birthday, when war meant they were forced to flee. They were lucky to find asylum in England.

I don't remember living anywhere other than here – this is my home – but my parents always had an aura of displacement about them. Not that they were made to feel unwelcome here. They were, if not welcomed, then certainly treated with a sort of apathetic tolerance; it's simply that learning a new language and culture is exhausting and relentless. Truthfully, they never seemed to fully commit to Britain. Wouldn't? Couldn't? I don't know, but they didn't. They missed their old life, the friends and relatives they'd left behind. I grew up to a chorus of sentimental (no doubt rose-tinted) reminiscing. They talked of their old home with such wistful joy: the summers spent at the lakes or mountains, the winters in the city, pastries and grilled meats that were apparently beyond compare. I was always vaguely embarrassed when my father played the gajde (it's a sort of bagpipe), and I wondered why, let alone how, they'd managed to bring it with them when they left their homeland in such a hurry. They tried to speak to me in their mother tongue, but I would always reply in English. I know this frustrated them, perhaps hurt them, so I made up by being an extremely studious child, grabbing every opportunity offered at the local schools that did well on the Ofsted reports. I became that cliché – the driven immigrant, determined, bright, dirt poor but with big dreams.

My father died of a heart attack when I was seventeen; my mother moved to Serbia not long after. I refused to go with her, because whilst my parents had been waxing lyrical about delicious baklava that melts in your mouth, I followed the trials of the war criminals on the news and in the broadsheets. The most recent estimates suggest that around one hundred thousand people were killed during the war we ran from. Over two million people were displaced. Horrendous. Obviously. No words. But the thing I read that disturbed me the most was that an estimated twelve to fifty thousand women were raped during the war. Brutalising women is not a new weapon of war, but what bothered me particularly was the discrepancy in the estimate, the scarcity of actual reporting. I was afraid of going to a country where women couldn't say what was done to them. So I stayed here. See how that's working out for me. #Peachy. I take a deep breath and a bruise on my ribs twinges.

Safe to say, Evan and I have had vastly different formative experiences. He has never been hungry, forced to eat cheap, tasteless, nutrition-free crap. He once told me that on his seventeenth birthday, his father gifted him a brand-new BMW. It cost over twenty-five thousand pounds. He wrote it off just three weeks after passing his driving test because he was driving at speed on a narrow, bendy country road. The important thing to take from the story is that Evan's father said Evan was in no way to blame for the accident; it was all his fault as he shouldn't have gifted a kid such a powerful car. Like any right-thinking parent, he maintained that the important thing was that Evan had walked away unhurt. The following week, he bought Evan another car. It was a more expensive model, but he did insist on putting a speed tracker on it. I bet he slept well that night, congratulating himself on his brilliant parenting. Evan is three and a half years younger than I am, so at the point when he was first running cars off the road, I was just twenty-one, had dropped out of drama school and was already turning tricks. Sorry for the dated expression; it's hard to be woke about selling sex.

Evan went to a good school. His words. Rich, posh people refer to schools with their own ski chalets, theatres, groundsmen and chapels as 'good'; the rest of us would call them 'un-fucking-believable'. He got decent A levels – decent, not brilliant – and went to university, where he drank a yard of beer on a regular basis, played rugby for his hall of residence and had sex with a lot of hopeful, excitable young women who had attended schools similar to his. He didn't feel under any urgent pressure to get a first or a 2:1, he did not have to fight and claw his way through the ferocious, endless competition to get onto a graduate scheme. He knew when he left university that he had a job at his father's company waiting for him. More than that, one day the company would be his if he wanted it and didn't completely fuck up. Sometimes Evan says he isn't really that interested in property and that he's a bit bored. He expresses a wish that his father was involved in something 'sexy' like film or social media. When he says this sort of thing, I have to concentrate really hard on not rolling my eyes. Instead, I suggest he tries to find work in one of those fields if they interest him more. 'Good idea,' he comments. 'Maybe I'll ask Dad if he knows anyone.' I know, jaw-drop. He doesn't even do that, though. It's not his fault. Not really. It's just his norm.

Besides the job, when he turned twenty-one he was handed a literal key to the door. The door of a two-bedroom penthouse apartment in central London that his father apparently described as 'a decent starter flat'. My guess, it cost close to two million. Evan was also given a shitload of money to help cover the bills (in case the salary he earned and the rent he charged his mate who had the other bedroom wasn't enough). Here is something we should all keep in mind. I had a psychologist client who once told me that there's a bit of our brains (I think it's called the prefrontal cortex) that helps us make responsible decisions. Imagine, a specific bit of the brain devoted to that function. Here's the thing, though, that bit does not fully develop until we are twenty-five years old. *Twenty-five*. WTF? Come on, evolution, catch up. Twenty-five years old is too late.

Like, for me. As if I had any choice by then.

For Evan? Well, let's just say he had enough resources and space to really fuck up by twenty-five, so it's to his credit that he didn't kill himself or anyone else. He could have. He has enough money to give him licence to do anything. But then I suppose even killing someone wouldn't be an insurmountable problem. He would always be able to bail himself out of jail, hire a cracking lawyer, and even if he did end up in prison, I guess he'd pay other cons to make his life more bearable inside. The only thing stopping men as wealthy as Evan from doing vicious, terrible things is their sense of decency and decorum, maybe a concern for reputation. His family's, if not his own.

Evan didn't kill anyone. He just partied. Hard. So, well done, Evan.

Evan's father has offices all over the world, and so when we first met, Evan glided from London to New York to Hong Kong to Sydney. First-class flights all the way. There were token business meetings in boardrooms at the top of skyscrapers, and profound parties in bedrooms at the top of luxury hotels. The parties were fuelled by alcohol, drugs and women; some of whom were possibly paid to be there, whether Evan was aware of it or not. At the time, he described the parties as 'awesome' and considered them his birthright. He is not wrong about that exactly, which shows we live in a fucked-up world.

Sometimes he asked me to go with him on these business trips. I always refused. 'I can't afford the time off,' I would point out.

'I'll pay for your time.'

'You'll hire me?'

'Not for sex, for your company. Just so you can have a holiday but you're not out of pocket.'

'Busman's holiday going to parties with creepy businessmen.'

'We wouldn't have to party. We could see the sights.'

'No thanks.'

I get the feeling Evan is tiring of the parties now. The pandemic put an end to his days (and nights) of bouncing from one continent to the next. Like nearly everyone, he was tasked with working from home, which made it more apparent that little of his working day involved actual work. Quite quickly he settled into a routine that meant he spent his mornings juicing kale and celery and flicking through his phone, smirking at not-that-funny memes. In the afternoons, he'd lift weights or maybe do an online yoga class with me. At his suggestion, we were in one another's support bubble throughout all the lockdowns. Thank God. I don't think I could have endured a year of seeing no one other than men who paid. The pandemic has been hard on sex workers, even top-of-the-range ones like me. The better clients followed government rules and recommendations and decided that meeting hookers, which might lead to infecting their wives with a deadly disease, a step too far. That left us with the less thoughtful clients. Bear in mind, I'm dredging a very shallow pool. Evan and I played drinking games together, we worked our way through a fairly complex soupology recipe book, and we did a few thousand-piece jigsaws.

By the time he was finally able to return to the office, he'd changed. He didn't rush back to partying; instead he began limiting drink to weekends only and not doing drugs at all. He demonstrated a keenness to be productive that had been notably lacking in the past. His colleagues don't actively depend on him, because he is still inclined to go AWOL, either to visit me or go shopping or indulge in a very long lunch (either with or without a client), but nor do they dismiss him entirely. It's progress.

My point is, Evan isn't a totally hopeless waste of space like people imagine trust-fund babies to be. He just operates within the confines of his experience. Don't we all. The difference is, despite his global travel and countless opportunities to meet the wealthiest and most influential people of our era, his experience somehow remains limited. Basically, he doesn't have a clue what it's like to be anyone other than him. But he means well.

'Does this coffee taste OK to you?' he asks now.

I shrug. 'Fine.' I don't have a very developed palate. If you think of the things I've swallowed – literally and metaphorically – it's a blessing. I find people who claim to be coffee connoisseurs and go on about the origin of a bean and the coffee bean journey pretentious, frankly. Whilst I've faked interest in more grim subjects than coffee and would normally humour Evan, I'm not in the mood today. 'I'm not moving, I hurt too much,' I state. 'If you don't like this particular coffee any more, then you can go thirsty or go get a fresh one from somewhere else on your own, but I'm not moving.'

'No, of course not. I wasn't going to suggest …' Evan doesn't finish his sentence. He leans back against the bench. I lie down carefully, my head on his lap. I close my eyes and let the sunlight land on my lids. I can feel the warmth of his thighs. It's comforting.

'What is it you want to talk to me about?' I ask. I could do with a distraction.

'OK, well it's big, and I've been meaning to talk about it for a while …' He breaks off. I freeze. For some time, Evan has been mooting the idea of moving to LA or, sometimes, NY. Totally dissimilar cities; the thing they have in common is they are not here. Whenever he mentions either place, I show support, fake excitement, tell him to pursue whichever opportunity he is contemplating. Whatever dream he is playing with. The truth is, I do not want him to leave and just wish he could make the most of what he has here. If he announces he's moving, I'll be broken. He wouldn't do that to me today, would he? He has to see that timing would suck. I hold my breath, he continues, 'You know being a trust-fund baby is pretty much a core part of my identity, equal with my sexual orientation and gender?'

'Yes,' I reply carefully, unsure where this is going but willing to indulge him. Evan talks about himself a lot this way. My clients talk about themselves a lot too. I'm a good listener. I settle in. Evan is constantly roller-coastering; even though he's clean now, his moods are still extreme. Sometimes supremely confident, other times beleaguered by self-doubt. It's because he's not busy enough. Existential crises are a rich person's indulgence, along with sourdough pumpkin-seed bread, and fresh-cut flowers being delivered weekly to your home. He often wonders whether he would have been a better person if he'd had to struggle. Should he donate more to charity? Hell, maybe the lot? Should he travel? 'Experience, you know, *more*.' He's tried to find meaning before. He's read a lot of self-help manuals, and there was that period when he thought about becoming a Buddhist. I don't dislike it about him. I hear people say, 'I don't know what I believe in', and I'm jealous of them because they are at least assuming there is something to believe in. It suggests an openness, a malleability. I'm calcified.

'I think people can't really understand me fully without knowing that about me – the fact that I'm a trust-fund kid so I have to let people know I'm wealthy. You know. Like it's not something I can hide.'

'Rich, you're rich, not just wealthy,' I point out. 'Wealthy suggests a level of restraint and modesty.'

'Right. Exactly, that's just it, you get it. You get me. But people find it overwhelming. Most people are jealous.'

'They are,' I agree with him.

'Not you.'

'I *am* jealous, I just bury it deeper.'

Evan grins. My eyes are still closed, but I feel it ripple

through his body. I know him very well. 'No. No, you are different,' he insists.

I am very used to men telling me they know me better than I know myself. Few of them think better of me than I do, so I allow Evan's misconception to slide.

'I think we should get married.'

# 7

# *Dora*

I laugh out loud and wait for his punchline. The air stays still, and the silence vibrates. I realise that was the sucker punch. 'You are joking.'

'Nope. Deadly serious,' replies Evan.

Slowly I open my eyes. He's staring down at me. It's not a great angle. Probably I don't look great either. Someone in my profession is very aware of angles and best sides. I sit up, face him.

'Hey, I could tell you that you make my heart race the way taking too many uppers does.'

'Please don't.'

'No, I won't. Look, Dora, I've given this a lot of thought. I think it's the right solution for both of us. None of the women I date interest me the way you do.'

I guess I am quite special. Or at least a novelty. Other than me, the women Evan hangs out with fall into two camps. Beautiful but assetless women who are looking for a rich man to marry so they can spend his money. Or women who, like him, are trust-fund babies with substantial assets who are looking for a rich and handsome man to marry so they can spend money together.

OK, so maybe the same camp.

He has dated lawyers and City bankers in the past, but they were never available to party with him; refusing to do coke through the week was a major inconvenience for Evan at a certain time in his life. As he's clean now, that's not an issue any more, but he still needs a woman who can drop everything at a moment's notice to pack her Fendi sunglasses and a Chanel bikini and hop on a plane to the Caribbean if the mood takes him. Career women can't do that.

I see his problem.

I can see how he might have concluded I'm the solution. Before I met Evan, I never believed having money could be a problem. But now I acknowledge that the combination of a massive surplus of cash and a dearth of real responsibilities can lead to lack of direction, degeneracy and self-destruction. Added to which, people who grow up obscenely rich might struggle to know which friends are real and which are simply enjoying the benefits of hanging out with incredibly rich people. So now, I do believe having money can be a problem; however I maintain, not as much of a problem as not having it. I mean, Evan hasn't even had to be fucked from behind to pay the mortgage, so my sympathy is limited.

'I know what you're thinking,' he says.

'I hope not.'

'Money is brilliant, Dora, but only if you make good choices. Like choosing the right people to surround yourself with, you know? Proper friends. And treating your body well. You were so there for me when I was getting clean.'

50

It's true I sat for hours with him every night; some when he simply swore and sweated, other times when he sank somewhere dark and talked about death a lot. His. I held his hand, made mocktails with Mr Fitzpatrick's cordials and told him I'd miss him if he was dead. 'Loads of people would miss you. But I need you more than the others.'

'You need me?' he asked, surprised.

'Obviously.'

'I thought it was the other way round.'

'It's both ways round.' Being needed is quite the imperative in life.

I took his phone off him so he couldn't contact his dealer or any of the people who would give him what he wanted; definitely not what he needed. He was furious with me for that. He smashed plates in his kitchen, one after another. I watched him thrash about with futility and frustration, and when he'd finished, I told him, 'I'm not clearing up that shit, Evan. It's your mess.' It killed me to watch him down on his hands and knees, sweeping the smithereens into a dustpan; he was so ineffectual and unpractised, he cut his hand twice. It took an age, but when he'd finished, I made us hot chocolate and cracked open a new jigsaw. Sorting the pieces into edges, corners and centres was therapeutic. It was a manageable task and offered a sense of progress. I told him I was proud of him.

'Proud of me? You've just watched me obliterate an entire fine-bone-china dinner set.' He looked sheepish.

'Cold turkey sucks. Clearly,' I replied. 'But fuck yeah, I'm proud of you. We both know you can buy a new dinner service tomorrow.' I didn't need to articulate that some things couldn't be bought no matter how much cash he had. Things like health, life.

I skipped a lot of jobs during this time because I didn't dare leave him alone. I hid from him the fact I was stony broke. It was important that I stayed by his side.

He might have been following a similar line of thought to mine, because he says now, 'Money is not the magic spell that fixes everything, but it does buy freedom from stress and worry. I have that. Well, almost. I still worry about you. That man last night, he could have killed you.'

He could have. Any of them could. I never really know what I'm walking into, despite the checks Elspeth runs. It's terrifying if you dwell on it. I try not to. But it's there, the threat. The fear. Ever present.

Evan looks pained, which I'm almost certain isn't how you are supposed to look when you propose. He adds, 'I'd like to give you the safety I have.'

'Marriage, though? You're not even going to start with an offer to pay me a salary. Keep me.'

'No.' Has he thought this through or is he acting on impulse? I mean, I know he says he has given this a lot of thought, but with Evan, that might mean he thought about it whilst I was queuing for the coffee.

'Why not?'

An unfamiliar awkwardness swells between us, tasking the air with challenge and, perhaps, hope. 'You know why not, Dora.'

Yeah, true, I do. I've known for a while. The reason he's never tried it on, I worked it out. He's not gay, or indifferent to my many charms, or even disgusted by how thinly I spread those many charms. He is in love with me.

It's the weirdest thing, believing yourself to be in love. The most complex fantasy humans have developed. Yeah, I said fantasy. I don't believe that being in love lasts. You see, it's a chemical thing (oxytocin or dopamine), or a social conditioning thing (all those novels, movies, love songs. Please!), or maybe an evolution thing (bringing up a baby on your own, that's hard. Human babies are dependent for so long; unlike giraffes, we're programmed to find someone who will stick around and help out – well, at least in an ideal world). You won't believe me when I say this – even though in the land of the blind the one-eyed fool should be right, and I am the professional when it comes to all matters sexual – but newsflash: that giddy feeling you get at the beginning, the *I can't live without them* thing, *I need to be with them every minute of the day, I resent having to sleep*, etc., etc., it goes away. It fades.

Every. Single. Time.

In fact, you are blessed if it fades. In the worst cases, you are betrayed, deceived, tricked and misled. The rug is pulled from beneath your feet with such violence that you fall and break both your legs, you struggle to ever stand up again, and even if you do, you always walk with a limp.

I've seen what believing yourself to be in love can do. I've watched perfectly sensible, composed people tear themselves apart with doubt and insecurity. I've seen them run up debts, deny their friends and family, steal, blackmail, commit arson, kill. Yup, in my line of work, you meet all sorts.

I once fell in love. It was a total shit show.

I almost feel sorry for Evan for believing himself to be in love with me. It leaves him very vulnerable, and when he stops thinking himself in love with me, I'll be very vulnerable. I consider the offer.

'You have to give it up, though, Dora. I can't bear it. Not just the thought of the other men having you – although honestly that's not great – but all the danger. That's what I want to stop. So if we are doing this, you have to call Elspeth straight away and tell her you won't be taking any more jobs.'

People have choices in life. They think they don't, but they do, and that's possibly why so many of the human race are terrified or depressed. We know we've chosen to be where we are. Even the lucky ones, like Evan, who have many options sometimes feel paralysed. Too much choice is overwhelming. All those beautiful heiresses must have merged into one for him, since he's been unable to pick his way through them. It is difficult knowing if the paths we have set off on are the right ones or not. And if they are wrong, have we anyone to blame but ourselves? Can we pick a better one? Are we capable of that? Few know what to do in the face of splendid choice. There was a time in my life when the choices were extremely limited. Limited to just two options. But I still made a choice, and I live with that every day. More, I make the choice again, every day.

It's tiring. So tiring that some days it's hard to tell whether it's choice or whim that dictates my day. Sometimes, in the middle of the night, I hear the wind blowing and I think I ought to get up to check the bins haven't tumbled over and that my rubbish is not spreading across the road: vodka bottles smashed on the pavement, empty packets of stockings and Tampax blowing down the street, exposing my life to random strangers. So, on a whim, I might decide to get up, go downstairs and check the bins; clear up if needs be. Other times, the wind blows, and I decide to pull the duvet closer around me and not get out of bed.

I didn't have to take the extra job last night. I chose to.

My choice right now is to marry a kind, rich man who loves me and have sex with him exclusively until he stops wanting it, until he changes his mind about this choice he has made. Because he might change his mind. He probably will. Or I can keep putting myself in danger and have sex with a number of different men, some of whom are very unkind, cruel even, until I am too old to appeal to them.

It seems like a no-brainer. 'OK.'

'You're saying yes?'

'I am.'

'You'll be my wife?'

'I will.'

He looks delighted. He reaches for my face and cups it in both hands, kisses me with determination, excitement and expertise. I kiss him back. There's no embarrassment between us. It's not awkward switching from friends to lovers. I'm too good at my job to allow that to happen.

We go back to my place and have sex without discussing it. We're both adult enough to be curious, and also to know if left any length of time, it will become a big deal. He's gentle with me because I'm bruised and battered. It's good sex. As we fall asleep side by side but not entangled with one another, I think to myself: good choice.

# 8

# *Dora*

Elspeth is surprised to hear I'm getting married. 'Is he a client?' she asks. I can hear suspicion and scepticism in her voice.

'No.' I wonder, if he were, might she believe she is entitled to a commission? Thirty per cent of the wedding gifts, perhaps? I'm surprised she asked. We both know life is far from a *Pretty Woman* movie. I've encountered hundreds of sex workers throughout my lifetime, and we've had thousands of clients between us, maybe tens of thousands. I've never heard of a single client proposing to their sex worker. It doesn't happen. 'So, you'll cancel all my appointments?'

She sighs dramatically. Elspeth doesn't like having to rearrange clients; it unnerves them. She may lose business. My regulars are not going to be happy that I've resigned. None of this is my concern. '*All* of them? Straight away? No notice?'

'Yes please,' I reply politely.

'Well, congratulations, darling. I'll send your final accounts once I know whether these late cancellations are going to mean I lose deposits or not. Don't delete my number.' She hangs up.

We've been working together for years, yet we are done. Just like that. Mine is not an overly sentimental world. As I carefully rub arnica cream onto my ribs, I ponder for a moment. What did she mean, 'don't delete my number'? Does she think I'll need to crawl back to her at some point? She's wrong. I won't let that happen.

In the following week, Evan comes to my flat every day, sometimes more than once. He doesn't have a regular time, which I like. Sometimes he pops around before work, or at lunchtime; usually he arrives here after work. He's stayed over twice. Evan is the only person I have slept with in the past decade; I mean actually *slept* with. Sleeping is such a risk. Being unconscious is agreeing to down tools, strip off the armour that we so carefully construct throughout our waking day. I've never agreed to it with clients. Even when I took jobs that spanned across a weekend in a villa or a hotel, I always asked for a separate room. Men who can afford to take me away for a weekend never blink at this request. They want to preserve the mystery too. When Evan sleeps, I feel his breath on my back, warm and rhythmic. It's nice.

I gave him a set of keys to my place a couple of years ago; it's usual for him to knock, and if I am not fast enough about getting to the door, he will let himself in. In the past, he would humorously shout, 'Make yourself decent, I'm coming in.' He doesn't knock any more, and he doesn't want me to make myself decent; he starts undressing at the door. He shouts, 'Honey, I'm home', a parody of a 1950s housewife and husband that has permeated our culture, although even our parents weren't born when those roles were played out for real. Eager, he comes straight through to the bedroom and joins me in bed, where I am spending most of my days, recuperating. After sex,

57

we order something from Uber Eats and he languidly stumbles to the door in a post-coital haze that is no doubt obvious and embarrassing for the delivery guy. I'm taken aback by how like every other couple in the early, delicious stage of a relationship we are. Infatuated. Insatiable. Engrossed. I don't understand it, but yeah, it's good.

It also surprises me how quickly I become used to Evan being in bed with me, and I find it isn't easy to sleep peacefully when he isn't here. When I am alone, thick hands chase into my dreams. Fists pummel down on me. I writhe in the sweat-soaked sheets to avoid the thumps and punches, the pain and degradation. I move too quickly, and then the actual agony of my real injuries wakes me. I open my eyes and listen to my shallow breathing. Alert for unfamiliar sounds. Relieved that there are no other signs of life in my flat. I miss my childhood, when my parents would run into the room if I had a night terror, rub my back and say, over and over again, 'It's OK, there there, it's just a dream.' I'm not generally the jittery, scared-of-my-own-shadow sort, but since the beating, I am inconveniently edgy. We have suddenly been thrust into a heatwave, and my flat is insufferably hot, so I keep all the windows open through the day. However, someone slamming a car door or shouting to a mate in the street makes me jump as though a doctor has tapped my knee to check my reflexes. I close the windows at night, even though the room is airless. Even though no one has my address. I tell myself I'm safe. People who have to tell themselves they are safe rarely are.

Thank God I don't have to force myself back to work with these bruises and thoughts; I'm not sure I would be able to. It's a relief, too, that I am not worried about income. Evan has already set up a direct debit to send money to my account; apparently a sizeable amount of cash will land there every month. A little more than I usually earned. I don't have to do anything for this money; it's not contingent on my behaving well in or out of the sack. I don't have to give anyone a commission. It's just mine.

On the fifth day of my recuperation, Evan arrives with a ring box. He stands in the doorway of my bedroom and pitches it casually in my direction. Underarm. I, equally coolly, catch it with just one hand. Both of us the very epitome of urbane sophistication, shy of intensity. 'I don't know if you had something in mind,' he comments with a shrug.

'I didn't.'

'Well, anyway, if you don't like it, we can take it back.'

I'm not a romantic person. I find the down-on-one-knee thing awkward; single red roses – or worse, a bouquet of them – are an embarrassing cliché, so I'm pleased when Evan doesn't wait to see my response to the ring, but instead says, 'Shall I fix us a drink?' and leaves the room, leaves me to it.

The ring is exquisite. The most beautiful piece of jewellery I have ever seen. I have worn incredible pieces of jewellery in the past. Some clients have asked me to wear particular necklaces, earrings and bracelets that may have been family heirlooms or on loan from a jeweller. Pieces worth tens of thousands. It was part of the fantasy, the story they had constructed for themselves or for their colleagues, never for me. Occasionally, clients have gifted me more modest pieces of jewellery to show appreciation; when I say more modest, I still mean pieces worth a few thousand. My clients are extremely wealthy people with hugely different measures of what qualifies as expensive from the rest of us. Not that I ever got the real value of the pieces when I sold them on. It's tricky without the proper certificates and receipts and stuff. Jewellers assume I've acquired them by dubious means. An assumption I can't really refute.

Evan's ring is a Tiffany ring. It says those exact words on the box. A dazzling solid diamond pavé band, with a six-prong setting that allows the enormous centre diamond to float above the band. It gleams and catches the light in a way that squeezes my breath. I know two things about this ring: it's beautiful and it's expensive. Very. I slip it on the third finger of my left hand. It looks great. 'They do the centre stones in different sizes,' says Evan as he re-enters the bedroom and hands me a G&T. 'This one is two carats. They went up to six, but I thought that was a bit flash.'

'Good call. Six carats would be flash. I'll struggle to lift my arm wearing this. This diamond is enormous.'

'Do you like it?'

'It's beautiful. I love it.'

'Good.'

'And it fits.'

'Yeah, I measured a ring in your jewellery box.' I'm touched. I kiss him, and he adds, 'The diamonds are ethically sourced, et cetera. Integrity and social responsibility boxes ticked.'

'That's nice.'

'Isn't it.' He grins. The giving and accepting of the ring feels like a hurdle we've leapt over. Cleared. There is a sense of relief. We're far from a conventional couple, and the beats that society expects us to hit are a stretch, but we are a thing. Our thing.

'If it doesn't work out between us and I have to sell this, I'll still be fine forever,' I say with a smile, because he must have thought about it.

'Well, not forever, but it will give you six months if you keep the box and the receipt.' He winks. We both laugh out loud. I'm so relieved things are still honest between us. He knows me. I know him. We're going to have to reinvent things for everyone else, but it's important to keep it real when we are alone. When we stop laughing, we have sex.

# 9

# *Dora*

By Friday morning, I'm feeling much more mobile, the cut on my lip has healed almost completely and the bruising on my face is fading – it could be hidden by well-applied make-up, I guess. I don't know, because I haven't felt the need to put make-up on in front of Evan, and since he proposed, we've barely got out of bed. It's an adventure that I'm up and in the kitchen helping him to make breakfast. I'm fixing us black coffee. As usual, Evan offers me an array of breakfast options – French toast, yoghurt, bacon sandwich – but I keep telling him I'm a liquids-only sort of girl in the mornings. I notice that in response, he's bought a juicer for here like the one he's got in his flat; he's whizzing up something that's a very vibrant green colour, waxing lyrical about the importance of my imbibing a lot of vitamins. Suddenly, he switches and starts making noises about me meeting his family. This is a worry.

I accept the green drink and gulp it down as though it is delicious. It isn't, it's the opposite, but I'm buying time. 'I'm not sure. Not yet.'

'Why not?'

A hundred reasons. 'We need to really think this through. Explain who I am. By which I mean lie about everything that I am.'

Evan laughs. He's getting the amount and sort of sex that makes a man perpetually good-natured. 'They are going to love you as much as I do,' he says, his grin sloppy, wide.

'God, you are naive. I'd like to say it's adorable, but I think it's dangerous.'

His smile falters fractionally. 'Dangerous? That's a strong word.'

Evan hasn't told me an awful lot about his family. Not facts, not really, which is odd because he talks about them all the time. Despite the dearth of specific information, I have clear impressions. I understand what he comes from. It's unlikely they are going to love me as much as he does; they are going to hate me. His mother is 'beautiful and sassy'; he often says of her, 'You can't pull the wool over her eyes.' He notes that she's cool under pressure and 'Always polite. Always.' I know this, but I don't know if she works, whether she has siblings, what her feeling were on sending her children to boarding school. I have never asked. I don't want to appear to be prying. People are often far too interested in wealthy families; it can appear rude.

He calls his sister Little Miss Jekyll and Hyde. He swears the ditty 'There was a little girl who had a little curl, right in the middle of her forehead' was written just for her. If you are not familiar with the nursery rhyme, it goes on to say, 'When she was good, she was very, very good, but when she was bad, she was horrid.' I'm given to understand that his sister is not only hideously spoilt and prone to tantrums that can last days and may involve her writing off cars – or once, a yacht – but also too beautiful for her own good. This has made her unbearably arrogant and hideously insecure at the same time. She is four years younger than he is, she does 'something in fashion', and she's had a nose job. These are the only certain facts he has ever revealed. I assume she has curly hair, because of the rhyme.

Evan adores his father. He talks about him so often, and always with incredible pride. Sons of multimillionaires are prone to be proud of their fathers; that, or they are intimidated by them. Evan's excess of pride and sense of ownership of his dad shines through every conversation about the man. 'My dad has a golf handicap of six', 'My father made his first million before he was thirty', 'Did I ever tell you the story about my dad learning Mandarin when he wanted to break into the Chinese market? He took daily lessons. I ask you, who does that?' His father is in the sort of business that I think I could understand if it were ever properly explained to me, but Evan hasn't ever explained it to me; probably because when we first met he didn't want to seem annoyingly privileged or patronising, then he had his druggie phase and lost sight of what was going on. I sometimes fantasise about us getting to grips with the company as a power couple. Madness, I know. The call girl and the playboy: who would take us seriously? All I know is that it is something to do with property and/or insurance, it's global, and it's made him very, very rich. Evan's stories have revealed to me that his father mixes with incredibly powerful and influential people. He does the season, attending a series of white-gloved charity events (think Elton John's White Tie and Tiara Ball), he feels at home in the royal enclosure at Ascot, he sits with the Beckhams or the Middletons at Wimbledon, and, I understand, he attends the Queen's garden parties often enough to be able to rate the sandwiches ('never as delicious as you'd hope').

All of the above is a problem.

'From what you've told me of your father, he's not going to want someone like me marrying into his family. He'll see it as me getting my nails into his precious son.'

Evan reaches his hand out for me to take hold of. I do. He kisses my fingers. 'Oh, I hope you do get your nails into me. Long scratches, the entire length of my back.'

'Be serious.'

'I know who and what you are, Dora. I don't care what they have to say about it.'

'You are kidding right? You're not thinking of telling them the truth about me?'

'Would that be so bad?' I can't tell if he is teasing me or if he is genuine about the idea. It's possible he'd like to startle his family, who he sees as boringly conventional. Ruffle feathers. Is marrying me like refusing to do the Oxbridge exam? A show of creative rebellion? I can imagine several of his similarly privileged friends might be entertained by his choice of wife. His family are less likely to be amused.

'Your family cannot know I am a former call girl. I can't think many families would welcome that prospect,' I say, rolling my eyes at the understatement. 'But yours are loaded; they are going to think I'm a gold-digger, at the very least, which is just a breath away from a whore anyhow. We have to do everything we can to hide my past.' I sit down at the small kitchen table, all but collapse into my seat, and stare at him with what I hope is a look pleading for sensible thinking.

'I love it when you get all serious. It's very sexy,' he says with a smile as he sits opposite me.

'I am serious, Evan. They are going to investigate me.'

He doesn't contradict me. 'What were you thinking then? What shall we do?'

The nature of our marriage will be that Evan always assumes I have a plan, a solution. He'll expect me to sort things out. I see that now. That's OK. I am better suited to chicanery than he is. 'Well, the first stage is obliterating who I am, and then the second stage is making up a new me. Luckily, I have no social media presence at all. I've stayed completely away from every single channel, so at least we don't have to clear up anything there.'

'I've always thought that was so cool about you. The fact that you've never been into it. Not even Insta or TikTok.' Evan lives on a merry-go-round where he obsesses about his likes and then deletes his accounts. He's working on it.

'Yeah, well in my profession, it's not a great idea to be traceable.'

'But you are Natalya at work. You wouldn't be traceable.'

'Different name, same face. You never know who sees a picture. Imagine if I friend someone on Facebook, even under my name, and someone who knows me as Natalya is also a friend of that person, or a friend of a friend, whatever; imagine if they spot me.' I shrug. To me, it's obvious. I don't need to keep a low profile; I need an absence of profile. Then I add, 'Anyway, even before I got into this sort of work, I was suspicious of the whole look-at-me ethos that social media promotes. I'm always telling you it's unhealthy. I don't want people staring at me. I'd be happy never to catch a glance again.'

'What about when you were acting? Surely a media presence was helpful then?'

'Yes, when I was a lot younger, I had a social media presence, of course. I closed those accounts a long time ago. Besides, they were under the name Teodora Dziewulski, so they're unlikely to be linked to me now, over a decade on.'

'Of course, you told me this before. Your tutor thought Teodora was a mouthful and no one ever knew how to pronounce the Dz sound, so she advised you to simplify your name.'

'Yeah, she said if I wanted call backs it was a good move.'

'When did you become Dora Wulski by deed poll?'

'I was about twenty. I didn't want to lose my heritage, but I could see the point that was being made.'

'Dora is so cute,' says Evan with a grin.

'Yeah, it works.' I shrug. 'Anyway, all good choices, as things have turned out. At least we only have to focus on inventing a new me, which is less tricky than having to obliterate the old me.'

Evan frowns. 'Obliterate is a strong word.' He hasn't given this enough thought. Not really. I suspected as much. I stay silent. I've learnt the importance of not rushing to fill every space, but instead to let it breathe. Let them find their way to me. Eventually Evan asks, 'So who shall we say you are?'

'I think we should say I work in a shop or maybe that I am a mature student. Something innocuous that doesn't draw attention. I'll need to think about it. Get it watertight. That's why we can't rush into meeting your family. Leave it with me.'

I am used to inventing different careers for myself. The guy who works in the dry cleaner's below my flat once commented that I kept funny hours. He might have just been making conversation, but most likely he was making a point. Sniffing around. 'I'm a reflexologist,' I said quickly, as though that explained everything. I should have said I drove an Uber. The estate agent who handled the purchase of the flat thought that I was a clairvoyant and I told the woman in my local café that I was a childminder. That was stupid, because she hadn't even asked what I did for a living, I never have kids with me and I never have chipped nails. Still, she plays along and sometimes asks after my small charges. Once she said to me, 'Remind me, what ages do you look after? I might know someone who is looking for a childminder.'

'Oh, sorry. I'm at capacity,' I lied.

I'm quite the expert in reinvention. I reinvent myself every time I enter a hotel bedroom. I have many versions. I am anyone I want to be. I am no one at all.

# 10

# *Daniel*

'Daniel, how lovely to hear from you.' He likes the way she does that, pretends they are friends. It makes him feel less grubby, less sordid. She is always willing to make small talk, have a chat about this and that; she avoids getting to the point too swiftly, as though it is bad manners. 'Did you get any golf in this weekend?'

He can't remember telling her he plays golf. It could be a lucky guess, or it could be something Natalya has shared with her. He doesn't doubt they keep a file on him, on all the punters; it's a business, after all. Sometimes, late at night, he lies awake and wonders what would happen if that file were ever discovered, by the police perhaps, if there was a raid or – more likely, although less dramatically – an investigation into Elspeth's business. Someone from HMRC. Someone from the vice squad. What had he got involved in? He comforts himself with the thought that it isn't illegal to pay someone for their time. He is not the criminal here. Elspeth is, Natalya is. He knows that is how the law works. He's heard people complain about that, women, obviously. He's glad for the institutionalised bias that is in his favour. Still, they have his name, and his credit card details. If the police ever did raid Elspeth's place, they would know where to find him if they wanted to. It causes him to sweat, that thought. Like a fever that quickly heats then freezes on his body, leaving an icy sheen. To be clear, it is fear, not a conscience.

'No golf this weekend, but a few games of tennis,' he tells her.

'How lovely.'

'Yes, I played rather well.' He doesn't want to sound smug, but he likes her to know he's not a loser. He sometimes worries that Elspeth (if that is her real name) must think he is a loser. Him and all the men who use her agency. She calls them her clients, appears respectful and charming, but he wonders, behind the warm telephone voice, is there steely judgement? He's a man who pays for sex, for fuck's sake, it's hard to get far from that fact. 'So, I'm just ringing to enquire about Natalya's diary.' That's how he likes to phrase it. Ideally, he'd like to call Natalya directly, cut out the middle man, then he could tell himself it was a date, just a date that was guaranteed to end in sex. A result, right? But calling directly isn't permitted. Not part of the system. Elspeth needs to take a deposit, she insists on filtering all calls, keeping control.

'Have you thought about branching out?' she asks.

'Sorry?' He's surprised. That's not the script. She's supposed to ask him if he has a particular date in mind, that's what usually happens, and whilst her question isn't wild or unreasonable, it disproportionately bothers him that she has deviated. He's more nervous about this entire process than he can acknowledge even to himself. 'Branching out?'

'We have some beautiful girls who I think you'll like.'

'I like Natalya.'

'Of course, but variety is the spice of life, that's what they say.'

'Do they?'

'Yes. They do,' she simpers. Actually simpers. It's such an outdated, little-girl sort of thing to do; probably only a madam of a brothel could even think of simpering in the twenty-first century. Then her tone turns all business, and she starts to run through a list of girls he might like to meet.

'I want to see Natalya,' he interrupts. 'Is there a problem?'

'No problem, no,' replies Elspeth. 'Natalya isn't available.'

'I'll wait.'

There's a pause. Daniel thinks he can hear Elspeth inhaling on her cigarette, but that might just be in his mind. He's never met the woman; he has no idea if she smokes, and even if she does, is she likely to smoke at her desk? Does she even work from a desk? Maybe she's sitting at a dressing table surrounded by cosmetics, sheer stockings and lace. It's a fantasy, of course, this image he's constructed of the madam, just a thought that's flitted through his mind, not real. He doesn't know anything about how she works. This is a need-to-know sort of business, which is bizarre when you think of what she is selling: the most intimate thing of all. And yet sensible, when you think of what she is selling. 'Natalya has left.'

'You fired her?'

'No, she quit.'

'Natalya quit?'

'Yes.'

'Why?'

'I can't divulge personal information about my girls. You know that.'

Daniel takes the phone away from his ear and scowls at it, as though the phone itself has caused offence. He doesn't like this woman saying no to him. He is sick of people saying no to him. He wants to see Natalya. He has to. He notes that his knuckles have turned white with pressure, his grip too tight. He feels anger and panic flood through his body. He needs to see Natalya. He must. If she has left, where has she gone? How can he get hold of her? He can't, he knows that in an instant. She's never given him her telephone number. He doesn't know where she lives. In the past, he's spent hours trying to find her on TikTok or Instagram, but she has no social media presence that he has ever discovered. The thought that she can just vanish, disappear out of his life, causes his insides to slosh. His instinct is to demand some information, force his will on Elspeth. The rules she has in place regarding divulging information about her girls are for other men, not men like him. The rules don't apply to him. His temper spikes, he feels it physically; it's a scratching in his throat, an ache in his back. He deliberately shrugs his shoulders, hears his neck crack. He has to stay calm. Elspeth will tell him nothing if he scares her.

'There are a number of other girls who get incredible reviews; one or two of them look quite a lot like Natalya,' she says. 'I'm sure they'll make you happy.'

He doesn't point out that in the past Elspeth has said how unique Natalya is, how individual. She's always implied that he and Natalya have quite a particular and special relationship. Now he feels like a fool, because he realises that she will have done the same with all of Natalya's clients. It's part of the sell.

'I'd like her telephone number.'

'You know I can't give you that.'

'I'd like to say goodbye, give her a gift.'

'You can send it to me, I'll forward it on.'

He doubts it. 'We were friends. Are friends.'

'I'm sure.' Her voice rolls with sympathy. He can tell she wants to placate him; instead, he feels patronised. Thwarted. Of course he is not a friend of Natalya's, because if he were, he wouldn't have to be begging her pimp to give him her contact details. The facts make him itch.

'I have to see her. I need the number. Who has she moved on to? Give me the details of her new madam. I realise it's unorthodox, competition and all that, so I'll pay you, handsomely. Make it worth your while. Money is no object.' That is a lie. Money is always the object. 'I have to see her,' he repeats. He wants to sound authoritative, even borderline threatening if needs be; he fears he sounds a bit pathetic, weak.

'Daniel, darling, I'd like to help you, but she hasn't moved on to a new place. She's getting married.'

Maybe she says it to close down the conversation completely. Help him put the whore out of his mind. The whore has gone, she's going to be a wife now. Natalya has vanished. He ought to move on. But he can't. It's impossible. 'I need the number.'

'I hear you, but I can't give it to you.' There is exasperation in Elspeth's voice now. If he hadn't spent so much money with her agency in the last six months, she would probably hang up on him. He thinks she might do so anyway, so he has no choice.

'The thing is, Elspeth, it's not me who is asking.'

'I'm sorry.'

'I'm asking for a friend. A mutual friend.' Then Daniel says his name. That's all he has to do.

She gives the number to him straight away. She repeats it, asks him to read it back to her to check he's taken it down properly.

There is no debate. No room for error. Not when dealing with him. Daniel knows this. Elspeth knows it too, apparently.

# 11

# *Dora*

Evan wants me to join him on a business trip to Hong Kong. This time I can't fob him off with my usual excuse of missing work and therefore income, but I still don't want to go. I'm not ready to meet his colleagues, for the same reasons I'm reluctant to meet his family. I need to get my ducks in a row first. This business trip is totally legit, quite dissimilar to the 'business trips' of old, which were basically wall-to-wall partying, so he is likely to be spending a lot of time in dull meetings. I point out that I'll be bored sitting around in the hotel, waiting for him. I don't want him to feel pressurised into having to rush back to me at the end of each working day, when meetings might overrun or colleagues might want to go for dinner; not when he's finally taking business seriously. But then, I tell him, nor do I want to immediately morph into the sort of woman who has time to waste, to squander, to kill. I value time too highly for that. 'It's just five days,' I point out.

'A week with travel. And I don't want to be apart from you at all. We've just got engaged,' he replies sincerely. I'm startled. It's so ordinary, no normal. It's exactly the kind of thing regular couples say to one another. For years, my relationships with men have been detached transactions; I've often had the feeling I operate behind a thick plastic sheet – something a bit like you might see in a hospital. A sheet that muffles sound, dulls touch, disassociates. Evan's intensity and desire to rip through that plastic sheet is disconcerting.

'Yeah, we have just got engaged. Ergo we have the rest of our lives or whatever, so I don't think we ought to worry about this one trip,' I argue.

'Don't do that.'

'Do what?'

'Don't say we have the rest of our lives or *whatever*. It's the first thing.'

'OK.'

He finally agrees to me staying in the UK when I say I want to start a Google search for wedding venues. This is a lie. I can't imagine the wedding yet. I feel we are quite some distance from that. Once his family know about our engagement, I might feel we can start planning the actual day; before then seems a leap. Evan kisses me, his stubble catching my chin in a strangely appealing way. 'I'll call you every day,' he says.

'Oh don't promise that. You'll be busy, you should focus, and there's a time difference. Just text.' He looks disappointed. We know each other so well, we both realise that I'm holding him at a slight distance. I squeeze his arm and hope he understands that I'll get better at this as I get used to our new being-a-couple status. But right now, I'm not ready to become the sort of woman who is glued to her phone, desperately anticipating a call from her fiancé. The thing is, I think maybe I might become that woman rather easily, for Evan. It's best if

I'm not expecting a call at all. That way I can't be disappointed. I don't articulate as much, but he reads my mind.

'I'm not going to disappoint you, Dora.'

'I know you're not deliberately going to, but if a meeting overruns or, I don't know, there's an alien invasion and they disrupt phone networks on a global basis and you can't get a signal, then I might be disappointed,' I joke.

'If there's an alien invasion, you'd have bigger things to worry about than my phone calls.'

I'm not sure I would. 'Just texts, OK?'

'OK, but I'll come straight here to your apartment when I land back in the country. I promise you.' He gently squeezes my bottom goodbye.

Now, on Sunday evening, when my phone rings, there's no caller ID. I think it's not worth picking up. Probably someone selling car insurance or wanting me to change my electricity supplier, but then maybe it's Evan calling from a different phone or from the air; maybe that would block his ID. So I pick up. Mistake.

It's Daniel.

'How did you get my number?' I demand.

'Oh, Elspeth gave it to me. Is it a problem?' He asks this question in a cheery voice suggesting he can't imagine it will be.

'Yes,' I reply stonily.

'I'm sorry.' He instantly sounds it, so I don't hang up. If it were just about any other one of my clients, I would hang up. I'm angry with Elspeth for passing on my number. She hasn't ever been as sloppy before in all the years we've worked together, since it's always a risk giving clients our numbers, both to my safety and her business. Since she can no longer profit from me, it's now patently clear which of those things mattered to her. Her carelessness of me stings. I will have to change my number, I'm moving forward into a new life with Evan, I can't afford any blasts from the past. That decided, I can be polite to Daniel now. After today's conversation, I'll see to it that he won't be able to reach me again.

'Elspeth says you are no longer available.'

'That's right.'

'What does that mean? You'll never be available again?'

'Correct.'

'Did I do something wrong?'

'This isn't about you.' My clients have this in common: they are very egocentric and think everything is about them. I guess I did my job well; they were supposed to believe they were the centre of my world. 'I'm not seeing any of my clients any more. I'm having a career change.'

'Really!' He sounds excited for me, which is nice, I guess. 'What are you going to do?'

'I'm retraining as a nurse.'

'Well, that's splendid. You certainly have quite the bedside manner.' He chuckles. They can't help themselves with this sort of fnarr joke. I don't laugh along. I wonder if he notices that this is the first joke he's ever cracked that I haven't appeared to find hilarious.

'It's not very well paid, though, you know, Natalya. Lots of students take up your profession whilst training or studying. They do it to cover the cost of the tutoring.'

I have heard this before. I think it is an urban myth put around by sleazy middle-aged men. I don't get into the debate. 'I have savings.'

'I see.'

'A girl can't stay in my line of work forever,' I point out.

'You have some years in you yet, though, two or three, surely.'

'Thank you,' I reply icily. Has he basically just said *there's life in the old dog yet*? Since accepting Evan's proposal, I haven't, not for a moment, regretted the decision. Remember, Daniel is on the palatable end of the scale of men I deal with. 'If Elspeth told you I'm out of the game, why are you calling me?'

'Well, I just wondered if you could do me one last favour.'

'No.'

'You haven't heard what it is yet.'

'It doesn't matter what it is. I'm out of the game. I just said so.'

'Will you hear me out? For old times' sake.'

And I do. This is also a mistake, and I know as much as I'm making it. What does that say about me?

Daniel tells me he has been invited to a chateau in the south of France to celebrate a friend's promotion to partner in a prestigious law firm. He explains it's just a Monday-to-Friday gig. 'A vineyard tour, private chefs, lots of tennis and time by the pool. That sort of thing, you know.' He explains that the invitation comes from his old friend Giles; someone he went to university with. 'Brilliant chap. He's done well for himself; the bash is a bit of rather understandable willy-waving.' He tells me that everyone else is bringing their wife or girlfriend along on the trip.

That's where I come in. Daniel has neither. 'Can't you go without a date?' I ask.

'No one likes being the spare part.'

'Then take a friend.'

'There's no one I can take. All my friends are going to be there with their partners.'

'Well, then if all your friends are there, you won't be lonely.'

'It's embarrassing, though, isn't it?'

I wonder what sort of friends he has if turning up at a celebration do without a girlfriend is such a social clanger. Most of the people I am friendly with are sex workers; we're not judgy types. My people turn up to parties alone all the time; admittedly, they rarely leave alone. 'If it's so awful going alone, just decline the invitation.'

He pauses and takes a breath. 'Sisi is going to be there.'

'And how is that relevant?'

He sighs. 'It's not, not really.'

'She's married, Daniel.'

'I know. But I crave her company.'

'Well, frankly, that's a bit creepy.'

He laughs. 'You were never this blunt when I paid you.' I can smell my bridges burning as I let him understand that. 'Well, gosh, this is awkward.' Then he tells me he's been lying to Sisi. He has told her he is dating; specifically, that he has someone special in his life. I don't know if he was hoping to make her jealous, or whether his lie was in response to Sisi getting bored or concerned about him hanging around her all the time. Apparently she is super excited that he has a girlfriend and is dying to meet her. Now he doesn't want to lose face, yet he's so obsessed with Sisi that neither is he prepared to forgo a trip away with her. He really ought to see a counsellor. I'm an expert on messed-up people. Most of my clients are messy and complex, grubby or angry. They all have secrets. 'Please come with. I thought perhaps you could, you know, pretend to be my girlfriend.'

'No thank you.'

'But I thought you did that sort of thing.'

'Yes, I have done, but I don't any more.' Indeed, I have accompanied men to wild sex-, alcohol- and drug-fuelled parties, holidays, 'business meetings' in penthouses, villas and hotels, in Dubai, Las Vegas, New York … Trips away are always great earners, plus they offer a break in the routine. They're a perk. Often, lots of girls would go along and I started to get to know one or two other women on the circuit. It was quite chummy, the nearest I've ever got to a girls' holiday. 'I can suggest some other girls who could do the job.'

'No, that wouldn't do. They wouldn't know me. *You* know me. They'd slip up. It would be obvious they weren't my girl-friend. You could pull it off.'

'Sorry. I can't. I told you, I've given it up. I've drawn a line under that life.'

'Can't you draw your line next week?'

'I wish I could, but—'

'We wouldn't even have to have sex. I'll pay you as though we were. More, if you like, but we wouldn't. The other guests wouldn't know what was going on behind closed doors, or more pertinently in this case, what wasn't going on.' I think about my promise to Evan. 'Why can't you come? Who would you be hurting?' Daniel pleads.

I can't explain. 'The thing is, I don't look my best. I walked into a door,' I add.

'Oh, I'm sorry to hear that. Is it the sort of thing you can hide behind make-up?'

'Well, yes, but—'

Daniel interrupts and names a sum of money for my trip to France. It's a lot. More than double the going rate.

'When is this trip?' I ask. I shouldn't ask.

'We'd need to fly out tomorrow.' Tomorrow. I consider it. Evan wouldn't even have to know. 'We'd fly business. Tell me you have a better offer.' Evan is putting money into my account, a generous amount. I don't need money, I understand that intellectually, but the perpetually poor person I was for so long kicks against my rational knowledge. My gut says you can never have enough money squirrelled away. It's important to be financially independent. It's hard to say no to double the going rate.

'No sex, you say. Promise?'

'Well, I'll try and not be very offended that that is the deal-breaker, but yes, no sex. I just need you to help me save face.'

I won't actually be breaking my promise to Evan. Not if the trip doesn't involve sex. His objection to my working is twofold. One, he doesn't like the thought of me with other men. Fair enough, few husbands get off on that (although some do, I've met them). And secondly, he's worried about my safety. Daniel is a pussy cat. I'd be chaste and safe. So not really breaking the intent of the promise I made to Evan, not at all.

'OK. I'll do it. I'll pretend to be your devoted girlfriend. I'll send you my bank details, and you need to transfer the cash up front, extra for the plane ticket.'

'I'll buy you that.'

'I prefer sorting out my own.' Because my passport reveals my real name, and he has no clue what that is. 'Send me your ticket details. I'll make sure we are sitting together.'

I give him Natalya's email address, and as I do so, I hope I won't live to regret it. At the moment when Daniel's email pings into my box, outside the sun scuttles behind a cloud. It seems ominous when the room is temporarily plunged into a gloomy darkness. I mentally give myself a shake. It's not like me to look for signs. People who look for signs are either hopeful or gullible.

I'm neither.

# 12

# *Dora*

OK, more likely than not, this is going to make you uncomfortable. Possibly make you like me a little bit less. Although am I kidding myself? Maybe you don't like me at all anyway. It doesn't matter; you've never paid me to like you. I promise if you had, you would like me very much indeed, because I am good at my job. Anyway, what I'm about to say isn't going to win me any popularity points, but I'm going to say it regardless, because it is the truth as I see it.

People in my profession are not the only ones who trade sex. We're just the most blatant.

Everything to do with sex is a transaction in some way, shape or form. People trade looks, wit, brains, wealth, social status, fame or security, all for sex. People trade sex to say thank you for a really great date and, more surprisingly, to say sorry for a pretty piss-poor one. Sex is traded for jobs, for attention, for power. Sex is traded because once, twenty-five years ago, you stood in a church in front of a God you don't believe in and made promises that you hadn't really thought too deeply about, to a guy with a cute grin and straight teeth. And now that guy – well, it's his birthday and he's washed your car and popped to the supermarket this week; he even drove your youngest up to university, helped her unpack, fixed a wobbly shelf, so you owe him a blow job. You trade sex. And you are a *good* wife, he is a good husband; society agrees on that. He did the weekly shop, looked out for the kids, it's his birthday, you'd be a monster not to put out.

Husbands, wives, girlfriends, boyfriends, bosses, colleagues, starlets, directors, *people* trade sex. People trade sex for hope and despair.

I'm not saying it's right. I'm just saying it *is*.

We're not necessarily very different. Not that far apart. I think what offends people is that I don't choose my sex partners for their physicality. I choose them for their bank balance. But really, is one thing more shallow than the other? I trade sex for straight cash and that might offend you. You think it gives you the right to judge me? Go ahead, if you must. People have been judged for far less: what shoes they are wearing, how they hold their knife and fork, if they have or have not read the novels on the Booker longlist. We're a judgy species. We judge everything, even desire. We probably ought to be nicer. Involve ourselves elsewhere.

It's been hot this past week in London, sticky, but arriving in the south of France is something altogether different. The heat feels heavy and permanent. Walking just the short distance from the steps of the aeroplane into the terminal and then out the other side to a waiting chauffeur-driven car gives opportunity for sweat to pool in the crook of my elbows, the back of my knees, the base of my back. I blink behind my sunglasses and discreetly blot under my eyes to catch any mascara that might

have run. I'm paid to be immaculate, perfect. The air conditioning inside the car is ferocious and therefore a relief. I wonder
whether it will dry out Daniel's shirt, which is blooming dark
pink patches under his arms, down his back. I never understand
why rich men travel in pastel-coloured shirts and linen trousers;
they arrive at their destinations looking wrung out. But then,
he does not have to be perfect for me, or anyone. The idea of
straining to be flawless has probably never crossed his mind. He
keeps dabbing his face with a handkerchief, mopping the sweat
that is bubbling like soup. He's more nervous than I've ever
seen him before, even when he first visited me. I am increasingly
curious about his friends, and Sisi in particular. Any woman
who can have this sort of effect on a man is interesting to me.

We drive for an hour, leaving the airport behind, skirting
around the dusty, noisy city, heading out towards the more
bucolic scenes that city dwellers love to step into temporarily
and romanticise. We trundle past rows of tall, proud poplar
trees and hand-painted signs advertising rustic vineyards and
weekend *brocantes*. We pass through small French villages
where attractive dark-haired children sit on picnic blankets
with their vivacious, gossiping mothers and wrinkled pensioners
play boules. The A roads slim down to B roads, and soon we
are travelling down the sort of rough tracks where potholes are
a concern. This place we are heading to is very remote. I already
miss the smell of the city. Wherever we are now smells of earth
and dust, not even grass. I close my eyes to counter the waves
of travel sickness that are beginning to swell in my stomach.
Maybe I doze off, because when Daniel shakes my arm, I feel
disorientated, and it takes a moment to understand where I am.

'We're here,' he says with an excited beam.

The chateau is breathtakingly beautiful. Not the mismatch of turrets of my imagination, but a Georgian-style sand-bricked manor. Elegant, symmetrical, purposeful. It's also enormous. I'm looking forward to roaming around the rooms. I imagine parquet flooring, high ceilings, feature fireplaces – all that sort of stuff interests me. Elegance isn't something that sex workers are oblivious to. We see the same as you do. More maybe.

Daniel points out Giles and his wife, Melanie, waiting in the distance at the door of the chateau. At first, they are nothing more than small dots to me, as the driveway is incredibly long, but as we approach, they start to loom into focus, and I have the opportunity to assess the hosts.

Daniel hasn't provided a great deal of detail about anyone I'm going to meet, other than Sisi, but this doesn't faze me. I'm used to walking into rooms and dealing with whoever and whatever I find. Every time I arrive at a hotel or a villa or a party, it's like the first day in a new office and I don't know where the photocopier is, but I can never let the client know that. Confidence is all. Fake it until you make it. They may be nervous. I can't be.

The couple are standing framed in the open door, artfully, like a tableau. They each have an arm slung around one another and their free hands held high in the air, waving a welcome to us. The very picture of marital harmony and warm hospitality, which is usually only demonstrated by a newly married couple, or if there is an issue with fidelity. I wonder who he's shagged. I'm not a cynic, but I am a sex worker, so forgive me if I don't easily buy into the myth of domestic bliss. The open door creates a black gap behind them, so they appear mounted or suspended. I wonder how long they have had to wait there to greet us, and I wonder why they aren't busy entertaining their other guests. I assume their self-conscious formality is because they are curious to meet me, or at least curious about Daniel's girlfriend.

Giles is wearing the uniform I would expect from a man his age and class: khaki shorts and a pale blue collared shirt – linen, of course. He is a wiry man, handsome until he smiles, and then I notice his teeth are too small for his mouth; I see a lot of gum. The wife is in a striped sundress. It's not especially flattering, nor does it look particularly comfortable; it clings around her gently rounding stomach. She's too old for her belly to be blooming with fecundity; it's engorged with evidence that she's at the other end of the reproductive scale. Her metabolism has slowed, her waist has thickened. If she feels loved, she'll be comfortable with the protrusion; if not, she'll be neurotic. Her curves will taunt her, disappoint her. Our bodies are rarely the friends they ought to be.

They move forward in unison, welcome us loudly. I'm introduced, Giles casts an appreciative glance the length of my body, Melanie smiles at me without her eyes – let alone her heart – bothering to get involved. I don't blame her. I'm suspiciously young and beautiful on Daniel's arm. Still, they talk of their delight at us being there, instruct staff to take our bags to our rooms, urge us to join everyone at the pool. 'Do you want a drink? Anything at all? How can we make you feel most comfortable?' Melanie asks solicitously.

'I'd like to change if I can,' I comment. I step into the cool entrance hall. It is large, impressive. The tiles are black and white, the walls are wood-panelled and painted a pale grey. There are benches where people presumably pause to swap flip-flops for boat shoes or hiking boots. There is an enormous fireplace, but because of the heat outside, it is not lit. A sweeping double staircase stretches left and right; it's designed for people who like to make an entrance. Or maybe an exit. Before I can ask to be shown to my room, I feel Melanie's hand firmly on my back as she steers me outside once again.

'Of course, of course you want to change, and you can, but after you've had a drink. Everyone is dying to meet you. They are all waiting at the pool,' she adds.

I see how it is. Behind the impeccable manners, there is a steely determination. I might be asked what I want to do, but I'll be doing exactly what Melanie wants. No doubt she's been planning and scheduling Giles's promotion party for months, and she doesn't want anything as inconvenient as free will to detract. 'We're just picking over lunch. Nothing special. Charcuterie and fruit, mostly. We're keeping lunches casual. Dinner tonight is seven courses.' She widens her eyes as though she has delivered bad news, but it's obvious that she's delighted to be serving such an indulgent dinner. 'You're not anything dreadful like a vegan, are you? We kept asking Daniel about your dietary requirements, but he never responded to our emails.'

'No, not a vegan,' I assure her. 'I like my food far too much to be a vegan.' I laugh at my own small joke, but Melanie's gaze just drops to my flat stomach, scepticism oozing from her face. I want to tell her it's my genes that have provided the enviable figure, but even if I do, she won't believe me. She'll think I stick my fingers down my throat after every meal, and that will probably be some comfort to her. Charming a heterosexual woman who isn't paying for my services is not something I've ever attempted. I have been paid to have sex with women her age because they or their husbands wanted it – those women I could charm or reassure, depending on what was required. I guess a whole new skill set will be needed with Melanie and the wives of Daniel's other friends.

'I'm sure Daniel told you I'm allergic to raw egg,' I add.

'No, he never mentioned it.' Melanie looks irritated. 'Well, we'll manage to work around that, I suppose,' she says in a manner that suggests I've just ruined not only her menu plans, but her life.

# 13

# *Dora*

As Daniel, Giles, Melanie and I walk around the side of the chateau towards the pool, I take in the beautifully manicured garden and grounds. It is a perfect example of a formal, symmetrical *jardin à la française*. A style of garden based on equilibrium and the principle of imposing order on nature. The epitome of this style is generally considered to be the gardens of Versailles, designed during the seventeenth century for Louis XIV. I was told this by a client of mine who was a professor at a prestigious Parisian university. I pick up quite random bits of knowledge shagging wealthy men; their hobbies and interests are varied. Their desire to hear their own voice is a constant. What I'm saying about the garden is, it's anything but modest. There are colourful planting beds in precise geometric shapes, various parterres leading to a fountain where fat cherubs are immortalised playing under perpetual cascades of gushing water. We walk through a series of stairways and ramps that unite different levels of the garden; Melanie points left and says there is a grotto that way – 'Strange little dingy place, quite frankly' – then right, where she tells me there is a labyrinth: 'Such fun, you'll love it.'

I gaze out past the formal gardens to see what lies further afield. The grounds are vast – there are no neighbouring properties in sight – so it would be impossible to tend the entire enormous space with the same level of attention and formality as the area close to the house. Consequently, the geometric spaces ultimately fall away and spill into fields or woodland. The expanse of corn and maize crops stretches as far to the horizon as I can see, until it becomes blurred with a heat haze. The woods are dark and closed. The leaves on the trees don't so much as tremble, as there's not a breath of a breeze.

I spot a gardener bent over a rose bed. I assess him. It's habit. I assess all men. He is dressed in baggy ripped shorts, no top. His skin is tanned to the colour of a polished mahogany table. He has grey hairs on his chest, arms, torso, shoulders, back. This I've seen before. The men I service expect me to be waxed within an inch of my life, but they don't hold themselves up against the same standards. The gardener's torso is muscled from manual work. That's new; none of my clients have that. He's shaking his head, irritated, muttering aloud to no one in particular. I don't speak French well enough to understand, but as we pass him, I see that the plants he is looking at are blighted with black spots on the leaves. A second glance and I notice that the entire bed, ten metres in length, is quivering; crawling with an infestation of a sap-sucking black bug. The garden's perfection is marred. That's why I'm not a fan of the countryside. You can't trust it. It's too mercurial. Full of living and dying plants and creatures. Moss, mould and weeds that overflow, climb, leach. Insects, mice and rats. Pests of one form or another that breed, chew, kill. Melanie doesn't acknowledge the gardener or his plight; I shrug in a way that I hope communicates my sympathy.

We hear the chatter drifting upwards from the pool area before we turn the corner and see the other guests sitting at a long trestle table, nestling under a cabana. The white table-cloth and the gauze curtains of the cabana hang poker straight, like walls, but the rest of the scene oozes animation. I don't like swimming pools. I can't swim; it's a regret of mine that I've never learnt. Bodies of water unnerve me unless I know I can put my feet flat on the bottom. I always turned down jobs on yachts, even though they generally paid brilliantly. I told Elspeth I got seasick, which stopped her putting me up for that sort of gig. No one finds a retching sex worker hot. This pool is bigger than most you find in private homes; the water looks black, because it's lined with trendy noir mosaic tiles. This makes an impactful contrast against the lush lawn, but I'm not a fan; water is scary enough without it appearing murky. I won't be telling any of the guests that I can't swim. It's been my experience at pool parties in the past that if I admit as much, there's always some jerk who sees it as a challenge. There have been several occasions when I've been picked up and hurled in the deep end, sometimes fully clothed, sometimes naked. I've always managed to scramble to the edge and haul myself up to safety, looking no doubt like a drowned kitten. Apparently, streaming mascara and blind panic is a good look on me, a number of men have said so.

Bastards.

There is a man swimming in the pool right now. He's cutting energetic butterfly strokes, breaking the water into a thousand dancing shards. Three women and two other men are sitting at the table. They are laughing at something someone has just said. Giles shouts to them, announces our arrival. For a moment everyone freezes, and then they seem to collect themselves, shudder like birds in a bath shaking off water, and in unison turn to us, smiling broadly. I'm so distracted by the strange artifice of their greeting – did I imagine it? – that I can hardly keep up with the blur of introductions that Giles is making. I struggle to pin a name to a face, work out who is with who. Were they talking about us when we arrived? It's possible. I'm sure Daniel bringing a new woman along is cause for gossip, but it felt like more than that. Daniel sits down suddenly, folds his legs beneath him, tucks his arms neatly into his sides, not taking up much space the way most men do. There's something about the gesture that suggests he'd rather not be here at all, which is odd when you consider how hard he worked to persuade me to come with him. He was determined then, but seems reticent now. I wonder if he is feeling overwhelmed by the charade he's constructed.

I'm introduced to Chen, who tells me he's Singaporean, and Liling, who says she's Chinese American. 'We just get that out there straight away, because you guys never know where we are all from and your ignorance embarrasses everyone.' Liling laughs as she says this, a hard, cold sound.

'Us guys?' I challenge.

'English people. You're all so phoney-polite and weird when it comes to talking about race. It's awkward.'

'Actually, I'm Serbian heritage. I'm not polite about anything much,' I point out. The moment I do, I want to kick myself. I never give away personal details when I am on a job – normally I'm scrupulously disciplined – but there was something about Liling's prejudice that irritated me; I just wanted to prick her balloon of self-righteousness.

Rather than be embarrassed by the inaccuracy of her own generalisation, she laughs out loud. 'That's brilliant. Well done. I like her, Daniel,' she announces, as though I have passed a test. Daniel looks startled. Unsure as to why her approval of me might relate to him. I reach for his hand, squeeze it to remind him that we're supposed to be a couple.

He remembers his role, kisses my forehead, nods. 'Everyone does.'

His eyes are not on me, though; he's looking past me at the leggy black woman sitting at the table. She's exquisite, and I don't blame him for being drawn to her. She's wearing a yellow bikini, and an orange silk headband is holding her magnificent afro off her face. Her limbs are supple, tapered, sexy. Her stomach is a wall of muscle. She's holding a half-eaten apple in her hand. When she takes a bite, I find I'm mesmerised by her wide mouth, generous lips. Sisi, I presume. Daniel is punching above his weight, even in his dreams. The only way he'd ever be able to have a woman as beautiful as her is by paying her, but Sisi is not in my game, so having her is an impossibility. I study Daniel and note a slight tightening around his mouth. He knows it too.

Sisi is the only one around the table who is wearing swim-wear; all the others are in sundresses, or shorts and T-shirts. Middle-aged people dress for lunch because they can't stand seeing their own bellies when they eat; younger people aren't as self-conscious. Daniel is ten years older than I am, although he thinks the age gap is bigger than that. His friends, I assume, are also around their late thirties or early forties, as they went to college together. However, Sisi is a lot younger, around my age in fact. 'You must be Sisi,' I say, smiling. She smiles back and nods. 'Daniel has told me so much about you. He talks about you all the time,' I add.

'Really? He's hardly revealed a thing about you.' This comment comes from the other man at the table. 'Neo, Sisi's husband,' he adds with a nod of his head. He doesn't wave or shake my hand; he's holding a penknife and busy peeling a kiwi. I think that maybe he is aware of Daniel's crush on Sisi. He's probably bored or embarrassed by it. I think his comment a tad blunt, since he believes he is delivering it up to Daniel's new girlfriend. If I weren't being paid to be here and my investment were an emotional one, I'd certainly feel intimidated or hurt.

Neo suddenly drops the knife and fruit, and shoots out his hand for me to shake. I do so. He clasps my hand tightly, pumps it up and down too vigorously. I've often found that an overly zealous handshake indicates someone who is a bit of an insecure dick. It's a shame that for many, wealth simply breeds greater insecurity, competition, and a vicious strain of ambition. Neo doesn't look like a comfortable match with Sisi. I can't quite put my finger on why – they are both incredible to look at: hard-bodied, chiselled, with great smiles. It's something about their energy. She is languid, self-approving; he is agitated, tense, and I can't imagine he approves of anything much, not even himself.

'And I am Amanda.' A slight, bird-like woman, possibly only five foot three, stretches out her slim arm, offering me her hand to shake. The jewellery she is wearing is sensational, breathtaking. Her engagement ring is a trio of enormous diamonds that sit somewhere between awe-inspiring and just-a-bit-too-much. My thumb automatically brushes my third finger. Obviously I had to leave my engagement ring at my apartment. I'm surprised how much I miss it, how easily and swiftly it's become settled on my finger. Amanda's wedding ring is a band of diamonds, as is her eternity ring. Differently cut and set diamonds, but each ring equally impactful. She is also wearing a diamond bracelet. It's thirty-eight degrees Celsius and she's enjoying a casual lunch wearing tens of thousands of pounds' worth of jewellery. Women who do this have either everything to prove or nothing at all. I wonder which she is.

Then I notice that her slight wrist is blooming a band of black and blue. The bruises are imprinted on her tanned arm and appear as a shadow to the bracelet of sparkling diamonds. She follows my gaze and flinches when she sees that I've clocked her injury. To avoid embarrassing her, I dart my interest towards the food laid out on the table: sweating cheeses flopping out of their bloomy rinds, slices of cucumber swilling in balsamic, ruby-red tomatoes glistening in extra-virgin olive oil, and thin pink slices of ham. 'This looks delicious,' I enthuse, giving Amanda the necessary privacy to quickly tug at the sleeve of her lace top, put her hands on her lap under the table and bury her indignity and anguish.

I see she is a woman with everything to prove. Her diamonds are there to tell us she is loved, even though the bruises shout otherwise.

She continues to look me in the eye. A challenge, or a request for understanding, for silence? Or maybe just her way of getting through. Getting on. 'And that's my husband,' she says cheerfully. 'The one splashing about, emptying half the pool.

Darling, you really must work on that butterfly stroke. Your technique is such that we are all soaked.' She rolls her eyes playfully. Of course her congenial show of marital exasperation is supposed to show she's a happy wife. Most people would buy it. Her husband emerges from the pool, a silhouette against the sun, his shadow falls across me. 'Jonathan, darling, come and say hello.'

It's a common enough name. There's no reason for concern. But as his shadow falls across my path, I know straight away. I know it's him.

# 14

# *Dora*

He doesn't flinch, his gaze doesn't flicker. There's nothing at all in this man's demeanour or expression that betrays the fact that just a week ago, he cuffed me to a bed, beat me, raped me. He smiles, affably. The widest smile I've been greeted with, in fact, but his eyes remain cruel slits. Instinctively I back away from him. Placing myself behind a chair so that there is a physical barrier between us.

'Fuck, Danny mate. You lucky sod,' he says, open-mouthed with apparent admiration. I stare at him, try to hold his face together, but it shatters, fragments like pixels breaking up on a Zoom call, and I begin to doubt myself. Is it really him? It is, of course, I know it is, but I so desperately want it not to be that my brain is rejecting the idea. It can't be him. 'How did you ever persuade someone so beautiful as her to date you?' He laughs, but it's not funny, especially when he adds, 'You must be paying her, right?'

And there it is. I freeze. Daniel giggles nervously, but the others don't seem to notice the comment; they look on genially as Jonathan pulls Daniel into a big manly hug, slaps him on the back and says, 'Well done, mate.'

He moves quickly around the table. Cat-like, he pounces. I'm a mouse he'll play with, rip apart, eat, leave my kidneys splayed out. Nothing else left of me. I feel nauseous and panicked as he pulls me into a hug too. His wet body pushed up against me, crushing my breath, my voice. He is large and picks me up, lifts me easily off my feet. I'm dangling, helpless. I feel his hot, sour breath on my neck. My gag reflex flickers as I am sure I recognise the smell of his skin. Then he drops me as quickly as he picked me up, turns away from me and reaches for a plate, a knife, the charcuterie board.

The conversation bounces on around me. Questions are asked about the journey, the weather forecast, is anyone up for a game of tennis this afternoon? The court is apparently stupendous. Exceedingly high-grade. 'Flat as a flounder,' comments Neo. I don't join in with the chatter. Although Daniel briefed me to be a vivacious and gracious girlfriend, I can't play that role. My mind is whirling. I believe in coincidence, or more accurately, I believe in the six degrees of separation. I think six handshakes away is generous; most of us are linked by two or three, and in my case it's usually something a lot more intimate than a handshake creating the links on the chain. I remember Elspeth saying that Jonathan asked for me by name, that he was a recommendation from an existing client. Indeed, that was the reason I decided to make room for him that day. So obviously Daniel must have been the person who recommended me. I suppose he can't be aware that Jonathan went ahead and made an appointment, because if he were, he would never have suggested I come here under the pretence of being his girlfriend. I realise he'll have no idea that his friend is a sadistic bastard who hurts women – few men ever notice as much about their friends – and yet I feel angry and betrayed. Eventually I find my voice, cough, and mutter that I want to go to my room and unpack, change into a bikini so I can sunbathe. In fact, I plan to go to my room, pick up my bag and call a cab. I'm heading straight back to the airport; I'm not staying here with Jonathan. I can pay back Daniel's fee.

Melanie offers to show Daniel and me to our room. Her presence means I can't warn Daniel that Jonathan knows who I really am. Instead, we keep up the facade of being a happy couple. Daniel makes a few comments about the size and beauty of the house. 'Wow, you could get lost in here,' he says affably as we wander through the long and winding corridors.

'We came up the main stairs, but obviously there are back stairs too, originally designed for the servants' access, I imagine. Using those will be quicker if you want to get out to the pool, although not quite as glam. I wanted you to see the place in all its glory,' explains Melanie.

'Isn't it beautiful, darling?' prompts Daniel. He nudges me in the back between the shoulder blades, presumably wondering why I'm not doing a better job of playing the giddy, gregarious girlfriend he requested.

I gaze up at the ornate cornicing and blink. 'Very nice,' I mumble in response.

We are shown into a spacious, elegant room, decorated in eggshell-blue and gold brocade. There is a four-poster bed. It's stunning, but the vintage fabric smells musty, heavy. There's a marble fireplace, an en suite bathroom with a copper claw-footed bath, and the parquet floors are waxed to a gloss. It's magnificent. I'm fleetingly disappointed that I won't get to enjoy it.

'Where's my case?' I ask glancing about.

'Probably tucked in the bottom of the wardrobe. The staff will have unpacked for you.' Melanie opens a drawer and reveals my underwear mixed in with Daniel's. The intimacy is incongruous. She giggles. 'See, all done. We want our guests to have a dreamy time here. Totally relaxed. We want to spoil you.' She stops short of bragging 'no expense spared', but the implication is heard, loud and clear. 'I'll leave you to get changed. We'll see you back by the pool as soon as poss, hey?'

The moment she closes the door, I dash to the wardrobe and fling it open, I grab my case, throw it on the bed and start to pile my belongings into it.

'What are you doing?' Daniel asks, obviously confused.

'Leaving.'

'Why?'

'I don't like your friends.'

'Oh, you mean that thing Liling said. She didn't mean to be spiky. You can imagine how much racist crap she puts up with. She was just trying to head it off. She said she liked you.'

'No, not Liling. She doesn't scare me.'

'They can all be a bit cliquey,' he admits.

'It's Jonathan.'

'Jonathan?'

'He's a …' I break off. What can I say? A psycho, a sadist, a rapist. 'He's a client.'

'Jonathan is?'

'Didn't you recommend him? Daniel, did you tell Jonathan what I do? Did. Who – what – I am?' I ask these questions

102

without slowing down the process of packing. I continue to rush around the room, opening drawers at speed, grabbing bikinis, underwear, vest tops; yanking dresses and shirts off their hangers. The clothes I carefully selected for this trip and spent all last night ironing are thrown haphazardly into my case.

'No, of course not. Why would I do that? It would blow everything.'

'I don't mean now, on the trip. I mean in the past. Have you ever told him you pay for sex?'

Daniel is blushing. He turns pink at the top of his cheekbones, making him look horribly like Piers Morgan, or Jeremy Clarkson. I know he has told Jonathan just that. Maybe not the specifics, but enough. Maybe one night after they'd had a few.

I stare at him coldly until he splutters, 'I think maybe I have mentioned you. Just once. He was having a pop about how dull I am and how I never get any.' He breaks off and then clarifies, unnecessarily, 'Any sex, that is. So I told him I had an arrangement with you. He was quite impressed by my daring, the novelty. He did ask for details. I gave him Elspeth's number, but I had no idea he had followed up. He's married.' I roll my eyes at his naivety but bite my tongue. He adds, 'Are you sure he's a client? He didn't seem to recognise you.'

'I am sure. It only happened last week.' He was wearing a mask, and then I closed my eyes trying to block him out, but even so, I'm sure.

'But he didn't say anything.'

'He said you'd have to pay me to be with you.'

'That was a joke.'

'It wasn't. Anyway, what was he supposed to say, exactly,

with his wife there? My clients aren't usually especially excited to claim me in front of their spouses.'

'Oh yes, of course.' Daniel brightens. 'Well then, we don't need to worry, do we? He can't blow our secret if he can't say how he met you. I'm really only concerned about what Sisi thinks.'

I roll my eyes, this time in despair. My problem is not whether Jonathan knows Daniel has paid me to be here, but what he might do to me while I am here. I'm not one for telling tales. Women like me suck it up, hold it in. Usually. But I need to explain this to Daniel. 'He frightens me. He's not a nice man. He hurt me.'

'Hurt you?'

'Yes.' I decide that if Daniel asks for details, I'll give them to him. I won't lie. I won't protect Jonathan – why the hell would I? Nor will I shield Daniel. I'll treat him like a friend, I'll risk the truth.

But he just nods, he doesn't ask. 'Oh, right.' He doesn't care. I zip up my suitcase.

'I'm going to call an Uber.'

'What will I tell my friends?'

'That I'm feeling ill, that we had a row, that my mother's sick. Tell them anything, I don't care.' I reach for my handbag and fish out my phone. 'Oh bugger.' The battery is dead. Frustrated, I look around the room, trying to locate the charger that I know I brought with me. I can't see it on the mantelpiece or the dressing table. I check the bedside drawer. 'I don't know where they've put the charger.' I moan in exasperation.

Daniel pulls his phone out of his pocket. 'I'll call. Of course, if you want to leave, I'm not going to keep you here against your will.'

'Thank you.' Relieved, I sit on the side of the bed. I can feel a sticky prickle running down my spine, pooling at the base of my back. Thank God Daniel is, at his core, a decent man. I see now that he was too embarrassed to ask for details about how Jonathan hurt me, and he's a bit overly trusting generally, which makes him appear weak, but in the end, he'll do the right thing.

He studies the app for a minute or two and then says, 'I'm really sorry, Natalya. They can't get here for another two hours. I guess we are in a very rural area, more farmers than Uber drivers. I'll google a local cab firm.'

I wait. I can feel my heart thumping against my ribcage. I start to imagine Jonathan coming up the stairs, walking into this room. He could cuff me, spread-eagled, to the bedposts. Momentarily, black splodges obscure my vision. I blink frantically. Am I having a panic attack?

'There's only one taxi company listed. They're based in the next village. I'm sorry, Natalya, they're not open on Mondays.' I start to sway. I'm certain the colour has completely drained out of me. Daniel looks panicked. 'Hey, don't worry, I'll book the Uber. It's only a couple of hours away. Should I look at flights for you too?'

'If you would.' I take a deep breath in through my nose. It's just a couple of hours. I look around the room and notice for the first time that there is an ice bucket, within which is a bottle of chilled champagne. The bucket glistens with condensation that looks like little diamonds, but I'm not in a celebratory mood, so instead I guzzle down a large glass of the elderberry cordial that's presented in a pretty jug. It's just a couple of hours.

# 15

# *Dora*

I want to wait in the room until the Uber arrives, but Daniel says he needs to join the others at the pool, otherwise it will look odd. I'm scared that if Jonathan realises I'm alone, he'll come and find me. The thought makes my stomach heave. I'm safer in company, even if it is his company. The plan is we're going to pretend I have a work crisis that I need to return to in London. I'm grateful to Daniel for being so accommodating and understanding; I thought for a brief, terrifying moment he was going to insist I stay here with Jonathan.

We change into our swimwear. Daniel modestly goes into the en suite to do so. Hilarious, when you think of the things we've done together in the past, but I'm grateful for his decorum. Something has changed. I'm not sure if it's because of Evan's proposal or Jonathan's beating, but I'm not the same. I put on a one-piece and a pair of shorts. I just wouldn't feel comfortable in any of my skimpy bikinis in front of Jonathan. If I could, I'd wear full PPE. Or maybe sixteenth-century armour.

'I'll give you the fee back,' I assure Daniel as we walk towards the pool.

'Well, you can keep a fifth of it. You have spent the day with me.'

I feel embarrassed for him. His division of the pie seems small, ungracious, although intended to be the opposite. I try to shrug off that feeling. It's not like me to bring sentiment into this sort of matter. I decide I will keep a fifth as he suggested. It's work. It's money. It's nothing else.

When we return to the pool, I'm relieved to find that Amanda and Jonathan are not there. They've gone to play tennis. Now that I know I'm going home, I don't have to make an effort with these people. My first impressions are that they are not great friends to Daniel; they are not especially good or interesting or lovely people. If these people are his emotional support, it's no surprise he visits sex workers and pays for intimacy. If I had been continuing with the job, out of professional pride and courtesy to Daniel I might have tried to charm them. Instead, I lie on a sunlounger and close my eyes. I let the sun cocoon me. My eyelids are heavy. I ask Daniel to wake me twenty minutes before the Uber is due, and then I fall asleep.

When I wake, I instantly know something is wrong. I'm not by the pool on the sunbed. Something heavy is weighing me down. I feel groggy, and it takes me a while to work out where I am. I'm back in the room Melanie showed us to. I'm lying in the four-poster bed. Despite the heat, someone has covered me with a quilt. I kick at it, panicked, hemmed in. It's a great relief when it slithers off the bed onto the floor. I kick at the top sheet, which has been firmly tucked in at the bottom of the bed, then sit up, breathless. Wipe away the saliva that has dribbled down the corner of my mouth. What is going on? It's dark in the room; someone has closed the shutters. I rush to the window and fling them open. Light splatters into the room, lands at my feet. But it isn't the solid yellow light of day; it's the peachy light of sunset. What time is it? I must have missed my Uber, maybe my flight. My eyes are still adjusting to the light flooding in the room when the bedroom door creaks open. I jump.

'Hello, sleepyhead.'

'Fuck, Daniel, you scared me.'

He shrugs, looks sheepish. 'Sorry for sneaking. I didn't want to wake you.'

'Why the hell not? You were supposed to wake me. I'm leaving.' I look around the bedroom, spot my suitcase, packed ready for my flit. I lunge for it. Hold tightly to the handle, ready to roll it out of the room right now. First, I ask, 'How did I get here? I fell asleep at the pool.'

Daniel looks confused. 'No, you didn't. You wouldn't come down to the pool. You said you didn't want to see Jonathan.'

I stare at him; now I'm the one that's confused. That's not what happened. But then I catch sight of my own reflection in the dressing table mirror, and I notice I'm wearing the clothes I travelled in, not my swimming costume.

'I don't understand.' I slump on the stool placed in front of the dressing table and try to ignore the fact my hand is shaking. My head pounding. I check my Fitbit. It's nearly 7 p.m. The Uber was due just after three. 'Why didn't you wake me?' I demand crossly.

'I tried to, but you were so exhausted. You just mumbled *send it away*. You said you were too tired and that you didn't want to go. So I did send it away.'

I shake my head, mystified. I must have dreamt that I went

to the pool this afternoon. God, how tired am I? Could this be something to do with the beating? Maybe a delayed concussion? Or perhaps something less sinister: an early start, the intense heat, dehydration. That combined with a few days of not sleeping well might cause me to crash. I am clearly exhausted.

'Did I do the right thing, letting you sleep?' Daniel asks, uncertainty leaking into his voice. I drop my head into my hands. It's not his fault, but I'm scared and angry. Angry with myself mostly. I shouldn't have fallen asleep. 'Look, Natalya, I had a word with Jonathan.'

'You did what?' I demand coldly.

'Well, once it became obvious you were staying overnight, I thought I'd better clear the air.' The understatement is ridiculous, insulting, but I remind myself that's not Daniel's fault. He doesn't know the extent of the damage Jonathan inflicted. How badly he hurt me. I wasn't explicit. Daniel is a middle-class man who represses his feelings; he's limited. I try to cut him some slack. He coughs. 'Look, Natalya, Jonathan isn't your client.'

'Yes, he is. Well, he was. Once. Last week.'

'No, he wasn't,' says Daniel carefully. His tone of voice is similar to one that you might use when reasoning with a child who thinks there's a monster under the bed, a bogeyman in the wardrobe. Sympathetic, but underpinned with a slight frustration that the child believes in that sort of nonsense. 'I asked him straight out. It was all a bit mortifying, actually. Because obviously doing so meant I had to make it clear what you are, and why you are here with me.'

What I am.

'Jonathan was out of the country all last week. He was

in LA. He insisted on showing me his itinerary to prove the point. He was a little surprised that I thought he might have used a woman like you. After all, he has Amanda, like I said.'

My gag reflex hiccups, but I keep my mouth clamped closed, swallow back the lunch I picked at earlier. I won't throw up. I'm not squeamish. I'm not heaving at the thought of these two men discussing 'using' a woman like me; I'm bewildered. I was so sure that Jonathan was the man who beat me. His name, his look, his smell. It *was* him.

'I'm certain it was …' I break off. *Am* I certain?

'It sounds as though you've been through something awful, Natalya. I'm really sorry. But Jonathan has nothing to do with it. I think you might need to see a doctor when you get back to England. Just to check everything is OK. I mean, might this be some sort of physical repercussion? Did you get hit on the head? Or maybe it's a mental reaction to the trauma,' he adds carefully.

'I don't know …' I was so sure. I start to doubt myself. Is it him? The man who beat me, raped me? *Was* it rape? I was there for sex. Sex he was going to pay for. He had sex. He paid me. Probably not rape in the eyes of the law. Except I sobbed and begged him to stop. He could call that role play.

'But it is awfully embarrassing for me, and for Jonathan too now. You can see that, can't you? Accusing the poor man of all sorts. Visiting prostitutes, beating them up. Awkward.' Daniel says the final word in a strange, high-pitched comedic way, then grimaces. Nothing in his life has probably ever surpassed awkwardness. He's never known the extremes: grief, humiliation, degradation. He's never even experienced the other side of the scale. He hasn't been in love, not really. He has a schoolboy crush on his friend's wife. An infatuation, nothing more sincere. 'Well, anyway, we don't have to worry. Jonathan is being very decent about it and said he won't mention any of it to anyone.'

'It?'

'Us. Our arrangement. Not even Amanda. That's a relief, isn't it?'

'I suppose.' I'm parched. It feels as though I've swallowed earth.

'So we're good, are we? Or do you still need me to book a flight home for you tomorrow?'

'I don't know, I—'

'Because truly, Natalya, I think you should stay. You need the break. A few days recuperating here might be just the thing. You are clearly not yourself.'

'Well, maybe …' I am usually particularly good at identifying what I want, what I don't want, but my head is throbbing; pulsing with such ferocity that I think it might split. I imagine it exploding, my brains splattered all over the damask walls, the silk bedding, the crystal chandelier. Such gore smearing such beauty. I might have made a mistake. It's possible. Going to the pool felt real, but I never left this room; that was a dream. I am traumatised by what that man – the real Jonathan – did to me. Perhaps I heard his name today, just after seeing the bruises on his wife's wrist, and my brain played a trick on me. How do I know he had anything to do with her injured wrist? She seems perfectly happy. I'm jumping to conclusions. I'm not being rational. I'm not being myself. But dare I stay? I glance at the bed and then at Daniel. He's a regular client. More trustworthy than most men I meet, but that is still a long way off trustworthy.

'You could kill me while I sleep,' I joke. I make the joke because airing my worst fear exposes it for what it is. Ridiculous.

Daniel grins at me. His glasses have slightly steamed up, because the room is humid. He opens the window. He struggles with the sash, has to stretch up. His fleshy belly pokes out from beneath his polo shirt, his efforts make him look momentarily incompetent. He doesn't present a threat. 'I think you are more likely to kill me. I'll take the chaise longue.'

He's going to be uncomfortable on that. It's a genuine antique, therefore of mean proportions, because our ancestors were slighter than we are now.

'We can share the bed,' I mutter. 'But don't think this means anything.'

'It means you are kind, and maybe that you know that if I don't have a good night's sleep, I'm a grumpy arse. So, you'll stay?'

'Yes.'

'Excellent. Well, I'll leave you to get dressed. Melanie told me to tell you that the women are all wearing cocktail dresses. She said you'd want to know. There's nothing worse than turning up in the wrong gear, is there?'

'No, there's nothing worse than that,' I reply with a sigh.

# 16

# *Dora*

'Oh, don't you look beautiful,' enthuses Melanie the moment she claps eyes on me. I'm wearing a black halter-neck cocktail dress; it clings exactly where it should. She watches from the bottom of the grand staircase as I slowly make my way down. I'm in high heels and so my progress is precarious, careful. I wear killer heels more frequently than most women and am normally able to strut and stride confidently, but the two-hundred-year-old staircase is ferociously polished; it's like walking on ice. I need to pay attention. I get a strange feeling that Melanie has been waiting for me to arrive – for my entrance – but that doesn't make sense. Why would she be interested in me? She has other guests. Get over yourself, I self-instruct.

'Feeling better?' she asks. I nod. 'Daniel said you were exhausted from travelling.'

I flew across the Channel in business class, I did not hike up Kilimanjaro, but I nod again. I let her think I'm a delicate, protected, cushioned woman, as she is. I'm certainly fragile. Although that's not quite the same thing.

As I reach the bottom step, she slips her arm through mine. Our bare skins caress one another, interlinked. Melanie trails a finger along the length of my arm. The intimacy seems peculiar, the action predatory rather than friendly, but I don't pull away. I don't want to appear odd, and I'm very used to being touched by strangers, so it's hardly an issue.

'Oh, your skin is so smooth,' she says with breathy admiration. 'Come on, the others are in the salon, drinking cocktails. They've all been there nearly an hour. You'll have to catch up.'

Since they've been drinking for an hour, I'm surprised that when I approach the room, I can't hear the usual sounds that signal good times. There is jazz music playing (which I always think a little pretentious; why not listen to some Ellie Goulding or Norah Jones pre-dinner?), but other than the tinkling of piano notes and the rasping, edgy sound of a saxophone, it is silent. No one is telling a story or laughing at one. Melanie swings open the wooden doors and sweeps into the elegant, high-ceilinged salon. I follow. There is a marble fireplace, three white sofas arranged around it, a baby grand piano. How is this a rental? I wonder how many mothers have scolded children and dogs for siting on the sofas, nervous of sticky hands and muddy paws. All heads swivel in our direction, and then – a fraction of a second later – the guests burst into a boisterous round of laughter. Are they laughing at me? What are they laughing at? I run my tongue over my teeth: a basic lipstick application error?

My confusion is not eased when Liling insists, 'You are hilarious, Neo. What a funny story.' Addressing Melanie and me, she adds, 'You've just missed the funniest story.'

Did we? Melanie smiles vacuously and nods. Her entire

demeanour is that of a woman who is used to missing things and doesn't mind. My vision swims fleetingly. My senses are playing tricks on me again. The room *was* silent, I'm sure of it. *Almost* sure of it. The ruby and orange light of the sunset tumbles into the salon through the long multi-paned sash window. The colour catches on the crystal drops of the chandelier and is flung in scattered fragments. The elegant greys and whites of the furniture and furnishings, the parquet floor and the portraits hung on the walls look as though they are splattered with blood. I take a deep breath. Try to clear my head. I am not myself. I accept the G&T that Daniel is proffering and down it in one. He looks startled but not concerned, and cheerfully returns to the cocktail trolley to refill my glass.

'Can you repeat it for me?' My request comes out jarring, not showing a pleasant interest, but something close to an interrogation. I feel uncomfortable and demanding. The crowd stop laughing. They hold their faces in wide, unconvincing grins. 'The story, can you repeat it for me? So I know what you were laughing at.'

'You had to be there,' says Sisi firmly.

'Shall we go through to dinner?' suggests Giles.

Dinner passes in a blur, a series of fast images, vivid, pungent smells, and clashing noises. I need to drink more water. However, I find myself repeatedly reaching for my wine glass. The water is at the other end of the table, near Jonathan. I don't want to ask him for it. The room is dark and indulgent. Fusty wood panels line every wall, from floor to ceiling; there is a long table that comfortably seats all ten of us; the chairs are red velvet, with gold brocade accents. It's like being inside a medieval castle. Or a coffin. I don't know why I leapt to that. It must be the smell of polish and oil. That, mixed with the heady scent of fat lilies opening to show off their proud stamens. Those are the smells I associate with my father's funeral. I'm being morbid. I'm not normally indulgent of any sort of illusion. Reality is frightening enough. I'm glad when those smells are replaced by the aromas from the dishes: piquant herbs and spices in salads and mousses, then the iron of the bloody steak that has been cooked so rare it's barely been wafted over the pan's sizzling heat.

As the evening wears on, I become more conscious of the expensive perfumes not quite masking the raw, perspiring bodies; the smell of wine, in my glass, on everyone's breath. If the gang were quiet in the salon pre-dinner, there is no sign of that reserve now. Besides the music coming from the iPod, the noise from the kitchen, and the constant clattering of feet as the waiting staff run to and fro delivering course after course, there are several conversations taking place at once. The noise around me is raucous; hilarity and excitement bubble up. There is a general sense of anticipation, even after we've eaten, suggesting it's not the food they were anticipating having. Everyone is buzzing with the energy you get from the sort of people determined to push limits, to go too far. I come across this careless daring, this need for highs, a lot in my business. I don't tell any stories, but I laugh loudly whenever anyone else does, even if I haven't got the joke, even if the words sometimes seem to be reaching me morphed and distorted, as though they are talking to me from under the sea. No one seems to mind that I don't contribute my own stories. Maybe they think I'm a mystery. Maybe they think I'm dull and have nothing to say.

I'm used to smiling, taking it in, not offering it up. It's safest and easiest. It's not just sex workers who do this; many women do. They do it to their husbands, and fathers, and colleagues because they haven't the energy to waste on getting to the truth of matters. These men have views on everything, from the naffness of e-smoking to the way the country is governed – no, scrub that, the way the *world* is. It's obvious that they like to hear the sound of their own voices.

It's a hot night. None of the other women are wearing make-up. Mine is coming off in places, exposing a shiny nose; it's caking in other parts. I don't often make mistakes like this one. Chen and Neo are sitting to my right and left, Giles is opposite me. I'm grateful I'm not seated next to Jonathan. I watch Amanda offer food to him, pile it on his plate without his permission, hold her own fork up to his mouth. She's like an insect hovering around a plate of meat at a BBQ; she has incalculable energy and persistence, but at the same time, she's annoying. He bites, masticates, swallows, but hardly pauses to thank her for her attentions. Regardless, she continues with the vigorous determination of a grandmother pushing treats on a spoilt toddler.

My stomach tightens. I remember that Daniel has explained that Jonathan is not the man who beat me. That man was wearing a mask; I tried not to look at him throughout the ordeal; there have been so many men, they tend to merge. Of course, it is possible I have made a mistake. Well, probable. Certain. Daniel saw Jonathan's itinerary; he wasn't even in the country at the time. I am suffering some level of physical or mental trauma, and yet still I find looking at him difficult. I try to put him out of my head. The Jonathan sitting at this table, and the man I thought he was. I need to relax, that is why I agreed to stay here after all.

After several courses, a heaving cheeseboard is brought into the room. It's ripe and pungent. Everyone insists they cannot eat another mouthful, and then, one by one, they reach for the knives and start to cut off small wedges of Brie and Camembert. Eventually Amanda and Melanie make noises about wanting to go to bed. Their husbands smile affably but show no intention of joining them. I know that as I'm working, I can only go to bed when Daniel says I can. Since we're playing the part of the newly involved couple, we can't drift off separately as older married couples do; it would be suspicious.

'We've had a long day, shall we hit the hay?' I ask. Daniel can, if he wants, pretend to interpret my suggestion as a hint that I can't wait to get him between the sheets.

Unsurprisingly, since he knows sex isn't part of the deal, he isn't interested in leaving the party. 'But you had a nap, you can't be tired.'

He'll stay up as long as Sisi does. I need to settle in, accept as much. 'What shall we do next?' I ask with the enthusiasm of a devoted girlfriend.

'Let's play charades,' suggests Liling. Her suggestion is quickly shouted down.

'Oh God, no, too much effort.'

'That's something to do when everyone's here.'

'How about cards?' offers Sisi.

'I'm too drunk to concentrate.'

'No, you'll take all my money!'

'Let's play truth or dare,' says Neo, his voice oozing a giddy excitement.

What are we, twelve? The question stays in my head, thankfully. The others clap their hands, shout out their concurrence.

Someone suggests we take the party outside, under the stars, near the pool. Someone else grabs a bottle of tequila and another person takes the claret. Daniel picks me up and throws me over his shoulder; he whoops and slaps his hand down hard on my backside. I am not sure if it was intended to be playful. My mind catapults itself to some old movie, set in the 1950s, when the handsome hero subdues the cute little wife. In the movie, that slap might have been delivered to chastise or to suggest desire. Then, it was all wry grins and winks: I know what's best for the little lady, she wants it really. Subjugation over generations of popular culture. Things have not changed, not really, and not fast enough. There are no knights in shining armour, but fuck me, damsels are still in distress.

# 17

# *Dora*

It's black out, but luckily the walkways are lit by modern, state-of-the-art electric uplighters, which help as we drunkenly stumble towards the pool, where we collapse heavily on sunbeds. Daniel and I take the luxurious double lounger; no one fights us for it. I notice that Neo and Sisi, and Liling and Chen sit separately. They do not twine their limbs around one another, announcing their devotion. Some couples do that at this stage of the evening; I guess this group are a little too cool for public displays of affection. It's helpful: I won't be required to be competitively overly attentive with Daniel. I position myself close enough to him to give the impression we are together, but not so close that I can feel the heat from his body.

Chen lights a spliff, Giles produces a small packet of white power, Jonathan and Sisi cheer. I don't do drugs – my world is precarious enough – but I'm often around people who do, so I don't feel fazed. I roll onto my back and look at the stars. Leave them to it. I don't doubt that the idea of skinny-dipping will be hinted at soon. It is a basic expectation at this sort of party. Why else has someone suggested truth or dare?

These people have been friends for years; they must know all they are ever going to know about one another by now. A thought occurs. Unless I am the focus. Maybe they want to fast-track getting to know me. Or at least getting to know Natalya, Daniel's girlfriend. That seems a likely theory; when the questions start, they inevitably follow a sexual nature. Everyone is always interested in everyone else's sex life.

The bottle spins, slows, stops. Giles asks Liling, 'Have you ever been unfaithful?' She shakes her head. Spins again and asks the same question of Jonathan.

'No!' He says it with the level of outrage that causes me to doubt him.

'Have you ever done al fresco?'

'Are you a member of the mile-high club?'

'Have you ever strapped one on?'

'Have you ever done a threesome?' This question lands at my feet. Chen's dark eyes are bright, alive.

'Yes,' I reply calmly, knowing I'm sending a frisson of excitement and tension out into the crowd.

'Really? Which way on? Two boys, or did you bring along a friend?' he probes.

'That's technically two more questions,' I reply with a smile, and then stub out the cigarette I'm smoking. 'You are a rule-breaker.' Everyone pauses and then simultaneously burst into riotous giggles. I feel Daniel let out a sigh of relief. If they were testing me, I passed. They now think I'm a cool girlfriend, possibly a bit too cool for Daniel, but they approve of me. I'm sure my attractiveness and poise will help his standing with Sisi. Sexual politics is a complex, wild beast, but I'm the ringmaster.

The garden lights must be on a timer, because at some point

we are temporarily plunged into a solid pitch black. The boys scrabble about, pulling vintage Dunhill lighters out of their pockets and then lighting the candles in the lanterns that are scattered about. There is enough light to see the men's fore-heads shine, the women blush and pout. Everyone is drunker than they ought to be. Keen to talk dangerously. Nights like this can go two ways. Within an hour they'll all be consumed with forbidden thoughts and so will scurry upstairs with their partners to pound out a bit of pent-up energy. Or someone might suggest a swap. I've seen it happen. I guess that's what Daniel is praying for.

It's my turn to spin the bottle. I do so with a flourish, and wink at Daniel. I'm drunk enough to be convincing. It slows to a stop in front of Jonathan. I shiver.

'Have you ever hurt anyone?' The question plunges out into the night. It jars. The others fall silent. I don't know why I asked it. The tequila, no doubt.

Jonathan looks confused. 'Hurt in what way? What do you mean? Broken a heart? Well, darling girl, look at me I'm irresistible,' he jokes. For the record, he is not. He's far from it. Generously, I'd say he will only ever have attracted women who are interested in his personality; more honestly, I think if he attracts people at all, it's because he probably earns a telephone number as a salary.

'No, I mean, blacked an eye, split a lip?' The friends stay silent. There is no boisterous whooping or lively teasing. A night bird hoots; there is a small plopping sound in the pool. I guess a field mouse must have run to its death.

'Well, yes,' he admits. 'I've broken ribs, fractured jaws, burst eye sockets.' The words rip at my skin. I feel each blow he's confessing to as though I'm enduring them. My head swims as I feel my body contract in cold dread. I can't breathe; it's as though someone is pouring sand down my throat. Why did I ask something that was obviously going to be triggering? I take a deep breath, blink slowly, force myself back into the here and now. Jonathan continues. 'You all remember I was a member of the Gentlemen's Boxing Society at uni. Stupid, when I look back. Macho competitive nonsense. No gloves, no protective headgear. I'm not proud of it.' He grimaces and looks sincere, a man in his forties embarrassed by his youthful violent antics.

I let the words into my head. I try to accept them. A boxing club. He was in a boxing club. That was where he hurt people. Not last week in a hotel room. As a young man, other young men being bloodied. Not great, ill-advised, but a sport, fought equally. He smiles at me. I force myself to smile back.

'Oh, this is heavy,' groans Sisi. 'Let's do some dares now. Jonathan, stop talking about blood,' she instructs with a big playful grin. 'Everyone has to either haul themselves up a tree or strip off and get in the pool.'

Climbing a tree requires effort and sobriety. Skinny-dipping entails opportunities to ogle and fondle. I'm not surprised when everyone starts to cast off their clothes, but I'm reluctant. I watch bare arses run away from me; they dive-bomb into the pool, opting for a short, sharp shock of cold water over a slow approach. I bolt towards the surrounding woods. Quickly off the manicured lawn, I speed across tough long grasses that lash and bite at my ankles. I hitch up my dress to around my waist, kick off my shoes and shimmy up the closest tree. Deftly, like a monkey, ignoring the pain in my still tender ribs. I've been climbing trees since I was a child, and it's a knack. Even so, I scrape my left foot on the rough bark and graze my right elbow. I'm hardly correctly dressed for the task. The others spot me and cheer my daring. I'm putting on a show of athleticism, and everyone always admires that. I know the men, at least, will be noting my firm thighs as I clamber and rise. I find a branch robust enough to settle on, and sit, shrouded in the green canopy, the leaves shaking. Disturbed by my presence, the others are calling for me to come down. Giles threatens to follow me, but he quickly gives up the idea because he can't be bothered to dress, and scaling a tree naked is obviously a precarious feat.

'You made short work of that! Well done you!' yells Neo.

'I was brought up on a farm, spent half my life shimmying up trees,' I tell them. Daniel needs to stop looking so surprised when I drop personal facts into our conversation. If I'm supposed to be his girlfriend, he would know this and more about me. He all but spits out the word 'fascinating'. I cut him off. 'It was a lovely childhood, roaming the fields, picking blackberries and watching baby animals being born.' There's a lot of death too, besides the business of taking animals off to slaughter: owls eating mice, foxes eating chickens, calves getting stuck in their mother's birth canal, nose and hooves tantalisingly on show but a too-long labour ending in a finish, not a start. I don't mention any of this. I know how to self-censor. That sort of reality is not pool-party appropriate.

Soon, they forget me. I am glad. I've had a strange feeling all evening that I'm being closely observed; something beyond curiosity. I don't like it. I wonder whether Jonathan has really kept his promise to Daniel. If not, and they know what I do for a living, they are likely to be intrigued. *Did*. Did for a living.

My mind drifts to Evan. I must be mad to be here, up a tree, when I could be at home in bed, texting my bestie. My fiancé. I should not have taken this job. I'm not well, and these people are not quite right. But then, who is? I took the job because for years I've been jabbed by the needling fear of poverty. An unthinking imperative to make money whenever I can, however I can, has absorbed me. But I shouldn't have come.

So much has happened in these last ten days, I can hardly keep track of it. I'm not a stranger to sudden pivots in fortunes; I pride myself on expecting the unexpected and certainly being able to absorb and manage the things that life throws at me. However, I'm still processing Evan's proposal. The Cinderella nature of it terrifies me. I always thought the only believable part of that fairy tale was that at midnight she turned back into a servant girl and the coach once again became a pumpkin. No one in their right mind believes in fairy godmothers or glass slippers, and certainly not in Prince Charming. Yet there is an engagement ring worth about thirty thousand pounds hidden under the mattress in my apartment in London.

I watch as Chen jumps back out of the pool. His body is lean and muscular. Much fitter than the average man his age. He clearly works out. He picks up his linen trousers, which lie discarded near the pool, fishes in the pockets and pulls out a small packet. Tablets of some kind, oxycodone or fentanyl, at a guess. Something middle class that can be got on prescription. But maybe I'm underestimating him; maybe it's something that's less regulated. He holds the packet aloft and the others give a cheer.

Chen settles on the edge of the pool, his legs dangling in the water, and doles out the drugs. He is completely naked. One by one the group swim up to him and tread water in front of him, their eyes level with his penis, as they wait for him to hand them a tablet. None of them seem abashed. I don't understand them. I think of myself as quite the people connoisseur, but I can't put my finger on their dynamic. The answers to the questions asked during truth or dare seemed to come as news, yet this level of comfort in their own skin suggests extreme intimacy. I had Daniel pegged as an intellectually brilliant but socially underdeveloped teddy bear. But despite the hoots of laughter that from time to time rise from the pool and pierce the blackness, this is no teddy bears' picnic.

They seem to forget about me altogether, and I'm glad. From my perch I watch silently, wondering what might unfold below me. Because in my experience, when people strip off their clothes, their masks of civilisation drop too.

# 18

# *Dora*

When I wake up the next morning, Daniel is nowhere to be seen. I didn't hear him come to bed. I don't think he did. Least, not this one. It may be that he found a spare room or that he slept outside, too drunk and spent to move. My perch provided exactly what I'd hoped. Out of sight, out of mind, they soon forgot about me. I stayed long enough to see Giles and Liling have sex – yes, that's right, *Giles and Liling*. Drugs and extramarital sex; the lawyer sure knows how to celebrate a promotion. His hypocrisy doesn't shock me, but it does sadden me a little. I would like to believe in the power of the law; I'd like to think that the people in charge are honourable, reliable, fair. Giles makes me think of that old quote, 'the law is an ass'. Of course it is. I am a sex worker who can be prosecuted for having sex with people who pay me, but those people can't be prosecuted, they aren't breaking the law. It's ludicrous.

Giles and Liling did it up against the wall of the outside bar, no more than twenty metres from the pool. Not exactly in your face, but a long way from discreet. Melanie was safely tucked up in bed, but Chen and Neo meanwhile floated on an inflatable swan and inflatable pizza slice respectively, Chen seemingly unaware of his wife's transgression, or if he was aware, then unconcerned, careless. I wonder if this is how she can say she's never been unfaithful; they might have an agreement. Or is she an out-and-out liar? Was that her first transgression? It didn't look like it to me. Interesting.

Jonathan, Daniel and Sisi also stayed in the pool. Initially there was some low-key flirtatious cavorting, as they casually threw a blow-up ball between them. Chances perhaps to touch her breast, her bottom; certainly an opportunity to drink in her shape. However, it didn't progress to anything extreme. When I carefully clambered down the tree and then sneaked away back to the chateau, they were huddled talking in low voices.

I've seen everything. I really think I have. I consider myself unshockable and it certainly wasn't the most unusual outcome of a party I've attended: drugs, nudity, infidelity are often par for the course. However, I find I am unsettled by these people. Whenever Daniel touched on his friendship group, his conversation centred on how rich and successful they all are, how they've known one another since they were at college, where they were all brilliantly erudite and notably athletic. His accounts were idealised, romantic even. I thought he was naïve, innocent. Seeing them behave the way they did last night was unexpected; it didn't quite fit in with the Richard Curtis scenes he had drawn. I'm not passing a moral judgement here – how could I? I don't care who sleeps with whom, I just feel somewhat blindsided. A pulse of anxiety keeps bobbing to the surface. I don't know these people. I wonder what Daniel, Jonathan and Sisi were talking about when I slipped away.

It looked serious. None of them was wearing the expression fitting guests at a chateau celebration; surely wall-to-wall giddiness is the order of the day.

I shake my head, pour a glass of water from the carafe by my bed. I take large gulps, pour a second glass. I must stop being so paranoid. It's not like me and it's not helpful. I wonder if I'm thinking this way because my life is finally coming together and I can hardly believe it. I don't trust my own luck. Probably they weren't talking about anything important at all. Their serious faces were most likely a result of drug- and drink-induced obsession and intensity. I've seen people come to blows about which is the most influential David Bowie song after one too many tequila shots.

My head aches this morning. I'm sure it's just a hangover, which is inevitable after the night we had. I dig out a box of paracetamol from my wash bag, swallow a couple down, then scrabble about for my phone, which is now fully charged, and send Evan a quick text asking him if he's arrived safely, what the hotel is like. Has he had any meetings yet? I have not told him that I accepted this job with Daniel. I wasn't sure how he would react. I know he would be concerned for me. He wanted me to go to the doctor's to be checked out after the beating, and probably I should have followed his advice, or at least stayed put, recuperated fully. I try to put him out of my mind as I shower and then hurriedly dress. The anxiety I'm feeling is most likely because of the hangover.

As I head downstairs, I can hear chatter swapped between the staff. The most senior staff members are French, the cleaners are Eastern European; irrespective, they greet me in English: 'Good morning, madam,' repeated often and sometimes accompanied by a small bob of the knees. I don't run into any of the other guests; the house is quiet except for the murmuring of the staff and the drone of a vacuum somewhere in one of the wings.

I mooch about, drifting from one elegant room to the next: a drawing room, a conservatory, a library. The windows are open; sunlight floods in and washes the shiny parquet floor. I can hear birds chattering. The gardener must have been up early to turn on the sprinklers, because the grass is wet, light catching the velvet lawns like glinting broken glass, but it's not dew, that's long since burnt off. The library is full of books with leather covers, navy blue, burgundy, bottle green. I run my finger along the spines. The covers have turned soft as cloth with age and wear. I find a shaggy biscuit-coloured dog. I'm not an expert, but my guess is a golden retriever crossed with a poodle. A goldendoodle. She raises her head when I walk past, looking for attention, which I happily give. The tag on her collar tells me her name is Marmalade. I wonder who she belongs to. I bury my face in her coat; indolent, placid, she lets me breathe her in. I wonder whether Evan and I will get a dog. I'd like that. I leave her sleeping on the rug and continue to roam. The salon and the dining room have been returned to a state of immaculate calm. All the debris from the night before cleared away, gone, as though nothing indecorous ever happened within these walls: no overindulgence, no drinking, no flirting.

I'm offered breakfast by the housekeeper, but I never eat breakfast. I accept a black coffee and then drift outside. I realise that I'm half looking for the others but also half hoping I don't find them. The grounds are large enough that we can all be swallowed up, entertained without crowding one another.

Ideally, I'd like to be left alone to read my book. I don't particularly like any of the group and I haven't the energy or inclination to find out if there is anything about them that is worth liking. Of course, if Daniel is around and wants me to join in, then I must, but if I can, I'll keep my head down.

It's half past ten and yet the air is already swollen with heat. I'm glad of the enormous brim of my sunhat. I head towards the pool. There are ten sunbeds, as well as a hammock and the double lounger, all laid out invitingly. I've only just got out of bed, but the urge to flop is strong. White towels, that have most definitely been professionally laundered, are rolled into fat cylinders at the foot of each sunbed. I pick a lounger under a sun brolly. There's a guy in his early twenties standing behind the outside bar. He's polishing glasses, oblivious to last night's antics, which were performed just where he is standing. Without my asking, he brings me a fruit cordial, offers me sun lotion. I accept gratefully, because mine is running low. The bottle he offers is an expensive brand and smells wonderful. I very much doubt it will be the sort that stains the hem of my sundress. I start to apply it to my legs. Slowly massaging the cream into my muscles feels good, but the respite is temporary.

'The others have all gone into the local town. There's a farmers' market.' Jonathan's voice cuts through the hefty hot air. I tremble. Just a fraction of a second, then my brain catches up. *It wasn't him.* Yet disquiet squats in my stomach.

'Oh, I wish they'd woken me. I like a farmers' market. All those free morsels, yummy pastries, spicy sausage.' I beam, pleasantly, but immediately regret mentioning sausage. Jonathan knows what I do for a living. Will he read more

131

into that comment than I intended? Men love to think women are constantly having lewd thoughts, and whilst few of us are (most of the time we are thinking about food, or current affairs, the TV show we're streaming or the weather), it's not an unreasonable leap to make about a sex worker. I feel a wave of something like grief wash over me as I wonder whether in the future, when I offer Evan bangers and mash and say I fancy a fat sausage, will he always think I am being suggestive? How is he going to forget my past? I mentally shake myself. Don't complicate this. Don't look for problems. It will be OK. Relationships are all swings and roundabouts, everyone comes with their own particular circumstances. I'll have to get used to the fact that whenever he sends me flowers, I'll know his PA chose them. We all have our burdens to bear.

Jonathan looms above me. 'Can I show you around the grounds? You didn't get to see everything yesterday.'

He is not the host, so it's not really his place to do so. I'm quite settled with my book and don't want to trail about in this heat, but I get the feeling there's an agenda. Maybe he just wants us to get on a more comfortable footing. I wish I could believe this, but I'm not big on trusting in people's better nature. However, I do believe in facing things down, and I decide I might as well accept his offer.

Alone together, Jonathan is amiability personified. He continues to keep up the polite pretence that I am Daniel's actual girlfriend. He tells me about the charming market the others are visiting: 'I feel dreadful you missed out.' He tells me a little of the house's history: 'Although I'm no expert, I'm only repeating what I've been told.' He is solicitous of my comfort: 'Are you OK in flip-flops? Watch that step.'

He walks me through the formal gardens, along the edge of the woods and across to the tennis courts. We visit the grotto; it is as Melanie described, dingy. A man-made cave decorated with a mismatch of mosaic tiles and shells. However, the dank, cool air of the caved area offers a brief respite from the blazing sun. He even takes me to look at some of the outbuildings. It seems we are the first visitors to these for a long time. The farm machinery and tools all have a cloak of dust on them. A shallow grave. As a child who grew up playing around a disorderly collection of sheds and outbuildings, I am not intimidated by the deserted, disused barns. I quickly make a mental note of what is stored here. A sit-on lawnmower, bags of fertiliser, ladders, a wheelbarrow, a metre-high pile of chopped wood, several axes, a chainsaw, pitchforks, spades, various other bits of machinery and tools, mostly rusting. Habit. I always assess my environment, check for exits and even weapons. In a hotel bedroom, that might be the ice bucket; here it is more obvious, should the need arise.

Jonathan also appears to be making an inventory, or at least I think so until he says, 'Not much to see here. Shall we press on?' I suppose his roving gaze was one of boredom rather than calculation.

I can't think there's much left to see. I'm hot and tired, as we walk I can feel the stones of the rough ground and the roots of the fat trees through the soles of my flip-flops, which are now dusty, as are my feet. My ruby-red pedicure looks like drops of blood at the end of my toes. I'd like a cool drink and to sit down, but good manners cause me to nod.

As the tour progresses, I begin to really believe he is a devoted husband to Amanda; that he is a good friend to Daniel and will keep his secret. That I am safe. Then, just as we enter the maze, he says jovially, 'So Daniel tells me you are a hooker. How much would it cost for you to give me a blow job.' He doesn't laugh as he asks this. The question squats fat between us.

'You couldn't afford me,' I say smoothly, and keep walking. I am not as calm as my quip suggests. It must be the heat, but I'm not thinking the necessary step ahead, and I find I've strode forward, deeper inside the maze. The bushes are tall, a couple of feet above my head, and thick. It's dangerous. I turn around, try to exit, but his bulk blocks me. I don't want to appear intimidated, so I choose to head further into the labyrinth.

'What do you think of the house?' he asks, seemingly return-ing to safer subjects. I decide to remain civil and humour him, because what else can I do?

'It's beautiful.'

'Yes, but a money pit, wouldn't you say? People think of a chateau, and they think, wow, what luxury! They don't see the moss, mould and mouse damage, or the wind and rain loosening tiles.'

'I suppose not.'

'It's like when men think of a hooker, and they think, wow, what fun! They don't see the filth and the squalor. The gold-digger.'

My breath catches in my throat as he says this, but I force myself not to show how much he's frightening me. Instead, I smile broadly and say again, 'I suppose not.' Then, after a beat, I find the nerve to add, 'You seem to know a lot about my profession.'

'Oh, only what I've been told,' he says with a modest smile, as though he is humbly refuting having a great understanding of a complex fiscal issue or a particularly insightful interpretation of a Renaissance painting.

I try to concentrate on the route we are taking. First right, second left, second right. I may need to be able to reverse it and get out, but I already feel disorientated, lost. I'm not sure if we go much further that I'll be able to keep it in my mind. All the hedges look the same. I should turn back now, while I have a chance.

'So why do you do what you do?' he probes. This is the same question they all ask. That's comforting. He's just another pathetic man who thinks he can bully me. Not a real threat.

'Why does anyone do anything? Money, obviously,' I reply. This isn't the answer they want. They want to hear I do it because I like sex. They want to think of me needing sex as much as they do. If he were a client, I might tell him that I do it because I love sex, because it would excite him. But he's not my client, and I owe him nothing at all. Not even a frisson of a thrill. I turn around. I've had enough. I'm going back to the pool. I don't care if I look rude. I don't care if he tells everyone that Daniel paid me to be here. He might not be the man who beat me, but he is a creep and I don't like being alone with him. I don't have to do this.

Jonathan must see something in my face that suggests I'm about to bolt, because at that moment he grabs my arm and pulls me sideways through a hedge. His bulk forces a gap where there wasn't one, but as I tumble through behind him, I am scratched by the rough branches. My hat falls off and lands in the dusty earth. I glance at his hands. Faces may blur, become indistinct, they can be hidden behind masks and smiles, but hands are harder to disguise. Some are square or long-fingered. Others have fat, podgy fingers. Hands can be smooth, clammy, hairy, liver-spotted, wandering. Curled into a fist. I try to remember the hands of my assailant in the hotel. I try to forget them.

We've plunged into the centre of the maze, but his shortcut means I have no idea how to get back out. I feel like Alice falling down the rabbit hole. I start to claw back through the bush, the way we've just come, but it's impossible; the branches don't seem to bend to allow it. I'm getting more cuts on my arms and legs, deeper this time. I look ridiculous, and worse, I look panicked. I know better than to show fear. I bend, pick up my hat and brush off the grime, but I don't put it back on my head. Instead, as I turn to face him, I use it as a fan, so he can't see my hands shaking.

'You don't look the type,' he remarks.

'You know a type?'

'You know what I mean. You're not how I imagine a whore to be.' I realise he's trying to humiliate me. He can't. I'm the only person who controls how I feel, how I respond. I've taught myself that. But I live in the real world and I know he can hurt me; I have no control over that. Words can never hurt me, but sticks and stones – well, everyone knows how the playground rhyme pans out.

'You can call me a whore if that makes you feel better about yourself,' I say calmly.

Sweat is collecting grotesquely on his top lip. He seems to become aware of it at the same time as I do; however, instead of wiping it away, he licks it. His tongue is long, thin, reptilian. 'You make a good show at classy, I'll give you that, but what you do is actually so very, very sleazy. So disgusting, you know that. Down deep, you know that about yourself.' He asserts this in a way that presumes a lot about me.

I don't reply. I hear echoes of the words that were said to me in the hotel. *You disgust me. Stop what you are doing.* He's right, sex *is* sleazy. Or can be. I know that better than most. The whips and synthetic costumes, the cheap peekaboo bras, the toys, the tricks. I try hard to keep away from all that, although I can't always manage it. After all, the customer is always right. I'm there for his needs, not mine. I'm an actor. It's not even me. I'm playing a role. I know admitting any of this would feed this horrible little man's fantasy. He is, no doubt, getting excited talking about this stuff to me. I won't give him the satisfaction.

'Sex can be glorious,' I reply steadily. I jut my chin a little. 'They pay to believe it's glorious.'

A sound escapes his mouth. A sound that conveys he is caught somewhere between thrilled and disgusted. 'I want you to tell me about it.'

'I'm not in a chatty mood.'

'I'll pay you to tell me about it.' He reaches into his shorts pocket, pulls out his wallet. He flips it open. It's fat, full of cash. As he flicks through the notes, I see dollars, sterling and Euros. All high denominations.

'No thank you.'

'Oh yes. I forgot. You're on a job already. Of course. One at a time, is it?' I don't reply. 'I bet it isn't, you dirty bitch.'

My eye hurts from where he punched and bruised me last.

This is imaginary. I don't really hurt. He's not hurting me. *He* never did.

Except I do, and he is. And I don't care what Daniel says,

137

Jonathan *was* the man in the hotel. I know he was. Itineraries can be faked.

My thoughts leap from one thing to the next, unable to settle. Opposing thoughts clash, making me feel dizzy, nauseous. It's the heat. It's fear. I need to focus. I can't afford to slip up.

'Is the sex the same with them all? All the same to you?' I know he wants me to say it is. If I confess that, then I'm admitting they are just pieces of meat, which makes me a butcher. The truth is, there are similarities, but they are all different too. The weight of them. How they hold me. *If* they hold me. I won't tell him. I won't bring this alive for him. I turn on my heel and start to walk away. I turn left and right randomly, hoping to recognise something but not doing so. It all looks the same. I worry he's going to suddenly grab me from behind, but running isn't any safer, as I may be running in circles. I know this, and yet instinct takes over and I do run. I run left and right. Round and about, into dead ends and over old ground.

It takes about fifteen minutes, but eventually I find my way out of the maze. Panting, I burst back out into sunlight not broken by the shadows of the bushes. I bend, put my hands on my knees, trying to steady my breath.

Liling and Chen are waving to me from a distance. 'Oh, there you are!' they call cheerfully. 'We've been looking for you everywhere.'

# 19

# *Dora*

'Where is she?' Liling asks.

'Who?' My breath is still fast and shallow. I'm dizzy, light-headed. The sun is too much. I think I missed a bit of my shoulders with the suncream; I can feel the uncomfortable prickle of scorching flesh. I pull at the collar of my dress to try to protect myself from burning.

'Marmalade.'

'Marmalade?'

'She's missing.'

'Missing?'

'Is there an echo around here?' asks Chen, laughing. His entire body is taut; even when laughing, he looks constrained.

'Oh, you're talking about the dog,' I say, finally catching up. They nod. 'I haven't seen her since earlier this morning. She was in the library.' Liling looks cross, but I haven't got the time or inclination to get involved in her problem. I head into the house. I need a drink, and to put space between Jonathan and me. I'm going to call my own cab and I'm going to do so now. I don't care what Daniel thinks. I want to leave here. Right away.

I bump into Melanie in the kitchen. She's fussing around a member of staff who is making fresh lemonade. I grab a glass and head to the kitchen tap. 'Oh, wait a moment, the lemonade is almost ready,' says Melanie. I ignore her. I've been trailing about in the blazing sun for nearly three hours with, if not a psycho, then at least a total dick. I'm parched. I want water and I need it straight away. I fill the glass, but just as I lift it to my mouth, Melanie knocks it violently out of my hand. 'I said *wait*,' she yells. The glass smashes in the kitchen sink. The maid and I stare at the splinters, shocked. 'Here,' says Melanie, smiling sanguinely as though nothing out of the ordinary has happened. 'Try this.'

The lemonade is delicious, and I glug it back. I don't know what to say about her show of temper. I ought to ask if the stress of hosting is getting to her, if anything else is troubling her. But I find I can't. She isn't open to that sort of confidence.

She continues blithely, 'We've all eaten crêpes at the market, so we're not bothering with lunch. You are not hungry, are you.' It isn't a question. I am, but I don't want to linger, I want to get upstairs, pack and leave. These people are crazy. I'll eat at the airport. 'I'm taking this tray of lemonade out to the gang. They're already at the pool. Daniel too. Will you carry the glasses?'

'I'm actually going to have a lie down.'

'Oh no you are not.' It's said faux playfully. 'We've seen nothing of you today. Pick up the glasses, please.' Whilst her voice is merry, her smile is icy and I feel the prod of steely determination that I identified yesterday when we first met. This woman is resolved that everything plays out exactly as she has choreographed it.

I reach my hand inside my dress pocket. I want to feel the smooth reassurance of my iPhone but it's not there. Panic surges through my body. I need my phone to text Evan, to call a cab. Where is it? I was sure it was in my pocket. Have I lost it? When did I last have it? I definitely had it when I was near the pool this morning. I pick up the tray of glasses and follow Melanie. I need to find my phone to get out of here.

It seems none of Melanie's guests are behaving exactly as she'd like. When we arrive at the poolside, no one pays much attention to her lemonade, even though she makes a big thing about it being fresh and homemade. The guests continue playing in the pool, listening to music, soaking up the sun. Sisi is dancing, swaying like a sapling in the wind. She reaches out to Melanie, grinning and coaxing her to join in, move her hips, relax, but Melanie remains stiff and sullen, determined not to be influenced by the joy. I see her shoulders rise with tension to around her ears. She lies and says she prepared the lemonade herself. I've just watched a member of staff make it and she knows as much but seems entirely unconcerned about telling this lie in front of me. The men ask for beers. She comments we should all probably pace ourselves. This call for temperance causes a hoot of laughter. Giles asks the bartender to 'Set them up.' It's the same guy who offered me sun cream this morning. I ask him if he's seen my phone, but he says he hasn't. I'm not that surprised. I don't think I'd have left it here. I'm pretty sure I had it with me when Jonathan was showing me the grounds. I remember feeling the reassuring weight of it in my pocket, against my leg. I concentrate hard and try to think when I was last aware of it. In the outbuildings, maybe. Which means I've most probably lost it somewhere in amongst the maze. A cold slither thrums through my body. I need my phone, but I don't want to go back in the maze.

It quickly transpires I'm not the only person who has lost something. Liling's dog is missing. She asks us all to help look for Marmalade and I agree. I mention my lost phone and ask everyone to keep an eye out for that at the same time, but no one seems particularly concerned about the phone.

'Are you sure it's not on charge in our room?' asks Daniel. I feel awkward pushing the point. Finding Marmalade is clearly a priority and whilst I've never had a pet, I imagine Liling and Chen must be very devoted to her; they wouldn't have brought her on holiday with them otherwise.

Amanda confirms as much when she shakes her head and under her breath says to me, 'That dog is like a child to them.'

Everyone agrees to look for the dog and we split off into groups and head in different directions. I haven't seen Jonathan since I left him in the maze, but I certainly don't want to bump into him, so I stick close to Daniel and Sisi. Neither of them speak to me much as we hunt for Marmalade. We tramp out into the woods, calling her name and whistling. In the distance we can hear the others doing the same. 'I hope we find her. She seemed such a sweet thing,' I comment.

Sisi glares at me. 'If anything has happened to her Liling will be devastated.' I don't understand her ferocity. She's intense, maybe she should be in therapy. Daniel looks apologetic, I get the feeling he's apologising for me, which I don't understand either. My comment was innocuous enough. I'm fed up with receiving the cold shoulder. I'm going back to our room. I'm going to pack and get a member of staff to call me a cab. I've had enough.

'I think I'll head back to the house. Marmalade might be inside, staying cool,' I say.

Sisi and Daniel simultaneously glance at their watches to check the time. 'We've been looking for an hour now; we might as well all head that way.'

As soon as the chateau is in sight, it becomes clear there has been a development, but not a good one. I can see the rest of the group gathering. Liling is sobbing hysterically; Chen is gently helping her into a waiting taxi. She is practically prone in his arms. Giles, in the meantime, is carefully placing a big box in the back of the car.

'What's going on?' asks Daniel.

Suddenly Liling notices me. She lunges out of the car and starts to run towards me. 'This is all your fault,' she yells.

Chen is fast to intervene. He folds his strong arms around her and guides her back into the car. 'Come on now, this isn't going to do any good. We need to get her to the vet.'

'What? What's my fault?' I ask. 'Is that Marmalade in the box? Is she OK?'

No one replies. No one will look at me. The taxi leaves at speed. Amanda says, 'We found Marmalade down the well. Luckily, as it's been so dry, there's not much water in there, so she didn't drown, but she's badly hurt. She looked in a very grave state.'

'Oh, that's awful – but how is it my fault?' I regret the question the moment I ask it. It's definitely insensitive. A dog is hurt, no one wants that, but I don't understand why everyone is angry with me.

'Well, Chen did ask you to look after her,' replies Amanda.

'What? No, no, he didn't.'

Everyone looks at the floor, embarrassed.

'Yes, he did, this morning, before we went to the market,' adds Daniel. 'Chen and Liling were debating whether to take Marmalade with us, but they decided it was too hot for her. You told Chen you'd look after her.'

'Did he tell you that?' I see now what has happened. Chen lied to his wife to reassure her that it was OK to leave their pet in the house, and now it's landed at my door. 'Did he tell you that?' I demand again.

Daniel shakes his head. 'No Natalya, I was there, I heard you offer to look after her.'

# 20

# *Dora*

I run inside the house and start packing my case for the second time in two days. This time I'm going. I don't feel safe at all. I don't trust Jonathan, or Melanie, or Chen, or Daniel. They have all lied about me, or to me, or bullied me, or threatened me. Things are crazy. Or at least something is.

*Me?*

I pause as the thought scuttles into my head. I'm used to not trusting other people, but I've always trusted myself. I've always had to. The thought that my mind is playing tricks on me, that I'm my own enemy, is terrifying. Sickening. Did Chen ask me to look after Marmalade? Surely I would remember that. Although yesterday I thought I'd fallen asleep by the pool but I woke up in this bed. I don't know what's real and what isn't. My head has ached more or less constantly since I arrived here. I thought it was the heat, dehydration, tiredness. Maybe it is concussion. Maybe I was damaged in that hotel room by that man. By the man I see in Jonathan. By Jonathan? As soon as I'm back in the UK, I will go to the doctor.

I pack my bag hurriedly and then push it under the bed. I don't want Daniel to see it. I'm not sure he'd bother to stop me leaving, I'm hardly proving to be a popular girlfriend with his friends, but I somehow think it would be better if he didn't know I'm about to flit. I need to find the telephone number of the local taxi company. I wish I could have just leapt in with Chen and Liling, but that is a vain hope under the circumstances. Without my phone, I can't check the internet. I'll have to ask a member of staff to call for me.

I'm about to head out of the room when Daniel walks in. He looks awkward, tired. He sighs. 'Oh, here you are. I wondered where you'd run to.' I don't know what to say to him. Is it worth reiterating that I can't remember Chen speaking to me about Marmalade? Will he believe me? 'Wow, that was intense.' He flops down into the armchair at the end of the bed. For a moment or two he doesn't say anything at all. Then he asks, 'Are you OK, Natalya?' His concern touches me. I nod stiffly, and then sit on the end of the bed, facing him. Maybe he can be trusted. Maybe he can help. 'What happened?' he probes.

'I don't know.'

'Did she slip her lead?'

'No, I didn't have her on a lead.'

'You should have had her on her lead. I heard Chen tell you that.'

'I wasn't with her. Not at all. Well, only for a bit in the library …' I catch sight of his face, emitting disappointment and maybe pity. I stop talking. I'm not explaining this at all.

'I'm not angry with you,' he adds. 'I'm worried about you.'

'You don't have to be.'

He looks momentarily stern. 'I think I do. Why won't you admit that Chen spoke to you about Marmalade?'

I don't answer. I can't. What can I say? I'm ill? I'm mad? Why would that matter to Daniel? He's paid me to come here to be entertaining and fun. He is not a friend, he's a client. It's best to keep this as brief as possible. Once I leave here, I'll never have to see him again. I have Evan and future plans. I can leave this mess behind.

Daniel lets out another long, frustrated sigh. 'I think you should go home, Natalya.'

I nod. 'Yes.'

'I should never have invited you on this trip. I wish I hadn't.' Only yesterday, he suggested I should stay, recuperate, but men change their minds about women with alarming speed, I know that. 'I've looked into flights, and there's one tomorrow morning, eleven fifteen. There is plenty of availability. You can buy a ticket at the airport. I know you prefer booking your own flights.'

'Thank you.'

'I've booked a taxi. It will pick you up at 8 a.m.'

'OK.'

'If you could just try to …' He breaks off.

'What?'

'Well, between now and then, if you could just try not to embarrass me again or make this any worse.' He stands up and leaves the room abruptly. The door slams behind him. The air in the room seems to wince.

I'm not unused to male disapproval or the feeling that men are trying to get rid of me. Daniel and I want the same thing here – me out of the way as quickly as possible – so I don't know why I start to cry, but I do. Silent fat tears glide down my face and splash onto my sundress. Then I hear the key turn in the lock.

I jump up and hurry to the door. I try to open it, but it won't budge. I rattle the handle. These enormous wooden doors do have a tendency to stick. I shake it hard, but I know it's locked. I slam my hand on it. 'Daniel! Daniel! Unlock the door! What the fuck, Daniel?' I don't want to go anywhere; given a choice, I'd be quite happy to stay in my room all afternoon and evening, right until the sun comes up tomorrow and the taxi arrives, but being locked in is something else altogether.

I thump on the door and shout for Daniel again. I call for Amanda, anyone. No one comes. The door is a couple of inches thick, and two metres high; there's no way I can break it down. I run to the windows and fling them open, but there's no one in sight. I yell for help anyway. One of the staff might hear me, someone might come. But no one does. All I can hear is crickets on the lawn, rubbing their back legs together. There must be hundreds of them, because the chorus they make is loud. I almost think it drowns out my cries for help. Where is everyone? I realise the friends might be at the pool or tennis courts, but where are the staff? Frustrated and panicked, I reach for a vase on the dressing table. I wonder just for a moment, is it an antique, is it valuable? But I don't care. The staff might think the cries for help are just one of us messing about, a game, 'help, someone is turning a cold hose on me', that sort of cry, but a crash, a smashing vase, can't be ignored. I fling it out the window.

Still no one comes.

I wait. I yell, I wait, I yell again. The sky slowly starts to lose its vibrant blue colour as a hint of honey creeps into view. I haven't eaten all day; there is water in the room, but I'm light-headed with the lack of food. Daniel probably isn't aware that I haven't eaten. He wouldn't lock me up hungry, would he? But why has he locked me up at all? It doesn't make sense. I crawl to the bed and close my eyes. No one is coming.

# 21

# *Dora*

When I wake up, the chirp of the crickets has been replaced by a shrill whiny sound, similar to a drone hovering. Mosquitoes. Bugger. It's pitch black outside, but the windows are still wide open. My bedside lamp is on, although I don't remember switching it on. Why would I do that and not close the windows? I'm susceptible to mozzie bites. Indeed, I glance at my sore and itching arm and see a cluster of five or six welts on my right bicep. I hop out of bed, regretting moving so quickly when the room sways. I'm woozy with the lack of food; I need to be more careful. I close the windows and the shutters too. But now the mosquitoes are trapped inside with me. I rummage in my toiletry bag and spray myself with the weird-smelling repellent that I brought along. I look for the cream that eases the irritation of existing bites, but can't find it. I thought I'd packed it; I suppose I must have left it behind.

I can hear voices coming from downstairs; the salon is just below my bedroom. Glancing at my Fitbit, I see it's 8 p.m. They have probably gathered for cocktails and will soon be having dinner. In just twelve hours, I'll be out of here. The thought of my own flat and Evan cheers me. I can't wait, but I am not going to manage another twelve hours without eating. My stomach rumbles loudly, emphasising the point. The gnawed-out hollowness that I feel is not just to do with lack of food, but that is the aspect I need to tackle first. I must build up some reserves. I will have to get out of this room and find something to eat. I try the door, not expecting any joy, but to my surprise, it clicks open. It's not locked. But it was. I am sure it was. I pull it wide. Neo is in the corridor, just coming out of his and Sisi's room opposite.

'Hello, sleepyhead,' he says with a grin. 'Feeling better?' I nod, although I'm not certain, and maybe that is clear, because he looks sympathetic. 'You've had a bit of a crap time of it, haven't you?'

'How's Marmalade?' I ask.

His gaze drops to his feet, uncomfortable, then he forces himself to look me in the eye. 'I'm really sorry. She didn't make it. Chen and Liling called. The vet said her injuries were too severe, that the kindest thing was, well …' He trails off.

'I'm so sorry.' I remember burying my head into the beautiful dog's fur just this morning, breathing her in. She was a comfort. I hate the thought that she's gone. Sadness sluices through me.

'We all make mistakes,' he says kindly. I'm not sure I did, but I am sorry anyway. I feel overwhelmed. I think I must sway a little, dizzy from lack of food. Neo reaches out and puts his hand on my shoulder to steady me.

'Hey, are you OK?'

'Just hungry.'

'Come on, let's go and get dinner.'

'No, really, I don't want to see everyone, I—'

'Liling and Chen aren't coming back here tonight, if that's what's worrying you. They've taken an Airbnb in town. I guess they're not really in the party mood now.'

They are not the only guests I want to avoid, but I'm too hungry to object, so I let him lead me downstairs. He clasps hold of my arm, very tightly. He's tall, broad and muscular. Is he trying to make me feel more secure by grasping me so firmly, or is he demonstrating my powerlessness? I am unsure about everything and everyone. 'Watch your step, you seem unsteady,' he says. 'Beautiful places, these old chateaus, but deathtraps too, wouldn't you say?'

'No, I wouldn't. I haven't noticed anything that the health and safety brigade would get excited about,' I reply, trying to sound as rational and non-alarmist as possible. I'm aware that women in particular are often called hysterical. It's never helpful and I have to avoid it.

'Really?' He raises his eyebrows. 'I see potential threats everywhere in this place. There was rat poison on the floor in a bowl in our bedroom. I said to Sisi that if the dog hadn't fallen down the well, it might have found a messy end anyhow, eating the poison. You'd think people would be more careful. The floorboards are polished so thoroughly they're like ice rinks. Just a few minutes ago, I was dashing about in my socks in my bedroom, looking for my formal shoes, and I took a tumble, slammed right into the wall. Hurt my shoulder. Imagine if I'd tripped on the landing; I might have been head first down these bloody steep stairs.' I'm not sure why Neo is talking about these things. It's odd; he's adding to my all-pervading sense of unease. He continues with his litany of concerns. 'And look.' He pauses, we're halfway down the stairs, and he vigorously rattles the banister. It quakes under his touch. 'This is pretty rickety. In a new house, the banister height is specified so that people can't easily tumble over. This is far too low to be allowed now. Then there are the open fires and candles in every room. They're all a risk. The whole place could go up like a tinderbox if just one person was careless.'

'Are you trying to make me feel anxious?' I ask.

Neo laughs. 'Oh God, no, it's just my job. I'm in film. Sounds glamorous, but in fact I'm at the admin end. I get sets and shoots insured. I assess risk as a profession.' He clocks my face, which is probably creased with concern, and laughs. 'Sorry. You must think I'm some sort of nutter, going on about dangers etc. since you didn't know that about me.' I smile, relieved. I'm jittery. 'Sorry, it's just a professional habit. Sisi says I can be unnerving, and that I have to stop telling people about what could go wrong. She says it ruins the party mood.' He grins, and then jokes, 'Have you seen the chef's knives? They're terrifying, and in every room there's a poker for the fire or a paperweight that could be a deadly weapon.'

I pick up the light-hearted tone. 'You've played too much Cluedo.'

'You're right. Come on, Miss Scarlett, let me take you to the dining room.'

'As long as you don't offer to show her your lead piping.' I jump at the sound of Sisi's voice. She's on the stairs behind us. I didn't hear her approach, even though she's wearing heels. She must have used quite some stealth. Why? Was she listening in on our conversation? Her expression is one of a vaguely disgruntled wife having caught her husband being overly solicitous to the new, younger woman in the gang. It's

153

not an unreasonable expression to wear. But Neo wasn't flirting with me. Sisi's comment about the lead piping was the only suggestive comment made.

Neo breaks into a hearty laugh, and then Sisi's face cracks into a big grin too. He kisses her cheek. Oh, they were just playing. A married couple making a harmless double entendre. Why did I think there was more to it than that? What's wrong with me? I allow myself to laugh too.

## 22

# *Dora*

'Nice of you to dress up,' says Melanie the moment she claps eyes on me. I'm still wearing my sundress from this morning. It's creased. When I turn my head, I think I can smell a faint whiff of my own sweat in my pits. My arms and legs are scratched from the bushes in the maze, and the mosquito bites are raw and unattractive. I'm not wearing make-up or heels; I'm still in flip-flops. I don't look like a woman who charges what I do. Dressing for dinner was not a priority when trying to escape from my locked room. *Except it wasn't locked.* Neo and Sisi, on the other hand, look amazing. He is wearing a pale blue shirt and light trousers; she is in a red clingy cocktail dress. They have both clearly just emerged from a hot bath; they look groomed and pampered. Melanie is wearing a more traditional black cocktail dress. Just a shift really, but it's obviously designer, the material suggesting it's expensive. Both women are dripping diamonds, fully made up and in heels.

'Should I go and change?' I offer.

'No, we haven't got time for that. The chef is already wait-ing for us,' replies Melanie with an obvious sigh of irritation.

I guess I've embarrassed Daniel again. I don't care, I just want to eat and then leave. I don't owe these people anything.

We file straight into the dining room and I find myself sandwiched between Neo and Daniel and opposite Giles. Daniel nods stiffly at me and then instantly turns away and directs all his attention towards Sisi. I don't care.

Just like last night, the drink flows generously. Four magnums of champagne bathe in a silver trough of ice in the centre of the table. The first bottle is opened and hastily poured into our glasses; champagne froths over the rims in a show of abundance and carelessness. I take a big gulp; it kicks the back of my throat, a cold, addictive, unquenchable dryness. The bubbles barely have time to dance on my tongue before my glass is refilled.

I don't quite make the active decision to drink heavily; I just find I am. I need to get through tonight any way I can. I tuck into the food the moment it is put before me. I don't bother joining in the conversation, which anyway mostly consists of casual obscenities and thinly veiled barbed insults flung back and forth between everyone else at the table. For a group of supposed friends, they don't seem to like one another much. I've seen this before. Friends behaving like competitive rivals, stags locking horns to establish who is most alpha.

Daniel and Giles seem to be prepared to argue over anything, from which vineyard they ought to visit, to what colour socks one ought to wear with light-coloured trousers, to which stock or share is worth investing in if you have some 'spare cash being lazy'. #Richpeoplesproblems. I gather that they played tennis together this afternoon. The score was close, a set each, and then Daniel snatched victory in the final set. As this is Giles's promotion bash, I wonder whether it might have been more politic of Daniel to allow him to win, or at least to have settled with the draw. I thought Daniel was more of a sportsman, more of a gentleman; it occurs to me that I don't really know him. Did he really lock me in the bedroom and then go downstairs and enjoy a game of tennis? Is he capable of that cruel detachment, or was my mind playing tricks on me again? Maybe the door was just stuck.

Melanie repeatedly asks Sisi if she is cold, and even goes so far as to dig out a tartan rug to wrap around her shoulders, despite Sisi's assurances that she's perfectly fine. I don't think Melanie is being solicitous; I think she's trying to dampen down Sisi's glorious beauty and perhaps make a point about her skimpy dress and the hard nipples that are poking through the flimsy silky material. She insists Giles lay and light a fire even though it's a warm evening. His efforts create chaos; the chimneys must need sweeping. First tendrils, then plumes of smoke bloom and billow into the room.

I hear Amanda ask Jonathan how he amused himself whilst they were all at the farmers' market; he tells her he swam in the pool and sunbathed. I wasn't expecting him to confess to negotiating the cost of a blow job, but he doesn't mention our tour at all. I feel trapped by a brittle unease lurking beneath the veneer. Tomorrow can't come soon enough. These past couple of days there have been so many times when it's felt like I've stumbled in on something not quite right. Like a family in a sitcom being an accepted version of something we all agree might be a family but is far from the reality of a family – the friends feel like that. They do not click or bounce; they clash and pounce.

The smoke in the room quickly becomes overpowering. My eyes are stinging, and Amanda and Daniel are both coughing quite furiously. We open the windows, but it's such a still night, the smoke lingers. It's decided that we should have dessert, cheese and coffee on the terrace. The waiting staff are instructed to load up trays; the men lug the champagne trough, not prepared to let the alcohol out of their sight even temporarily. I see my opportunity to slip away, but as if reading my mind, Daniel grabs my hand and whispers, 'Come outside, play nicely.' They are the first words he's said to me all evening.

'I'd have thought you'd rather have me out of sight now.'

'I need you to even up the numbers, amuse Neo.' I scowl. 'I'm paying, remember.' I nod reluctantly.

Outside, I choose to sit as far away from the others as I can politely manage without appearing odd. Everyone else settles around the table, so they can easily reach the chocolate pudding and the champagne. I pile my plate and then perch on an enormous Perspex bubble chair that is swinging from a tree just at the edge of the terrace. I'm hoping that once again I'll be out of sight, out of mind. This isn't to be. Neo sees me sitting on my own and comes to join me.

'Room for a little one?' he asks.

'You are hardly that,' I point out.

He smiles, a man rightly proud of his impressive physique. 'I brought some pop with me,' he says, holding up one of the magnums of champagne. It's still over half full.

'I left my glass over there.'

'We can drink from the bottle. You're not above that, are you?' he challenges.

'I'm not.'

'Good girl. I had you down as a woman who is willing to embrace life.'

'Did you.' I arch my eyebrows. It's not a bad assumption to make.

'Yes.' He grins at me, fast and loose. I wonder how many women he has said the same to. A few, I imagine. It's a great compliment, original enough to cut through, but the way he delivered it struck me as practised.

The bubble chair is designed for two, I suppose, a cosy two. I'm far too used to agreeing to what men want, and so I shuffle to one side and he squeezes in next to me. I can feel the warmth of his thigh through his trousers against my leg. He gulps from the magnum and then gives me the bottle. I take a swig, hand it back to him. He has long legs, and they reach the ground. He drags his feet forwards and backwards, to create some momentum. The chair oscillates left and right and then starts to twirl.

'You never said, what is it you do?' he asks.

It's the first time I have been asked this since I arrived. I had expected this question to sail my way frequently, and I planned to say that I work in an art gallery in Mayfair. There's a certain type of woman who does this sort of job, and people like Daniel's friends understand that. More likely than not, she has a rich father or is waiting for a rich husband. They are unlikely therefore to ask my views on neo-Dadaism or relational aesthetics and participatory art because they would assume I have none. They will assume they know all there is to know about me. It is a solid and safe cover. But I can't be bothered with it. I decide that I might as well tell him the truth. At the moment, the hiccuping uncertainty of working out what is real and what isn't is so concerning to me that I don't want to add another layer of duplicity and confusion. I'm leaving first thing tomorrow; what does it matter if Daniel's secret is out? It doesn't. Not to me. So instead of rolling out the fake identity, I say, 'I'm an escort.'

Neo stares at me with a crazy intensity. He's hollow-cheeked, his deep-set eyes red-rimmed. I wonder what he has taken; although there was no evidence of drugs at dinner, it doesn't mean they weren't consumed, just that a little discretion was used in front of the staff. This is surprising. People like these are usually too entitled to concern themselves with discretion.

He says, 'Well I'll be damned.'

'Technically, that's more likely to be me,' I joke. He laughs. I get a sense of satisfaction from that. I like making people laugh. It's my job to be entertaining, and I pride myself on being about more than the tricks I can pull between the sheets. I haven't delivered what Daniel wanted this week. It's my fault; after the beating, I should have rested. I wasn't ready to take this on. It's been confusing and messy. I wait a moment. I wonder whether Neo will ask about my fees, or Daniel, or my past experiences. I don't believe he'll choose to move off the topic.

'So, Daniel?' The question lingers in the warm night air.

'A client,' I confirm.

'I wonder if he'll offer to pay my wife?' Neo muses. This comment is borderline offensive, if you think about it – offensive to Sisi, insinuating that she can be bought, and to me, insinuating that I'm not enough – so I decide not to think about it. I've been successful at my job for all these years because I choose not to be offended by almost everything that is said to and about me. Neo's comment also shows a reasonable amount of astuteness; it's best I concentrate on that. So, he realises Daniel is interested in Sisi. We both glance towards where they are sitting, huddled as usual, heads together, talking in low voices. Neo doesn't react. He doesn't seem particularly concerned.

'Any good stories to tell?' he asks, revealing that his thoughts are on me.

'Some.' Because I'm relieved that he didn't ask how much I cost, I decide to tell him some peculiar but fascinating anecdotes, share a few truisms and reveal the occasional comical situation. 'I get to travel a fair amount, which is fun. But my God, the conditions.'

'Conditions? You mean travelling economy?'

'No,' I laugh. 'I mean the things they ask of me. There was this one man who took me to LA for a week but insisted that I wore Barbie pink for the entire time, and that I call him Ken.'

'For real?'

'Would I lie to you?'

Neo grins. 'Probably.'

'Pink is not my colour. Then there was this other guy who was a jewellery designer – really high-end, beautiful stuff. Diamonds mostly. He had hired three of us to wear his collection for the entire weekend to showcase to his potential clients. But that was all he wanted us to wear, nothing else. The air conditioning was vicious, and I was so worried about losing an earring.'

I present it as glamorous, powerful and amusing, but honestly, if you think what I do is any of those things, you probably are not thinking about it hard enough. However, Neo and I are drinking champagne in the grounds of a chateau in the south of France; it's not the moment to go deep. I want to be entertaining, he wants to be entertained. I need a break from all the weirdness and intensity. The soupy-warm night is soothing; we listen to the cicadas in the distance and I allow the champagne to wring some of the tension out of me.

'So what are they like? Your clients? Are they all like Daniel?'

'I'm not sure what Daniel is like.'

'Oh, you know, he's pretty straightforward, isn't he? Uptight. Square.'

'He skinny-dipped with your wife yesterday; he's not so uptight,' I point out.

Neo laughs, takes a swig of champers, passes me the bottle again. I should probably have insisted on us using glasses. Drinking from the same bottle is at the very least unhygienic; some might think it flirty. Provocative.

'Repressed, then,' he clarifies.

Those adjectives are exactly the ones I would have chosen for Daniel. I find it reassuring that Neo has him pegged where I do, as they've known one another for much longer. I'm not losing my mind. Would an uptight, square, repressed man lock a whore in a bedroom because she's embarrassed him in front of his friends? I ask myself. I realise that the answer is yes. Possibly. Probably. Outside, with food in my belly and drink running to my head, this doesn't seem as frightening as it did earlier. It seems a bit pathetic. It's certainly not as frightening as thinking I imagined the situation, that I can't trust myself. I have to be able to have that.

'Many of my clients are repressed,' I admit as I take another gulp from the bottle. 'Repressed or insecure. But then, many are arrogant or risk-takers.'

'So there's not a type then, that's what you're saying?'

'I guess I am.'

'Except they all like sex.'

'Not even that,' I confess wryly. Neo raises an eyebrow. 'I suppose what they do have in common, these men, the sort that pay for sex, is they expect to make the rules. They think they've bought your soul, not simply a few hours of your time.'

'That sounds scary.'

'It can be. Often, it's just boring. The stuff I've had to listen to.' I shake my head, trying to communicate the exasperation, the tedium. 'And I guess the other thing they all have in common is that they seem to have a secret longing to be understood.' I use my fingers to draw faintly sarcastic speech marks in the air around the last word.

'We all have that in common,' observes Neo, quietly.

I shrug. I don't feel that. I'd settle for being ignored, left alone, unjudged. Unharried. I just want to live my life. I don't need anyone to understand it. 'Do you think? It strikes me as the ultimate in self-absorption, hoping for understanding from others to give meaning to your life. Get over yourself, I say.'

Neo whoops. 'Whoa, that's cool.' He beams at me and then prods me in the shoulder. 'You're cool.'

Is it? Am I? I think we must both be quite drunk by now. Still, I like it that he admires my amateur philosophy. Encouraged, I plough on. 'Some clients try to not tell me about their insecurities. I find I work them out anyway. Some of the girls don't care. To be clear, I don't *care*, but I am *interested*. Other clients go the opposite way: they want to own up to exactly what makes them feel small; they want to use me like a perverse confessional. I have to pretend to be surprised by what they tell me.'

'And you're not?'

'Rarely. It's usually the same stuff that makes them feel bad about themselves.'

'*They* feel bad about themselves?'

I guess Neo thinks I'm the only one who should feel bad about myself. That's lazy thinking. 'Everyone feels bad about themselves,' I assure him. 'Which is a tricky starting point, because it's all about them being in the mood. They aren't always, which may seem peculiar to you, when you reflect on what they're paying. But I think some are ashamed that it's come to this. You know, paying for it.' I shrug. 'But then, others find that the entire turn-on. There's no accounting for taste. *That* I do know.' I glug some more champagne.

'You can't have any problem getting them in the mood.' Neo's gaze drops, grazes the length of my body. My shoulders, breasts, waist, hips, legs. Is he flirting with me?

'It's not always a physical thing,' I say, meeting his eyes. 'It's more about their own confidence. I praise them a lot. The size of their penis is a good place to start. It's amazing what they'll believe. "Oh big boy. Whoa."' I pout and flutter my eyelashes, re-enacting the scene for Neo. I'm just having fun. He enjoys the show and almost falls off the bubble chair, he's laughing so hard. 'If their penis is ludicrously small and I just can't be convincing, I simply rave about their prowess in the sack – you know, the way a parent praises a talentless child's drawing. With gusto and hopelessness. I'm good at faking stuff.'

'I bet you are.' More laughter.

I don't know where it comes from. The absolute truth.

Information volunteered, not even mined, but I find myself telling him, 'I was going to be an actor, so I sort of enjoy that part of it.' I think I share this information because he's in the movie business. OK, the administrative side, but since he told me that, my sliding-doors moment has played on my mind.

'No way,' Neo comments.

'Way.' I allow myself to imagine it for a split second. The brilliance. The potential. What it could have been like. A life devoted to auditions, callbacks, rebuffs, and small parts. Greasy stage make-up, learning lines, sitting in the wings, standing in the spotlight, taking a bow. And then close it down. It's not helpful. It's not where I am. I stay in the here and now with Neo. 'So what I do, it's no big deal. I see it as just another role,' I tell him.

'Of course. I get that. I really do.' We sit in a contemplative, solid silence. I notice that we are alone. The others must have gone back inside, or maybe they've moved on to the pool, planning on a little more skinny-dipping. We're too far away from neighbours or a road to hear any passing traffic or signs of life. Occasionally I hear a rustling animal in the bushes, a bird flying overhead, its wings flapping.

'I can still be surprised,' I admit. I don't know why I confess this. It's probably better to develop the persona of unshockable, worldly-wise tart with a golden heart. Best not to tell him anything too awful, too awkward. But it seems dishonest. 'There was this man who arrived with a snake in a box. He surprised me. I am not ophidiophobic, so it wasn't a horrifying experience, but I'm not a snake-lover either. Who is? Nor am I a snake expert—'

'I thought you'd spent all evening telling me you are,' interjects Neo. We both laugh, him more than me.

'It was unnerving.' I add. 'You see, I didn't know what this man intended with the snake and I didn't know what damage it could do.'

'Is it poisonous?' I had asked.

The client had shaken his head, but his lower lip was trembling with excitement, I wasn't sure I believed him. I reasoned it was unlikely; he would have been at risk from a bite too. He might have liked that, of course, the fear, the threat. I mean, I'm in a profession where men might ask for a whipping; self-harm isn't the exclusive domain of mixed-up teens. From a distance, I scanned the snake for red markings – I'd read once that they indicated poison – but I knew at the time I was possibly lying to myself, trying to find comfort where there was none. That is another skill of mine, another professional necessity.

'I like him being here. Watching.' The man sniggered. 'It's a bit of fun. I'll pay you extra.'

'I don't need the extra.' But I did need the basic, and if I left, then the basic would not be earned. He wanted the snake to roam over my naked body. I could see the erotic appeal. I'm fairly generous and open-minded about understanding what turns other people on. Snakes are not slimy; their skins are dry, smooth. I told myself I was just being asked to do what every celeb on *Get Me Out of Here* has been asked to do. And that's true. Up to a point.

'He fucked me vigorously as the snake slithered over my breasts,' I tell Neo. 'The more vigorous he became, the less comfortable the snake appeared; it swiftly slithered away. Thank God.' I shiver at the memory. I left the minute my time was up. As I closed the door behind me, I felt swamped with concern that he might not hunt about for the snake, retrieve it before he left. I imagined a poorly paid chambermaid discovering it curled around a tap or a bedpost. Her screams echoing through the hotel.

'Oh my God, that's horrible,' says Neo.

'Yes, it was.'

I've broken the mood. Neo can't think of what to say to me now. Or maybe that isn't because I've forced the reality of my profession into his consciousness, rudely ousting the fantasy; maybe his silence is more to do with how much he's had to drink. He can't focus on me; his eyes are spinning around his head, I think, or maybe I'm seeing double. We're definitely both very drunk.

I need to find some water. We stand up unsteadily. Wobbling strikes both of us as hilarious. We collapse onto one another, giggling. It's no longer clear if we are holding one another up or pulling each other down to the ground. His body is hot and heavy on mine.

'Fancy a game of pool?' he asks. I spotted an enormous purple pool table in one of the many salons when I was mooching around this morning.

'I don't think I can be trusted with a cue.' I mean because I'm drunk, and it could be dangerous, but my comment causes Neo to laugh disproportionately.

'Oh, I think you can be.'

I ignore the innuendo, if it's there. I may be imagining it; either way, I shouldn't be encouraging it. Evan, Daniel, Sisi – three good reasons right there to stay on track. 'I mean, I might rip the cloth or break something. I need to get to bed, Neo. I'm really drunk and I have to – absolutely *have* to – get up early in the morning. Let's call it a night.'

# 23

# *Dora*

My alarm goes off at 7 a.m. It feels like it's ringing inside my head. As I sit up, I feel a wave of nausea rush through my body, and I know today is going to be a hard one. I don't often drink to excess; I'm normally very careful, always pacing myself to be just a little bit more aware, a smidgen more sober than my clients, so this hangover is a shock. An unwelcome one. Ideally, I'd like to roll over and pull the sheet up above my head and go back to sleep. I fight that urge. While I still feel dizzy, maybe even still drunk, I know this isn't the best place for me to be. Far from it. Neo was kind and fun last night, possibly some sort of an ally in this crazy place, but really, I need to get home. See a doctor. Move on with my plans with Evan.

Daniel is asleep next to me, eyes closed, mouth open. Still keeping up appearances that we are a couple, although I'm not sure who believes that any more. His breath drifts towards me, sour, acidic, suggesting that he too drank a lot last night. He's snoring. I don't remember him coming to bed, but then I don't remember getting into bed either. He's lying on top of the sheet and I'm underneath it, a fact I'm glad of when

I realise I'm naked. Of course, he's seen it all before, from every angle imaginable, but the idea of him seeing it again feels uncomfortable and might lead to the sort of complication I could certainly do without. I carefully ease myself out of bed. I don't wake him as I dash into the bathroom. I want to shower, clean my teeth and dress before I have to interact. I turn the shower up to as hot as I can stand. The water drills into me. I open my mouth and let water run in and out again. I wish I could feel clean inside and out, but I don't. I feel filthy, but I'm not certain why exactly.

Once I'm showered, I sneak back into the room, with a towel wrapped around me, in order to get some clean clothes, but my stealth is not required; the room is empty. I touch the bed – it's still warm. I'm relieved. It sounds mad, but I needed to check I hadn't imagined Daniel sleeping next to me. I know, insane, but well, I just needed to check. I slip on the first pair of shorts and T-shirt I lay my hands on, and head down the stairs. As I do so, I hear the scratch of paws on the wooden floor. My first thought is mice, but I glance up and catch sight of the tail and hind legs of a dog scampering out of the open front door.

'Marmalade?' I call. I quickly dash after her. The dark coolness of the hallway is abruptly replaced by the dazzling glare of sunshine as I rush outside. I am temporarily blinded. I blink once, twice. The dog has disappeared. Was it her? Well of course not. She's dead, Neo said so. The thought is like a punch. Sometimes I think I like animals better than people. Not such a wild statement when you consider my profession and the sort of people I meet. So whose dog was it? I'm not aware anyone else here has a dog. It looked like Marmalade. 'Marmalade,' I call out again. This time louder. My voice shatters the slow silence of the morning. In the far distance, I see a young deer in a field. We seem to lock eyes for a moment, and then it dashes off. I watch, feeling a strange sense of loss and desperation.

'Oh, you're up.' His voice causes me to jump. It's stern, like a schoolteacher's ringing through a classroom of rowdy children. I turn and see Daniel standing at the other end of the hall, near the kitchen. He looks as austere as he sounds. I assume he is also struggling with a hangover. 'Who were you calling?'

'I thought I saw a dog.'

'Oh Natalya, for fuck's sake.'

'It looked like Marmalade.'

'How is that possible? It was probably a deer or a fox.'

'It was here in the house.'

He shakes his head, clearly not believing me and openly irritated. 'I need to speak to you. In here.' He points to the dining room. I check my watch. I really need a coffee, and must not miss my cab, which is arriving in ten minutes. I suppose he wants to talk about his reimbursement. By this point, I'm happy to return the lot. I just want to get out of here. I follow him through to the dining room, with the intention of making it snappy.

The elegance of the room is submerged under a haze of lingering smoke from Giles's attempt to build a fire, and the other debris from last night's partying: dirty plates, discarded linen napkins stained with food and lipstick, glasses, some still half full, others upturned, overflowing ashtrays and upended bottles. The room holds the smell of cigarettes, beer and wine, but not necessarily good times. Just indulgent ones. The previously beautiful and luxurious room feels grubby, defiled. I'm surprised the staff haven't already straightened it.

I turn to Daniel. He holds a phone out towards me. At first I think he has found my phone and is handing it back to me. I'm delighted, relief rushing through my body, but then I realise it's a slightly different model, newer. Anyway, the way he's holding it is challenging, aggressive. Sex workers live with an ever-present sense of all that is wrong with the world. It's best not to dwell or it will drive you mad. My body flushes through with adrenalin or horror, I can't quite pinpoint which. I'm unsafe. Acknowledging as much causes a bone-deep dread. I focus on the screen. It's a video. I've seen hundreds like it before: flesh – white, pink, red; breath – hot, fast, shallow. In and out. Up and down. He's asking her, 'Do you like that? Do you? I bet you do, you dirty bitch.' 'Yes, yes, I like it,' she's reassuring him. Tits and arse and cock. It's all very predictable. As I say, I've seen hundreds of videos like this before.

Except it is me in the video.

My blood slows, freezes. I think I'm going to throw up. I snatch the phone from him, and press delete. It's an instinct, but I know the act is toothless.

'It was emailed to me this morning. To all of us, actually. The whole group. There are multiple copies, you can't get rid of it,' says Daniel. I can't quite decipher his tone. Is he furious, disappointed, turned on? Is he threatening me? He's right, though, I can't get rid of the image, because whilst it's no longer on the screen, it's playing on a loop in my head. Me bent over the purple pool table, him hammering into me from behind.

'Who filmed this?' I demand.

'That's hardly the pertinent question.'

'It is to me.'

'How could you do this to me?' Daniel says, plaintively.

'Oh Daniel, don't play the wounded boyfriend. You are paying me to be here.'

'I am. Which is why I can't understand why you've sabotaged this trip for me from the moment you arrived. Are you trying to alienate all my friends? Accusing Jonathan of God knows what, killing Chen and Liling's dog.'

'I did no such thing. I saw Marmalade this morning. She's not dead.'

'And now you're fucking Giles.' Daniel glowers at me. 'It was supposed to be a smart and rather special celebration for his promotion.'

'Well, the lawyer looks happy enough,' I quip. I'm trying to sound more confident than I feel, because yes, it is Giles in the video. Not Neo, which might have perhaps added up, or even Jonathan, which would have been horrifying but a possibility. Not Daniel, who is paying me to be here, but *Giles*. It makes no sense. And worse, I have no memory of it at all. None. Daniel grabs me by both shoulders, shakes me hard.

'What the fuck is wrong with you? You need help. Aren't you sorry? What the fuck is wrong with you?' he repeats. I'm a rag doll in his grasp, too hung-over and too used up to fight back. I feel my brain slam about in my head. My bones rattle in my body.

'Hey, hey, stop. Leave her alone.' Neo is suddenly between us. He pushes Daniel off me and stands in front of me like a shield. I want to be grateful, but a thought occurs to me, and I can't allow myself to feel comforted or protected, not even for a moment. I step away from him. The three of us stand in a tense triangle; it seems we are each ready to bite. To blow.

'Did you film this?' I ask Neo.

'You asked me to. You wanted me to,' he replies.

He sounds sure of himself, unrepentant. Shameless. 'And who sent it to the others?'

'Melanie. I filmed it on Giles's phone, and she must have found it.' He shrugs. 'Do you really care?' he asks. I know what he's about to say. Maybe not the exact words, but I can guess at the gist. 'I mean, you're a prostitute. This can't be the first time you've been the A-lister in this sort of film.'

There we have it. What everyone thinks when it comes down to it. My career disqualifies me from any decency, respect, honesty or sympathy. I push past him and stride out of the room. From across the hall, in the kitchen, I can hear voices. I hear someone say, 'What was Daniel thinking, bringing a woman like her here? Of course, she's ruined everything.'

'It's disgusting. She should stop what she is doing. Stop it now.'

The words slap me. I want to walk away from them, but I can't. They are too familiar. Too close. I push open the big wooden door into the kitchen. It creaks back on its hinges. Sisi, Jonathan and Amanda are seated around the table. They are eating croissants; the smell of freshly brewed coffee drifts towards me. The normality of the scene strikes me as almost sinister. But then, what was I expecting? A masked sadomasochist crouched on the table, ready to torture me again?

'Morning,' says Sisi. She throws me a look of amusement. I've noticed that certain women who believe themselves to be edgy, open-minded tend to treat me with a droll tolerance. She'll no doubt be fascinated to have discovered she's shared the house with a sex worker. She'll be looking forward to getting back to England, where she can dish up the anecdote to her chums at her private media club. The other two stay focused on their breakfast plates. Fat globules of raspberry jam are apparently fascinating.

'Where's Giles?' I demand.

I think I hear Jonathan snicker. Amanda forces her gaze up to mine. Her expression is mostly pity, and yet tinged with an undeniable veil of revulsion. Everyone pities someone. I pity the people in my trade who don't have it as good as I do. The ones who have to take clients back-to-back. The ones who do it in the street, or in dirty council flats, next to needles. I pity them, but I don't patronise them. They don't sicken me. I've seen Amanda's expression before. I tell myself it doesn't matter what she thinks of me, what she believes she knows about me. But if it doesn't matter, why does it hurt so much?

'Giles and Melanie have left,' she informs me. She can't resist adding, 'Understandably.'

'They didn't need to do that. I'm leaving now.'

'Good riddance.' She mutters this under her breath. Sisi smirks; Jonathan sniggers again.

'What did you say?' I challenge.

'I said good call. It's all very awkward for everyone. They've paid for this place to the end of the week; we think we'll stay on, but after everything, it probably makes most sense if you …' Amanda trails off. She clearly thinks it is so obvious, it doesn't need stating. It probably makes most sense if I leave.

'Giles is no saint. I didn't seduce him.' I don't know why I'm trying to defend myself to these people. They're right, I should just go. They are nothing to me. Yet I find myself saying, 'He had sex with Liling on Monday night.'

Amanda shakes her head. 'Oh, really, that's too much.

Throwing accusations around when people aren't even here to defend themselves because you've driven them away. Haven't you done enough harm?'

I exit the room, closing the door firmly behind me. I can't fight the compulsion to lean close to the wood, put my ear up against it to listen to what they are saying about me. This, after a lifetime of trying to avoid hearing what people are saying about me.

'She is disgusting. She should stop what she's doing. Stop it now,' says a man's voice.

I want to fling myself back into the room, demand he say it to my face, but I don't. I daren't. I fear that I might open the door and find them all simply, silently, sipping their coffee. There is a real chance Jonathan hasn't said anything at all. That it is all in my head.

# 24

# *Dora*

I run upstairs and grab my suitcase. Most of my clothes are packed. I carelessly throw in the last few bits and pieces of mine that I can see scattered about the room. Other than my passport, I don't care what I leave behind. I check that it is in my handbag, and then strap the bag across my body so I can't drop it or put it down accidentally. Not exactly the most fashionable way to wear an Osprey Hendrix, but I've lost my phone, I think I'm losing my mind; I *need* my passport.

I bounce the case down the stairs. No one comes to offer help. I didn't expect any of the group to make an appearance, but the place has been teeming with staff up until this morning. I haven't been able to move more than a metre without someone offering me a drink or asking if they can do anything for me, yet there's no sign of help now. I listen, but I can't hear the chat of the staff or the hum of the vacuum cleaner. Where is everyone?

I stand outside the enormous front door at the top of the sweeping stone steps. The sun is blistering, pricking at my skin. I don't have any sun protection on, but I can't bear being in the house for a moment longer. I pray the taxi comes on time. I pray it comes.

I don't remember having sex with Giles. That is a first for me. It's horrifying. The lack of control I feel because I can't trust my own memory is devastating, debilitating. Without that certainty of knowing what I've done, seen, said, I have nothing. I *am* nothing. Was I drugged? Oh God, I must have been. Am I ill? Did I simply drink far too much? Did I agree to sex with Giles? Did I really ask Neo to film it? Why would I do that? So many questions. Every one of them leaves me feeling unbalanced, unsteady, because I don't have any answers.

I think hard, rack my brain, but I don't remember anything after telling Neo I didn't want to play pool, that we ought to call it a night. At least, not clearly. Flashes of half-formed, shattering images pummel their way into my head. I try to piece them together. Maybe I can remember the purple baize of the pool table, my face pushed into it. I think I can feel the imprint of hands on my body. I don't mean during sex; I mean being manhandled into position. And there were a number of hands, weren't there? Not just one pair. My mind turns black. I want to remember.

And yet I don't want to.

I daren't.

I look longingly into the distance, willing the taxi to come into sight, but there is no sign of it. It could just be late. I want to believe that so much, but I also fear that Daniel has cancelled it again. Would he? Surely he wants rid of me, but maybe he has already washed his hands of me and doesn't care how I make my way to the airport. I feel vulnerable waiting outside the chateau doors, so I start to walk along the sweeping driveway towards the road. There is only one way in or out by car, so I'm bound to meet the taxi. I'm so shocked by the existence of the video. I only watched it once, but the content is branded into my mind and plays back on a loop. It's in the world; an inescapable, eternal taunt, because that's what digital images are. I've always been extremely careful to avoid anything like this. Clients ask all the time. They want to take photos of me mid act; I've been offered large amounts of cash for them to do so, but I never allow it. In fact, if I think they are a bit too keen to do so, and unlikely to accept my rules, I make them put their phone in the room safe for the duration of my visit.

There has only ever been one time, early on in my career, that there were photos. When I signed with Elspeth, she made it clear that she had to put something on her website to advertise my wares. Those photos changed the course of my life forever, in such a dreadful way I try not to think about it. I've never allowed there to be any photos since. I remember asking if she could make sure my face wasn't in any of the shots. She simply replied, 'Funny girl.'

'Well, at least not at the same time. Tits and bits in some shots, face in others. Is that so hard?' I asked.

'No can do, I'm afraid,' she replied. 'You're either in or you're out. I need these initial shots to launch you.'

So I agreed.

The shoot was in a hotel, the sort I've since become familiar with but at the time found overwhelming or impressive or something. The photographer, a man, said I wasn't wearing enough make-up, my hair was too flat and my lingerie all wrong.

'Wrong?'

'Too subtle.'

'I'm looking at the expensive end of the market,' I pointed out when he handed me a pair of orange latex pants with a zip at the back.

'I know,' he said, without any apparent irony.

It was a good learning curve, the shoot. He taught me a lot about angles and illusion. My stomach ached with keeping my legs in the air. He suggested I might want to do crunches regularly. 'After all, your legs are going to have to defy gravity quite often, from here on in.'

Afterwards, Elspeth assured me the photos were 'Just gorgeous. Very tasteful. They offer the sizzle, not the steak,' she added to reassure me. They were explicit enough.

Now there is this video, the full barbecue.

I don't have any practical shoes with me, no trainers, and I could only find one of my flip-flops when I looked around my room this morning. The right one had vanished. The kitten-heel shoes I'm wearing were my best bet out of a limited choice; everything else in my suitcase has a three- or four-inch heel. Still, kitten heels are not the ideal footwear for dashing down a long drive in the rustic countryside. They rub, and I can feel blisters forming on my right little toe and my left heel. I'm in a bad way physically; besides the hangover from drink – or probably drugs, if one of them did slip me something – my mosquito bites have swollen into painful lumps that look a bit like bruises, and the sun is irritating them, causing them to itch ferociously. I scratch and scratch at them, only stopping when I realise I've made one or two bleed.

I reach the gates of the chateau and there is no sign of a taxi. In fact, there are no cars at all on the quiet little dirt track of a road. I look left and right, unsure which direction to set off in but certain I need to keep moving. Daniel said the cab company were based in the nearest village, but he wasn't specific. I don't know the name of the village, and without my phone, I am lost. I am utterly parched, so dehydrated I think I can feel my brain shrinking, so the thought of walking miles is overwhelming, but what choice do I have?

I decide the best plan is to walk along the road in the hope of hitching a lift or finding a farm or cottage where I can ask for help. I look about me; as far as I can see, there is nothing but fields and woodland, yet I know there has to be a farmhouse somewhere. I set off in the direction from which we arrived, dragging my case behind me. Its wheels keep catching and bumping on the uneven road; it's making my arm sore and I wonder whether I should just dump it. I'm tempted, but if I want a farmer to help me get to the airport, I can't afford to look any more odd. I'm bruised and scratched; I don't have a phone. I'm aware that I don't present the picture of respectability. I'm always vividly aware how important it is to present the right picture. So I plod on with my case.

I walk for over twenty minutes before I see a farmhouse in the distance. It's off the road and I loathe the idea of deviating, but as only two vehicles have passed me by in all the time I've been walking, I think my chance of catching a lift is slim. Especially as one vehicle was a painfully slow single-seat tractor and the other was a truck, carrying logs and trundling in the wrong direction.

It takes me another fifteen minutes to reach the farmhouse. I almost collapse with relief when I meet a woman in the yard and, in my schoolgirl French, manage to explain that I need to call a taxi, I am going to the airport and I have lost my phone. Like all farmers, she is industrious and gives the impression that she can't linger. She calls to her husband, who emerges from an outhouse. He looks suspicious of me, or maybe he's simply irritated that he's been called from his work. He listens as his wife explains my predicament to him in fast French. He goes inside the farmhouse, and I hope he's calling for a taxi; in the meantime, the woman offers me a glass of water. When she sees how quickly I drink it, she says something to one of her children, a gangly boy aged about ten. The boy returns with another glass of water, an apple and a banana. I gratefully take the food and drink from him. The woman shoos him away. As I was brought up on a farm, I know there is always more to be done, and anyone who can help out has to. Reluctantly the boy picks up a pitchfork and heads off down the lane. I suppose he might be moving hay.

Two younger children stay in the yard, watching me with open curiosity. The woman also goes back to her chores; she moves backwards and forwards between pig pens, filling troughs with food. I can't see her feeding the animals, but I can hear and smell them. I sit on the doorstep of the back door of the farmhouse. The concrete steps as unyielding as the hospitality. No one suggests I take a seat inside. It seems the help I'm being offered is cautious. Enough, but not an abundance. This place is nothing like the neighbouring chateau, although some of the outbuildings may have been built around the same time. The chateau is elegant, ordered, primped and primed for luxury, indulgence and extravagance. This place has derelict, tumbledown buildings; tools and machinery lie about, suggesting it's a place of industry and hard graft. It's dank and smells of animal faeces, and yet I feel safer than I did in the graceful, opulent rooms. It's my experience that people make a place congenial or threatening. Heaven or hell. Not that this place is qualifying as either. The reception I'm receiving gives it more of a purgatory, limbo vibe.

I wait for twenty minutes and then the farmer re-emerges. He is carrying keys and points to an old truck parked up in the yard. 'I take you to taxi. It close but can't reach, track too …' He breaks off, his English exhausted, but makes hand gestures. I understand: the taxi driver is unlikely to negotiate the undulating narrow track. I hop into the farmer's truck, thankful not to have to walk another strep. The two youngest children try to get in the back, but he sends them away impatiently.

He drives me to the end of the track and points to a waiting car. Gratefully I scramble out of the truck and dash to it. I fling open the back door and throw in my case, quickly sliding in after it. I pull on my seat belt. 'A l'aéroport. Rapidement.'

It's only at that point that I look up and catch the driver's eyes in the mirror. Sly, small eyes, like rips in fabric, like slits in a steaming pie. I scramble for the door handle, but it's locked. Jonathan starts the engine. Waves affably to the farmer and pulls away. I bang on the window of the car and shout, 'Aidez-moi.' But the farmer can't hear my pleas, because he is already part way back along his track. The tyres of his truck obscured by the dust he leaves in his wake.

# 25

# *Dora*

'Calm down. What are you saying? I don't speak French.' Jonathan smiles at me in the mirror, his eyes retreating yet further into his head, but I don't detect any warmth in the smile. It's an expression, learnt and delivered, not felt. I have no idea whether he speaks French or not, but I'm certain he must have understood my frantic banging on the window, and it wouldn't take a genius to guess at the meaning of '*aidez-moi*'.

'Where are you taking me?' I demand.

He looks surprised. 'The airport. That's what you want, isn't it? I understand you missed your taxi.'

'It never arrived. Daniel must have cancelled it. If he ever booked it in the first place.' Jonathan's eyebrows rise, the picture of concern. I don't buy it. 'Why did the farmer call you? I asked him to call a cab.'

'Ah, Monsieur Dupont does some work at the chateau from time to time. He called the landline there because he guessed you were most likely a guest. He was worried about you, a lost Englishwoman.' It sounds reasonable: a logical, concerned man. It sounds threatening: a network of spies and traps. I don't know which it is. 'What time is your flight?' Jonathan asks with another insincere smile.

'Daniel said eleven fifteen.'

Jonathan glances at the clock on the dashboard. 'Cutting it fine. Have you checked in?'

'No, I need to buy a ticket.'

'You could do it now online.'

'I've lost my phone.'

'Oh.'

'In the maze,' I add pertinently.

'That's a shame.'

Is it? Is it just that? A shame? Nothing more than an unlucky accident? I don't know. I add, 'I'm not even sure if the flight is to Heathrow or Gatwick. I'm assuming British Airways, because that's who we flew over with.' I shrug, feeling helpless with the weight of the gaps in my knowledge. 'Daniel has all the details.'

I suppose we must both see that isn't much use to me right now, because all Jonathan says is 'Right.'

'Just get me to the airport,' I mutter, exasperated. Stuck, I look out of the window. I don't want to talk to Jonathan. I don't want to be with him at all, but I don't have a choice. I have to believe that he is nothing more than a creepy middle-aged man who I met for the first time this week, who tried his luck in the maze, but who will, ultimately, deliver me to my destination. Thinking he's anything more insidious, anything more powerful will cause me to spin. I need to stay in the moment, keep a grip. I open my handbag to check I have my passport and money. The relief is enormous when I find I do. I gasp when I notice that my purse is nestled next to the letter

184

knife that I remember seeing on the library desk. Did I steal it? I don't remember doing so. It's a long, thin, sharp blade. It could be deadly if wielded correctly. It would certainly do some damage to a neck, an eye.

Jonathan grins at me. 'Got everything you need?'

'Yes thank you.'

He keeps one hand on the steering wheel, and with the other reaches for a packet of cigarettes on his dashboard. He taps one out of the carton, puts it in his mouth.

'Light it for me, will you.'

'I don't have a lighter.'

'Not one in your bag?'

'No, I don't smoke.'

'I think there's one in the side pocket of the car.'

I don't want to be compliant, but I am. I feel about for a lighter and there is one. Not one of the smart Dunhill vintage lighters that I've seen used over the past day or so, but a cheap neon-pink plastic one. I lean forward and light Jonathan's cigarette. He inhales deeply. 'Thank you.' The moment is more intimate than I'd like. I slip the lighter in my bag. If I get as far as the airport, I'll have to dump it and the letter knife before I can check in, but who knows if I'll get that far.

Evan's face bounces into my consciousness. I remember him trying to persuade me to go away with him. I wish I had. It hurts to think of him. So close and yet, maybe, still too far away. Out of my reach now. I shake my head. I can't think of him. I have to stay focused. I have to survive this if I ever want to see Evan again. I scan for a landmark that I might recognise from the journey here, or a signpost that might give me a clue as to where I am, or where we are heading. I hope to God

Jonathan is taking me to the airport, that he is done with me, but he could be taking me anywhere to do whatever the hell he wants with me. I have no control. No choices.

We drive in silence for a while. It's a hefty, volatile silence, the sort that seems about to burst, but my only desire is for it to continue. I would like to fast-forward the next couple of hours. All I want is to be safely on the plane back to England and Evan. It's frustrating that my life is stuttering and spilling at the moment, that time isn't reliable, but I can't speed it up at will.

Of course, the silence doesn't last. Jonathan breaks it, commenting, 'You've had quite the experience, haven't you?' I sense him looking at me in the mirror again. I don't want to meet his eyes, but I feel compelled. I glare at him but refuse to answer. He coughs. 'I'm sorry. I realise I've been part of that. We've never met before, Natalya. You believe that now, don't you?' I don't know what to believe, but I realise that admitting as much will give him more power. 'The thing I said in the maze, it was just supposed to be a joke. I didn't really expect you to go for it.' I tut and once again turn away from him, concentrate on the countryside beyond the car. Fields of sunflowers and grape vines speed by, a blur. Then, before I can even allow myself a moment's hope that he really is repentant, just a crass but harmless man, he adds, 'Although you did go for it with Giles. What's he got that I haven't, eh?'

The tone is jocular, but the words are not. Men never joke about other men having something they lack. Envy, competition, rivalry, they are not laughing matters. 'I don't remember anything about Giles.'

Jonathan laughs. 'Really? It all seems so muddled, doesn't

186

it? What and who you think you remember. What you don't. And now there's a video.' He's practically licking his lips.

'You should all delete that.'

He shakes his head. 'I don't think that's going to happen.'

'Why not? What do you want from me?' I don't have any money and these people do, so they can't be thinking of blackmailing me for cash. Sex is the obvious currency they could demand, but that doesn't seem logical. Why would they film me having sex to demand more sex? They could have all had a go when Giles did. It's a disgusting thought, I know. But I don't shy away from it. I can't; everyone else can, but I can't. 'I have nothing to give and nothing to lose,' I state, but even as I say it, I know this isn't true. I have Evan. I could lose Evan. For the first time in a long time, I really do have something to lose. My heart starts to speed up, thumping against my chest. I feel dizzy. I breathe in deeply, but my lungs just fill with the smoke from Jonathan's cigarette. I hold tight to the edge of the seat, feel the fabric under my fingertips. Stay here. Stay in this moment.

Jonathan pauses, then sighs. 'I don't want anything from you, but a friend of mine does.'

'What does your friend want?'

'He wants you to go away.'

'What are you talking about?'

'He's prepared to pay you to leave England. To give it up. He doesn't want you to get hurt. Not if he can avoid it. In the boot of this car there is another suitcase, not unlike the one you are carrying. In it there are new, more sensible clothes: jumpers, jeans, trainers. There is a new phone and some money. Enough to get you started. More will follow once we have your bank account details. When we arrive at the airport, you can get out of the car and catch a plane to Canada. There's a flight to Toronto at one fifteen. If you agree to this, I'll buy you a ticket.'

It's insane. What he's saying makes no sense. Who would pay me to leave the country? Why would anyone do that? 'Who is your friend?' I ask.

'That doesn't matter. All that matters is that you get on the flight. Go away. Stay away. Never come back. Leave your life behind.'

'Is he some sort of evangelist? Does he want to save sex workers?' I once had a client who claimed he'd found religion. He started booking us girls for sessions where he did nothing other than preach. He wanted us to see the evil in the path we'd chosen, to repent and be born again. Some of the girls accepted multiple sessions with him, reasoning that being paid not to have sex was easier than being paid to have it. I didn't see him again once I heard he'd found religion. In my line of work, nothing is as dangerous as unpredictable. If one week a man pays women to spank his arse with a cocktail swizzle stick and the next week says he's going to sit at God's table, he is definitely what I'd call unpredictable. My gut was right on that one. The girls who did continue to visit him told me his ultimate goal was to baptise them; naturally this ritual was to be performed by him. Apparently he needed to be naked to do the job, and they needed to be naked for the rebirth. Not a real desire to save anyone, then, just a variation on the theme of desire. 'Are you talking about Daniel? Is that why Daniel brought me here? Are you some sort of cult?'

Jonathan chuckles, shakes his head. 'A cult. What an imagination you have.'

'Why start with me? There are women in worse positions than I am.'

Jonathan stops laughing. 'Are there?' he asks.

I shiver, because there's something about his tone that suggests he thinks not. I am in the worst position imaginable.

Mentally I flick through possibilities of who might want me to leave the country and who has the sort of money to not only get me on a flight but create a new life for me. Many of my clients are wealthy, very wealthy; some are obscenely rich, so that is not much of a filter. Who would want me to give up my life? A wife of a client? It's possible, but it seems like a stretch. There are easier ways to stop your husband using sex workers. Divorce, for one. I wonder have I embarrassed someone. Some of my clients are politicians; are any of them in line for a promotion, perhaps the top job? If so, might they want me far away so I can't cause any trouble? But no one comes to mind. Besides, I've never been anything other than discreet. I don't rock the boat. I'm not a threat.

Yet I am being threatened. Because whilst the suitcase in the boot and the plane ticket are carrots, the video is a stick. There may be worse to come. I wonder whether I might have a chance if I appear compliant. I can get to the airport, alert someone at security that I'm travelling against my will. I can buy another ticket back to England, back to Evan. My tentative optimism is quashed when Jonathan adds, 'Of course, I'll have to come with you to Canada. It's not that I don't trust you.' He chuckles, 'Actually, it's exactly that. I don't trust you. So I'll stay with you just to see that you do get across the ocean.'

He's playing with me.

I want to tell him that I can't go away, I can't start again;

that I won't, because I have a fiancé and I'm going to get married. I swallow down the words, try not to move a muscle in my face so that he can't guess at the rebellion simmering in my head; he has to believe in my submission. But I reach for the thought, I mentally stretch and grab for it, clasp it to me, the one thing that might save me in the end. Evan. Evan loves me. It's a pure, honest love. He'll find me. I can depend on him.

Can't I?

My head starts to spin again. I frantically press the button that ought to lower the window, but it doesn't. I realise Jonathan has control of everything. 'Can you open the window; I'm feeling a bit car sick.'

'We're about to go on the motorway. I can't open the window.'

'Then put out the cigarette or turn up the air conditioning,' I suggest.

'Here.' He chucks a foil packet onto the back seat. 'Amanda made me some beef sandwiches because she knew I'd get hungry driving all the way to the airport and back.' I want to tell him that I don't need anything from him, but my head is pounding and I'm dehydrated, and I know eating something will help. 'Smothered in melty provolone, and the garlic aioli is home-made. She made it herself. All those maids running around that chateau, and my wife made the aioli herself.' He smiles fondly. 'She's a keeper,' he says with a laugh.

The panic rises and tightens in my chest. I am breathless, suddenly uncertain whether the conversation about flying to Canada ever happened. How could it have? From new countries to beef sandwiches in a matter of breaths. I don't know. My hands shaking, I open the foil and salivate at the succulent meat folded into a golden baguette.

'She slices against the grain. That's why it's so tender. What are you waiting for? Knock yourself out.'

I want to resist, it's a matter of pride. 'How long until we get to the airport?'

'About an hour.'

I feel too unwell to wait another hour on a matter of pride. I'm too sensible to do that. *Pride comes before a fall. Don't cut off your nose to spite your face.* These expressions are ones my parents used to recite to me when I was a child. I can hear their voices ringing in my head, and I remember their own pride, which they tried to hide, in their ability to grasp complex foreign idioms. I spot a sign for the airport. Seventy-five kilometres. Thank God. Relieved, I bite into the sandwich and sit back. It's almost over.

# 26

# *Dora*

*Eleven years ago*

The first contraction rips through my body, waking me from an unsettled, dream-fuelled sleep. The pain is filthy. I think I am going to die, and for a fraction of a moment, I think maybe that would be easier. My life is a shit show. Death would at least mean it was all over. But not really. Not really. Really, I always want to fight on.

I don't imagine anyone in the northern hemisphere plans to give birth to a child in January. It is such a relentlessly grey and bleak month, not the welcome into the world a child deserves. But snow is something different altogether. It wipes away the dank blur and gifts magic. I've never seen it snow in London, but as the pain of the contractions pushes me to my feet, I glance out of the window and see that snow is falling. As thick as glue.

I think it is a sign. A good one.

Whilst I boil the kettle to make a cup of tea, I look out of the window and watch the flakes fluttering. I feel excited by the muffled hush that is symptomatic of heavy snow. She is three days overdue, so the contractions aren't a surprise, and yet they are still a shock. I panic, suddenly horrified at the thought of the hours ahead of me. I wish my mum was with me. Fleetingly I toy with calling her, but it is a ridiculous idea. Even if she is able to get over the news of my pregnancy and then decides to be supportive, by the time she flies here, the labour will most likely be done. Better that I wait and tell her in a more considered way. Although what that might be, I don't know. I've been looking for the right words for nine months.

I time the contractions and then call the hospital to ask what I should do. They tell me the contractions are still too far apart; they warn me that there is no point in arriving too early, that there won't be a bed. I get the feeling I'll be in the way. I hate being in the way, so I decide to stay put for as long as I can. However, once the contractions gather force – by which I mean I think I'll vomit with the pain – I don't want to be alone in my bedsit. Two reasons. First, it is too poky; I don't want her born into a room that, at best, is only ever an apology for a life. Second, I am terrified of being alone, aware that births can be tricky, a lot can go wrong.

I take the bus to the hospital because I know it will lumber slowly through the London streets, take its time, but I will have people around me if I need them. I sit up top, at the front. I watch the snow dance in the headlights of the cars and buses coming towards me. I take in familiar sights made unfamiliar by the surprise coating.

There is the Flamingo Bar! A kitsch place that sells cheap cocktails and plays sentimental, mawkish but somehow irresistible 1950s music on Tuesday afternoons. My friend Lizzie and I once danced on a table in there, having taken advantage of the cocktail deal and a gap in our timetables. We danced until the bartender lost patience and kicked us out. There is the theatre where I saw a production of *Cat on a Hot Tin Roof* when I was fourteen years old. My first visit to London and my first visit to a proper play; Christmas pantomimes don't count. That was when I decided that I had to be an actor. And there is the academy where I auditioned in a vault-like room for my place on the extremely prestigious course. My heart speeds up at the sight of the building, even now. I remember being so terrified that my soliloquy just wouldn't cut it. I was certain that if I messed up, I'd miss out on more than the place, but on life itself.

I was offered a place, though.

I thought that was the beginning of everything. Everything marvellous and possible and wild.

Yet here I am. Another contraction seizes me. No way can I breathe through it.

As I sit on the bus, pregnant and alone, panic claws at my throat, I swallow it down. I can't contemplate how it was or even how it could have been. There is no point. Since the two little blue lines turned up on the pee stick, I've stopped believing that life is one linear trajectory of brilliance; that if you set off on the right path, you are guaranteed greatness. You are not. Your greatest dream can be realised, your most fervent wish can be granted, but then you can be blindsided by the unexpected. I wish I didn't know this at my age; it is a bit like being the first in your class to discover that Santa Claus doesn't exist. I am scared that this will set me. Define me. Make me cynical, weary. I wish I still lived in blissful, ignorant belief of unlimited possibilities and progress, like Lizzie and all my other friends at RADA. But what is the use of wishing?

It isn't any easier thinking about the future. The imminent birth of my baby girl terrifies me. What am I going to do with a baby? How am I going to be a mother? It's not what I planned. I suppose at some level I had a vague notion that I might be a mother one day. I don't know, I hadn't given it any real thought. What am I going to do? I can't look back, it's too painful; I can't look forward, it's too scary. I groan out loud. There are only a few people on the bus; two have earbuds in, the third respects the fact we live in London and refuses to meet my eye or acknowledge my despair in any way. I wonder can I stay on this bus forever, just driving around on an eternal loop? It's unfeasible, though, as the contractions are coming closer and closer and harder and harder. It's impossible to pretend I am just a kid on a bus, going for a ride in the snow, planning to dance on tabletops later. Impossible even for me, someone with enviable acting skills and a propensity to self-delusion. I will not be meeting up with friends in retro bars, or to lie in the park and carve angels into the freshly fallen snow, I will not throw snowballs or draw hearts on the windscreens of parked cars tonight.

I have a baby to deliver.

When I get off the bus, the driver says, 'Mind how you go.' He looks worried for me. I force myself to grin at him, hoping to reassure him that I am fine, because I want people to believe I am fine; I want to believe it myself. However, my calves have swollen so much I haven't been able to fasten my boots since November, and I am wearing the only pair of shoes that still fit, summer trainers. They are not designed for heavy snow, and as I clamber off the bus, I almost slip over, right under his gaze. A middle-aged woman offers me her arm, and walks me into the hospital. I smile gratefully, but I'm not able to say much. I'm gritting my teeth, trying to keep my mouth clamped shut so I can hold in the screams. Still, it's nice to note – strangers are not always strange.

# 27

# *Dora*

'Come on, sweetheart, you're almost there. Just one more big push. It's almost over.'

'I can't.'

'Yes, you can. You're doing brilliantly, Teodora.'

'I can't.' I've been in labour for sixteen hours, the last eight in the hospital with this nurse or midwife, whatever she is. I am not sure of everyone's proper title, and I don't dare ask. I feel stupid asking too many questions, so I limit myself to only asking for essential information. She seems like a kind woman; she is about my mother's age, which renders her at once reassuring and a little terrifying. Another contraction seizes me, making my body convulse. I scream. It is blood-curdling. I see the nurse flinch, even though she must have heard louder and worse. Surely I am not the loudest or worst. But maybe I am. My mum has always said I am too dramatic, a bit over the top.

The sounds that come from me are violent and crazy. I am scaring myself and am ashamed that I can't be more measured and restrained, but here I am; legs splayed, blood, mucus, faeces easing out of every orifice, I am stripped back. My body is waging a war on itself. Punishing is the right word. 'Aarghhh!' I let out another scream. It feels good. It feels like that noise has been caught inside of me for too long and I had to let it out. Fuck stoicism. Fuck decorum.

'Get the fucking baby out!' I am crying and I wish I hadn't said that out loud. I shouldn't have called the baby a 'fucking baby'. Will someone make a note of that? Will it get me into trouble? Throughout the pregnancy I have been racked with fear that they won't let me keep my baby. That I'll be judged too young, unfit. After all, I am both, so why wouldn't they think it? 'They' being a vague and horrifying body that clouds my mind: authorities, the system, the people in charge.

'You're doing brilliantly,' says the midwife kindly. Not acknowledging the rush of expletives.

I haven't told any of the nurses my fear; it's too awful to articulate. At the check-ups, I just nod, say as little as possible, try to appear calm and reasonable, or if not that, then at least functional. I tell myself it is an irrational fear – most fears are. No one has actually suggested I give up my baby; no one has tried to make me feel small, pathetic or wrong.

The nurses tend to fall into two camps. Some ooze compassion; they have gentle, smiling eyes and sense my skin hunger, my need for reassurance and comfort, so they keep their hands on my arm for a moment longer than necessary, squeeze my fingers when they tell me to get dressed. Others are cooler; they have an efficiency about them that betrays their boredom. I am never sure what they are bored with. Their own lives: cleaning bodies, taking blood and urine, administrating vaccines? Or mine? A knocked-up college drop out. Oddly, sometimes I find it is a relief to be looked after by nurses who don't make small talk but give instructions in crisp voices. Sometimes it is harder to see the compassion in the smiley-eyed nurses, because compassion is just a hair away from pity, isn't it?

I have scrupulously attended all the prenatal appointments I've been offered. The nurses keep praising me for doing so, constantly reminding me how important it is; hopefully they think my attendance shows I am committed to raising a healthy, happy child, despite my age. And I am doing my best to ignore the internal monologue that occasionally erupts. A baby! A baby! What will I do with a baby? Shush, whisper it. It's a dreadful thought. Selfish. I'm not thinking clearly. That's the pain. I really do want to do everything I can to give her the best start. I've read up on it all. I practised breathing exercises, I talked and sang to my bump, I took the vitamins, but the problem is, even whilst I eat apples and spinach, I know really that I am bailing out the boat with a thimble. How can I give her the best start? She doesn't have a daddy. And me? Am I the best start? Hardly. I've had to drop out of drama school to give birth. It's not the best start, it's just not, and only a child or an imbecile would think otherwise. I am neither. I am young, but old enough to know better. Another one of my mother's favourite sayings.

I have liked going to the antenatal appointments, not only for the reassurance that the baby is OK, but because the nurses *see* me. I've found that since becoming pregnant, no one else does. It seems that outside the health centre's walls, I disappear. I've known for a long time that pretty girls are noticed with a frequency that can be flattering, overwhelming, even irritating. I've actually complained about being ogled! But I've discovered that being ignored is so much worse. I know, not a great moment for the feminist movement. I feel unsteady, not really involved in the world. If I am not seen, am I here at all? It feels like a death. A vanishing. I am too young to vanish.

The only other people, besides nurses, who seem to still notice me are other pregnant women. When we cross in the street or bump into each other in the supermarket aisles, they cast a glance over my bump, then their gaze drifts to my left hand. Maybe they blush through embarrassment for me, or outrage at me. Not sure. I see them think it. *Too young, too stupid.* I don't disagree. Nurses are different. They look me in the eye. They interact with me. I am integral to their day, or at least to ten or fifteen minutes of it. They get me to pee in pots, they give me injections and vitamins. They wrap a black band around my arm and pump air into it to take my blood pressure. Tighter and tighter; it seems like a metaphor for my life closing in on me. But hey, can't be picky. At least I'm there. They rub freezing gel on my bump, and then laugh with me when the ultrasound machine hums out a heartbeat. Once, a nurse blew my fringe out of my eyes because her hands were busy elsewhere. 'You should get that cut before the baby arrives; there'll be no time afterwards.' She said this with a grin; she wasn't telling me off. She was having fun with me. Noticing me. I didn't have the money to get a haircut, so I did it myself with a pair of IKEA scissors that were designed to take off bacon rind, or maybe chop herbs. When I went for my next check-up, I expected her to say something like 'nice hair', because I had done a decent job. She didn't, though. I guess that was too much to hope for. It was silly of me to be disappointed.

'You're crowning. One more big push, Teodora. Nearly there, sweetheart!' The nurse delivers this news with a grin that doesn't quite wipe away her all-pervasive expression of concentration. She glances at me, briefly, but then straight back to the messy end.

From the books, I know that crowning means that the baby should be out soon; no more wrench-in-two contractions. I will stop sweating, and crying, and bleeding, and cursing. My stomach has been hard to look at, a veiny mound that appears alien to me; with the baby out, my body will be my own again. It won't frighten or surprise me. Yet the news that she will soon be out of me and in the world doesn't make me feel brave or relieved. *One more big push* seems idiotic. Better the baby stays in there. What am I supposed to do with a baby?

But I don't get time to think about it, because my body takes over. 'Aarghhhh!' I push down with redoubled force and strength. A wild, animalistic urge. It's filthy and cruel. The pain. Immense. Unthinkable. And then she is here! Real. There is a space in my stomach and my arms itch, craving her. She has arrived!

They hand her to me. She is a mess. A slick film coats her, blood and a sticky veil of mucus. Such a mess, and yet so perfect. There she is, *life*! All of it. I can't take my eyes off her. I drink her in. She curls into me as though she doesn't know yet that we've separated, that she is on the outside, and I count her tiny, tiny fingers and toes. She seems to sense that I am her harbour, and I swear I will be. Always. I promise you, baby. I promise.

I started labour in a flimsy paper gown. I only brought one nightdress with me; normally I sleep in pyjamas, but the books said you needed nursing nighties for hospital. I could only afford one. A hideous navy thing; the books said a dark colour was a good idea because of the blood. It is shapeless but comfortable, and front-fastening for easy access to my breasts. When I arrived at the hospital, there wasn't a right moment to change into it. The nurse said I should keep it for home, and gave me the paper gown, which I ripped off about four hours in. I am as naked as the baby. I don't care. Nudity never bothers me. My veiny boobs and my floppy, recently evacuated stomach are unrecognisable. My body, her vessel and her launch pad.

The nurses buzz around me, cleaning things, stitching things. Stitching *me*. Then they take her away to assess her Apgar scores. I want to shout out, to object; however, I am grateful that the words catch in my throat, because I have to behave normally. Rational mums want their babies to have Apgar scores. I just want to hold her tight. Nothing more. I very much doubt I am a rational mum, but I must appear as such. I wait impatiently, the few minutes stretching like hours. 'Is she OK?' I ask, irritated that they are assessing her, judging her, and yet valuing their opinion, yearning for them to tell me she has passed this first test.

'She's perfect,' says one nurse, as she hands her back to me.

'And beautiful,' says the other.

She is perfect and beautiful! I love her so much I think I might explode. Explode with the responsibility and joy of her. I just can't believe she is mine and that she grew inside of me.

'Have you thought of a name?'

'No.' I glance at the midwife and see that she is watching me closely. 'I have a few. I just can't decide. I thought I'd know. She is so small for a name. Just a dot. Maybe I should call her Dottie?' I offer the name up, waiting for approval. A thumbs-up or thumbs-down. Dottie is not on my list. I had been thinking about Cordelia, Francesca, Amelia. They all seem too much for this little thing to handle. 'What do you think?'

'There's plenty of time to pick a name,' replies the midwife, not conveying much confidence in my choice. I feel silly. Does she think I am impetuous? My mother's name is Radmila. It is my middle name too. I briefly wonder whether I should give it to Dottie as a middle name, but I give up on the idea before it is even completely formed. Doing so seems presumptuous, as my mother has no idea that I am pregnant. I would never want her to think that I chose the name to ingratiate myself with her. That wouldn't be the reason – it would be to offer Dottie a sense of continuity, of history – but I couldn't bear it if my mother thought I'd named my child as some sort of apology. My daughter will not be an apology.

'You won't drop her.' I'm not sure if the nurse is giving an instruction or asking a question. Her tone isn't confident enough to be an assertion. I tighten my grip. Dottie snuffles and roots into my breast. I put my nipple in her mouth. It just seems like the thing to do.

'You're a natural.' I hear approval, or if that's a stretch, then at least relief.

'Is there anyone you'd like us to call?' I shake my head. 'You're sure?' I feel the nurses' scrutiny. Just minutes before I thought they were supporting me, now I wonder. A young, pregnant, unmarried girl is vulnerable, a priority. A baby just minutes old is more than that. She is everything. She is their priority now. They have swapped teams. I want to explain that I am on Dottie's team. I am captain and cheerleader and coach, and anything else she needs. I'll do it all.

Maybe I should let the nurse call my mother. For nine months I've been trying to find the right way to tell her I was pregnant; maybe a nurse telling her I am a mother is the answer. At least that way she can't yell at me. Not straight away. But I doubt the NHS stretches to international calls, and I know she will insist I return to Serbia, to live with her. She'll knit for Dottie, pink bonnets and cardigans, feed her baklava and superstitions. One too sweet, the other too sour. My life will be over. There has to be another way.

I don't bother answering the nurse; confirming my complete and utter isolation isn't going to help anyone. I can't be bothered with what is missing and lacking, I must focus on what I have right in front of me. I just stare at her. My baby. Dottie. She is perfect. We will be all right.

# 28

## *Dora*

I only spend another eight hours in the hospital after delivering Dottie. Sixteen hours in total there, and then I leave with a new person. An extra person. It is extraordinary. Unbelievable! By the time I – we – leave the hospital, the snow has hardened to an inhospitable ice where footfall has been scarce, and where cars have relentlessly ploughed on, it has melted to an ugly slush. I scan the pick-up-set-down parking bay for the cab the nurses booked for me. I watch as a middle-aged woman pulls up and then, with a painful mix of frustration and love, eases out an elderly confused man from the passenger seat: her father, I suppose. Then my attention is pulled to a man in his late thirties who is dropping off his wife and young son. The son is wearing sports kit; his head is bleeding. The mother has blood on her coat, from cradling him, I guess. 'Get him inside, I'll park the car and come and find you.' The father barks the instruction, and yet his voice is infused with concern.

Dottie will never know her father, so I suppose she won't ever have to watch him become old and feeble, help him when he is cantankerous. That should comfort me, but it doesn't;

she is being denied a fundamental relationship and I can't pretend otherwise. I tell myself that this is not my fault, but I don't know if that is true. Whether it's my fault or not, it's certainly my problem. All her problems are mine, and mine entirely. I already know that. If she ever gets injured on a sports field, who will rush us to a hospital? I need to learn to drive. Although even as I have this thought, I realise it is unlikely to happen. I don't have the money.

Dottie makes a sound, a sort of snuffle or mew like a kitten, reminding me of her presence. Already, I realise I'm aware of her on two levels. I'm thinking of her and I'm holding her. She is in my head and my reality. I suppose this is mothering. Consequently I see that learning to drive is not only unlikely because I don't have the money, but now I will be short of time too. I didn't bother to learn in sixth form like some of my friends did; I was too busy at rehearsals, dance and drama classes. I shrug my shoulders, trying not to let that particular regret settle. I can't take on any more regrets. I will snap.

I watch these family units with a stiff envy; it causes an ache in my lower back, or maybe that is just the weight of Dottie. I can't let the envy take hold and solidify either. It won't help. I kiss Dottie's head. 'You have me,' I murmur.

I'm glad the nurses called a cab for me. Initially I was worried about the cost of the fare and argued that I could take a bus, but they said the cabs have baby seats installed and it is the only safe way to leave hospital. Of course. I should have thought about that in advance. I haven't bought a car seat because I don't drive. I thought that was one expense I could avoid at least. Looks like I was wrong about that. I already have the feeling there will be plenty I'm wrong about. Nothing I can avoid.

A cab blinks its lights at me. Relief sloshes through my body.

I am grateful for the specialist taxi company, whose service extends to the driver showing me how to put Dottie in the seat. His hands are confident and assured. *Click, click, click*. A little tug at the belt to check that she is secure. There is a school photograph of three kids under the age of ten Blu-Tacked to his dashboard. He clocks my face, confused and overwhelmed at the mechanics of the car seat fasteners, at everything. 'It's just a knack, you'll get the hang of it,' he says cheerfully.

He drives slowly through the slushy streets. I can't take my eyes off Dottie, who has fallen asleep. The driver offers to help me carry things up to my flat. I live on the second floor and have my handbag and hospital bag with me; with Dottie to carry as well, I have run out of hands. However, I turn down his offer; I am shy about him seeing the communal entrance. Often the door needs to be forced back with a shove because of the build-up of fliers advertising pizza deliveries, the walls need repainting, the carpet is threadbare in places and pocked with stains in others; sometimes it is actually spongy underfoot. I'm not sure why. Probably because the place is damp. The hallway always smells of fried onions. I think it is the family in number 3.

'I'll be fine, thank you,' I say, throwing my handbag into my hospital bag, putting that over my shoulder and then carefully scooping Dottie out of the car seat. She smells awful. I inadvertently pull back from her, wrinkle my nose.

The driver laughs. 'You get used to that too,' he says confidently.

I am sweating by the time I climb to the second floor, and Dottie is crying. Crying doesn't cover it. She is screaming. An urgent, hiccuping hysteria that suggests I've let her down. She needs her nappy changing, I need my sanitary towel changing. The moment I open the door to my flat, I drop the bags and collapse onto the only armchair I own. I scrabble to pull out my breast and urgently push my nipple into her mouth. She clasps her tiny rosebud mouth around it, sucks hard. The crying stops immediately. Silence, except for the gentle sucking sound. She doesn't seem to care about her nappy, happy to sit in shit, which is not an un-useful skill. I stay in that chair for forty minutes, then I wind her, change her, nurse her until she falls to sleep.

The entire process is terrifying. I trembled as I eased her out of one baby onesie and into another; terrified I'd bend her limbs in the wrong direction, that she'd break. I am slick with sweat, and my head is pounding. I forced myself to breathe slowly, as I have been taught to do in the wings of a theatre before a performance. I talked to her throughout. I have enough control over my voice box to at least sound calm. I owe her that. By the time I manage to get to the bathroom, my blood is everywhere. I take off my skirt, tights and pants and leave them on the bathroom floor. I find clean knickers and fresh sanitary products. I put on the nursing nightie that I took into hospital, and two jumpers on top of that. I crawl into bed and close my eyes. Exhausted.

# 29

# *Dora*

As I was leaving the hospital, someone told me that the health visitor would be calling by the next day.

'Tomorrow?'

'Is that a problem?'

'No.' I am not confident enough to present problems. Are there new mums who dare to? The thought of a health visitor scares me. An inspection, a judgement. Luckily, late in my pregnancy, I was surprised to discover that the concept of nesting is not a myth, and I cleaned my little flat from top to bottom. I scrubbed floors, windowsills and tiles, I tackled in and behind the old fridge and the oven. Everything about my life is cheap. When I sit on the bed, the mattress groans because it is so thin. Lots of things are old and worn, but they are at least clean.

However, Dottie and I have been in the flat for twenty-four hours now, and nothing looks clean or tidy by the time the health visitor presses the buzzer. As she walks up the stairs, I pull my greasy hair into a ponytail. I can smell my own scalp. I haven't found time to shower, which I regret but can't do anything about.

The health worker turns out to be motherly and kind. Thank God. She takes Dottie from me, weighs her, while I stand by, helpless. After twenty-four hours of holding her more or less constantly, I don't know what to do with myself; my arms feel useless, pointless. I offer to put the kettle on.

'Oh, don't bother yourself, dear.' I pick up a nappy sack and throw it in the bin, but the smell lingers. 'Oh, don't worry about the flat, sit down. Rest whenever you can, that's my advice.' She says this with a laugh. I begin to hope that she isn't here to judge me, but perhaps to help. She asks questions and nods and smiles in a way that suggests I am getting the answers right. I am grateful to Dottie for falling asleep, for not screaming. Still, I can hear my own breath, too fast and shallow. The health visitor's eyes graze the room. 'You seem well kitted out.' It is kind of her to see what I have, not what I lack. I've done my best to make sure I have all the essential things a baby might need. A changing mat, a baby bath and a bassinet, I do not have a full-sized cot yet, or a highchair. I plan to get those as she gets bigger. I don't have a pram either; they are too expensive, and anyway, there is no room to keep one in the communal hall downstairs, and how would I get it up and down two flights of stairs? I do have a baby papoose. It cost fifty quid! Two slow shifts in the coffee shop for a sling, but it was cheaper than a pram by a long stretch. I found everything else in the Cancer Research charity shop. I got lucky there. I was picking out baby clothes a couple of months back, and a woman who volunteered there said she had a few bits and pieces that might be useful. After that, she secreted away all the decent baby stuff that was donated. She found me a bottle-sterilising kit, a baby gym, a breast pump, which she assured me was immaculate, lots of clothes, some books and toys. Some of the stuff looks brand new.

'Well, Dottie is doing brilliantly,' declares the health visitor. Before I can feel relieved, she adds, 'I'll pop in again in a few days' time, and then every week, just until you find your feet.' I nod, although I'm unsure as to whether I want this intrusion, but it doesn't seem like a matter of choice. I am in a system. 'And how is Mummy doing?' It takes a moment to understand she means me.

I nod. 'Fine.' I'm surprised to feel a knot in my throat. I suppose it is nice to be asked.

Over the next month, I become more used to her visits. I stop worrying about tidying up for her arrival. Actually, I don't so much stop worrying about the state of the flat; it is more that I stop caring, or maybe even stop seeing the mess. All I can see is Dottie. I am on a carousel of screaming, nappy changes, feeding, burping, sleeping, screaming, changing, feeding, burping, sleeping, screaming, changing, feeding, burping, sleeping. It just goes round and around. She doesn't like to sleep anywhere other than in my arms, and so I doze in the armchair when she does. Pinned. Some days it is an achievement if I manage to get to the loo. The health visitor's visits begin to merge.

Today she is talking to me about vaccinations and going to the health clinic for those when she suddenly comments, 'Dottie is a beauty, isn't she. Like her mummy.' My hair is greasy, I am wearing sweatpants, but I guess there is always my bone structure. I know she is trying to be kind, but I don't know how to react. I stare back blankly. She continues, 'You're lucky. Girls your age snap right back.' I am not sure if she means my vagina or my figure. Does either thing matter any more, anyway? I don't want to ask which she means. I don't want to be caught out having trivial thoughts about trivial things like my body shape. It could be a trap. Or at least a test. Am I sensible enough to be a mother, or am I self-involved and frivolous? I keep this thought in my head. It sounds ludicrous, paranoid. A red flag. If they think I am paranoid, they might start to be concerned about postnatal depression. I mustn't draw attention. The health visitor seems nice, but she is always probing. How am I feeling? Am I coping? Do I feel happy? Content? It is possible to think people are on your side, that they are being nice, but then find that they might not be. I remember my tutor at RADA. I was her favourite student, always bagging the best roles, always being praised for my intuitive acting, my original interpretations, my fierce imagination. It annoyed the other students that I was so clearly favoured. And then, suddenly, I wasn't.

She called me into her office. The formality was unusual. 'Come in, sit down, close the door.' Her tone suggested it wasn't good news. 'I want to talk to you about your plans.'

'My plans?'

'Well, it seems your circumstances have changed.'

I wrapped my hands defensively around my belly. 'In what way do you mean?' She paused, and her eyes dropped to my stomach. I was five months pregnant at that point, and no matter how I dressed to disguise it, it was becoming obvious. I knew I couldn't hide it forever. I was not deny-ing it, but I was ignoring it. Or rather, I was hoping that everyone else would ignore it. I didn't want to have to let it go, all the possibility, my dreams, my hopes. I knew that the moment I acknowledged my situation, that was exactly what had to happen.

'Can we do anything?' My insides were scrunched up so tight I thought I was going to implode. 'We're here to help, but to do that, we need to understand your thinking in order to put in place some sort of plan. We should talk about timings, whether you're going to take some time off.' I didn't reply. 'Or childcare afterwards? If, that is, childcare will be necessary?' She was fishing. 'You might have plans in place. Your mother?'

I bit my lip – it was barely perceptible – and shook my head a fraction. My tutor's brow furrowed. The window was open, the noises of the street drifted in and her hopes for me drifted out. I showed promise, but then so did many, many many other young female actors. Showing promise was only relevant if it was flanked by one hundred per cent commitment and stringent, single-minded focus. I watched as her face hardened, as her mind whirled.

'There is insurance to consider. Some of the classes must be taking their toll now. The dance? The ballet? You can talk to me, Teodora.'

'Do you have a tissue?'

She rummaged in her desk drawer, pulled out a packet of tissues. I took one, handed back the pack. She shook her head. 'You can keep them.'

'Thank you.'

I left that day. I never went back. I don't imagine I ever will. I picked up more shifts at the coffee shop. I was on my feet all day; my back ached, the skin across my belly stretched so taut that I thought it might burst.

The health visitor brings me back to the room. What is

she saying? I have to tune in. I must listen and stay in the now. 'She's a good little feeder, isn't she?' I nod. 'And that's been straightforward for you? No problems?' I don't confess to how much I like it, Dottie's hungry, urgent tugging at my breast. I let her stay on my boob for as long as she likes; sucking at first furiously, then contentedly, then sometimes losing interest, sometimes falling asleep. I am worried that it might sound weird or just lazy if I tell her this. But as there is never anyone to see us, I don't always feel the need to unlatch her, put my breast away and pop her into her crib. I just let her stay there, joined to me, needing me. Me needing her. I like feeling her so close. The health visitor weighs her. 'Oh, very good.' She writes down the weight gain, nodding with approval. I feel like I've just won an Oscar. 'And you? Are you eating?'

I smile, nod again. 'I have a huge appetite too,' I reassure her. 'I'm starving the whole time.' I am, because I've rarely managed to stumble out of the flat since we arrived home from the hospital. Getting groceries on a regular basis is proving harder than I imagined. The corner shop, downstairs and two doors along, charges prices that make my eyes water. Literally. The supermarket, a Tube stop away, might as well be in the Sahara desert, it seems that inaccessible to me right now. I drink my tea black, eat cereal without milk. I wonder what I'll do when the cereal runs out, when the paltry stack of tins does. Before Dottie was born, I built a pile of nappies so high it was a tower. I remember thinking I'd overdone it, that we'd never use them up. I am down to my last four.

'Is there anyone dropping food by, helping out?'

'Oh yes,' I reply, smiling. 'Lots of people.' I lie because I don't want to appear friendless or hopeless. A person without friends is suspicious. I am glad that she doesn't ask who, exactly.

I change Dottie's nappy and she seems appreciative. She kicks her legs and gurgles. I swoop down on her and kiss her, over and over again. Her face, head, tiny body and chubby thighs, her arms, her wrists and hands. Her skin is like butter left out in the sun, so soft. She loves me kissing her this way and laughs. I could kiss her all day, every day. I could really. And that doesn't cost anything. But after a bit, my lips seem dry and scratchy, and she seems bored. I have to think of something else to do with her.

# 30

# *Dora*

The man next door, who is in his thirties, basically ancient and a sad fuck because he plays video games all night, bangs on the wall because she is screaming and has been for four hours straight. Or two weeks straight. I am not sure. I've fed her, changed her, burped her. She won't stop crying. I've cried too. It didn't help, but maybe it did. When he bangs on the wall, I hammer right back, hard. Really hard, so my hand hurts.

I yell, 'Fucker, sad fucker, you sad fucking fucker. I'm on my own here. I'm doing my fucking best, you fucker.' Almost certainly, that excessive amount of anger is not really directed at him, and I feel guilty as soon as the moment of rage passes. So I cry some more.

I'm not sure whether it is me or Dottie who stops crying or falls asleep first. Both things must happen at some point, though, because at five in the morning, she starts crying again and wakes me up. 'OK, baby, OK, Dottie,' I murmur, and pull her to me. My body aches to the very bone, especially my hand. I flush with shame as I remember hammering it against the wall, and hope the gamer didn't hear me calling out expletives.

I don't want to be that person, and if I am, I don't want anyone to know. Turns out he did hear, though, because at 8.30 in the morning, there's a knock at my door. It's him. He's carrying a pint of milk, eggs and some orange juice.

He looks to the floor, not at me or nosily past my shoulder. I'm glad of his social awkwardness; anyone looking past my shoulder would see how bad things are getting inside my flat. It looks like it does under various London bridges, where homeless people have to make settlements. His nose curls involuntarily. My flat smells funky. The smell of nappy sacks is almost as repellent as the smell of actual faeces; sort of sanitised noxious lemon and plastic. Besides that, there is the smell of milk, first time around and regurgitated, feet, armpits, hair. People always talk about the new baby smell. I guess they don't mean a new baby trapped inside a two-room flat, a few metres square, with a mother too exhausted and alone to find time to shower regularly. If I had a bath, we could have got in there together. I don't. So when I want to get clean, I have to lie her on a towel on the cold lino floor of the bathroom while I shower as fast as I can. She screams throughout the process, missing my arms. It is exhausting and heartbreaking, so I don't bother unless I know the health visitor is stopping by. 'Sorry,' he says.

I nod. I am too. About a lot of things. I don't know where to start. I eye the groceries greedily; could they really be for me? He follows my gaze and offers them up. Whether that was his initial intention or not, I grab them, too done in to be proud.

'Can I do anything?' He looks exactly like you imagine a man who plays video games all night might look: he is tubby, sweating, he wears glasses and is prematurely balding. A year ago, I would have been freaked out by having him as a neighbour; I'd have thought he was a creep. Lizzie and I might have made up stories about him drilling holes in the bathroom wall so that he could watch me shower. There would have been no need for any evidence of this in order for us to make up these stories. Being giggly, over-imaginative, fairly self-obsessed girls, stuff like that leapt into our minds. We rarely believed the nonsense we made up; we were just amused by it. After we'd talked about how weird it was for a man his age to play video games all alone, night after night, we might have talked about a new album, or our punishing rehearsal schedule; we might have discussed something in the news or a storyline on a TV show. Our minds were able to flit around from thought to thought with glorious, speedy freedom. It is different since Dottie's birth. My mind flits as though I'm being subjected to shock treatment; I am fried. I can't hold onto thoughts even when I want to. I don't watch the news or TV shows. There is no time to do so, and yet there is nothing but time.

At this point in my life, the gamer doesn't look like a weirdo; he looks like a port in a storm. I don't have any loo roll, or instant coffee. I really need a coffee. I couldn't ask him to buy me coffee and loo roll, could I?

'Write a list. I'm going to the supermarket at eleven, I'll pick up what you need,' he instructs. It is exactly what I want to hear, but I can't just agree to it.

'I can't pay you. I don't have any cash in the house, and I'm not giving you my card.'

He doesn't flinch at my rudeness. 'You can owe me.'

'I don't like owing people.'

'You have trust issues.'

'No shit. I'm a single mum, college drop out. The world so far? So untrustworthy.'

He considers my point. 'I'll run a tab. When you feel up to it, we can walk to the cashpoint, you can pay me back then.' I'm not sure what to say in the face of such kindness. I think if I speak I will cry. He takes my silence as resistance and offers an alternative. 'Or you could get shit delivered.'

'I resent the delivery charges.'

'So, do you want help?'

'I need it,' I admit.

'I'm Graham.' He doesn't hold out his hand for me to shake or anything. I'm glad. It would seem wanky or formal or somehow uncomfortable.

'I'm Dora,' I say. Reinventing myself in that moment. I need to leave Teodora behind. I don't want anyone to find me or Dottie if, in the unlikely event, anyone comes looking. 'Dora Wulski.' And no matter how exhausted I am, I realise that one job I have to do for myself, and do it soon, is get my name changed by deed poll.

# 31

# *Dora*

Graham becomes a lifeline in those following weeks.

Weeks that feel like months.

Weeks that become months.

He and the health visitor are my only two visitors. I never stop being slightly nervous about the health visitor popping by; I grow to actively look forward to Graham doing so. When Dottie was first born, I texted Lizzie and my other friends from RADA to tell them the news. They sent back emojis, the baby face and the milk bottle. Their messages were variations on a theme. And I can't judge them, as they are exactly the same sort of messages that I might have sent before I'd laboured for hours and brought a being into the world.

*CUTE!!!!!*

*OMG, so hard to believe you are a mummy!!!*

*Do you wear matching outfits? It's so Suri Cruise and Katie Holmes. You should!!*

They promised to visit. They didn't. At first, they sent excuses: they had rehearsals! Dates! Then the excuses dried up. I had thought they would all visit at least once. You know, out of curiosity. Jesus, it is hard to accept I am not even an object of curiosity any more. So, without friends or family to depend on, I bounce from one stranger to the next, depending on their random acts of kindness: the woman in the charity shop, the taxi driver, Graham. As I do so, I am aware that it is a precarious position to be in. It isn't much. I wonder will it be enough?

As unlikely as it might have once seemed to me, Graham becomes as close as I have to a best friend. We start going to the supermarket together. Dottie strapped to my body, he helps me lug the shopping home. Sometimes we have a coffee in his flat. It doesn't smell much better than mine; it is stale with discarded pizza boxes and the dank waft of musty weed. When we are out on the streets, we gratefully gasp at the fresh air. Although really, I find his questionable hygiene reassuring. I don't have to try too hard with Graham, I don't have to pretend. He doesn't ever offer to change Dottie's nappy, as he says that is 'totally gross', but he plays with her; when she moves on to bottles, he starts to feed her, and sometimes he just holds her, when my arms or back or calves ache with striding up and down the corridor, jiggling her, begging her to sleep. As she's got bigger, we've travelled further on the Tube, sometimes to libraries for parent-and-toddler reading groups, often to markets or charity shops, where we hunt out bargains together. Graham was the one who spotted the Bugaboo pram and pushchair in the British Heart Foundation shop. It was selling at just a fraction of its retail price. He also dropped in on the people living in the three ground-floor flats and told them that we would be storing the pram in the hallway. He didn't ask for permission, as I most certainly would have done, so no one said we couldn't. As soon as Dottie started sleeping through, I began doing a night shift at the local pub, and Graham babysat for me. The money I earn barely covers my rent, but with benefits as well, I manage. It is OK; not the life I expected to be living, but OK. It is a life.

Today, Graham tells me that his company are moving their office to Nottingham. He has a choice of moving there too or taking redundancy. He likes his job and tells me, 'I'm a bit fed up of London anyway. I live in a shithole.' It is true, although depressing to hear articulated, because his flat is bigger than mine and smarter inside. 'It's too expensive, and getting another job isn't a given. Will you be all right if I go?' he asks.

'I'm getting out and about more now. Don't worry about me.' I smile at him. An enormous beam. I learnt it in an acting class when I was about fourteen. I remember the instructor singing an old song; the words bounce into my head: *Smile though your heart is aching.*

'You could move too. Flats are cheaper in Nottingham. We could rent together, like as mates.' I don't know what to say. Suddenly our months of friendship vanish and I feel like I did the day he offered to buy me groceries: overwhelmed. Like that time, I fall silent as I try to gather my thoughts. He jumps in and adds, 'Or not.' It isn't clear if he means we can rent together but not as mates, or not rent together. It doesn't matter; neither thing will work.

'I can't leave London,' I tell him.

'Why not. What's keeping you here?'

I shrug. I can't explain it. I need to stay here, near what might have been, because whilst that is on one hand torturous, it is on the other hand my last glimmer of hope. I daren't say it out loud, I barely let the thought play in my head, but it is there. Maybe one day, when Dottie is a little older, I might be able to find a way back into acting. Admittedly, I won't be formally trained, but that doesn't have to stand in the way. If I move to Nottingham, it is a declaration that it is all over. I don't think I could get out of bed in the mornings if I admit it is all over. 'Don't worry about me. I'm fine,' I lie.

I don't know if I'm imagining it, self-esteem issues and all that, but he looks relieved to be off the hook.

Graham moves quite quickly after that. 'Not much to pack up,' he points out. Dottie and I stand at the end of the street and wave to him. We're still standing there long after his rented Transit van has disappeared from view.

# 32

# *Dora*

I miss Graham, his visits, his company, but also practically his help, specifically with babysitting. That sounds selfish. However, I'm so exhausted and worried about money that I can't find the energy to be more nuanced. I have to give up my shifts in the pub because there isn't anyone I trust as much as I trusted Graham to watch Dottie. I register at babysitting agencies because I know that at least those people are vetted, but I can't find any work that pays enough to justify babysitting costs. Waitressing, office temping, positions in retail all earn less than childminders, certainly once I deduct tax and factor in the cost of travel. I look for work where I can take her along with me; there isn't any. It would be easier if she were a dog; they are welcome in all sorts of trendy offices. I need money. I am desperate. Hungry. And I don't mean hungry with ambition, as I was when I arrived in London. I am literally hungry for food. *We* are hungry.

When she just wanted to feed from me, it was easier. Only I had to eat, and I could manage. Not necessarily getting the most balanced diet – back to handfuls of cereal, sometimes pasta with tinned tomatoes on top – but enough to get by on. Now she needs food first. I am a mother, and so it excites me to see her push mushy food into her little rosebud mouth. She needs to eat things with vitamins and minerals. My baby is growing. I have cut the feet off her onesies because she can't stretch out her legs when she is wearing them. My hip bones and ribs reappear. Initially, I'm quite pleased about this. I'm a woman living in the Western world, I'm programmed to think weight loss is a bonus, but my flesh continues to melt away and soon my thinness is worrying rather than attractive. We go to food banks, but I feel uncomfortable, as the volunteers always ask questions. Maybe they are just making conversation, maybe they are nosy, but I find it threatening. *How old is she? Bonny little thing. Is your mother around to help? Is anyone?* Same questions over and over again; the implication is that I need help. That we aren't managing. I suppose we are not, but I can't allow anyone to notice as much. Before we set off for the food bank, I carefully check over Dottie, I examine her. I make sure she has a clean nappy and a clean face, laundered clothes. She is perfect, so why do they keep asking questions about who is helping? Maybe it isn't her, maybe I am the giveaway. I can't risk being noticed by social services. I live in fear that they will take her off me.

Being a mother is the greatest privilege life can offer, but at the same time also terrifying. When she was born, I became aware of my inefficacy when it came to describing what I felt for her. A powerful, all-consuming rush like the strongest tide. A love I did not know I was capable of. More than that I'd felt for my parents, or her father, because she was my responsibility. I created her. She didn't ask to be born. I owe her everything.

But I can give her nothing, or next to it. I am constantly failing her. Dottie's life is literally in my hands. If I drop her, she will break. Bones will smash. If I drop her emotionally, she will break in a different way. We don't all get to choose NCT groups and Montessori pre-schools. Some mothers' choices stay with food or nappies? Heating or baby shoes? She keeps growing. Growing out of things. She always needs more. I am trying. I buy things in cheap shops, things made by babies on the other side of the world who are probably paid about eleven pence an hour. I hate myself for that. I buy second hand from charity shops, but it is never enough. She grows and I shrink.

I am sitting in the flat, eking out a meal of beans on toast, when I recall a girl I used to share occasional shifts with at the pub. Frances left because she said she'd found more lucrative work and that she could do it from home. I wonder if I can get in on it. I call the pub, flirt with the manager to get him to give me her number. Then I call her. My guess is it will be some sort of pyramid selling scheme. Kitchen gadgets or beauty products. There are women in this world who have so much money and time on their hands that they think a soft-boiled egg timer is a must-have. Frances tells me she takes her bra off online on live feeds; men pay five pounds directly into her PayPal account to watch her do it.

'Oh, right,' I mutter. Not sure how to respond.

'It's really easy. It's fun,' she tells me. I doubt it. Then she adds, 'You get used to it.' I hope not, but it's a more honest observation. I respect her for that. I don't have another choice.

I quickly carve out a niche. I attract men who like big breasts that they know are that way due to lactation. I know, it's disgusting. *I'm* disgusting, but I am desperate. My look proves extremely popular. My breasts appear even bigger than they are because my ribs are like a glockenspiel. One of my clients describes me as 'council estate hot'.

*What do you mean?* I ask in the digital chat, regretting the question the moment I type it.

*Too thin, low expectations*, he replies.

I tell myself his comments say more about him than they do about me.

I put on and take off my bra five, ten times a day, if I am lucky. Some of the men want me to play with my nipples, others want me to take off my pants and shake my arse at them. I say no, until an unexpectedly high electricity bill arrives.

Before it all happened – him, and then Dottie as a consequence of him – I was one thing. Now I have become another. Transformed forever. The before me was breezy, daring, fearless. I had developed a confidence in the world, in my environment that I knew my parents didn't have but I knew was needed. Sometimes, when I am nursing Dottie, I wonder what my parents must have been like before. Before the war, before giving up their country. Maybe they too were breezy, confident. I have become cynical, cool, careful. I keep waiting for the old me to shoot through again, bloom, but she never does. I worry that some things can't be repaired. You are what you are. It is best to avoid thinking about it too much. There are streets that you don't walk down after dark. It shouldn't be that way. But it is.

The days, weeks, months pass, merge. The baby needs feeding and changing and feeding again. I am flattened with weariness and loneliness. I have no one to talk to, even if I had anything to say. I've become two-dimensional, paper-thin. The flat doesn't have a washing machine, but because of showing strangers my tits, I can now at least afford to go to the launderette, rather than wash clothes in the kitchen sink. I like the launderette. I like the smell and the warmth. I always try to time my visits to coincide with Dottie's naps, but today, when we arrive, all the machines are full. I decide to wait, but that is a mistake. The cycles take too long to finish. Dottie wakes up and she is hungry. She cries and cries and cries. I pick her up, desperately feed her from one boob and then the other. She is eleven months now and my milk just isn't enough to satiate her. Stupidly, I haven't brought snacks with me. I thought we would be done by now and there wouldn't be a need, but it's obvious that she is keen for a bit of mashed sweet potato or baby rice. I try to distract her: I show her the buttons on the machines, I walk about jiggling her on my hip, I throw her in the air and then catch her, but the crying continues. I put her back in her buggy, but then the crying just escalates. Finally, I hoist her over my shoulder, pat her back. Her outraged, frustrated constant wail settles into exhausted hiccuping before it eventually stops. I feel everyone in the launderette release a collective sigh of relief. My sigh is more pitiful. I guess my daughter is learning that sometimes the food just won't be there, no matter how much she cries for it.

I don't know how it happens. The warmth, the rhythmic whirl of the washers and dryers, watching the clothes spin around and around.

I fall asleep too.

My grasp slackens. She slides down my body; luckily that jolts me awake. I catch her when she is an inch from the floor, save her from hitting the cold tiles. She isn't hurt, but the shame

I feel at having almost dropped my own baby explodes in me. Detonates from the inside as though I've swallowed a grenade. The Polish woman who runs the launderette yells at me. I don't even mind. I deserve to be yelled at. For a moment, I believe she is going to snatch the baby off me.

For a moment, I think that if she tries, I will let her. It's for the best.

The guilt, grief and fear have got through. Like water seeping in a fault, unrelenting. Dottie lifts me up, but paradoxically, I am at the same time weighed down. I can't do what I have to do. I can't look after her, no matter how hard I try. She is a burden, a responsibility. I thought at first that she might anchor me, but now I understand that the weight of her means I am just going to drown. Because motherhood is simply me endlessly treading water in a deep, deep pond. I need to get to the water's edge. I need help.

I go home and email my mother. I tell her she is a grandmother. That Dottie is almost a year old, that I am not about to graduate from RADA any time soon. It takes two days to get a response. I try not to read too much into that. I know she doesn't check her emails with any regularity; she might not be ignoring me. Still, it is two days of hell.

Her message, when it comes, is simple. *I'm coming.*

# 33

# *Dora*

My mother is shocked about everything. Dottie's existence, obviously, but not just that. She is shocked that I am so thin, that the flat is so small, damp and expensive – inadequate in every way. She can't believe London prices. She thinks I am lying to her or that she has made a mistake in the rate-of-exchange calculation; she does the maths four times. It never adds up to anything better. She is shocked that there are no friends on the scene, that I have dropped out of college. That I hadn't told her that I was pregnant. That I won't tell her who the father is.

She thinks Dottie is perfect. We agree on that. It is enough, for now.

There is never a moment when either of us suggests that I could go back to college; there's a tacit agreement that I've had my shot. I've blown it. My mother is prepared to save me from starving, save my child from neglect, but she is no longer prepared to indulge my dreams. Fair enough. We agree she will care for Dottie and the flat and I will find work. She has no idea what sort of work I have been doing to bring some money in. Telling her that would be a shock too far. She thinks I've been living on government benefits. She calls them 'handouts' and blushes when she mentions them. 'You need to pay your own way, Teodora. You need to take responsibility. God gave you two feet; stand on them.'

I need to look for something new. I can't continue taking my bra off for cash in my flat, because there is only one bedroom. My mother and I share a bed, all three of us in one room; sometimes if Dottie doesn't settle in her crib, we all end up in one bed. We are together twenty-four hours a day and my mother has just a fleeting awareness of the concept of privacy. It is not unheard of for her to follow me into the bathroom when I go to take a shower or a pee. I have to ask her to leave and I close the door on her; then she talks to me through the door while I go about my ablutions.

I approach the coffee shop and pub that I used to work at. The coffee shop reports that there's nothing going, but the manager at the pub offers me a few shifts on minimum wage. He makes it clear he's doing so as a favour; I wonder when he's going to call the favour in, and how.

I pick up work as a shot girl at a nightclub, which I can do after my shift at the pub. Even though I pull all the tricks – such as watering down the vodka I am offering and drinking water myself when punters buy me a drink – the money I earn still isn't enough. It keeps the three of us off the streets, but not much more. One of the other shot girls, who is exceptionally pretty and studying economics at UCL, quits suddenly. She tells me she is going to be an escort. 'You could do it too,' she says casually. 'You're pretty enough, even without make-up.' She casts a glance around the nightclub, taking in the other shot girls. I admit there is a higher-than-average propensity for hair extensions, false nails and lashes. 'Most of these girls wouldn't make the cut,' she adds dismissively. 'Not at the rate I'll be charging, anyhow.' She makes it sound like a career opportunity, a progression, a position to be coveted, and in a way, it is just that.

I now earn three times as much as I did at the pub and the nightclub combined. I am no longer asked to clean the loos at the end of a shift, although admittedly I still have drunken men slobber all over me. I am in the eye of the storm. I know this, but I don't know what else I can do, except ride the waves, see where I wash up.

# 34

# *Radmila*

I am pleased Teodora is doing the right thing. She got herself into trouble, silly girl, but she isn't the first and won't be the last. So, it is what it is. I'm not trying to make it small. I was shocked. All right, I say it, horrified. But it's water under the bridge. She is my daughter. What is done is done. What is it the English say? No point crying over spilt milk. I try to talk in English again now. Second time leaving my home, leaving my friends and language. I miss it. Of course I do. London is nothing like Serbia, nothing like the farm in north England either, think of that. London is scruffy, expensive, so much, much money needed to live here. Well, not live even, just exist. Teodora and Dottie should come back to Serbia with me. We explain she had husband and he died. No one would believe but everyone would pretend they believe and that is enough. But Teodora, stubborn, says opportunities are here. Future here.

'What opportunities?' I yell. I look deliberately around the poky flat. Smells of last tenant no matter how much I scrub. They had dogs. I smell their dogs and their sweat on the furniture, in the air. Teodora works, but in a pub; no one ever get rich working in a pub. We can't manage. I say this, many times. She listens, eventually. A good girl really. Gets a promotion, now a manager, this means long hours. Often she at the pub until three or four in the morning. I ask, 'What do you do all these hours?'

'We have lock-ins, Mum, you know for the regulars.'

'I have to do the inventory.'

'I stay behind and do the cleaning.'

'You take the salary for the manager *and* cleaner too?' I ask. She nods. Not too proud to work hard, my girl. 'Good girl. Hard work never killed anyone,' I tell her when the alarm goes off early morning, when she returns home late, and she listens to me. Nods, knows I'm right.

I worry about her walking home alone at night from the Underground station. I don't suggest a cab, though, I know we can't afford it. She knows it too. I just tell her to take flat shoes to change into as she leaves the bar. She's a fast runner, if it came to it. Dear God, I pray it never does.

The extra money she earns is a big help. Very lovely. She spends it all on Dottie. Not herself. Some girls would buy dresses and shoes for themselves, but not Teodora. She buys lots of new clothes for Dottie, though. Really new, not just ones bought from the charity shops. At first it is enough for her to buy Dottie clothes from supermarkets, then she buy from Gap, then she start to buy hundred per cent organic cotton onesies from 'independent retailers'. She says this phrase to me, the pride in her voice obvious. I think the onesies same in Tesco, but it makes her happy and she works hard, so this is her choice. 'Dottie deserves the best,' she say to me, like I said the opposite, which I didn't. I wouldn't.

We find somewhere better to rent. A place with two bed-rooms, no smells. I tell Teodora that it make more sense that Dottie sleeps in my room, because Teodora keeps such funny hours and there is a risk she wake the baby when she comes home after a very late shift. I had to say this because once I hear her come home late when Dottie still asleep in her room. I watch from the door and I see her ease Dottie out of her cot to cuddle her. It's sweet but selfish. A baby shouldn't be woken. So the next morning I suggest the baby sleep with me.

'But she's a good sleeper,' Teodora protests. 'I didn't wake her.'

'Not this time, no.'

'And even if I had, she would quickly go back over.'

'It's not good for a baby to be disturbed. You want the best for your baby, don't you?'

'Of course.'

'Well, it is unfair disrupting a baby's sleeping pattern. Sooner or later it will cause problems.'

Teodora can't argue with my logic. The next day, she helps me carry Dottie's cot into my room. I know she thinks I am interfering and controlling, but she doesn't say it and that's for the best. I'm not interfering and controlling, I'm look-ing out for her, for both of them. Because look how things turned out for her when she had no guidance. She needs me. Dottie needs me.

I don't ask many questions. No point. When I do ask Teodora evade me and so I tell myself she is an adult. She has her own life to live. She knows what she is doing. But that is a mistake. I see now I should have asked more questions.

These pictures! Her bottom, her breasts. My own daughter.

I never thought I would ever see such a thing. I don't understand what I am seeing on her laptop! I was looking for her work address. I thought I should take Dottie to her. She didn't answer her phone. Dottie is sick. I wasn't snooping, I was searching for her address. But I find this!

The angle, someone must have taken the photo of her, for her. She's very beautiful, that is a fact. Even like this. Her skin is a lovely tone and it's tight. I remember being young and having skin like that; we look a bit alike. She is more beautiful, though. At first, I think she must be sending these to a boyfriend. I've read about that; girls do that now. Foolish, but the world is. One boyfriend I could have understood. But then I notice she is emailing the photos to a woman. I don't understand this. Is she a lesbian? No, the woman sent her the photos, but they are of my daughter. It's confusing me. Dottie is limp next to me. I take her temperature one more time. It's higher than last time. I strip her to vest and nappy but then worry because her feet are ice. I put on socks. I take them off. She mews, she does not cry. It's worse than wailing, this silence. Then I notice the spots on her neck, cascading down her back. No time to find Teodora's work address. No time to understand these pictures. I snap closed the laptop and I take my granddaughter to hospital.

It's echoey and busy. Disconcerting. I rush through glass sliding doors, talk to women in blue uniforms who look comfortable and serious. They dash me along corridors; they insist on holding Dottie. I feel breathless with panic for my granddaughter and also grubby. The thought of my daughter's flesh pixelated, exposed.

Dottie is with the doctor now and I am worried sick about

her. I tell myself at least now there is someone looking after her, finding out what is wrong. They told me to wait here. Wait, wait. So I am in this room with the buggy and the laptop. I don't want to be here with these photos. I want to be with Dottie. Innocent, precious, sick Dottie. 'You can get a cup of tea from the vending machine,' says the nurse. I glance about the room, uncomprehending. I can't see a vending machine; there are rainbows painted on the wall, cheerful, colourful, but the image of my daughter's nipples, her thighs, her buttocks keeps assaulting my mind. I must look like I am in shock. I am. My head buzzes and my limbs feel loose, unreliable. The nurse smiles sympathetically, tries to be reassuring. 'You'll be more comfortable waiting here. This room is especially for sick children and their parents.'

'I'm the grandmother,' I clarify.

'It's OK,' says the nurse kindly. 'You can still sit here. You should settle in.' I stare at the laptop; it is pushed in the basket under the pram, it's nestled up against the spare nappies and bottles I brought with me. Irrationally, I imagine the nurse can see the pictures as though they are being projected out of the computer onto the wall, superimposed, splattering across the pretty rainbow. My daughter's shame squashes me, I feel breathless. I think of Dottie. She's all that matters right now.

'I mention I'm the grandmother in case this is a problem for legal things. If you need to treat Dottie.'

'We'll cross that bridge if we come to it. In the meantime, if you can get hold of one of her parents …'

'My daughter, her mother.' Both relationships so fiercely elemental, and in this moment remote. That bottom pushed up, those breasts pushed together, where her fingers were, fingers that pop food into Dottie's mouth, it's unimaginable.

The nurse smiles encouragingly. 'Good, if you can ask your daughter to meet you here if at all possible.'

'I have tried. I've called her mobile and her work this afternoon but no answer.' The mobile must be switched off, and the pub she said she worked at said she does not work there any more, that she left weeks ago. She is not the manager; the man I spoke to says *he* is the manager. 'I'm trying to find other contacts on her laptop,' I explain. The nurse nods, but she's already turning away from me; her attention has to focus elsewhere. These people are busy. Honest. Hard-working.

'Well, keep trying,' she urges.

Basically, she gives me permission. I don't have any choice. You think I want to look at that filth, to know more about that world? Of course not. It kills me. But I must go back to the computer and comb carefully through everything. I'm not snooping, I'm trying to reach my daughter, but I can't because by the end of my search, when Dottie is finally returned to my arms, I conclude I don't know who my daughter is.

# 35

# *Dora*

It is hardly the dream, working as an escort and then returning home to my mother and fatherless daughter every night, but it is OK. It is workable. It is what I have.

I don't know how it's possible to live with two people in such close quarters and still feel lonely, but I do. Telling lies to the ones you love cuts you off from them. They seem separate, apart. It's not just the fact that when I catch up on sleep during the day, my mother takes Dottie to the park to feed the ducks, play on the swings; it's more than the lack of shared experiences. I've started to notice that I smell different from them. Dottie smells of baby lotion and fabric conditioner and milk; sometimes she smells of raspberries or ice cream, her favourite treats. My mother smells of a designer perfume I bought her a month after she arrived at our door: roses, verbena and cherry blossom. A treat to say thank you for everything she is doing, and also to mask the odour of the old apartment, which she used to say smelt of other people's dogs. Sometimes she smells of baking, sometimes of Radox bubble bath. These are all good scents, but try as I might, I can't catch them. I always stink of the night before. A cloud of staleness smothers me: sour cigarettes, coffee, aftershave, sex. It gets in my hair. The stench lingers in my head after it has in reality been scrubbed from my body. Initially, my mother waited up until I came home from work. Two or three in the morning, I'd find her propped up in the armchair, TV on for company, although muted so not to wake Dottie. The moment I walked through the door, she would try to pull me into a hug. I had to jerk away from her, because of the smells. When she stopped waiting up for me, I was relieved.

When I come home from work – exhausted, dirty – I like to rush into the bathroom and shower. That first. But I've discovered that the sort of dirty I feel can't be rinsed off by even the hottest shower. Only one thing can make me feel really clean again, whole, justified. A Dottie cuddle. So in the dead of night, often still damp, too impatient to dry myself properly, I silently edge into my room and scoop her up out of her cot. She snuffles up against me, her breath and mine mingling. I love the feel of her body next to mine, her chubby legs dangling down my hips, her smooth, bare feet tapping the sides of my body. I delight in her, cushiony and soft with sleep. When I hold her like that, in the darkness, it is possible to believe that my life is different. I'm not sure exactly how it would be different. Maybe it is just the two of us, or maybe there is a father; I daren't think of her actual father, but a father in a more abstract sense. Maybe I am not a hooker. Maybe.

But my mother recently said it was bad for Dottie, me waking her in the night. I don't know how she knew that I was. I thought she was already asleep when I did so, especially as she's no longer waiting up for me, but I guess she has been lying awake, listening to my movements through the paper-thin walls. Sometimes it's possible to believe the thing she used to tell me when I was a kid, that she has eyes in the back of her head. She insisted we move Dottie's cot into her room. I didn't know how to disagree. I mean, if it's best for Dottie. Yet I miss the ritual, our pitch-black cuddles. I have to go to bed without touching the moonstone that makes me feel renewed, and so now, every morning when I wake up, I'm still dirty.

Tonight, when I arrive home, the apartment is empty. I sense as much before I know it for a fact. I can't feel their breath, their warmth. The rooms seem vapid and intangible without my family. Their bedroom door is open, but a peek confirms what I feared: there is no sign of them. The curtains are open, which is unusual; normally my mother draws them and puts on side lamps the moment it gets dark; she likes things to be cosy. There is no sign that she has cooked supper; ordinarily there are pots neatly stacked on the drainer. I scan around for a note on the kitchen unit or coffee table that will explain their whereabouts. Nothing. The absence is galling. I check my phone, expecting a message saying where they are. There are five missed calls from her. A surge of impatience charges through my body when I realise that despite the numerous missed calls, there isn't a message. She never leaves messages; she doesn't like talking to machines. Why not even a text? My heart beats in my throat. I call my mother's mobile, but she doesn't pick up and I am sent straight through to voicemail. I leave a hurried, terse message. 'Where are you both? Call me back.'

My impatience blisters into concern. My mind starts to race; horrible scenarios punch their way into my consciousness. My brain won't be soothed into reflecting on anything reasonable. They can only be in one place. A hospital. I know it. That's why her phone is off. Of course a hospital, because Dottie is ill or has had an accident. Worse. Oh God, there is worse than ill. The room swims around me, morphing and inconsistent. I wish I didn't always feel a sense of overwhelming dread and despair, but I do. I just do. Since the moment I knew I was pregnant, I have been haunted by a terrible certainty that Dottie will not be mine forever. She will be taken from me. Maybe other mothers fear this, maybe I'm not insane, but I feel the helplessness of insanity, the powerlessness and unreasonableness.

I nip the flesh on the back of my arm to shock myself back into the now. I need to be logical and hold it together. I need to find my daughter and my mother. However, it's impossible to fight the belief that something is wrong, because we don't have people they could be visiting; where would they be at two in the morning? The blood slows in my body. I feel dense and solid, as though I'm setting like concrete. I want to rush out onto the street and scream their names, and although that makes no sense, I am reaching for my coat when I hear my mother's key in the lock. I fling open the door and demand, 'Where have you been?'

She puts her finger to her lips. 'Be quiet. She has only just fallen asleep.'

I understand instantly. Relief floods through my body and soul and I'm nearly washed off my feet. My mother has been walking the streets to soothe Dottie to sleep. I am relieved for about a nanosecond, then I return to my more usual emotion, one of concern. We don't live in a particularly safe area; where *is* a particularly safe area? I'm not sure such a place exists. I know bad things happen everywhere.

'You shouldn't walk the streets to get her to sleep. It's dangerous.'

My mother doesn't reply; she pushes past me, takes Dottie into her room and lowers her gently into her cot. I notice Dottie is still wearing day clothes, not pyjamas. If my mother had been trying to get her to sleep, she would have been wearing pyjamas.

'What's going on?' I ask.

'You tell me.' Her eyes drop the length of my body. Scouring me. I am wearing a black cocktail dress. It is short and strapless. I can see her disapproval in her brow. Normally, my mother doesn't see me in my 'uniform'. When she used to wait up for me, I was always careful to change into trainers and jeans before I got home. Since I no longer expect to see her at night, I've become sloppy about that habit.

I pretend not to be aware of her questioning gaze. 'Do you want a cup of tea?'

'She had a fever.'

'Dottie did?'

'Yes. High, very high.'

'When did that start? Did you give her Calpol? Why didn't you call me?'

'I did give her Calpol. I waited. Her temperature went higher. She was crying. In pain. Then by teatime, she was not crying, but floppy. I did call you.'

I feel sick. I am usually home most of the day; even if I take a nap, I'm here if they need me. However, today's job was in Oxford. I left just before lunch; I went by coach, because it is cheaper than the train, although slower. I remind myself that Dottie is safe and asleep in her bedroom. Whatever the problem was, it has passed. It is all OK.

'Then there was a rash. I think of meningitis.'

'Jesus, Mum.' I imagine her fear, her panic.

'Yes. So, I need to take her to hospital. But how? I didn't know where it is, which bus to take.'

'You should have taken a cab.'

'I did in the end. I took the money from the saving jar in the bottom of your wardrobe.' The jar where I keep my cash tips. It doesn't surprise me that my mother has found the secret stash, and it doesn't matter that she has. I'm not hiding the money from her, but from burglars. Still, she might wonder where that amount came from. It's more than is likely tipped in a pub. 'I called you again, to check this OK. To tell you to meet me at hospital. You didn't answer.'

'We're not allowed our phones on when we are working.'

'I called the pub. They said you left months ago. They don't know where you work now.'

I feel the air in the room slow and still; my mother edging closer to my secret, to my shame. I try to be breezy and bluff. 'Oh you must have called Libertines. I moved to a different bar. I told you, didn't I?'

'No, you never said.'

'Oh, I thought I had.' I need to get her away from this. 'The fever? It wasn't meningitis. It can't have been if you are home.'

'No. Thank God.'

'Yes, thank God. So, what is it?'

'She has a viral infection. They gave her a prescription. She'll need fluid and sleep. The doctor and nurses, they were very good. Very concerned.'

'God, it must have been scary.' I keep busy, filling the kettle with water, reaching for a couple of mugs, sniffing the milk. Avoiding my mother's eye.

'Yes. It was.'

'Well, thank you for taking care of her. I'm not working tomorrow, so I'll be here. You've had a long day. You should sleep in and I'll take her all day. I want to.' My mother remains silent, and I decide to give up on the idea of making tea. I suggest, 'You must be really tired. I know I am. We need to be getting to bed.'

My mother does not move; instead she asks, 'What is adult-seekfun.com? You email a woman, Elspeth.'

'I don't understand what you're asking.' I do understand exactly what she is asking, but I don't want it to be true, so my mind is stuttering, hoping somehow to avoid this reality.

'I went through your emails.'

'When Dottie was sick?' Maybe sounding indignant might deflect, at least temporarily.

'I picked up your laptop as I left for the hospital. I thought I could find a way to reach you as you were not at the work you said you were at.'

'It's an agency. Elspeth is my agent.'

'An agent? You work behind a bar.'

'Well, I'm more of a waitress, really. I work at events. You know, corporate functions. Freelance.'

'As a waitress?'

'Yes.'

'Dressed like that.'

'They are high-end events.'

'Stop it. Stop lying. I have seen the pictures.' I know instantly which pictures she means. 'And the addresses of the hotels that Elspeth sends you to. You are not a waitress.'

The hairs on my body crawl. 'You had no right to go through my things.' Attack is the best form of defence.

'I have every right.' Her eyes bore into me. 'I'm your mother and her grandmother.'

'Yes, her *grandmother*. I am her *mother*.'

'You are not fit.' She turns, leaves the room and closes the door to her bedroom behind her. Locking Dottie in. Me out. Cutting me off from my daughter before I can so much as check on her, kiss her goodnight.

Her words float around me; they drift into my head and settle. I can hear them, loud and dark.

The thing is, I believe her. She is right.

My mother isn't a bad person. She's a good one. She flew here to help me the moment she heard I needed her help; she is wonderful with Dottie, so patient and practical. I know Dottie adores her and trusts her. My mother provides a routine for my daughter that I can't deliver. And it's not just Dottie she's rescued, but me, too. Food in the cupboards, loo roll and Tampax in the bathroom, clean pots on the drainer; she provides all these things. Despite long days with Dottie, she stayed up each night to see I arrived home from work safely. She wanted to wrap me in a hug, congratulate me on my fine work managing inventories and cleaning loos, but I pulled away from her. I had to, because I thought I smelt of sex. When she said that I am unfit, I saw her naked anguish. It was haunting.

Truth is a bit like depression: it creeps up on you. You don't notice it, you can keep denying it, but once it lands, it's indisputable. Weighty and fucking scary. I am sitting on the ledge, teetering. My world is precarious. Dangerous. If I fall into the abyss, I'll drag both of them down with me. Being an escort who sometimes drops to her knees for an extra twenty quid isn't a place for ageing mothers and baby daughters. They have to go elsewhere. I know it, and my mother – because she is my mother – knows it too.

The next morning, I wake up early, planning to make breakfast and amends. I want to try to stave off the inevitable, but my mother is already up and dressed. By beating me to the early rise, she has already scored points in the intangible, silent battle. Her air is one of grim, fatal determination. She is wearing her usual get-up, relaxed trousers and a roll-neck jumper, but rather than appearing familiar and comfortable to me, she seems resolute and stiff. She is hand-washing some of Dottie's clothes. This flat has a washing machine, but she likes to wash the delicate things by hand. I'm glad she's staring at the wall; I don't have to meet her eyes.

Dottie seems quite well. Not one hundred per cent, but bright enough. She is muttering in her own, fairly incomprehensible baby speak; she stretches her podgy hand out to wave at me. When I sweep her up off the floor for a cuddle, she momentarily struggles because she wants to stay on the rug playing with her soft rabbit. Then she relaxes into my body. I feel the weight of her melt into my hip. She turns her bright eyes to me and I see her love shine my way. She tangles her fingers into my hair and I want the world to stop. Just to stay in this moment, her on my hip, merging into me, entwined with me.

'She seems much better today,' I comment to my mother. Hoping our shared love for Dottie can drag us onto common ground and away from the explosive revelations of last night.

My mother does not comment. Unprepared to chat. I try again. 'Little kids do that, don't they? They bounce back.'

'It gets harder as you get older to bounce back,' my mother responds, darkly. I'm not sure she is talking about illness when she adds, 'Everything will get harder as she gets older.'

Dottie pokes her fingers into my mouth, and I play-bite them, grateful that she's stopped me answering. What would I say? It *will* get harder. A lump of regret, exhaustion and fear swells in my throat. I can't swallow, I can't breathe. I won't be able to keep my job a secret from her. No one believes hookers are role models.

'I'm taking her home,' my mother says. Her words lethal and unfathomable.

'She's mine.'

'She is also mine.'

'You can't, she hasn't got a passport. I won't let you.'

She sighs. 'Yes, you will.'

'I love her.'

'That is why you will get her a passport.' The room shivers. I think it's hope exiting completely, leaving a vacuum in my life. My mother continues. 'I'll tell her you are her sister. You are her brave, clever sister who makes money in an office in England and sends it home to us in Serbia. As soon as she is completely well, we take her to post office for photo and passport. I will not stay here and watch you do this.'

'I could do something different.' But as I say it, I wonder what.

'I will take her with me. You can stay here, earn money, however you like. Or you can come home with me too.'

'I don't speak Serbian. What would I do there?'

'You could be a cleaner.'

'But we still would have nothing.'

'We'd have our pride.' My mother says this as though she's in some sort of mid-twentieth-century movie. It is that dated superciliousness, the judgement and condemnation that decides it for me. I know that it doesn't matter what I choose now. If I go with her or not. She has made her mind up about me. I am done and she is moving on. On to my baby. She is not a terrible person. I can't outrun the truth. She is right, I am not fit. Not just because I smile at fat men at parties for a living, not even because I suck dick for a living. I am just too small to do it all – the job and the mothering. I am too thinly spread. Before my mother arrived, I thought we might starve, I thought I might literally drop my baby.

The hardest decisions are often the best. That's what people say, isn't it?

The thing is, in my experience, the hardest decisions are just as often the worst.

# 36

# *Dora*

I start to stir as I feel the road beneath me change from the smooth strum of motorway travel to a rough and rutted track. In the fraction of time before I open my eyes, I panic. We shouldn't be travelling along any bumpy tracks. I feel sick and groggy, something heavier than car sickness. I am slumped on the back seat. I can smell provolone cheese and a distinct undertone – vomit? Mine? My lids are like hefty sandbags; I'm reminded of the heavy tiredness I felt during pregnancy. When I do force my eyes open, the first thing in my view is the remaining part of the sandwich Jonathan gave me. The beef, rare and bloody, is sweating. Instantly, I realise it was laced with something. I have been drugged. I'm furious at myself for ever thinking this could be anything other than a nightmare; anything other than the worst-case scenario. Perhaps since Evan proposed, I've become sloppy. Sloppy in the sense of sentimental and hopeful as well as sloppy as in not wary and careful. I should have known. It is always the worst-case scenario. Experience has shown me that. As I slowly sit up, I see that yes, I have been sick. With the back of my hand, I wipe my mouth and neck, but not the car seat, and then – desperate – I wipe my hands on my shorts. I'm not sure anything is any better or cleaner. I'm a mess.

'What's happening?' My words are slurred, my tongue thick and swollen. It doesn't matter anyhow if the question is indistinct; Jonathan isn't going to tell me anything useful or honest.

'Oh, you're awake,' he says with faux brightness. His announcement sounds as though I've just had a little refreshing nap in the back of the car as he kindly drives me to the airport so I can catch my plane. We both know this isn't what is happening. As the chateau looms into view, my fears are confirmed. I'm a captive.

Jonathan half pulls, half drags me out of the car. It's not that I'm resisting him; my legs won't work well enough to let me stand straight, so I have no chance of running. Where would I go anyhow? 'It will wear off soon,' he says, confirming what I know.

I'm scared, because he's not hiding the fact that he drugged me; he's no longer pretending to be any sort of friend. Through the blurred memories of the past few days, I realise that most probably he has been drugging me throughout. Him and who else? Which of the others are involved in this? What *is* this? Some sort of sex slave ring? The possibility is horrifying but real. I've known of women who have disappeared: no body, no trace. One day a working girl, the next just gone. Nothing. Some are reported missing – the fortunate ones. Very, very rarely are women in my line of work lucky enough to be recovered.

My mind darts to Evan. He would look for me, wouldn't

he? He has the resources to find me. Except he doesn't know I'm in France; he thinks I'm in my flat above the dry cleaner's. How would he ever find me? Jonathan blatantly admitting to drugging me means the danger is ratcheting up. Pretence was some sort of protection. The lack of it shows a riotous confidence that he is in a clear position of power.

He roughly hauls me out of the car and drags me into the chateau as though I am a sack of potatoes. Once over the threshold, he lets go of me and I dead-drop onto the cold tiles. The place is silent. My breathing echoes through the halls, high up to the lofty ceilings.

I remember that this morning there was no sign of the staff. 'Where is everybody?' I ask.

Jonathan crouches down next to my head. I can smell the mud on his shoes. I think he is going to kick me, and I want to roll into a tight ball, but I don't have the control over my limbs to do so effectively. I move slowly, flopping about like a fish out of water, tossed on a riverbank, waiting for the angler to bring down a final, lethal blow. I now know, with absolutely certainty, what I have not wanted to believe for the past few days. Despite his protests, and Daniel's reassurances, Jonathan is definitely the man who beat me in the hotel room. I loathe myself for doubting it. Why did I want to believe Daniel and not trust my own judgement? Just to save him embarrassment? Or was it because thinking that Jonathan was my attacker was too dark, too insidious? Either way, I have to face the fact now. Flashbacks to the hotel room slam into my consciousness: the gag, the cuffs, the punches raining down on my ribs, my spine. *You disgust me. Stop what you are doing. Stop it now. Or next time will be worse. Next time will be the last time.*

There are black patches at the periphery of my vision, looming in and out, making it difficult to focus. My body wants to shut down, pass out. I can't let that happen. I need to fight this. Jonathan gently moves a lock of my hair that has fallen over my eye. I flinch, quiver like a wet animal. His gentleness is as grotesque as his cruelty. It's as clear a threat as if he were holding a clenched fist above me. He trails a finger down my cheek, my throat, between my breasts. I inch away from him. That just makes him smile, because we both know I have nowhere to hide. 'Where is everybody?' I ask again.

'Gone.'

'Gone?'

'Yes. I hired them until this morning and now they are surplus to requirements.'

He's not making sense. '*You* hired the staff?' I don't understand. It wasn't Jonathan's party, it was Giles's. Surely Giles ought to have been the one who hired and fired. And why are they now surplus to requirements? The party was supposed to last until Friday.

'Yes, I hired everyone and now I've sent them away,' Jonathan snaps.

My thoughts are taking too long to process. But who hired the staff is not important right now; it is just another oddity. The part that is important is the fact that they have been dispensed with. Other people could help, they could save me. My heart is thundering in my chest. 'Where are the others?'

'Others?' Jonathan asks, frowning.

'Melanie and Giles—'

'I just told you. I hired everyone and now I've sent them away.' He sighs and looks impatient, the way a teacher might if a pupil wasn't keeping up with an explanation on calculus. I stare at him, perplexed. 'Why? Are you missing your sex buddy?' he asks with a nasty, taunting tone. It's such a pathetic question I don't bother to respond. I suppose that because there is a film of Giles having sex with me, Giles and Melanie will be mid-domestic row. It will be messy, but that doesn't account for what Jonathan says next. 'Can I make it any plainer? No one is here. They've all cleared out.

'What about Amanda. Your wife, has she left without you?'

Jonathan laughs. 'Wife?' He shakes his head and seems amused. What exactly is amusing him? I know he is holding all the cards and is enjoying playing his hand slowly. My mind is racing, trying to pull together everything I'm being told, trying to understand what is not being revealed to me.

'Where have they gone?'

'Back to England. You just don't get it, do you? They've all gone. It's just you and me, princess. No one can help you.'

'Daniel wouldn't leave me,' I bluster, but as I say the words, they seem hollow. A deep sense of aloneness and abandonment sinks into my bones.

'Yes, he would. You know he would. You don't trust anyone. You, more than most, are aware that no one is trustworthy.' The icy words slice like blades, because he is right, that is exactly what I believe. 'Daniel brought you here for me, and now he's left you for me.'

'Why? Why would he do that?'

'He owed me a favour. Actually, he owed me several thousand of them. Has a bit of a gambling problem, does our friend Daniel. Didn't you know that?'

No, I didn't. I suppose I know extraordinarily little about my clients, other than what they choose to tell me. The pieces start to plunge into place, each one like a door being slammed shut. I recall the car journey that initially brought me to the chateau. Daniel kept dabbing his face with a handkerchief, mopping the sweat that was bubbling like soup. He was incredibly nervous. At the time, I thought it was something to do with Sisi. That was idiotic of me, I see that now. Daniel did recommend me to Jonathan, and whilst he may or may not have known when he brought me here what Jonathan had done to me in the hotel, he should have believed that Jonathan was a threat once I told him what had happened. He could have protected me then, helped me, before it was too late. My thoughts tumble over one another. Maybe he did believe me; if he did, but still left me here, that is worse.

With great effort I push myself up so I'm sitting rather than lying on the cold floor. My eyes are at least now on a level with Jonathan's, a little further away from his heavy boots. I still feel groggy and disorientated, but I have to fight that. I must focus. I listen again to the silence of the house. Nothing, not even a creaking floorboard to give me hope that someone has lingered; no comforting music coming from the pool that would suggest people bathing and frolicking. There is a breeze that indicates all the windows are open as usual, but the sprinklers are not making their habitual whoosh and splash outside. I can't even hear any traffic; we are at least half a mile from even the barely used B road, further still from the neighbours, who anyway seem to be in the pay – or at least confidence – of Jonathan.

I am alone. He is right. There is no one who can help me or save me. I have only myself to rely on. It's not an unprecedented position for me to be in, but my God, it's a lonely one. The large, ornate grandfather clock in the hall ticks ominously.

I glance at it: it's ten past four in the afternoon. I must have been drugged for quite some time. I suppose Jonathan drove around waiting for the others to pack up and leave. His careful planning troubles me. His words haunt me. *You disgust me.* *Stop what you are doing.* Most horrifying of all: *Next time will be the last time.* 'Are you going to kill me?' I ask.

'Yes, I am.' His words are matter-of-fact, dropped like stones. 'Why?'

He doesn't answer, but asks a question of his own. 'If you die, who will miss you? No one. Your existence has been as meaningless as it is temporary.'

'My fiancé. He would miss me.' I throw this out because I know that personal information can sometimes help to bring a captor on side. Elspeth taught all her girls this technique in case we ever had to use it with clients. I remember her telling me, 'If they think of you as a real person with loved ones, they might treat you better. Only use it in an emergency, though. Otherwise much better to keep quiet about your home life. Business and pleasure never mix.' I recall noting the implication at the time. Our clients did not think of us as real people. It is clear that Jonathan thinks of me as nothing but a prostitute. Dispensable beings for millennia.

'You think so?' he challenges.

'Yes, I do.' Evan would miss me.

'That's a shame, because I am going to kill you anyway.' His assertion is calm and has total conviction. Not a threat. A promise.

# 37

# *Dora*

Jonathan grabs hold of my hair and yanks me to my feet. My hands go up to my head to try to somehow shield me from the pain of him tearing my hair out. I think, this is it, I have moments to live, and the thought is surreal, because if it's over now, then what has it all been for?

However, at the same time, something instinctual and bigger disagrees. Maybe this *is* it. Maybe. But maybe not, and I'm not going without a fight. I forcefully jab my elbow into his ribs.

My limbs are still not completely under my control, so my struggle is uncoordinated and not as effective as I'd like, but I do resist. I kick out at him, managing to make contact with his shins; I bring up my knee hoping I can get him in the balls. He dodges my move and punches me, hard in the stomach, violence coming to him with slick and practised expertise. I'm bent double, the ground pulling up towards me. Black dots swim in front of me again. I blink furiously, dispelling the patchy darkness, grasping for the actuality, however harsh. I need to stay with this, I can't fall unconscious. I grasp and grab at door frames as he drags me by my feet through the tiled hall.

My hands clutch the woodwork, turning white with pressure and then red as blood oozes from the scratches and scrapes that I'm picking up. My hope is to delay him from taking me wherever it is he wants to take me. To stop his progress and plan. I can't think beyond that. It might be enough. It has to be. He smiles, as though he is enjoying my struggle, which is not encouraging. Then he kicks me in the belly, which means I automatically curl like a hedgehog rolling away from a fox, and lose my grip on the frame. Before I can scramble away from him, he pulls out a gun.

A gun.

I freeze. Panting. The sound of my breath, my life, desperately echoes around the cavernous hallway.

I have seen many things, but never a gun. Isn't that strange? In this moment when I have no time left, something peculiar happens. My life does not flash before my eyes. I don't see Dottie, a chubby and gurgling baby, flesh like a blooming dusty-pink rose, folds of fat around her wrists and knees; or even Dottie a stretched and skinny girl, legs folded up as she jumps a skipping rope. I don't see my mother's face splitting into an encouraging smile or even pulled tight with concern. I don't see Evan chucking the ring box across the bedroom towards me, inviting me to be his wife. I want to have these people in my mind, by my side, offering motivation, comfort or hope. But I can't feel the essence of them. I am hollow and alone. They are not here with me. Which is no doubt a result of my years of ruthless compartmentalising. I've never wanted them near any of this.

Instead, the moment stretches, morphs. I am stuck in this atrocious last second, hung up on the fact that I have never seen a gun before. I think about that and nothing more. It's remarkable, incredible, considering what I do for a living. Considering the sort of people I mix with. Sex, money and violence often go hand in hand; for so many they are intrinsically linked. Not for me. Until Jonathan, I had largely managed to stay away from cruelty and bloodshed. I had been aware that it was permanently on the fringes, that it could at any point seep my way, but I had walked a fraught tightrope. Until Now. Seeing the gun pointed directly at me is paralysing. The magnitude of what it means takes my breath away. It is solid, brutal, undeniable. Punches and kicks I can dodge or absorb. A shot from a gun will destroy me.

Now, I do think of Evan, though not how I wanted to. Not head thrown back, laughing so loudly people turn and stare at us, slightly envious that they are not in on our private joke; not flinging open the door to my flat, arms full of fresh pastries, head full of a madcap plan of a way to spend a Saturday afternoon: 'Let's go wakeboarding on the Thames, Dora'; not even ducking his head under the sheets then re-emerging, lips wet, smile cracking. Instead, I think of him discovering that I died on a job. His hurt, his sense of disbelief and betrayal. The press will have a field day. A sex worker murdered at an orgy is how they will play it. It will be reported for titillation, to sell papers, not with any concern or gravitas. Women like me often come to a bad end and no one really cares. Will Evan be furious with me for taking one last job? Will that stop him grieving for me? Will he think I asked for this? Had it coming? Got what I deserved? There will be people who will think all those things. People I have never met will make those judge-ments over their breakfast tables as they read the headlines or slumped on sofas as they watch the news. Jonathan is right. I won't be missed. That has to be the greatest tragedy there is. Not being missed.

I think I have stopped breathing even before a bullet has hit me. I raise my hands above my head. I am on my knees. Begging. 'Please, please, no.' I'm begging for a few more minutes. Any time at all is a chance.

Jonathan stares coldly. 'Will you behave nicely?'

I don't care in this moment what that means exactly, what he will ask of me. I nod, vigorously. Spurt out reassurances. 'Yes, yes.' The words barely audible through my panic.

He pulls me to my feet and pushes me in front of him, the barrel of the gun pressed between my shoulder blades. 'Walk.' I walk. I do not punch, kick, claw or try to run. Running from his gun isn't bravery, it's stupidity. I walk through the passage as he instructs. I behave nicely.

He directs me into the kitchen. I assume he's going to put me in the basement, as all hostages in books and movies seem to be held captive in basements. However, in this chateau, the cellar is full of wine bottles. Jonathan must realise he'd be handing me an arsenal of weapons; a lot of damage can be done with broken glass. Instead, he places a wooden chair on the kitchen table, instructs me to climb up onto it. I stare dumbly at the table, hardly able to believe that just this morning I saw him, Amanda and Sisi gathered around it, eating croissants with cherry preserve. It seems a lifetime ago. I glance around the kitchen. There are knives on a block, heavy iron-bottomed pans hanging from a rack attached to the ceiling. I know these are all weapons that I can use given the opportunity. But they are also weapons that can be used against me. Far too easily.

'Come on,' he urges. 'Let's have you where we can see you. You like to be looked at, don't you?'

I don't reply; I just clamber up and sit on the chair. He tells me to put my arms by my sides, and then he uses a thick rope to tie me securely to the chair back. He works neatly and quickly, binding me in the same manner that I wrap the electric cord around my hair curling wand. Tidy, secure. The rope was under the table. Again, this suggests that everything has been meticulously planned. Jonathan is a professional. This thought is confirmed when he walks into the pantry and emerges with a bowl full of eggs. I quiver. Inside, I wilt, shrivel. I must not let my shoulders collapse, bend in on themselves, drop altogether. I force myself to seem bigger than I am, bigger than I feel.

'I understand you are allergic to eggs,' he says menacingly. I neither confirm nor deny it. What's the point? He's already decided what he's going to do next. 'I thought that was a thing kids had,' he adds, almost conversationally.

'It is, mostly.'

'You never grew out of it, hey?'

I get the feeling he will have done his homework, this professional killer. He will know that reaction to eggs usually manifests in skin inflammation or hives. Some people are bothered with nasal congestion, runny nose and sneezing. A few suffer digestive symptoms, such as cramps, nausea and vomiting. I get all these symptoms. That would be inconvenience enough, but I wonder if Jonathan knows it's worse than that for me. I watch as he walks to the door that we just came through and throws two eggs on the threshold. He crushes a third in his hand and smears the gunky mess onto the door handle. I have my answer. He knows. He obviously listened when

I repeatedly asked the chefs whether there was raw egg in the dishes I ate; when I patiently explained that my allergic reaction is so extreme that I don't even have to imbibe the eggs. For me, simple contact will lead to anaphylaxis, a life-threatening emergency that requires an immediate epinephrine shot and a speedy trip to the hospital. Touching an egg or even, on some unlucky days, inhaling it may cause my airways to constrict, my throat to swell so it is difficult to breathe. My pulse can speed up and I might fall into medical shock characterised by a severe drop in blood pressure and ultimately a loss of consciousness. Untreated, I'll die. That is what can happen on an unlucky day. It's hard to classify this day as anything other than unlucky.

Jonathan cracks several eggs along the windowsills and again smears them over the latches. White, yolk and shell creating a sticky prison. There is a back door leading to the garden. He throws three or four eggs at this door and once more daubs the handle.

He meticulously rinses his hands under the kitchen tap, scouts about for a tea towel, locates one and then thoroughly pats his hands dry, being careful to reach between each finger. His fastidiousness is mind-blowing. Chilling. Turning back to me, he says, 'Well, be good. I'm going to wait just outside this door.' For a fraction of a moment, I'm relieved – I just want him away from me – but then he adds, 'You have a visitor coming.' He glances at his watch. 'Not long now.' He leaves the kitchen, banging the big wooden door behind him.

My mind whirls as I try to think who is coming to see me. Who is behind this? I realise that Jonathan must be working for someone. That makes sense. He could have killed me five times over by now if this were just about him and me. He hasn't.

He's waiting, but the questions are, who is he waiting for, and why? I wriggle but am bound fast. Miraculously, my bag is still across my body. I remember that inside it I have the letter knife from the library. Knowing it is in there but I can't get to it increases my frustration and anxiety rather than helping it. I try to keep my breathing shallow. In times of panic, people are advised to take deep breaths, but deep breaths might trigger the allergic reaction.

Deep breaths can kill me.

# 38

# *Dora*

I do not trust what I am seeing. I can't believe it. And yet, I can. I should have known. I should have guessed. There's a moment when you go for an eye test when the optician rolls the big machine towards you, asks you to rest your chin, look through the lens and stare at the letters on the screen. At first everything is blurred, and you feel disorientated, vulnerable, then the optician alters something, turns a dial up by a notch, and suddenly it is all crystal clear.

He is standing in front of me in a well-cut dark suit that I know will have cost a fortune; his crisp white shirt is linen, like all the other wealthy men I've met this week have worn, but somehow his has not gone limp at the collar. He looks box-fresh, not in any way crumpled or dishevelled. A stark contrast to me. I am bruised, beaten, covered in vomit and – literally – blood, sweat and tears. This is not how I wanted him to see me, ever. This is not how I imagined a reunion. He pulls at his cuff, a habitual move. As if things could get any more surreal and unfathomable, suddenly Marmalade bounds into the kitchen. She looks as right as rain. She starts to sniff at the egg on the floor and then she laps it up; yolk, white, shell all indiscriminately gobbled down. He doesn't do anything to stop her.

I don't know where to start, so it might as well be with the dog. 'She's OK?' I ask. 'She recovered? They said she died.'

'Did they? Marmalade is quite well, as you can see,' he replies crisply, calmly.

'Liling and Chen are here too, then? They've come back?' I'm suddenly hopeful. I didn't especially warm to either of them, but they did not seem like killers to me. If they are here, it means that this situation might not be as dire as I fear. It might just be a strange, macabre game that I'm part of.

'I have no idea who you are talking about.'

'Liling and Chen. Marmalade is their dog. They were guests here. Daniel's friends. They claimed I was looking after their dog, on their instruction. I wasn't. She fell down the well.' Suddenly I'm not sure. I didn't see Marmalade in the box. 'Everyone was furious with me. Especially Daniel, he said I was an embarrassment. They said the dog was dead …' I trail off. Terrified. I don't know what is real and what isn't. I wonder, am I going mad?

His face is bland. 'Marmalade is my dog. She stays here all year round.'

'This chateau belongs to you?'

'Yes.' I try to process that, but can't. I'm too battered.

'The staff take turns looking after her. It's better for her than being dragged backwards and forwards across the Channel, which is just cruel.' He stoops and ruffles the dog's fur playfully and with affection. He looks exactly like a kind man, a decent person. Which just goes to show, you can't believe anything, not even your own eyes. 'There's more space to run about here too.' He stops. 'Is this really what you want to talk about?'

'No, it isn't.'

'I thought not.'

'Jonathan works for you?' I ask.

'Correct.'

'You paid him to hurt me, at the hotel?'

'Correct.'

'Daniel works for you too?'

'In a way. He owes me money.' I realise that my captor's influence stretches further than I can even process.

'So, he brought me here because he owes you money.'

He laughs at this. 'Deeper, it goes deeper. It goes way back. He started hiring you because he owes me money. I arranged that.'

'You're lying. I've been seeing Daniel for six months.'

'I know.'

I absorb what he's saying. Can it be true? Is his power so wide-reaching? His preparation so thorough? It's possible. 'You started planning this six months ago?'

'Not *this* exactly.' He gestures at me; he looks pitying and disgusted at once. 'I laid the groundwork months ago. I didn't know it would categorically come to this.'

'What were you expecting then?'

'I just wanted you to stop. I hired Daniel and Jonathan to stop you.'

I think of the times Daniel used to casually say I should do something different with my life, that he'd lend me the money to leave the country. Hell, he'd *give* me the money. But he never offered to help me write a CV. He wasn't interested in that.

266

Now I see that his brief all along was to get rid of me. 'You sent Jonathan to the hotel to beat me? To rape me?' My tone is a mix of incredulity and horror.

He sighs, seemingly bored of explaining things to me. 'Well, Jonathan took matters into his own hands somewhat. He does tend to get carried away. I wasn't explicitly directional. You were warned,' he adds. 'You could have put a stop to this. In a way, I wish you had.'

'You've been torturing me.'

He tuts, as if to say *oh come on now*, shakes his head. 'I'd say I've played with you. Fair play at that. What's that saying? All's fair in love and war.' Which is this? I wonder. Both? 'I offered you a chance. Several, really. Torture is a strong word.'

'You had me beaten and drugged – several times, right? I was threatened, raped by two different men. Everything that has happened here, *you* are behind it.'

'I was trying to get you to stop what you were doing. You must understand.' He shrugs, dismissing me.

'I thought I was losing my mind. Were they all in on it? Giles, Melanie, Liling and Chen. Neo and Sisi?'

'To an extent.'

'I only came here to help Daniel, you understand that, don't you?' I think it might help me if he does. If he knows that I didn't come here as an escort, or at least not one who was planning on having sex. 'Daniel is in love with Sisi. He said he needed me,' I explain.

'Brilliant backstory.' He chuckles. 'You see, the funny thing about you, Teodora, is that despite everything – your protestations, your profession, your experiences – you are at heart a romantic.' He chuckles sardonically. 'It's actually very endearing. I knew you'd go for that impossible love thing.'

'Backstory?'

He looks amused. 'Daniel isn't in love with Sisi. They hadn't even met until this week. None of them had. They didn't go to college together. I hired them. They are all actors. Don't you get it yet? They think you are an actor too. They thought they were indulging a very rich, bored man. A sort of immersive drama, if you like.'

He thinks he is shocking me, terrifying me, and in a way, it *is* horrifying what people will do for money. To unquestioningly play the parts they did was certainly extreme, dangerous, but I understand; after all, it's what I do. Chen and the women didn't cause any real harm; they were bullying, aggressive, weird, but if the fee was high enough, they would have comfortably told themselves they were simply following the character guidelines. That it was all a game. Giles, though? The video? How does he sleep at night? And Neo, I really thought he was OK. I sigh. It's sickening, but maybe they were told I had consented to everything, even the drugged sex. Perhaps they thought I was just acting drugged, and that I was into it. Did they even care? I think that Giles is most likely a chancer. Pathetic, exploitative, cruel. I witnessed him hook up with Liling that first night; he clearly is the type who, driven by his want for sex, would have very few boundaries or morals. And Neo, well, he will have told himself he didn't actually do anything, he just stood by. I shudder.

Still, for all that this is horrifying – extraordinary – I am relieved. I am not going mad.

The strange silences can be explained because they were

actors waiting for cues, and the truth-or-dare game that had seemed so forced was exactly that, as they didn't know one another. Taxis were not called. I did not fall asleep at the pool edge. I was not told to look after Marmalade. Doors were locked and then opened because they thought they were playing a game, but the whole thing was orchestrated to destabilise me. Knowing this helps. The extreme gaslighting was just that. Tricks to make me think I was mad, but I am not. There is power in knowing that.

'Well, the good news is, I am not a dog killer,' I say with a resistant smile.

My smile obviously annoys him, because he snaps back, 'You soon won't be anything at all.'

'You are going to kill me.'

'Yes, I am. Or rather, Jonathan is.' He says it coolly.

'Why didn't you just have me killed at the beginning?'

'Looking back, maybe I should have – it would have been much cleaner – but no one wants to be a killer, do they?' He looks something approaching troubled; not torn, not as far as that, but maybe inconvenienced. 'I thought you'd give up. You are very stubborn. I thought you'd go for the Canadian passport thing, but Jonathan texted me, said you couldn't be trusted, that you seemed determined to return to the UK, so I'm afraid we had to go to the drugged sandwich plan.' He shakes his head, mystified. 'I'd have been just as happy setting you up in a new life. But it has come to this. You really have no one but yourself to blame.'

This isn't true. Why should I believe anything he says? He is probably just hoping I'll beg him to let me go because he wants the fun of turning me down. Another sick play. People don't just happen to carry drugged food in case their victim won't get on a plane. It's no truer than me killing Marmalade. This situation I am in, I do have someone to blame for it, someone other than myself.

*He* is to blame. Shaun Beaufoy is.

# 39

# *Dora*

I think of him as my first client. Shaun Beaufoy. The father of my child. Technically, he wasn't a client. He was an affair. A love affair, I thought. But when I told him about her, he offered me cash to make it all go away. Her, me, all of it. He made us into a transaction. A business. A shady business at that. He identified a figure that would cover the cost of the abortion and also 'compensate for the discomfort'. He biked the cash in an envelope to RADA. It was left with the receptionist, who handed it to me when I was passing her desk. I was between classes: sight-reading and expressive movement, I think. It's funny the details that have stayed with me all this time later.

I wanted to burn the money. You know, make a big *fuck you* gesture. I wanted to set fire to it and send him a video of me doing so. I didn't burn it. I paid my rent for the next month and bought some vitamins. Big gestures were an indulgence I couldn't afford.

I was just nineteen when I met him. A peculiar, neither one thing nor the other age. If you ask any nineteen-year-old how they see themselves, they will tell you they are bouncing on the balls of their feet! They are standing on the cliff edge, ready to leap! They don't think, for a moment, that they will plummet – despite science and precedent. If they jump from a cliff, gravity won't rule them and pull them to a bloody death. Nothing rules them! They believe they will fly, soar up, up, up and away! It is a tremulous, tremendous age, balancing between childhood and adulthood. Legally allowed to do what they like, young enough to believe such a notion exists. Nineteen-year-olds are so *ready*. Ready to pile into the world, make a mark, make a mess, make history!

I'm not sure it's fair to say he seduced me. That suggests a level of reluctance on my part, and there wasn't any. But he did lie to me. His bad.

I was in my second year of college, first term. London was still sweeping me off my feet; I was still dazzled by everything. Naive. No one ever knows they are naive, though, do they? That's the point. You don't know what you don't know. My personal tutor was excited to take our class to a much-vaunted production of *Doctor Faustus*. She also dangled the carrot that a handful of us would be picked to attend the final-night after-show party. It was an opportunity to network with real working actors and musicians, as well as meet the people behind the production: the director, the theatre manager, stage managers, make-up artists, even the theatre trustees. It was a tremendous honour. As I mentioned, I was my tutor's favourite, so of course, an invite floated my way. I remember Lizzie was almost crazed with jealousy, but still she let me borrow her pink mohair cropped jumper that exposed my flat, toned and tanned midriff. I paired it with a purple maxi skirt. Her loan of her favourite top was generous, since she longed to attend herself. The moment I arrived at the party, I realised we'd got it wrong anyway. I was overdressed; everyone else was wearing jeans and a T-shirt. I brazened it out, telling myself that as an actor, there was no such thing as drawing too much attention.

I was wrong about that.

Everyone noticed him the moment he arrived. There was a ripple throughout the room; energy seemed to heighten, the air seemed clearer. Certainly, when I spoke to him, I felt light-headed, as though there was an altitude change. I believe everyone felt something similar; we were all buzzed. You could see people trying to catch his eye, pretending to be absorbed in their own conversations but really not at all bothered about their companions, only wanting to strike up a conversation with the rich, sexy trustee, Shaun Beaufoy. It was rumoured he had saved the theatre by making an obscenely large donation that covered refurbishments, essential maintenance and some insurance thing that none of us cared enough about to understand. All we knew was that he was a hero, a saviour, the good guy.

The best.

I remember Lizzie discussing the donation before the party. She claimed that it wasn't a big deal. I thought she was just downplaying the man's generosity and reputation to somehow show she didn't care about missing out on the after-show party and the chance to meet him. 'Of course he can save the day. He can easily afford it, he's like really old,' she pointed out. And he was, at least in comparison to us. Older than we could imagine being. Older than I am now; or, it seems, older than I will ever get to be. Shaun Beaufoy is twenty-five years older than I am. I realise now that made him still young to be as rich and successful as he was at forty-four. I can't deny it. He's exceptional.

At the party, he didn't head straight towards me, although I noticed him clocking me almost the moment he walked through the door. Initially he swapped pleasantries with the director and the lead actors. About an hour in, he was suddenly by my side. He handed me a glass of crisp, chilled champagne. I don't know where he got it from. There were trays of basic red and white wine scattered about; no one else was drinking champagne. His first words to me were, 'You look like the sort of girl who enjoys a glass of champagne.'

'I am.' In fact, at the time, I'd drink anything anyone offered. Nineteen-year-olds rarely have the chance or need to be picky or careful about what they imbibe. But I liked the idea that I looked like the sort of girl who might enjoy the finer things in life. It was a look I wanted to wear.

'Then champagne is all you should drink,' he asserted.

I took the glass off him, lowered my eyes, sipped, eyes back up at him. I don't know if I was doing it for real or whether it was simply something I'd learnt in a class. Do any of us ever know when we are authentic or when we are working at it? Isn't it possible to be both things at once? I didn't know what to say and he didn't rush to fill the silences, but instead kept his eyes trained on me. Undressing me there and then, in the room full of party people. He asked me what I'd thought of the play. I'd anticipated that someone would ask this question, of course, so I had a thoughtful response prepared. He asked what I was doing at the party, how I was connected to the troupe. I explained I wasn't, but that my tutor at RADA was a friend of the director. I knew the effect of dropping RADA into conversation; people couldn't fail to be impressed. He immediately showered me with praise about my talent. 'You haven't seen me act,' I pointed out.

'But RADA.' He shrugged, my aptitude a given, enough said. He commented that I was very pretty. Just asserted it, didn't bother to slide the compliment in amongst other observations; he stated it, as an assessment. I had been called pretty before. Many times. So many, I can't remember the first time it was said to me, the way I can't remember my first period. These big moments women are supposed to cherish and rate, or be traumatised and worried by, have been lost to me. But I do remember how I felt when *he* said I was pretty. I was disappointed. I felt my lack. I wanted to be beautiful. Beautiful suggests gravitas, importance. Pretty is lightweight and suggests 'somewhat'. I needed him to think of me as beautiful. I felt challenged, as though he had thrown down a gauntlet.

'You're married,' I replied. It wasn't exactly an objection. More a statement of fact. Was I testing him, or grasping at a sophistication I certainly didn't possess? Pretending I was totally OK with flirting this way with a married man; that I would sleep with him anyway? Maybe I would have. Eyes wide open. That would have been a different playing field. But what he said next changed my world. Changed our flirtation into something else, something with possibility, hope and a future.

'No, I was. We're separated. I'm a free agent. I've moved out. I live in a hotel at the moment.' He let me take in the fact and then added, 'It's very smart. I think you'd like it.'

It was magical. We barely left his hotel room all weekend. We didn't need to; we had everything we could imagine needing within those four walls. Well, more than four walls, because his room was a suite. I'd never seen anything like it, except in movies. The magnificence and luxury didn't intimidate me; it just added to the fabulousness of the situation. The perfection. Everything seemed natural and straightforward. Right. *Of course* the first time we made love it would be between crisp white cotton sheets, *of course* the first meals we ate together were brought to us on silver trays by discreet staff members who were appropriately pleased when he palmed them notes for tips. *Of course* we drank nothing other than champagne. The glamour and opulence all added to the illusion I wanted to be swept up in.

There are some particular conditions in life when time and other forces of reality can just be forgotten, you can be suspended. It happens in hospitals, in casinos, and it happened in that hotel suite that weekend. The world may or may not have been going on around us, we didn't know or care. Or even ponder it. We were totally absorbed with one another. I felt so comfortable and confident. The sex worked; our bodies got each other. Naked, I walked around the hotel room in front of him, perched awkwardly on the end of the bed to eat room service food. The awkwardness coming from the height of the table, not my nakedness. I was in awe of him. I craved him. Adored him in a way only nineteen-year-old girls can yearn for lovers. Unreasonably. Unguardedly.

He brushed six foot, had broad shoulders and was muscular. He definitely devoted time to the gym. I liked that level of vanity. He was hirsute and I liked threading my fingers into the thatch of hair on his chest, as though I was sewn to him. He had blue-black hair; it flopped over one eye in a way that had probably been fashionable when he was a teen, but it was a classic look that suited him. Made him timeless and closed the gap of years between us. His voice was low, measured. He dropped out his thoughts with determined restraint that meant I, and everyone else, stopped and listened to every word he had to say. He never had to fight for attention. The passion I felt for him was something I didn't know how to manage. I knew as much when I was right in the middle of it. It felt too extreme and mercurial for me, like frothing champagne bubbling up over the rim of a glass, down the stem, through my fingers, messy and gorgeous. Irresistible.

We had sex. I see that now. At the time, I thought we were making love. I didn't have enough experience to discern the difference. My years of dance classes meant that energetic and flexible sex was my norm. Because of the soft-focus lighting, the plush interiors, the free-standing roll-topped bath, I thought him bending me over and banging me hard over the dressing table, where he could watch in the mirror; or me straddling him on the high-backed leather chair was romantic. I didn't expect a thousand butterfly kisses up and down my body.

I think.

I thought.

I'm almost sure.

It's hard to be absolutely certain. It's so long ago, nearly twelve years.

I thought I was special. How many women, girls – men too, I suppose – have said the same? Allowed the same self-delusion? We are not special. The people married men pick up, play with, drop. None of us are special. What happened to me is laughably commonplace.

After we'd had enough sex that he was exhausted, he asked me what my ambitions were. Was I interested in theatre or film? What sort of films specifically? I shyly told him, knowing he was someone who could make all my dreams come true but not wanting to appear like the sort of girl who was hoping he might. He wasn't in the movie world – not a director or producer – but he had a number of fingers in a number of pies. He was connected. He knew people. But I didn't care that he knew people; that wasn't why I was with him. I was so sure of that, I thought he would realise the same. Maybe he didn't; maybe he thought I was well aware that I was just a bit of fun, that what we were doing was a transaction.

On Monday morning, he got up early and said he had to get to work. He told me I could stay in the room until eleven o'clock, but that it would be better if I vacated by then to allow the cleaners in; we'd been sending them away all weekend. The very first thing I did when I got back to my student flat was google him. I was excited to know everything I could. His net worth was extraordinary; the businesses he was involved in were complex, his charity work impressive. I was disappointed that there were no details about his split from his wife, not even on the gossipy tabloid sidebars of shame. Wikipedia was out of date and still had his status as married. I felt a strange flicker of delight at being in on a secret that wasn't public knowledge; I knew something about him that others didn't.

But I knew nothing.

It *was* a transaction.

I guess other young women might have realised as much. A weekend of sex might have led to a useful introduction; several weekends would have led to a guarantee of an audition, perhaps an actual part. I wasn't entirely naive, I was aware those things were put on tables, I just didn't think they were on our table. I thought if I benefited from our connection – our *relationship* – it would be through an entirely organic, natural and honest process. I believed what we had was authentic. I thought we'd start dating. Then, perhaps at a party we attended together as a couple, I might meet someone who wanted to audition me. Perhaps my lover might point out my in-depth understanding and command of Stanislavski's acting technique, or my incredible spirit and energy, my hunger and work ethic. Maybe, because we were in love, I'd glow in a particular way and somehow just get *seen*.

I know, idiocy. Nineteen, practically a child.

I didn't hear from him for six days. It felt like sixty. I checked my phone hundreds of times a day. I thought of all the reasons he might not have contacted me. He was busy at work, I must have given him my number incorrectly, he might be ill. When he did text the following Sunday morning, I was so relieved to hear from him, I didn't ask why he hadn't called all week. I told myself a week was not a long time to wait to hear from him after all. I'd hoped he'd say we could meet at a bar or a restaurant. I knew he had to know all the best places. He told me he'd had a full-on week, that he was exhausted; would I be happy to come to his hotel? 'We can order room service.' The third week he texted me on Sunday afternoon, and that became the pattern. I'd obsess about him all week but only hear from him on Sunday afternoon, then I'd go to the hotel and we'd spend the evening and night together. There was always room service and champagne, as he'd promised.

On the fifth Sunday, at 11 p.m., just as I was dozing off after another round of sex, he woke me by shaking my shoulder. 'You can stop here tonight if you want, but I'm getting on my way. My wife is arriving from the airport. She'll be home within forty minutes.'

'Your wife?' I mumbled, too groggy to instantly comprehend.

'I have to shower.'

'Ex-wife, you mean.' He looked confused. Reached for his watch, which was on the bedside table, slipped it on. 'I thought you said you were separated.'

'She's been visiting family in Australia, yes.'

'No, that's not what you said.'

He looked at me as though I was insane. As he'd jumped out of bed, he'd thrown the covers back off my body, exposing me to the chill of the air con. Simply exposing me. He stared at me. Embarrassed. I wasn't sure who he was embarrassed for or at. Himself or me.

'It's complicated,' he said with a sigh. Perhaps laboured breath was to be expected when pushing out such a tired excuse.

'Well, explain it to me.' Although he already had, really. I scrambled out of the bed and stooped to pick up my lace panties; aware of my nudity in front of him for the first time, I got dressed as quickly as possible.

He turned on the tap in the shower and called from the bathroom, 'We were going through a tricky patch, but we've sorted it out.' He sounded buoyant. 'This has been a lot of fun. If you want to leave a bunch of cards, I'll see your name gets around the industry. Girls with your talents are always popular.' He laughed. I was a joke.

My face screamed a blood-red roar of humiliation and disappointment as the door clicked behind me.

It isn't ground-breaking; being stung by the time you are nineteen is par for the course, I believe. I think I could have walked away from it. Called him a bastard to my friends, called him out some years later when the #MeToo campaign was putting heat and headlamps on such behaviour; behaviour that had for too long been accepted as the norm. But things got complicated when I didn't have my period like I was supposed to. I'm usually clockwork.

'You're on the pill, though, right?' asked Lizzie. She was wide-eyed and incredulous. She lived for drama both in and out of the classroom.

'No. It makes me feel heavy. I can't afford the extra pounds. We used condoms.'

'Every time?'

'Yes. Maybe. Probably not.' I tried to think back through the blur of alcohol and lust.

I sent him a text. Well, several. I don't know what I expected. Then the envelope arrived at reception, with the cash and a typewritten note: *This is enough to deal with your problem and a little extra to compensate for the discomfort.* There was the telephone number of a private abortion clinic. Very thoughtful.

I called the clinic. I even made an appointment, but then two things occurred to me. Firstly, the donation he had made to the theatre was thousands of times greater than the amount he'd put in the envelope that was delivered to me. He was able to put a price on us, and it wasn't a very high one. Secondly, having an abortion was his idea, not mine. His solution to an inconvenient consequence, a problem. I thought the little being inside of me was a person, a life. Priceless.

In all the years since, I haven't once seen him in the flesh, and yet it doesn't surprise me that here he is, standing in front of me, calm and glorious. He has aged well. I can admit that. He's a little greyer than he was, and certainly a bit broader, but clearly he's benefited from a private chef, a personal trainer, a gym in his home. He must be fifty-five years old by now; he looks younger, and still extremely attractive. I hate it that I can see that. Despite everything. Even now, I feel a lick of something towards him. My body betraying me.

'Why did you come after me after all this time?' I ask.

'You know why. Any parent would do the same.'

# 40

# *Shaun*

*Eleven years ago*

He has two phones. He thinks nothing of that. Nothing at all. It's just practical, like having multiple jackets to wear or mugs to drink tea from. He needs more than one phone. There is the phone that his wife, his PA, his friends and family use to contact him on; along with his legitimate business associates, people from trusts, foundations and charities, his buddies from the golf club, the guys he plays squash with. Then there is the other phone. The number he gives to the sort of people he wouldn't like his wife to meet, not in a dark street, not ever; some of his other business associates, and the girls. Unless there is a time-sensitive deal going down, he leaves his second phone in his office; he doesn't need his wife finding it, and of course, she goes through his things. He doesn't resent her for doing so; he respects that she's not a pushover, that she tries to catch him out. Thing is, he's just cleverer than she is, so whilst he admires her effort, she's unlikely to ever find a thing.

There are no urgent deals going down now. No reason for him to check his phone, except that he's feeling a bit randy. He wishes there were a better way of saying it. Something more refined or more PC. He doesn't like the coarse, unsophisticated connotations of 'feeling randy', but that's what it is. He thinks of the various expressions they used at school to describe how he is feeling now: his balls are breaking, nuts cracking, he needs to get his rocks off. All so crude, but honest. He doesn't say any of those things out loud any more. Not for a long time. But he still thinks them. He just needs to slide one in, a quickie, get his end away, dump his load.

His wife is being uncooperative in that department at the moment. It has never been her thing. He married her because she came from a wealthy and respectable family, she lent him the propriety and credence that he was undoubtedly lacking. He brought wit, charm, and a feral, urgent can-do attitude to the relationship. It was a fair enough exchange. He is tall, dark, handsome; she is slight, smiley, pretty. They look impressive together, even now, when they are in their forties. Only thing is, they used to look incredible together. But his point is, she has never really been that into sex, not even when they *did* look incredible together, when he couldn't keep his eyes off her, let alone his hands. She made it clear from the beginning. Vanilla, once a week, and be grateful. But now, he can't even rely on it being once a week, not any more. A sleepless night because she was waiting up for the kids to get in from some teenage party, or she has her period, or a good book. Any of these flimsy excuses might trump his needs, his desires. She *never* sucks his cock any more. Not even on his birthday; they're not even at it enough to be that cliché. No one could blame him for looking elsewhere.

So he picks up his phone thinking he might flick through

the contacts, find someone easy and willing. Easy in the sense of loose morals and easy in the sense of having no delusions about this being anything other than a casual hook-up. He tries to make that crystal with all of them, but frankly, some of them don't want to hear and refuse to understand even if he speaks to them in one-syllable words. He makes it clear he'll buy them dinner, champagne, pay for their entry into clubs and their cab home. He'll show them a good time, a fun time, but it's a treat, not something they should expect to repeat.

He notices he has three unopened messages. Hers is the last he glances at.

'Fuck!' The word explodes, angry and spiteful, out of his head and mouth into his office.

'Boss?'

He looks up, surprised that Jonathan is in the room with him. He's very stealthy, Jonathan is. Shaun tends to forget he's there at all, it's disconcerting. Jonathan is a relatively new hire, came via a murky deal. He was working for the other guy but recognised where his bread was buttered and started feeding Shaun information that turned out to be valuable, really especially important, albeit a bit grubby and unsavoury. Therefore, Shaun is well aware of two pertinent facts about Jonathan. One, he is useful, and two, he is a mercenary. So not a man you can trust, but a man you can buy; that works for Shaun, as it happens, because Shaun has deep pockets. Even so, he doesn't like the way Jonathan is always sneaking about, like a shadow. Yet it's worth remembering that the man is discreet and resourceful; so far Shaun has not found a limit to what he is prepared to do. Sometimes that bothers him; other times he feels the relief and release of that knowledge. It will come in handy one day.

He weighs it up for a moment: is this something he should confide to anyone else? Even discreet and resourceful Jonathan? The words on the text seem to flash in front of his eyes, like a blue light of a police car approaching from behind, spotted in the mirror, and then in front of you, blinding you. Forcing you to pull over. The message is bald, blunt.

*I'm pregnant. Can we talk about what we should do next? Can we meet for a coffee? Teo xx*

Stupid bitch. Two questions shows weakness. *Teo*, as though he has a nickname for her. He does not. If he were to call her by her name, it would be Teodora, he supposes, but generally he doesn't bother with names, sticking instead to casual ubiquitous endearments – he's less likely to slip up that way. Gorgeous girl, honey, cutie. That kind of thing. Interchangeable, no matter who he's with. The two kisses, they're an embarrassment. They leave him exposed. Yes, him, not her. The two kisses have an air of desperation about them, and he hates to admit it, but youth too. He doesn't want to dwell on that. How young is she anyway? Has she ever said? Twenty-three, maybe more; they dress to look younger, don't they. Especially actresses, because they never want to reveal their age. She could easily be twenty-five, for all he knows.

'You remember that girl I met at the theatre party?'

Jonathan nods. 'The RADA student.' That's another thing about Jonathan: he has a good memory, good with detail. Shaun wonders if he takes notes, and the thought makes him uncomfortable. As does being reminded she's a student; unlikely to be twenty-five then, or anywhere near it.

'Well, she's got herself into a bit of trouble.' And that's a fair assessment, thinks Shaun, straightening his shoulders, because in the end, her body, her choice and all that must also mean her body, her responsibility, right? So, she's got herself into this. She should have been more careful. He thought she was on the pill; aren't all women on the pill? They should be. He was being polite using condoms as often as he did. Obviously he doesn't like condoms; show him a man who does. They're messy, ruin the moment, and most importantly, cut down on the fun. No one could blame him for sometimes going without.

He puts the phone on the desk in front of him, nods towards it, indicating that Jonathan can read the text. Jonathan does so, his face remaining inscrutable as he asks, 'Like me to sort it out, boss?' Shaun nods, a slight movement. Enthusiasm would be tasteless. 'I'll need some cash,' Jonathan adds.

Again, a barely perceptible movement as Shaun nods towards the safe nestling behind the David Hockney that hangs in his office. He's not sure what he thinks about Hockney's bright, colourful landscapes. They are certainly noticeable; they do the job of catching other people's eye. The more gauche might ask, 'Is that an original?' which he likes. He also likes watching those in the know check out the signature, the size, make an educated estimate as to what it might have cost.

Jonathan has the code to the safe. It's not a risk, him having the code; it is in fact a test. Shaun currently has four thousand six hundred quid in there, petty cash. It's a thing he does, as he's letting people into his inner sanctum: gives them the code, gives them the opportunity to show their honesty. He adds to the stash, a grand every week, quickly becomes haphazard with it, or appears to, sometimes deliberately suggests there's less in the safe than there actually is, to see if his new employee will correct him, or whether he'll just pocket the excess, believing no one will be any the wiser. People can be shifty around money, and if they are untrustworthy with your money, imagine what they can do to your reputation, your honour, your confidence. Shaun has found it an effective way to weed out those hooked on drugs or drink or in debt, whatever; those too desperate to be dependable.

'How much do you think you'll need? A grand?' he asks.

'I think this could come in at less than that. Maybe seven hundred. Leave it with me, boss. Don't give it another thought.'

Shaun grins. Jonathan is proving to be extremely helpful indeed, and also canny with money, a promising combination. All being well, this could be a comfortable long-term arrangement. Publicly Shaun courts men who went to Eton and are now CEOs of the blue chips and the financial companies, or are in ministerial positions. He likes to receive Christmas cards from the Lord Mayor of the City of London, a few bishops and archdeacons, the PM and some of the royal cousins. He attends dinners with the men who govern the country. He didn't go to Eton, or Harrow, or Westminster. He met these chaps at Oxford. He admires them and despises them all at once. It's complicated. He is having to buy his way into the old-boy network, and the old boys are aware of this. They admire him and despise him too. He is cleverer than many of them, richer than most of them, but his family isn't as old as any of theirs. Bullshit, of course; we all have ancestors. There's just a difference between what those ancestors did.

Shaun resents his ancestors. They must have been sleeping on the job, digging ditches when they ought to have been aspiring to ride in carriages. It's all been left to him. He's had to raise his family. He's doing well. His children are everything to him; they are his legacy. Look what he's done for them, look at the opportunities he's afforded them. He's not so much given them a leg-up as taken a gigantic leap. And it hasn't been easy. He's had to graft hard. Damn hard. Every hour of the day for as long as he can remember. Not just the academic work he had to do as a boy to get him to the spires of Oxford, or even in his businesses. There was other work too. All the associated skills that he needed to pave the way; the little lessons he had to be constantly open to: the right way to speak, dress, joke, eat, gamble, marry. It has been a lot of work. Who could blame him for indulging in a spot of recreational sex from time to time? Every man deserves a bit of fun.

So, the idea that this messy girl might hijack all that work, destroy his reputation, is vile, impossible. It cannot happen. His lineage matters. He can't have this sort of chaos. It's unthinkable. So yes, publicly he courts one sort of man. Privately he also needs to court a different type. He needs Jonathan.

'Can I borrow your phone, boss?'

Shaun nods again. Jonathan picks up the phone, pockets it. Truly, little has been said, yet everything is understood. Mentally, Shaun shrugs. Who is to say which group of men governs really?

# 41

# *Dora*

*Now*

I have always longed for things. I am ambitious. I want, I crave. It might seem odd; people don't expect sex workers to have ambition, but I do. I told you before, my ambition is not for something as simple as just money. Money is nice. It offers choices, freedom, but what I crave is deeper than that. *More* than that. I want a big life. I want to experience, to feel, to grow, to know. That's why I wanted to be an actor. I thought it would give me the opportunity to be a hundred different people in one lifetime. That's why I can bear being a sex worker, because in some ways I do get to play many roles. People have always said I'm complicated. Some say this with a sardonic or admiring smile, some with frustration or even dread. My mother was always fearful of the fact. She thought it was a dangerous quality to have. I don't know if I'm complicated. I'm just me. I wanted a lot: love, fame, power, recognition, revenge, a reckoning. I wanted it all.

Now it seems I'm going to get a lot less than average.

The average life expectancy for a British woman is eighty-three years. But here I am, age thirty-one, some way off the allocation that is doled out – taken for granted, squandered. It tastes bitter, the reality. I thought there was still a lot ahead of me.

My chest is rasping, I can hear my breath. That's not good. I try not to think of the eggs or the gun. The rope is digging into my arms; if I move – wriggle just the smallest amount – my skin is scratched, sawed.

Wanting more is uncomfortable. I look at contented people and they astound me. I'm not dismissive of them, I'm envious. There must be so much joy to *not* yearning; I believed that even before I was beaten and held at gunpoint. But a person can only be what a person is. That's for sure. Thinking back to my childhood, my parents always seemed content. A fine day, a tasty supper, regular work; they were thrilled by these things. I remember when I was six or seven and I first realised I wasn't like them, or really anyone else I knew at the time.

There was a bike shop I had to walk past to get to school. I never paid much attention to the window display, as I couldn't even ride a bike at the time. That all changed one day in the run-up to Christmas, when the window was specifically dressed to attract the attention of as many children as possible. There were a number of bikes displayed, all different sizes and colours; most were black or grey, one or two were pink or blue, gender appropriated. My friends and I started to pause at the shop window on our walk home from school; we'd press our noses up to the glass, ignoring our mothers, who urged us to hurry up. Then I spotted it. The canary-yellow bike, not centre of the window, but towards the back. Hidden, almost. Shy. Still, it called to me. It wasn't the most expensive – I'm not greedy, that's not the point. I wanted the yellow bike because it was different from all the others. I wanted the extraordinary. All the other kids spoke excitedly of the pink or blue bikes; no one even seemed to notice the yellow one, no one other than me. I longed for that bike, pleaded for it. My father teased me, 'What use will it be? Will you walk next to it and push it? You can't ride a bike.'

'I'll learn,' I promised him, which I did, and quickly. I borrowed other people's bikes until I could ride without stabilisers and my father was convinced; moved by my determination and grazed knees to buy the yellow bike for me. Other kids could not see the attraction. They teased me about the bike, said it was the colour of wee, asked me why I didn't ride a pink one. I was told I couldn't join the Pink Ladies Bike Club. This rejection was supposed to spell social death; I remember feeling relieved. I certainly had no desire to be in their stupid club, I didn't want to be like everyone else. I didn't understand why they all wanted to wear their hair in the same style, dress in the same clothes, even say the same things as one another. And so it started, my abhorrence of conforming, blending or melding. I experimented with different hair colours and styles, pushed the limits when it came to fashions, said things that seemed to shock.

It was lonely, a little, I admit it. Being odd. I endlessly caught shared eye-slides passed between the other girls, who thought I was confounding; I saw teachers raise their eyebrows as they found me exasperating, and I watched my parents trying to hide the fact that they thought of me as exhausting. But what can I tell you? Different has always been my more.

I guess being murdered by the estranged father of my child is different. I suppose, thinking about my life philosophy, that should be some comfort. Of course, it isn't.

RADA delivered different and more. My God, in *spades*. It was everything. Prestigious, a stretch, the opportunity to reinvent myself not once, but many, many times, every time I took on a new role. When I walked into the lofty halls of RADA, or along the crowded, buzzing streets of London, I knew I had finally found *it*. This, *this* was what I had always wanted, what I needed. This was what would finally satiate all my uncomfortable cravings. A place where everyone understood the desire to be extraordinary and no one was judged for it. People didn't notice my outlandish hair or clothes; in fact, I started to develop a more conformist look – I let my natural hair colour grow through, most often I wore leggings and a sweatshirt – because that was the way to stand out at RADA. Appearing normal was eccentric. People talk about it, don't they? The moment you know you've arrived. Well, for me, it was being at that institution and knowing I deserved to be there. That I was good. One of the best. Maybe *the* best. Oscars were joked about, people whispered excitedly about my promise and potential. My future stretched. My life mattered.

He took all that away from me.

RADA couldn't survive the faulty love affair, the surprise pregnancy, the bleak desertion and the single-mother struggle. The agony is he didn't take *everything* away from me. In a way, it would have been easier if he had. But he didn't cull the longing, the craving. I could not learn to settle. The ambition within me still rolled and roared. He couldn't douse that fire, destroy that intrinsic part of me; he just obliterated the path I had found to channel the impulse.

So, I changed tack. For a time, all my ambition was funnelled into Dottie. I accepted that I'd screwed up my chances, my life, but she was a second chance. The work I did would provide her with opportunities.

When my mother first took Dottie back to Serbia, she made me sign a power of attorney document giving her legal rights over my daughter. We agreed it was important to get the paperwork squared away. If my mother was going to adopt my daughter and bring her up as her own, it was critical that Dottie never discovered the truth about me. She argued that it was a case of the sooner the better in terms of my committing to her plan. The less time Dottie spent with me as her mother, the less likely she was to remember me as such. And my mother was right. You can't put that on a child, that level of confusion and nuance. I never wanted Dottie to think I gave her up or that I gave up. I just wanted her to feel loved.

I didn't kid myself that once my mother had left the country with her, I could resurrect my dream and go back to RADA. I needed to bring in money, not rack up student loan debts. I had responsibilities. I'm a realist. I knew that them leaving just meant that I'd have more time to whore. I use the word 'whore' a lot. I make it into a verb as well as a noun. The word's familiarity – its recurrence on my tongue and in my ears – takes away the sting when other people fling it about. I won't let it cling to me, the humiliation everyone wants to pour my way. Remember, I'm just doing a job.

By the time Dottie was two and a half, my mother had legally adopted her. It wasn't easy. God, that's an understatement. Take my word for it, no one lightly makes the decision to let a child go. The plan was that I would sink into the background; my new role would be the wayward big sister in London. Fun but flighty. It was a solution, but it felt like a punishment. You see, despite the role my mother had cast me in, I was not flighty; I took my responsibilities very seriously and I kept my side of the bargain. I never revealed to Dottie that I was more than a sister to her, even though there were times when I ached to do so. I let her grow up in peace and stability. I sent money home to my mother. Lots of money, enough to ensure Dottie wanted for nothing. I planned for her to attend the best school in the country; I wanted her to have chances and opportunities. She would never have to make the choices I had made.

She was on her way to enjoy one of those opportunities when it happened. She was going on a school ski trip. Imagine! Learning to ski at just six years old! The school had its own chalet, and even the little ones got to stay there. Dottie had been so excited about the idea of going to ski school. Chattered about it to me on FaceTime. The coach departed from the school at 6 a.m. So damned early. Why did they have to meet so early? It was dark, raining hard, I've been told. My mother shouldn't have been driving in the dark; she was always a nervous driver. She could have put Dottie in a taxi and told a teacher to meet her at the other end; or better yet, they could have both taken a taxi. They had enough money to take taxis everywhere if they wanted, I saw to that.

I imagine her briefly toying with that idea but shunning it before it was even fully formed. She didn't like to squander the money I sent; too well aware that it was hard earned, perhaps. I was always urging her to treat herself, indulge a little. 'No need to be flashy, Teodora,' was her standard response. In my more reasonable moments, I realise that most likely she simply wanted to keep up with the other parents, who were all dropping off their girls personally. She didn't like Dottie standing out. She would have wanted to wave her off. Shout last-minute instructions up to the coach: to clean her teeth, stay warm, wear sunblock on her nose. My mother had her faults – she was old-fashioned and stubborn – but she loved Dottie, she was devoted to her. She would not have knowingly put her in danger. Like me, she would have protected her with her last ounce of strength, her last breath. It would have been her final wish. I know that. Although knowing as much still hasn't quite stopped the fury I've felt. The fury, the regret, the grief.

The other car came out of nowhere and was speeding. Maybe it was inevitable, unavoidable. Or maybe someone younger, with quicker reflexes, could have sidestepped the head-on collision. A mother, rather than a grandmother, might have managed that. When it first happened, I sometimes got drunk on whisky and grief and tearfully confided to other working girls what had happened. They all said the same thing: 'It was over quickly, at least they didn't suffer.' But these women weren't there. How do they know if my mother and daughter suffered? I realise they said as much hoping it would bring some comfort.

Nothing has ever brought comfort. Nothing ever will.

The rope is digging into my wrists. My breathing is shallow and laboured. My bruises ache, my cuts sting. I wonder whether there is an afterlife. I wonder whether I will see my mother and daughter again soon. If there is a heaven, and I get in, I'm going to tell Dottie that she is my daughter. That's the first thing I will do.

I make myself look at Shaun. The devil incarnate. He looks bored, impatient. He has no idea that I am grieving for our child. He has no idea what he has lost. I envy him that. I'm jealous of that enormous inequality between us. That is the one that rips, that burns. That, more than jealousy of his family, his career, his wealth. I am jealous of the fact that he is oblivious to the pain of losing a child; that, more than I'm jealous of the fact that he is the one holding the gun. It isn't fair. He should have to feel some of the loss too, but he hasn't got a clue.

It wasn't my mother's fault she was driving my daughter to school in the dark and the rain. It was mine. I let her take her. I should have taken better care, held onto Dottie, held tightly, no matter what. I should have taken all the responsibility. That's what I think on my bad days.

And on my very worst days, I think the fault was his.

My choices, or lack of them, when peeled back, begin and end with him.

# 42

# *Dora*

'This place is a mess,' Shaun snaps. 'Jonathan, get in here.'

Jonathan scurries into the kitchen. He's been lurking outside the door, waiting for instructions. I've felt his intrusion throughout my conversation with Shaun; I don't doubt he's been listening. His presence has seeped into the silences too. In front of his boss, his demeanour changes somewhat. He's still a bulky, violent man, but he's no longer quite as showy; he has stepped back into the role of supporting actor, leaving Shaun to play the leading man. His obsequious manner is even more repellent than his former arrogance.

'Yes, boss?'

'Get her down. Get this place cleaned up. You know I hate mess.' I remember that about him. The fastidious way he would fold up his clothes and lay them over the back of a chair before we had sex. At the time, I remember thinking it was charming; now I see it as the mark of a psychopath. Why didn't he just throw his clothes around the room with wild abandon? 'I'm going for a walk,' he adds. 'I want to look at the new flower beds the gardener has been working on. See how they're flourishing.'

'They're not. They've got black bug,' I interrupt. It's satisfying to see his cheek pulse, a little flicker that betrays his irritation. I'm glad I've managed to point out a flaw, to show him he's not a god; no matter how much control he currently wields over me, he is not omnipotent. Despite all his money, power and influence, he is just like the next man – his bloody hedges can still be plagued.

He stares at me coldly but continues to speak to Jonathan. 'I'll come back to her. Put her in the salon. I'll be back in fifteen. We'll finish it then.'

'Yes, boss.'

I can only assume the fifteen-minute stay of execution is to demonstrate his ultimate power, to prolong my torture. He can rush this through or he can take his time. Jonathan cuts me free from the rope. I wiggle my fingers to get the blood to circulate again; I shrug my shoulders, which ache because my hands have been tied so tightly behind my back. He pulls me roughly from the chair. Through the kitchen window I see Shaun head towards the formal gardens; once I'm certain I'm alone with Jonathan, I beg in a frightened whisper, 'Just let me go. You could. I'd do whatever you wanted.' I hate myself for stooping so low, but I haven't any choice.

'No chance. I've already had anything you can offer up,' he replies with a sneer.

He holds the top of my arm and marches me out of the kitchen. He no longer has the gun; he handed it to Shaun when Shaun first came into the kitchen. Shaun didn't hand it back as he headed out to the garden, but instead slipped it into a holster inside his jacket. This tells me two things. Firstly, gun handling is not something new to Shaun. Therefore, secondly, if

I have a chance, it's now. Later might not be an option. Fifteen minutes and it's likely to be all over for me.

So I run. I bolt. My feet slap down hard on the tiled corridor, and I feel the shock and power of my panic reverberate through my body. I run faster than I ever have before. I run for my life.

For a moment, Jonathan stands still, surprised by my resistance. I suppose he thought he'd beaten and scared the defiance out of me. A surge of challenge lights me from the inside. Fuck him. I'm down but not out. Men like him have no idea; they think they can terrify women into submission, they think they can convince us we are mad or valueless. But they are wrong. I'm sane, and there's a point to me. They think we are weak and can be cowed, but we are strong and resilient. After I lost my mother and Dottie, there were months when I lay in bed at night and wished that I'd stop breathing, that it would all just end. The dawn of each new day seemed cruel, taunting. I blamed myself. I had an itemised list of 'what ifs' and regrets that I ran through the way other people count sheep or say prayers at night. If only they had stayed in London. If only I hadn't become an escort, my mother would not have wanted to remove Dottie from my care. If only I could have found other work. If only I had been in the car instead of them. I wanted to die, but I didn't.

I don't want to die now.

I run so fast that I can feel my heart banging in my chest, thunderous, as though it wants to escape from my body as much as I want to escape from these men. My lungs feel inflated, then squeezed, as I push myself. I'm grateful now for my self-discipline, which means I've always made myself pound the London streets for at least five kilometres every day, rain or shine. I glance right, but the enormous front door is shut; I imagine it will be locked. In a split second, I calculate that I can't risk heading in that direction and being cornered. Instead, I head up the stairs, my feet slapping out a desperate hasty rhythm. For all my effort and determination, the truth is I'm in a bad way. The adrenalin careering through my body can only go so far in countering the beatings I've taken recently; I'm slower than my optimum.

Jonathan proves to be surprisingly fast; he's gaining on me, he's only a few steps behind me now. I climb higher, taking two steps at a time. My hair streams out behind me, and I imagine I can feel him grasping at it. One step closer, an outstretched arm, he could grab it, yank me down the stairs. The thought is terrifying. I realise what I must do. It's not a choice, it's not a decision; it's an instinct, a reflex. I stop. I turn, and with both hands, I shove him as hard as I possibly can in the chest. The weight of my body and the weight of my grief combine to push him right over the banister.

I watch his arms and legs claw at the air for a fraction of a moment, an upturned beetle suspended, and then – *crack*. He smacks to the floor and smashes, his frail shell shattering like the eggs he threw to imprison me.

All the king's horses and all the king's men.

I watch as a pool of blood seeps from his head. There is no question he is dead. I start to quake, my body acknowledging what my mind really can't. Slowly I head back down the stairs. I glance at the body and then at the front door. If I run, how far can I get without a car? Not far, as I found out this morning. I need to take his car; I assume he has the keys on him. I edge towards the twisted corpse. He looks like a puppet with tangled strings, thrown down in impatience. I realise I'm thinking of him as a beetle, an egg, a puppet, anything other than human. I killed *a man*. It's always made to look easy and remorseless on TV. It doesn't feel like that. I'm shaking as though I have a fever. He was a bad man, wicked. Unequivocally. And it was him or me. It might still be me. But I've just killed a man.

He is warm, of course, too soon to lose the heat. Am I imagining the stiffening, his blood slowing? His eyes are open, bulbous and staring, not at me, past me. I shiver. I can feel something: not his soul leaving so much as his evil lingering. I don't check his pulse, I can't bear to touch his flesh; it's bad enough that I have to squeeze my hand into his trouser pocket. The left one is empty. I roll him onto his side to get to his right one. It takes effort, but I manage to shove hard to budge his heft. As I do so, his phone falls out of his pocket. I take that, it might be useful. Finally I find his keys. There are two sets, car and chateau.

I stand up and run. It is as I expected: the huge front door is locked. I slide back the bolt and then scrabble to push the large old-fashioned key into the lock. My body betrays me; I'm shaking and sweating so much that I nearly drop the keys several times. Finally it slips in, and I turn it and swing open the door. The low, early evening light floods into the dark hallway, blinding me. I blink once, twice.

His silhouette looms larger than life in front of me. His shadow falls, tall, ramrod straight and narrow, like a stake pegging me to the spot.

'Evan?'

'Dora?'

And then in unison we ask, 'What are you doing here?'

# 43

# *Dora*

I eye him warily. There is a dead body behind me, clawing at my consciousness and still creating fear. And there is this live one in front of me, the last person I was expecting to see. What next? Do I collapse into his arms? Is he here to rescue me? Or – for a moment my mind goes to the darkest place possible – is he here to hurt me too? Is he in on this, part of this horror? The thought almost floors me. Is that possible? Anything is possible. I know that. My legs wobble, my stomach churns. If he is here to hurt me, I wouldn't be able to physically escape him, but more than that, I wouldn't be able to mentally carry on. If Evan is mixed up in this horror, there is no good in the world. There is no point. We stare at one another for a fraction longer than feels natural.

'What are you doing here?' he asks again.

'Some men are trying to kill me.' The sentence blurts out of my mouth. It sounds ludicrous, but that can't be helped. It's true.

'What? No.' He looks horrified and disbelieving at once. The contradictory emotions playing out on his face concern me. Why be horrified if he doesn't believe someone is trying to kill me? Unless it is *me* he is horrified with. Does he think I'm mad, a fantasist? But his gaze trails the length of my bruised and scratched body. There can be little doubt that I've been hurt and abused. 'What happened to you?' he asks. Compassion swims in his eyes, and I breathe again. It is OK. It is Evan. He loves me. I love him. Of course he is not in on this. What a despairing, unfair thought.

I start to gabble an explanation, but I'm panicked and struggling to make sense, as I'm conscious that at any moment Shaun could re-emerge. 'The owner of this chateau is trying to kill me. We have a history. It's complex. I haven't got time to explain it now. We have to get away.' I start to pull at the sleeve of his jacket, trying to drag him towards Jonathan's car. He is dressed immaculately. He looks cool and unflappable, the absolute opposite to my dishevelled, desperate state. We look worlds apart.

We are.

I continue, 'Did you come in a taxi? Can we catch up with it? If not, we need to steal this car.' He isn't getting it, he doesn't move. I try to drag him, but he's so intractable that my feet just slide in the gravel beneath me, moving me towards him but not allowing either of us to get away.

'Dora, breathe. You're not making sense.'

'Someone is trying to kill me,' I yell.

He is wearing sunglasses; he takes them off and pinches his nose, up close to his eyes. He looks weary. He repeats the question. 'What are you doing here?'

'Why is that relevant?' I demand, stalling, not wishing to confess.

'Why don't you want to tell me what's going on?' he asks.

'I am. I'm trying to.' I realise he is going to need to understand this completely to get on board. 'I came here with a client,' I admit, sighing. His nod is terse, but he doesn't interrupt. 'I know I promised I'd give it all up.'

'You did.' He looks saddened, and I feel a slug of sorrow deep in my gut. I've disappointed him. It hurts, in a different way to how the punches hurt, perhaps more. I haven't got time to explain the no-sex caveats I struck with Daniel. I push on.

'The man who owns this place planned it all. We have a long and complicated history. He hired people. I thought they were guests, but they were here to fuck me up. One is an actual assassin. He wants me dead.'

'I don't believe you,' says Evan flatly.

'I know it's a lot to take in, but why would you doubt me? Look at my bruises, my cuts.' I thrust my arms out in front of him; there are red welts where I was bound. I lift my top to show him the purple and brown bruises blooming on my ribs. I turn slowly. I know he will see each knot of my spine, my skin transparent and vulnerable; he's always saying I'm too thin.

'You say the man who owns this place did this to you.'

'Yes.'

'That's not possible.' Evan sighs and shakes his head. 'My dad owns this place. It's our summer family home. Well, one of them, I've been coming here since I was a kid.'

'This is your father's place? Your place?' I shake my head. 'No, it belongs to Shaun Beaufoy.'

'Shaun Beaufoy *is* my father.'

'But your surname is Smyth-Cooper.'

'My mother's name is Smyth-Cooper. They gave me her name because my dad had this thing about her having heritage. In fact, my legal name is Smyth-Cooper-Beaufoy. Can you imagine? I work for him. It's best if the first impression everyone has of me is not that I'm a treble-barrelled twat who works for Daddy. How didn't you know that?'

How indeed? We both fall silent for a moment. Shaking my head from side to side, I start to edge away from him. 'I didn't know because you've never mentioned it.'

'I must have, you've just forgotten.'

'No,' I say firmly. Then, trying to suppress panic, I ask, 'How did you find me? How did you know I was here?'

'When you stopped answering my texts, I used Snap Map.' I'd forgotten that years ago Evan insisted we both get this app. I've never been aware of him using it in the past – he's never mentioned it – but now I wonder, has he followed me before? Has he always been privy to my whereabouts? Does he follow me for my safety? Or ... I can't let the thought fully form in my head. He continues, 'I was worried there must be something wrong when your phone popped up in the south of France.'

'So you just hopped on a plane?'

'Yes, of course.' It is possible. Evan catches planes frequently, drops from one country to the next, no biggie. But what if he is lying to me? I edge stealthily closer to Jonathan's car. I want to believe him, but it's best I decide whether I do believe him or not from a distance. I need to get out of here.

I'm not looking where I am going. I'm concentrating on

what I have to leave behind. Bumping up against Shaun makes me react as though I have been tasered.

He, on the other hand, is statuesque, solid. Immovable and impenetrable.

'Oh, look who's turned up. What kept you, son?'

# 44

# *Dora*

As my gaze falls between one man and then the other, father and son, Shaun carefully eases the car keys out of my hand. His action is gentle, stealthy, and I don't realise I've relinquished them until he waves them in the air. He is triumphant. I am trapped.

'You're not thinking of leaving us so soon, are you?' he asks, amusement oozing in his voice. 'I've a better idea. Let's all go to the bar, have a drink, talk this through.'

He's such a fucking psycho, able to behave normally in front of Evan when really he's a ruthless, vindictive control freak who is prepared to kill. He puts his hand on the base of my back, and I feel the cold heaviness of the grip of the gun he is holding. He's not pointing it at me; that would be too obvious. He's just reminding me of its existence.

We all trudge around the house, and head towards the bar next to the pool. We walk in silence. Instinct makes me want to reach out to Evan, take his hand and reconnect, but that's impossible, foolish, since I have no idea what he is thinking. I try to catch his eye, but he's not looking at me, nor is he looking at his father. He's staring at the sky, as if looking for answers there. A flare of irritation flashes through me like a firework. Evan is four years younger than I am; it sometimes feels like the gap is far greater. Premature ageing is rarely something the privileged and wealthy have to worry about. I'm often aware of his immaturity, his dependency on others to manage his life: me, his staff, his colleagues, his father. I've regularly heard him mention that 'so and so is dealing with it', or 'blar blar will fix it.' I need him to be *more* right now. Not a boy in a man's body but a behemoth in a man's body. There are no answers in the darkening sky, just an indication that the day is fading. Time is passing.

Shaun gestures to the sunloungers, 'Take a seat.' His voice is clipped, a command not an invitation, and yet I sit, too weary to protest. Evan sits down opposite me but still out of reach; Shaun goes behind the bar. We form a bizarre and troubled triangle. Shaun puts the gun on top of the bar. I don't know if Evan has seen it. Surely if he had, he would say something. How can his father carrying a gun be normal to him? If it is, I'm done for. 'Bloody Marys all round?' Shaun asks, genially.

It's bizarre, he's playing the part of host after being my torturer. What can I do other than respond by playing my part as a guest, albeit an awkward and unnerved one? Somehow, he has always managed to silence me. When we first got together, he set the tone and shaped the conversations; I was never able to find the words to declare the passion or, later, the fury I felt. He always had stories to tell. He did ask questions, but only the ones he knew the answers to, meaning I never really did more than whisper. So when he wanted to walk away from me, he was able to do so without me being able to protest. He muted me, as simply and effectively as pressing a button on the screen.

I cough and force myself to say, 'I don't want a Bloody Mary. May I have a water?' Shaun holds my gaze expectantly and I find myself pathetically adding, 'Please.' He then nods as though that was what he was waiting for – the magic word, good-girl manners. I realise the whole thing is a game, a feeling confirmed when he hands me a Bloody Mary regardless of my request. I put it down on the ground untouched; alcohol is the last thing I need. I notice that Evan gulps his back, alcohol clearly being the first thing he needs. Then he silently hands his father the empty glass. A small domestic ritual that has probably played out between them hundreds, maybe thousands of times. Shaun will have passed Evan milk bottles when he was a baby, sippy cups when he was a toddler, then cans of pop when he became a tween. The two of them are intrinsically linked, their intimacy a given. I am an outsider.

'Another?' Shaun asks. Evan nods.

'Take mine,' I offer.

'No, don't,' says Shaun. 'I'll make another.' I wonder whether my Bloody Mary is drugged. Probably. I can't trust anything.

We sit in silence as Shaun carefully measures and pours the vodka and tomato juice, then adds Worcester sauce and celery to garnish. Evan accepts the second drink, though this time he takes careful sips.

I know him so well. Four years of trust and friendship. Love. I want to believe in him still. I want to think that his silence is coming from the fact that he's struggling to process this; who wouldn't be? I am his fiancée, and I've just accused his father of trying to kill me. I wait. Evan, if he can be trusted, is my best chance of surviving this. I have to let him work this out for himself. There is no doubt Evan adores his father, he is in awe of him, he has a desire to make him proud. He is going to struggle to believe Shaun is the murderous bastard I know him to be.

Unless he is already aware. In which case, his struggle will be that those murderous bastard tendencies are pointing in my direction.

Unless he's already aware of that too.

Is he? The thought makes my stomach churn. I think of the beautiful engagement ring nestled under my mattress in my flat, and I ache with longing to trust Evan. I need to be able to rely on what he said he felt for me. That's everything right now. But people say all sorts. I know that.

'It's so obvious now,' I mutter. I look up at Shaun defiantly. 'You didn't come after me because you are some insane moral crusader who wants to close down the sex worker industry.'

'Oh, come on, you never believed that for a moment.'

'You didn't come after me because …' I stumble here; there's no easy way to be explicit in front of Evan. 'It wasn't even because of our history,' I add cautiously. 'You came after me because I am engaged to Evan.'

'Don't play this game with me,' says Shaun.

'That makes total sense,' I add. 'Or at least as much sense as this complete madness can make.'

'So who is going to explain this to me?' Evan asks, interrupting. His tone is spiky; shards of confusion and pain splinter the air. 'What the hell is happening here?'

'You are engaged to a whore. Everything else is a natural consequence of that ridiculous decision you made,' says Shaun curtly. He glares at his son. A complex mix of despair and love. I can see that, and it pains me, but of course he loves Evan. That's the whole point. Evan's choices over the years may have frustrated his father – the decision to marry me very obviously does – but the parent–child bond is bigger than frustration or disappointment. It is all-encompassing; it is everything. 'Look at the sort of person you are mixed up with.' He spits out the words, exasperated, desperate. 'She is literally a whore, Evan. What were you thinking?'

'I know what she does for a living. Or did. She's given it up,' replies Evan, carefully.

'No, that's just it, son, she hasn't.' Shaun falls over his words, agitated. 'It doesn't matter what she promised you. She's here, isn't she? She came here with a client.'

I interject hurriedly. 'I did accept a job, I've already told you that. But I was never going to have sex with him. Daniel and I agreed it would be a platonic relationship while I was here. I didn't break our deal, Evan.'

Evan still isn't looking at me, but he's no longer looking at the sky; now he's looking at his feet. His shoulders rounded, he appears slight and gauche. Odd, because he works out, and normally his chest width is comment-worthy; women swivel in the street to check him out. Now he is reduced. Less.

'You can't believe a word she says.' Shaun reaches into his pocket and pulls out his phone. He holds it so Evan and I can both see the screen and then quickly shuffles through numerous photos of me with Daniel: at the airport, in the car, by the pool. We are holding hands in one; in another, his arm is slung around my shoulder. I look like a woman out with her boyfriend. Of course I do. That's what we agreed. I'm good at my job.

I try to plead my innocence. 'It's not what it looks like. I didn't sleep with that man. Or rather I did, I used to, but not once you and I got engaged. I came here to do him a favour. Or at least I thought that was why we were here. I was pretending to be his girlfriend, but we didn't have sex. I didn't lie to you, I promise.' I hear my own voice, whiny and unconvincing, rattle through the air. I am exasperated that I might be tripped up on whether I have or have not slept with Daniel, why I came here with him in the first place. It's hardly the biggest crime that has been committed this week, yet it could be the one that decides my fate. It isn't fair.

Evan looks bemused. It's clear he still doesn't know what to think. Even if I explain everything his father has done to me, and why – blow by blow – he still might not believe it. It's extreme and insane. And blood is thicker than water. But if he doesn't believe me, then I'm finished, so I have to try. 'That man who beat me up in the hotel, your father paid him to do that. He was trying to scare me off. Off you, presumably. Then he blackmailed the man in the photos to lure me here. He was a client of mine, but I've since discovered that your father arranged that too, ages ago. Since I've been here, an entire gang of people have drugged me, abused me, subjected me to gaslighting.'

'Oh for fuck's sake.' Shaun rolls his eyes.

Evan looks up at me, then at his father, and back to me again. He is confused; dismay and chaos ooze from his every pore like sweat. He's unsure what to do next.

Shaun pushes on. 'OK, if you and Daniel were platonic and you are no longer whoring, how do you explain this?' He holds the phone aloft again. The video plays into the darkness. Giles thrusting into me, bent over the pool table. The grunts, sighs and words that play out shatter any residual trust there may have been between Evan and me. His face is the colour of wet concrete, and hardening just as quickly.

'*You like it, don't you, you dirty bitch? You like it when I fuck you hard?*'

'*Yes, yes, I do, big boy, yes.*' My response is slurred and unenthusiastic. It is something I've said time and time again over the years. It doesn't surprise me that I managed to dredge up the rote phrases even when drugged. It doesn't surprise me, but it horrifies Evan.

'OK, I've heard enough,' he snaps, dropping his head into his hands. Still Shaun lets the video play on. More breathless gasping, more four-letter words sprinkle into our history. Eventually he stops it.

'I don't remember that,' I say quickly.

'She was too drunk.'

'I was drugged. I would never have—' Evan holds up his hand to silence me, but I can't be silenced, not now. '—I wouldn't have done that of my own accord. I've stopped. I promise you. That was rape,' I plead. 'Your father paid those people to do that to me. I have no memory of that incident.' I pick the word 'incident' to try to make it clinical, cool and distant. It doesn't work. Evan looks broken. Shattered. I've hurt him, and despite all the hell and pain I have been through recently, I think the look on his face right now cuts the deepest. Hurts the most. He doesn't believe me. If he doesn't believe me on that first fact, how can I get the rest of the story to stick? It's no good, he doesn't trust me. I hoped he would. I was counting on it. His shoulders slump still further as he collapses lower into the sunlounger. He's unravelling in front of me, retreating back into being a boy, a child, and his childhood belongs to his father. I realise that saying anything else is pointless. It will look pathetic, unconvincing.

'A leopard never changes its spots,' says Shaun, sensing his victory over me. He returns to the bar, pours himself a whisky, downs it. He fingers the gun, then mutters, 'Where the fuck is Jonathan?'

'Dead,' I respond.

'What?' I don't know which of them says this. Their tone of voice is indistinguishable. It's funny; now I notice similarities between them.

'I killed him.' I shrug. 'It was him or me.' My voice is jagged, gravelly one moment, squeaky and thin the next. What does it matter what I confess to now? Evan hates me anyway. I'm not going to win this. I'm unlikely to get through the night. I should give up.

'How did you kill him?' Shaun asks.

'I pushed him over the banister.' Evan makes a sound deep in his throat, a gurgling that makes me think he's about to throw up. 'If you want me dead, it looks like you're going to have to do your own dirty work,' I add with fake bravado.

# 45

# *Dora*

I expect Shaun to reach for the gun immediately, but instead he mutters, 'Fucking bitch.' He looks repulsed. The idea of killing me himself is not as appealing as I might have imagined. Perhaps he has never actually had to get his hands soiled before. A man with his sort of wealth is unlikely to have to do his own dirty work. He pours himself yet another whisky, suggesting a lack of control, a loosening of command. I feel his angry energy quiver through the evening.

We sit in a bleak silence, for how long I don't know. Time is dragging, or it may be whirling. I can't cling to anything as normal as estimating time passing. Not when the three of us are sitting here like this. Father, son, lover. Soon to be murderer, witness, victim. None of us could have ever imagined this end. We stay still for an agonisingly long length of time. I don't move or say anything at all, fearing anything I say might hasten my end. Shaun and Evan are also silent and contemplative. I suppose Shaun is thinking about the logistics, how he is going to finish me off and then hide the fact. Without Jonathan, he will have to deal with it all; not only murder me, but dig my grave too. I find myself thinking through his problem as though it is mine. Perhaps he will stage something: a fight between me and Jonathan, or an accident. Then he won't have to get rid of my body, but just report something to the police. He is no doubt turning his monstrous mind to these practicalities. He'll be weighing up whether the police will believe him, or at least take a bribe. He has options. He's just figuring out which one he'll take. The whisky won't be helping, though; it will be making it harder to focus, or perhaps it will be making it easier to be fearless.

And Evan? What can he be thinking? I keep my eyes on him, but his face is neutral. A face I've been reading for years and thought I knew as well as my own: a raised eyebrow to suggest scepticism; a millimetre or so higher and it indicates joyful surprise. He has a way of flaring his nostrils when he is tired, and there's something just below his right eye that twitches when he is angry. I thought I knew every inflection, but looking at him now, his face is unrecognisably passive. A blank page. As the light fades, it becomes harder to distinguish his features, and I'm almost grateful – staring at his face but not knowing it at all, not recognising his thoughts, intentions, or soul, leaves me feeling so entirely hopeless.

The sky slowly turns a rich navy, leaving behind the solid cobalt it has been all day. I didn't even notice the sun setting, and feel slightly regretful that I missed my final sunset. It seems careless of me. I should have paid more attention to that; I should have been more aware of everything. All along, forever. Midges cloud the air and I stare at them, transfixed, as though they are a thing of wonder and beauty. In the past, I've only ever seen them as a mild irritant. I listen to the sounds of the countryside, industrious crickets and the liquid warble of birds that I've never learnt to identify. Too late now. I'll never be the sort of person who can identify birds or trees. I know my Zara from my Chloé. It doesn't seem enough.

I think about the last time Evan and I made love. I didn't quite let myself go. Not really. I was still shocked by his proposal and didn't trust my luck. I remember waking in the middle of the night, sweating and ranting, reliving the attack in the hotel. Evan held me tightly, kissed my forehead and murmured, 'It's over, it's over. The worst is over.' He kissed me and we made love slowly. I gave as much as I was able, but the thing is, my experience has always been that the worst is never the worst. It's never over. So I held back a little. And I was right about that after all. It was not over. The worst is now.

So I just wish I'd given him my all when we made love.

I think about his kisses, his hopes, his dreams. Those thoughts replace the ones of abuse and horror that have dominated this week. I think of my mother and Dottie. I remember hugging them, the last time. It was at the airport in Serbia, six years ago. My mother was fussing. She had made me a packed lunch that included a flask of green tea. I told her I couldn't take the tea through security. She snatched the flask back off me, looking pained, as though I had rejected a gift – rejected her – rather than just followed the law. When I hugged her goodbye, her body remained stiff and irritated with me. Later, when I thought about that moment, I understood that she felt impotent when I left her, left *them*, to go back to my big bad world – because she was very aware that my world is big and bad. As a mother, she just wanted to do something, *anything*, to nurture, to make my journey more comfortable. This is the first time since her death that I've been glad she isn't alive. I'm glad she won't have to hear of my murder.

I remember Dottie's last embrace too. She hugged me tight. Flung herself at me, then clambered and hung on me like a monkey, demonstrating the sort of abandon only happy kids ever muster. It's a great memory. She was wearing head-to-toe purple that day, her favourite colour. Purple leggings, a big baggy jumper, purple raincoat, even purple socks, although her shoes were black. Patent leather. I thought they were a bit old-fashioned. I used to worry that my mother dressed her in an outdated way. I tried to tell myself that fashions were simply different in Serbia. That it didn't matter anyway, because Dottie was happy. I remember that she smelt of lavender. 'You are a proper little flower!' I told her, and she laughed, loving the compliment. These precious memories slide into my head. For once, they don't bring me pain or regret; instead, they hug my soul. I have loved. I have been loved.

'Why do you hate her so much?' Evan's question splatters out into the blackness, pulling me from my thoughts. 'Why do you care so much about Dora and what she does for a living?' He is staring at his father; he hasn't caught my eye for a long time. I wish he would, I'd find it easier to understand what he's thinking, and yet in some ways I'm glad he hasn't. Knowing what he's thinking might be too much.

'I'm doing this because you proposed to her. I'm doing this for you.'

Evan shakes his head. 'No one would need to know. We could have hushed it up if you'd wanted to. You could have done that for me. Would it really be the worst thing in the world if I married a sex worker? Even if people did find out,

319

so what? Couldn't it have just been a scandal in the tabloids one day, papers that line cat litter trays the next?'

'It's not just the sex worker thing,' Shaun admits.

'Then what?'

Shaun sighs, he turns to me and asks in a tone dripping with sarcasm, 'Darling, do you want to tell the story or should I?' A parody of a happy couple debating who should reveal the 'meet cute' story that all couples have. He cackles to himself and drains his glass. 'Tell him why I care, Natalya, Teodora, Dora … whatever the hell you call yourself. Tell my son why I care so much about getting you out of our lives.'

I won't. I don't have to. He can't rip the words from my throat. I have nothing more to add. I'm done. But then he stands up and charges towards me, arm outstretched, the gun in his hand. He holds it to my head. The cold barrel digs into my temple, just above my ear. 'Tell him!'

And if I don't, this is really the last second, so I spit out the words. 'Because your father and I have history, I told you that,' I gasp. Tears start to roll down my face.

Violently Shaun presses the gun harder against my head. He's not holding me down, I'm not tied up, but I don't move away from the jabbing barrel. 'Tell him *everything*. Admit it! You're not with him because you're in love with him. You came after him because he's my son. He could have been fucking Quasimodo, but you'd have "fallen in love" with him, right? Because you want to get some sick sort of revenge on me. You're here because you chased me down.' He is losing control. The thought of killing me himself, especially in front of his son, must be sending him wild. It was obviously not his

320

plan. He jabs the gun sharply into my skull again. 'You don't fucking love him. Tell him. You're just with him because you want to ruin things between him and me. You thought you'd take him away from me.' He roars his explanation.

'She didn't know you're my dad. I never told her your name,' interrupts Evan. He's leapt to his feet and is at my side now. If his father pulls the trigger, Evan will be injured too. At the very least he'll be left cradling my bloody body. Both men tower above me. I can smell the fabric of their clothes. Dry-cleaning fluid. It makes me long for my flat.

'She knew!' Shaun yells. His spittle lands on my bare shoulder. I'd like to brush it off, but I dare not move a muscle.

'Jesus, Dad. Not everything is about you,' Evan yells.

'This is,' Shaun counters.

'Did you do all this to her to control me?'

'Not to control you, to *protect* you, son. To protect you from a vengeful, gold-digging little bitch.'

'Which is it? Which do you think she is? A gold-digger who is after my fortune or a nutter who wants to hurt you because of some ancient history?'

'Both!'

'I love her.' The words are a balm; they sing like a hopeful gospel choir. He is going to save me. I am going to save him. If we believe in one another, we have a chance. If he loves me – and he says he does – his father can't kill me, can he?

Then I hear Shaun cock the gun. *Click.* Quietly, he says, 'You love fucking her, Evan. That's not the same.'

Evan shakes his head. 'You have no idea what I feel for her.'

'I do son. I do. I get it. She's good in the sack. Very athletic. Very convincing. I've had her too. I can see her attractions.

She tried to trap me as well, son. She got pregnant. Can you fucking believe that?'

Slowly I turn my head, fraction by fraction, to look at Evan's face. His usually kind and open face. Watching carefully, I see it. I don't want to, but the thought slithers into his head and is projected out through multiple rapid twitches just below his right eye, the thought of me with his father. I see the idea take hold, and there is a slight darkening of his eyes, maybe something about the way his mouth tightens. There it is, the tiniest shadow of doubt. A flicker. It almost instantly becomes tangible, like opening the fridge and detecting food that has gone off. Before you can find the mouldy cheese, the milk that has set, or the vegetables that have liquefied, you know that whatever is making the stench is past its best, beyond saving.

Evan's mind is clouding, filling with uncertainty. 'Pregnant?'

Shaun must see his son's disappointment in me and pushes home his advantage. 'We got rid of it. As soon as she realised she couldn't catch me that way, she had the matter cleared up.'

Evan glances at me. 'Dora wouldn't do that.' He sounds unsure. He wants me to clarify, deny or explain. This time I'm the one who looks away. I can't tell him the truth, not in front of Shaun. Not like this. I won't drag Dottie into this.

Shaun continues. 'She did. Look, son, can't you see this has gone too far to change course now?' He shrugs, feigning regret, which I don't buy for a moment. 'Things have got a bit out of hand, you see that. If she goes to the police, the firm wouldn't survive the scandal. Your mother wouldn't survive the scandal. We have to finish it.'

Evan turns away from both of us, looks out at the black

horizon. 'You can't shoot her,' he says with a tired, accepting sigh. 'How would you clean that away without Jonathan to help you?'

Shaun is glassy-eyed from the whisky, but even so, his face radiates delight and triumph. 'That's my boy. Good thinking.' He folds Evan into a one-handed hug. Slaps his back, heartily, the way men do when they've won at a team sport. He's waving the gun carelessly behind my back. I'm terrified it's going to go off accidentally. Evan is clearly thinking along the same lines.

'Hey, Dad, give me the gun.'

Shaun walks back to the bar and carefully lays the gun down again. 'I've got it, son. Why don't you go to the kitchen? Get some eggs.'

# 46

# *Dora*

Evan doesn't have to walk far before he disappears from my view. As soon as he's away from the immediate vicinity of the pool lights, his shape pours into the blackness. Vanishes. Although he disappeared before my eyes moments before, when he took his father's side and accepted that I had to be finished off. I blink ferociously. I don't want Shaun to see me cry.

'Drink?' offers Shaun. 'Might as well be civilised about this.' He chuckles to himself, knowing he has the result he wanted. He wins.

Despite my attempts to stem my tears, I find they are rolling down my face, dripping from my chin onto my lap. It's funny to have so little control when I have spent most of my adult life hiding what I actually think or sense, while feigning something I don't believe or feel. Now, at the end, it seems my emotions and body are finally in sync. I am exposed. Raw. I quickly wipe the tears away. My movement catches Shaun's attention.

'Oh, don't cry. You must have known that the odds were against you when you first got involved in all of this. You must have weighed it up and known there was a real chance that he would choose his family in the end. That he would choose me over you. No one's pussy is that irresistible.'

'I didn't involve myself in this,' I point out, snappily. 'You dragged me into this.'

'Oh come on!' He throws his head back, a parody of an exasperated laugh. 'He's not here. It's just you and me now; you don't have to keep up the act. You can tell me the truth. I know you came after him to get at me.'

I stare at him coldly. 'You are insane. We were years ago. Twelve years. I only met Evan four years ago. What do you think happened in that intervening time? That I sat about and plotted your downfall?'

'Maybe.' He walks back to the bar, picks up the whisky bottle, looks disappointed to see it is empty. He reaches for the closest bottle to hand. It's red wine. He starts to open it. It's an old-school cork; he clearly prefers the theatre over the convenience of a screw top. Of course. He is going to have a hell of a hangover tomorrow; you should never mix grain and grape. That thought flitting into my mind is so surreal. What do I care about this monster's hangover? How can I be thinking about ordinary things, like corks versus screw tops, and hangovers, when the axis of my world has been tipped, when I'm heading for my own personal Armageddon? It suddenly strikes me that I should probably have gone into therapy a long time ago. When I became an escort, or when I had to give up Dottie to my mother; certainly after the car crash. My ability to compartmentalise isn't healthy. It's too extreme. This common sense seeping into my mind at the eleventh hour is laughable. I haven't got time for regrets or what-ifs; I have to do my best with now.

I continue to try to reason with him. 'If I'd wanted some sort of revenge, why would I have waited all these years? Think about it, Shaun, it doesn't make sense.'

He doesn't answer my question, but demands, 'Am I supposed to think it's a coincidence that with all the men in London available to you, the one you make your best friend and ultimately your fiancé just happens to be my son?'

'Yes. That's exactly what you are supposed to think, because that's what happened.'

'Bullshit.' He laughs and knocks back the glass of red as though it's water. 'Hats off to you, though, you're a better actress than I imagined. Impressive the way you're sticking to your story even though Evan is out of earshot. Excellent commitment to your role.'

'You're mad,' I assert.

'You thought you were so clever coming after me, trying to ruin things for me and my son, but you're not. You're just a silly little whore with limits. I'm his father. I'm a multimillionaire. I have no limits. What were you thinking?'

'I love him,' I reply simply. 'He doesn't even have your name. How would I have connected him to you? Why would I want to marry into your family? You are crazy.'

'Money. You want to marry into our family for money. Besides being an embarrassment to me, and no doubt scuppering my chances of getting on the Queen's honours list, you'd get a pay rise. Flat on your back as usual, but making millions off my son.'

'You're disgusting.' I clench my hand so tight that my knuckles seem luminous in the dark; my nails are digging into the flesh of my palms. The words echo around my head, banging against my skull.

Suddenly he hurls the open bottle of red wine at me. He throws it overarm, like a cricket ball. It spins, creating an arc, leaving a bloody spurting trail. Then the bottle smashes on the patio; slivers of glass skittering everywhere, glinting coldly, some bits tumbling into the pool.

'You don't scare me,' I lie.

'You're not scared of me?'

'No.

'Then you are very stupid. I never had you down as stupid.'

'I didn't think you even remembered me well enough to have me down as anything.'

He spits out a short, sarcastic laugh. 'Honestly? I didn't, not at first. You were one of a number of women I'd spent time with in that way.'

'In that way' isn't said with a leer or even with disgust; it is smooth indifference. I didn't matter to him. Of course not, that isn't news. 'Did you send all of them money for abortions afterwards?' I ask.

'One other.'

The response is so audacious I think I might collapse. A cool fact. Even in that particular detail, I was not unique. I wonder what she did, the 'one other'. Did she abort, or is there another half-sibling to Dottie on this Earth? Because that's what Evan is; he is Dottie's half-brother. Did the 'one other' get to keep her baby? Did she get to be a mum? I loathe the thoughts that ambush me. It's all so complex.

Shaun continues, 'I didn't think of you for years. Do you understand?'

I do, fully. His life went on without me. Of course. I had never imagined anything other. He didn't give me a second thought. While my body became unrecognisable to me, skin stretched and limbs swelling, my stomach growing from a plain, to a hillock, to a mountain, month by month as Dottie lay cocooned inside me, I thought of him all the time. I thought of him when I was flat on my back, pushing hard, alone in a delivery room, and when we were hungry and I'd hopelessly shake the last of the cornflakes into my bowl, milk sour, baby screaming. I thought of him when I put on another layer – the baby wearing so many she could barely bend her limbs. I thought of him when I was flat on my back again, accommodating client after client. When I handed my mother Dottie's passport and signed the adoption papers. I thought of how his life was, no doubt, carrying on uninterrupted. He would have had people to stay for weekends in the country, attended board meetings, laughed with his wife, played golf and tennis with his children, gone on holidays to far-flung luxury resorts, drunk champagne and red wine. I imagined him in those and a million other scenarios. He offered plenty of thought fodder. His life was big and expansive, whereas mine was small.

I breathe deeply, and slowly under the cover of the black sky I start to edge my fingers towards my bag millimetre by millimetre. If I can unbuckle it without him noticing, if I can retrieve the letter opener, I will lunge at him. He's quite drunk now; that might slow him down if he reaches for the gun. I can only hope so. A knife against a gun isn't a fair fight, but it's my only chance. Slowly, slowly, I move towards the fastener. The only sound is the pump of the filter on the swimming pool, humming.

Shaun sighs, shakes his head. He seems weary suddenly.

'I didn't think of you at all until my son came home and told me he had met the girl he wanted to marry.'

'I don't believe you. The timings don't add up. Evan didn't propose until after Jonathan beat me in the hotel room. Evan proposed to me as a *result* of that attack,' I point out. I want to keep him talking; distracting him right now is paramount. I need to retrieve the letter knife before Evan returns.

'Yes, that's right, that is when he proposed, but he had already been thinking of it for a while. He mentioned it to me last year sometime. We were here, actually, sitting by this very pool.'

'He did?' Despite everything, I can't help the swell of happiness that ambushes my body. Rushes through me like a wave, almost drowns me. I had known for a while that Evan loved me, was maybe *in love* with me, but I'd thought his proposal came about through panic and pity. It's strangely lovely to hear it was something he had determined on some time ago. Except I can't forget that he is currently walking to the kitchen to find eggs that will kill me. I can't reconcile it. I think of the countless occasions we've stood in supermarket aisles and checked ingredients together, and the times he's grilled waiting staff about the ingredients of a dish. Have I really miscalculated his nature so entirely? Life – at least my life – hasn't been one where I've dared to hope for miracles or second chances. Yet Evan's proposal was just that. I should have grabbed it with both hands, held on tightly and not let it go. I should never have accepted Daniel's proposition. I walked into a trap.

'Yes, last summer, that little gap between lockdowns, we came here. It was such an idyllic holiday. At least it was until he told me his plans.'

The conversation is so normal, so sedate. Shaun is talking about lockdowns and love in the same sentence. Yet he's going to murder me. So, love and death are a breath apart. They are planning to do it together. The man who fathered my child and the man I agreed to marry. I've been up close and personal with so many people who defy understanding. Men who tell me about their wife's labour experience just moments after asking me if I do anal. Men who talk to me about having their garden returfed after having a tennis court or swimming pool put in, then within seconds tell me that they'd prefer it if my lady garden was a very fine landing strip. It's tricky to negotiate. Sometimes too much. Sex and life and death and love squashed up together, meshed and inseparable. It's all so very human. Are we ever able to absorb it? My mind wanders to these questions. I have seen more than most people do. It's been a lot to learn. I have fought and struggled and survived for so long now. I reflect that it might be peaceful to let it go. If I let go.

Shaun stays on point. I tune back in to what he's saying. 'The rush to actually pop the question was my fault, since I got Jonathan to move in on you, and my son – just a puppy, really – turned all protective and sentimental. Ironic, hey?' He laughs to himself, but it's mirthless. He shakes his head, the phrase 'pop the question' sour on his lips. 'I've been planning this for months.'

'This?'

'The end of you.'

'For months? Wow.' I have nothing left other than sarcasm.

'I had to get every detail right, whatever path you took. If you'd left the country – great. If you didn't – well, let's just say plan B needed to be watertight.'

I get it. I understand about the long game and revenge, a dish best served cold. I shiver. It's not that the night has developed a nip, it hasn't; it's airless and close, but I'm chilled to the bone.

Shaun continues. 'It was frustrating that I had to move everything up when I inadvertently became a catalyst for my own worst nightmare. I'd thought Jonathan would scare you away after that beating. I've never seen anyone stand their ground against him in all the years he's worked for me. I fully expected you to just up and run away. Not run into my son's arms. Or if you didn't do a bunk, I thought maybe after the beating and seeing the sorts your work brought you in contact with, Evan would realise that what you did for a living made you unsuitable as a friend, let alone a wife. I did not expect him to propose.' Shaun shakes his head, regretfully. 'I thought he had more self-respect than to attach himself to' – he breaks off and slowly waves his hand in my direction – 'to all this mess.'

I *am* a mess. Bruised and battered. Cut lips, chafed wrists. I am a mess because he made me so. My fingers stealthily unfasten the buckle on my bag, then caress the smooth leather and root around furtively until I find the cold hardness of the knife.

'But it doesn't matter now. He's come to his senses. Sees you for what you are. Thinking about it, if I'd killed you, he would perhaps have spent the rest of his days grieving for you. I'd have made you into a martyr. If you'd disappeared, he'd have spent his life looking for you. It's better this way. He's more likely to reach closure.' Shaun shakes his head, bewildered. 'Of all the things to become fixated on, a whore. Still, perhaps, properly channelled, that focus he's shown might turn towards something worthwhile. If not distracted, he can help build the family company, continue to grow it. I think he'll make me proud. He's like me, my son.'

'He's nothing like you. He's taking ages. How do you know he hasn't gone for help, or called the police?' I hope I can unsettle Shaun, but he is impenetrable.

'He hasn't,' he says confidently. 'He now knows what he is dealing with. He had to see for himself that you were using him to get at me, and that even though he had offered you everything, you'd still betrayed him. Once a whore, always a whore.'

'Sticks and stones, Shaun.'

'I have those too, Teodora, don't you forget it for a moment.' He glances towards the bar, where the gun is lying in the dregs of whisky and red wine. 'It's unfortunate that it's come to this, but I'd do anything for that boy. He's my son.'

I understand. I understand better than anyone. I leap to my feet and charge at him, arm outstretched, the silver letter knife glinting in the moonlight, looking beautiful rather than deadly. I stomp through the glass shards, hearing them crunch under my feet. I know the knife isn't going to cut through his suit and his flesh. I need to stab him in the eye, the mouth or nose to make an impact. It's gruesome, but it's my only option.

He turns to me, sees the slice of metal I am holding. He dives towards the bar; I bring the knife down into his face. I can't look to see where I am landing my damage. He lunges towards the gun; blindly his fingers stretch to grab it, the tendons in his hand translucent with effort. The tips of his fingers land on the cold barrel as I pull the knife out, then plunge it in again. Blood spurts through his fingers as he brings his hands to his face.

# 47

# *Dora*

Evan grabs my wrist, his firm grasp rendering me helpless. He came from nowhere. My hand is still in the air. I didn't want him to see me attempt to kill his father. It all happens simultaneously. A long moment in the longest night. An instant that decides everything. I drop the knife, and as it falls to the ground, clattering onto the tiles, it spins in the shards of glass and pools of red wine and blood.

Evan releases his grip. Looks me in the eye. A flicker of recognition passes between us. Yes, he knows me for what I am. And we will both have to live with that. Forever.

Shaun, bleeding and moaning, lunges towards me, roaring with disgust and outrage. I shove him away. Away from the gun, away from me. I don't push him in any particular direction. I simply repel him. I put my shoulder into it as though loosening a stiff door. I do this with all my strength. With all my hate.

He stumbles backwards, loses his footing, too drunk to right himself. His reactions have slowed, as I expected, as I hoped. Suddenly I am soaking wet. I think I am in the pool, and panic surges through my body. But no, it is Shaun who is in the water; I am at the edge. The splash his descent created shudders over me as I watch him sink like a stone and then rise, rear up, spluttering, seething and stuttering. A kraken, soaring monstrously. His limbs flail, lashing the surface like tentacles. Then he sinks under the inky water again, only to break the surface once more, the smugness gone from his eyes, panic swelling, along with his clothes, which bloat. They seem to pull him downwards. His suit jacket, an albatross.

'He can't swim!' I yell. I'm not sure if I feel triumphant or terrified. I holler out the fact, bald and uncompromising; I remember he once told me as much. It stuck with me, because we had that in common. Most people can swim. We could not. We had so little in common, I clung to this fact.

'Yes, he can. My father can swim,' insists Evan. That is all he does. He stands to the side of the pool, next to me, and watches Shaun whip and thrash at the surface. He does not dive in. He does not kneel and offer a hand. Shaun's mouth is open, cries for help tumbling out, water pouring in. He's sinking like a stone.

'Evan, you have to dive in. Save him.' I don't know if I want this, even as I ask for it, but he can't stand and watch his father drown.

'Come on, Dad. Why isn't he trying?' he asks me. He appears to be in shock. He stands, no longer a man, certainly not a son, but a statue. Turned to stone by the horror.

'He can't swim, Evan.' This time I don't yell. There is no one to hear us anyway. I say it quietly. I tug at his little finger. I dare not take hold of his hand, but I need to reach him somehow.

'No, that's me you're thinking of. *I* can't swim. *He* can,' Evan insists. 'I can't save him because I can't swim. Why isn't he trying to save himself?'

I stare at him, confused. My head is a mess. Have I got it wrong? I remember swapping that confidence. Yes, certainly with Evan; he knows I can't swim, but I don't remember him telling me he couldn't either. I thought that was Shaun. Although it's possible, isn't it? I don't know. I can't remember.

I want Shaun to stop splashing, I want him to die. This man who has ruined my life and wants me dead. This man who will, if he lives, take Evan away from me. I want him dead, and yet I run for the net that the pool boy uses to sweep out leaves and mice, I seize it and stretch it towards him.

'Grab this,' I scream. 'Shaun, take hold. Wade in, Evan. Wade in from the other end. The other end is shallower.' But it's too late. Shaun is no longer thrashing in the water. His shirt is ballooning around him, and he bobs to the top of the pool. Face down, spread-eagled.

Dead.

# 48

# *Dora*

Evan still has not moved. I rush to the steps at the shallow end of the pool and start to wade towards the body. Soon the water is up to my neck, even though I am on my tiptoes. Shaun is floating two metres away from me. The pool is extravagantly large, an idiotic decision when the owner and his son can't swim; even in this moment the arrogance infuriates me. I helplessly lift my feet off the bottom and lunge towards him, but panic immediately seizes me, and I splash and flail in the exact way Shaun did just moments ago. I retreat, put my feet flat on the bottom of the pool. I can't go forward, I can't reach him; the thought makes my heart thump and swell painfully. The truth is, he was always beyond my reach: emotionally, socially, and now physically. It's a tragedy. The blood from his face, where I stabbed him, curls towards me, a slithering eel through the water.

'Get out of the pool, Dora,' says Evan quietly.

'But we could do CPR. We could …' I break off. I don't know what we could do. Or should do. I carefully climb out of the pool. Evan takes a towel from the neat pyramid stack and hands it to me. I wrap it around my shoulders, but it doesn't stop my teeth chattering. We stand side by side, looking at the carnage in front of us, not at one another. I wait for him to reach for his phone and call the police. I have killed two men. One is his father.

'It was self-defence,' he mutters into the blackness. I hear his breath catch in his throat. A jagged hiccup of a statement. 'You did what you had to do in self-defence.' He repeats the phrase as though he is trying to convince himself.

'Well yes, but they will never believe me. I stabbed him in the eye with a letter knife, a weapon I brought outside from the library. That seems premeditated.' I state the brutal horror of what I've done so that neither of us can hide from it. Then I add, 'Your father is an important man.'

'Was,' interrupts Evan.

I shake my head, sorry and sad. Not sorry for killing Shaun, exactly. Not even sorry that he is dead, but sorry for Evan that Shaun is – was – his father. The word *was* is so final, so absolute. 'A bit of digging, and my career path will soon be unearthed; that will work against me.' People will be disinclined to believe anything I say; they'll want the important, powerful businessman, sometime philanthropist, to be better than he was. They'll think I am worse than I am. I sigh. 'No one is going to believe what has gone on here over the last few days. Frankly, I'm surprised you do.'

'I do.' Evan drops his head in his hands, rubs his eyes aggressively. 'I didn't go for the eggs.'

'You didn't?'

'Of course I didn't, Dora.' He sounds hurt that I might have thought he would. 'I heard everything you both said,' he mutters. I look to the ground and notice that puddles of water are forming around me as I drip dry. 'I heard my father's mad insistence that you were only interested in me because of him, and I heard you tell him I'm nothing like him.'

'I meant—'

'I know what you meant. Thanks.' We both fall silent and stare at Shaun's body bobbing on the water. Our collective will can't make it vanish. 'We can leave, just run away. I have money. We could simply disappear,' Evan suggests hopefully. He looks me in the eye at last, and I see his boyish urgency, his childlike desire to flee this mess rather than face it down.

I allow myself to gently take his hand. He is warm and I'm icy. I squeeze his fingers. 'My prints are everywhere. There are photographs on people's phones of my visit here. The police will hunt me down. I'm trapped. He got me in the end. But you can leave, Evan. You don't have to be anywhere near this. I can say I was here on my own. You don't have to be involved.' I can gift him that at least. A release, a way out. His father is dead, bloating in the pool; I owe him.

'No,' replies Evan firmly. 'We'll say that Jonathan stabbed my father and pushed him in the pool, that I chased Jonathan down in retaliation and you were upstairs at the time.' My heart surges and breaks as I realise that he's trying to protect me, despite the fact that I'm a killer. Worse, that I killed his father. 'We can say that when Jonathan saw you upstairs, he turned in panic, missed his step, and fell.' Evan is speaking quickly, making it up as he goes along, piecing something together, hoping to stumble into a credible story. 'Clearly they were both involved in some nefarious dealings. There will no doubt be a paper trail of bad business deals. They could have had an argument. We are just a newly engaged couple, here because I was introducing you to my father.'

I want to believe it could work, I long for a way out, a reprieve, but my subconscious mind is already rooting out the flaws, pinpointing the things that will trip us up and bring us down. I don't want Evan to get involved in any of this. He doesn't have to.

'There must be security footage. A place like this?'

'We can delete it. I know where it's stored.'

'But the others? Chen and Neo, Daniel, Sisi.'

'You said he hired them?'

'Yes.'

'All two-bit actors and extortionists. I can't imagine they want to step up and say they are involved here.'

'Extortionists, yes, so one of them will come forward sooner or later. Maybe not getting involved in the investigation, but perhaps they'd blackmail us. It seems messy.'

'It is, but not impossible. Things go away.' There it is again. A rich man's confidence. I don't believe things go away. What happened between Shaun and me happened twelve years ago, and yet it never went away. The past hunts and haunts. 'You didn't ask for any of this, Dora. I'm not letting you suffer any more,' says Evan firmly. And oh God, I want to be wrapped in his invisible invincibility cloak. I see the joy of being the wife of a rich man who can save the day. I crave that peace and rest and ease. But I am a sex worker with a past and a very visible vulnerability cloak of my own that I can't quite cast off.

'How accurate are they when they record times of death?' I ask.

'What?'

'Well, if our story is going to be that Jonathan killed your father and then you chased him down, we need to make sure that the autopsy won't expose us and reveal the fact that Jonathan died first.'

Evan looks at me with something like respect, but he also looks frustrated. 'I don't know. Can they be that accurate?'

I shrug. 'Possibly.'

We sit in the black silence for a long time. Normal people, now criminals. Murderer and accessory. An owl hoots, Shaun's body bobs on the water. I ache. I'm weary, but I'm also wired. Evan is right, I have suffered enough. I shouldn't have to suffer any more. Tentatively, I make a suggestion. 'If we could get your father to the house, we could set fire to the place. Fire will remove evidence.' It's a horrible idea and I expect Evan to need to process it. Instead he replies instantly.

'OK.'

'You're sure? It's your house.' I can't bring myself to add, *and your father*.

'I'm sure,' he says. His strong chin set.

# 49

# *Dora*

It's a grim process. I remember Jonathan showing me the outbuildings and there being a wheelbarrow in there. I send Evan to retrieve it while I tackle the problem of getting Shaun's body out of the water. I try to poke him towards the shallow end with the skimming net, but it simply bends and gives on contact; it's not rigid enough to have any force. I lower myself into the pool for a second time and wade towards him in the hope that he's drifted close enough to grasp. He hasn't; if anything, he has drifted further towards the deep end.

Evan returns with the wheelbarrow and a solution. He has remembered that there is a rubber ring tucked behind the bar. 'We can both wade into the pool. If you're wearing the ring and I hold onto you, we'll be able to get closer to him, maybe grab hold of him.'

'Why was the rubber ring hidden away?' I ask in frustrated disbelief.

'I guess my dad prioritised the look of the place over safety,' says Evan with a bitter sigh. I know he must be heartbroken that he didn't remember the ring when his father was drowning.

I squeeze his arm, trying to communicate the depth of my sympathy and sorrow at what he is going through. Tricky, when I caused it.

'Take your clothes off before you wade in. It will look odd to the police if your suit is wet,' I point out.

'And you?'

'I'll get some fresh ones before we set fire to the place.'

I see Evan's Adam's apple jump. I guess he's swallowing his surprise that I'm able to think clearly, think of everything. He's never had to think on his feet, save his skin, yet my mind is working nineteen to the dozen. I'm used to avoiding catastrophes, or at least trying to. It's up to me to hold this together.

He follows my instructions and takes off all his clothes, even underwear. Naked, he slips into the water. I follow him with the ring around my waist. He wades in as far as he can, until my feet are off the ground, then he holds onto the ring and, stretching, I'm able to loop my fingers into the waistband of Shaun's trousers. I drag his body after me as Evan guides me back into the shallow end.

I get out of the pool and tug at Shaun's mass, trying to get purchase on him as Evan pushes and shoves from beneath. Wet and dense, stiff and unyielding, he isn't easy to manoeuvre. He never has been. Evan's face is set with grim determination as he heaves and grunts. Finally, Shaun is splayed on the poolside. His blood smeared on the tiles looks blue-black not red. Evan nimbly hauls himself out of the pool too, then lifts his father into the wheelbarrow. It's an unwieldy load, and his face is a hard mask as he steers the barrow towards the house. I pick up the letter knife and wipe the blade and handle on my T-shirt.

As soon as we are in the chateau, we call for Marmalade and are relieved when she bounds towards us. I tell Evan to take her outside and tie her up out of harm's way, then to find the box of tricks that holds the security footage and delete the past few days. I put the letter knife back in the library. Together we place Shaun's body in a chair in the salon; I put a whisky decanter on the side table next to him, and a glass. I have no idea if it will melt to nothing in the fire, but I feel a need to be thorough. I'm imagining a scenario where he drank too much and passed out cold, therefore wasn't woken by the smell of smoke. We deliberate lugging Jonathan's body into the same room and positioning him as though he had fallen asleep on a chair opposite. I'm nervous of doing so. 'How would we account for his injuries? If there's anything left, they might see broken bones or his smashed head from the fall.'

'Will there be anything left?' Evan asks. He looks haunted, beaten.

'I don't know.' We have to hope not, because an autopsy would show that Shaun drowned, but I don't know for sure.

There is so much we don't know about the whole thing, but we have to push on. I clear my throat and say, 'We should leave Jonathan where he is. He could have fallen during the fire while, you know, trying to escape.' Evan needs me to stay focused and firm.

We light candles throughout the house, and then I tip over one that is positioned near a curtain in the salon. The fire quickly catches, the flames licking the velvet fabric, the floorboards, the wallpaper. The intensely hot summer means everything is bone dry and basically tinder. *Whoosh*, the fire leaps; a playful imp quickly becomes an angry devil. I move the side table closer to the flaming curtain and watch as it catches fire too. I need to shunt Shaun's chair towards the curtain but can't bear to articulate the thought. Instead, I take kindling from the woodpile near the fireplace and put the sticks in a trail from the burning curtains to below his chair, under which I build another pile and add logs.

The heat is becoming overpowering; a few sparks snap and singe my skin. I step back and watch the blaze. 'His damp clothes,' I mutter. 'We can't afford for this fire to peter out.' Evan looks like he wants to howl. The fire scorches my face, and my sunburnt arms and shoulders flare and sting, as though the flames are actually reaching me. I'm in hell.

'Should I do the same in another room?' Evan asks.

'No. It will be more realistic if there's one source. I'm certain they can work out that sort of thing.' I start to cough. 'Come on, we need to get out of here.' I take him by the arm and pull him out of the room, through the hall and out the front door. He looks back over his shoulder and I pretend not to notice.

Outside, I take my suitcase out of Jonathan's car, find fresh clothes and change into them. I throw my wet ones back into the blaze. The flames are dancing through the salon now. I can see them through the window, a brightness against the blackness. I sniff the air and wonder whether I am imagining that I can smell burning flesh. I need to get Evan away from the house. 'Go and throw the gun down the well. I'll meet you back at the pool. I'll bring Marmalade.' He follows my instructions wordlessly, seemingly grateful to have had the responsibility of decision-making taken from him.

Returning to the pool, we sweep up the broken glass that is scattered across the patio. We wash blood from the sunloungers

344

using wet towels, then dip the towels in the pool to clean them too. We reassure ourselves that the pool filter will have removed all traces of blood by the time the fire engines arrive. We leave the empty whisky and wine bottles where they are; a night of excess will help to explain slow reactions. I glance towards the house and see smoke above the trees. I pray that no one alerts the fire service too swiftly. We then lie down together on the double sunlounger. Marmalade climbs on top of us, creating a welcome blanket across our legs. 'We have to pretend we fell asleep here,' I say.

'I can't sleep,' replies Evan.

'No.' I put my arms around him, and he rests his head on my chest as though he is a child I am comforting. I gently caress his back and hair. Eventually he does fall asleep, and even as I am wondering how, I must do the same. I only know this because a little later I am shaken awake as I feel Evan's body shudder. He weeps, but I continue to pretend to be asleep. Grief is a very private thing. What can I do? Nothing. Leave well alone. What's done is done. I think I finally know that sometimes doing nothing is everything you can do.

# 50

# *Dora*

Sleep must have overwhelmed us again, because the next time we wake, it is to the sound of sirens. At first I don't recognise them as such. I think it is Dottie crying, screaming, the way she did when she was a hungry baby. This dream is one that haunted me for a long time when I was younger, but I haven't had it for a while. It's disconcerting that it's returned. No, in fact it's devastating that it has returned. I wonder what am I going to be haunted by from now on. We run towards the house and the sirens; Marmalade barks her distress, adding to the confusion. I keep her on her lead and close to my side. Flames are towering above the treeline now, lighting up the sky. The smell of smoke and desolation lingers in the air, cloying. Choking.

We're distraught and disorientated enough for the authorities to accept our story without question. It's made particularly compelling because Evan tries to run into the house. He screams, 'Dad, Dad, Dad. My dad's in there.' Over and over again. He's so convincing I think for a moment he really has forgotten that his father is dead. That I killed him by stabbing him in the face and then pushing him into the pool, and that he was powerless to save him. He's going to have to learn to live with being powerless, as I had to, and the thought makes me sad. Now that his innocence is lost, I realise how much I valued it. I always thought I resented it.

Powerlessness is torture. My baby girl would have been eleven and a half now. A child on the cusp of being a teen, then she would have stretched into womanhood. Who knows what she would have achieved, who she would have influenced or inspired, what she would have seen, thought and felt. If allowed. I am sure she'd have loved Evan. My mum would have adored him too. But there are some things that can't ever be changed.

As expected, the heat is ferocious, but the noise surprises me: timber groans, the roof and floors crash loudly like thunder and then fall into oblivion. Despite the valiant efforts of the firefighters, we watch the house burn to a blackened skeleton. Eventually there is nothing left other than a few partial walls, charred and unrecognisable.

The next several hours are a blur. A translator arrives and helps Evan explain who he is, who his father was, what happened. 'We had all had quite a bit to drink, we were celebrating our engagement. Dad and Jonathan – his employee, but really more of a family friend – turned in at about eleven. Dora and I wanted to stay out under the stars for a bit longer. I guess we fell asleep.' I absorb sympathetic glances from firefighters, medics and the police.

Evan keeps his arm around my waist or shoulders almost constantly; he ushers me into a hired car that seems to arrive from nowhere but was most likely organised by someone from

Shaun's company, a PA or lawyer, I suppose; both have been called, along with Evan's mother and sister. He made those calls alone and he doesn't share details of the conversation with me; I guess he wants to spare me their pain at his lies. Lies my actions have forced him to tell.

We're taken to a hotel. There are fresh clothes waiting for us. We are offered an array of food and drink, but neither of us manages more than a coffee. Concerned people constantly urge us to eat, sleep, rest, talk, cry if we need to. Evan watches me with wary concern. I imagine he thinks the guilt will be too much of a burden and that I'll crack under pressure or pleasantries, suddenly confess to the double murder. When we are alone, he tries to reassure me. 'It's OK that we lied to the police. Morally it's justifiable. We know the truth and understand it. Others might not. As long as we're always honest with each other, we'll be OK.' He kisses my forehead. Then, turning from the subject, he adds, 'Look, there's a note here from the hotel manager offering you a complimentary massage. Do you fancy that?'

'Not really.' I lie on the bed and wonder whether we will be OK. Should we be? I wish the hours away until someone says it's time to get a taxi to the airport. Despite the clean clothes and constant kindness, I feel dirty and fraught. It's a relief when we are on the plane.

Like the staff at the hotel, the air steward is overly attentive. He asks if we want extra pillows or blankets; is Marmalade settled? She has a business seat to herself, so I'm assuming she's fine. We're offered food and champagne; when we refuse both, he runs through a list of teas (breakfast, fruit or herbal), coffees (latte, cappuccino, Americano, all available caffeinated or decaf), or water maybe – still or sparkling? To show willing, I finally accept a sparkling water.

I suppose this is the power of Evan's gold card. I realise this is the life I will live from now on, one where other people make an effort for me, try to impress me. My comfort will be constantly and solicitously enquired after, prioritised. After a week of being so brutally treated by the people Shaun employed, and years before that of dismissals, slights, insults, restrictions and abuse, that are part and parcel of being a whore – or maybe just being a woman – this constant thoughtful attention is extraordinary. At the moment it feels awkward, since people are being especially kind because of Evan's loss, but I'm practical enough to know I will get used to it. I will enjoy it. It will be a relief. Shaun accused me of being a gold-digger. I doubt he will be the last to call me that. Women who marry rich men are always treated with suspicion. I don't care. I've been called worse, and besides, I know it's not true. What I have with Evan, well, it's never been about the money.

Shaun wasn't stupid, though. He got some things right.

There's something you need to know – or rather, there's something I need to tell you, which is almost, but not quite, the same. I must confess it to someone, and a glance at Evan – transparent with shock – tells me he's not up to hearing it.

I did know Evan was Shaun's son. I knew all along, despite the different surname. And yes, if he had looked like Quasimodo, I would still have tried to make him mine. It took me two years to plan how to best destroy Shaun Beaufoy, and four years to do it. He bragged of plotting his revenge on me for months.

Amateur.

After Dottie and my mother died, I could barely get out of bed, but when I finally did, I started to look for Evan Smyth-Cooper. Shaun was absolutely correct. I did want to ruin things between him and his son. I wanted to make Evan more mine than Shaun's. A child for a child has to be the going rate by anyone's reckoning, right? Something else Shaun said comes back to me. When justifying what he put me through, he said, 'Any parent would do the same.' It's perverse but if he had known about Dottie, I think he would have understood my actions. My need to make him pay. A parent's love is boundless, bottomless. Infinite and forever.

At the beginning, I thought it would be a straightforward seduction. Evan being a few years younger than me was an advantage. I fully expected him to be easily beguiled, bedazzled. I mean, I know a trick or two. I imagined him falling in love with me, embarrassing his father. I thought they would row about me. I imagined Evan cutting himself off from his father, at least for as long as he was infatuated with me. I had no idea how long his interest would last. Forever was a stretch; I was hoping for six months to a year. I could create a scandal and bring pain and shame to them all. Especially to Shaun.

However, those were my thoughts before Evan became real. When he was simply a face on various photos at the end of a Google search, a mass of pixels and headlines, a regular on the sidebar of shame, it was easy to imagine making him a pawn in my game. When I met him, something changed. I *liked* him. He made me laugh. I made him laugh. I soon realised that I didn't want to use him or hurt him. Truthfully, it was inconvenient to find I felt this way, but I suppose not unexpected. After all, I had fallen in love with his father; I suppose I should have accounted for an attraction to the younger, kinder son.

As the months went by, Evan and I became closer; our relationship blossomed and deepened while staying platonic. I realised that he brought a warmth to my life that helped me heal a little from the devastating grief that swamped and consumed me. For a time, that became more important to me than seeking revenge on his father. I lost faith in my plan. I didn't see the point any more; it seemed like self-sabotage. I had already lost Dottie and my mum; why risk the only other person I had found to care about? I came to think that I didn't want to risk Shaun finding out about us, as I knew he would inevitably try to prevent us seeing one another. Worse was the thought of Evan finding out about my history with his father and being so disgusted by it that he abandoned me. I decided to keep my head down. I thought maybe I could quietly maintain the friendship without Shaun discovering it. I stopped asking Evan about his family, I refused all invitations to family events, and yeah, I allowed myself to be loved and to love a little once again.

I suppose I could have turned down his proposal. I knew I'd have to if I wanted to hide from Shaun forever. You have to believe me, I really wanted to love Evan more than I hated Shaun, but I couldn't, not quite. The persistent grief and horror, it's always there with me. What happened to my mother and daughter was Shaun's fault, and he had to pay. So I accepted the proposal and waited to see how things might unfurl. I knew there would be trouble, though there were things even I could never have anticipated, consequences I could never have imagined. But honestly? Even if I had foreseen the pain I'd endure, the conclusion for Shaun, bobbing in that dark pool, I think I would still have chosen the same path. I wanted to rattle Shaun's cage, make him feel less secure, less comfortable, less bloody smug. He would have hated living with me as a daughter-in-law. You know, that's about the only reason I regret his death. I'd have liked to watch him squirm.

Everything I have been through was because I put myself in Shaun's path. I guess therefore he'd have maintained it was my own fault, that I asked for everything that came my way. He'd have probably coughed up something trite like, 'If you play with matches, you're going to get burnt.'

And I'd have said back to him, 'Touché.'

I glance over at Evan. He's sipping on a small plastic glass of red wine, provided by the air steward. I can't imagine it's a decent year; I don't suppose he cares. He keeps picking up the laminated safety instruction sheet, even though as a frequent flyer he must know it off by heart; and more pertinently, he must know that you can't ward off disasters anyhow. I reach out and squeeze his arm; he pats my hand. We seem old, weathered, but also solid, or at least bound, substantial. That's enough right now. It's a start. We just need to get through the funeral. And then our wedding. We have our lives ahead of us. We do.

'You OK?' he mouths, for the hundredth time. I nod, also for the hundredth time. It's obvious he doesn't really believe me. 'I've got you,' he murmurs. I'm not certain if he says this to reassure me or to comfort himself.

I love Evan. Finally, I am free to love him unreservedly. There is no hate or revenge clouding my vision, pulling at my heart. I'll be a good wife to him. However, I daren't tell him that truth about me. Not the entire truth. He thinks he knows the worst, since he's seen me kill a man. He doesn't. How can I tell him everything about my history with his father? How can I tell him about Dottie? It's an idealistic view of marriage, isn't it – being one hundred per cent truthful with one another. Idealism, that's the ultimate rich person's privilege. Not the schools with chapels and multiple sports fields, not the jobs that Daddy finds for them, not even the trust funds that afford a deposit on a swanky flat. The ultimate privilege is idealism. That, and optimism. They know it will all work out in the end. Because it does, for them. The rest of us feel foolish thinking there is room in the world for such things; we feel safer doubting and dreading. At least that way we can't be disappointed.

So, the question I'm left with now is: am I finally one of them? Am I a privileged person who dares to optimistically believe that it will indeed all be OK?

When I was sitting by the pool, a gun literally and metaphorically held to my head, I tried to bluff Shaun. I demanded to know why I would have waited all these years to avenge my disastrous love affair. I said it didn't make sense. His vanity meant that he believed I might have held onto a grudge about being dumped for over a decade. But who would do that? Not me, I promise you. Shaun believed I was madly in love with him and had never got over him, never stopped thinking about him. As if! There were months, years when I barely thought of him. But then there was the accident, and I did think of him.

Hatred surged through my body; hatred at the person driving the other car, who got away with a broken leg and some bruises. However, the hate I felt for that driver was fleeting and insignificant compared to the hate I felt towards myself for the choices I'd made. The choices that had ended in a chilly morgue, the two people I loved most in the world gone. Maybe if I'd had someone else to talk to, someone who could have picked through my grief with me, helping me make sense of the different stages – denial, anger, depression and acceptance – things might have been different. As it was, I faltered at anger.

My anger – my fury – grew, swelled to gigantic proportions. I didn't even get to attend their funerals. The authorities couldn't find me, because I had changed my name, something I'd done to hide from Shaun. I had been emailing my dead mother, cross with her for not responding. Then I called her telephone for days, becoming increasingly concerned when I couldn't contact her. Weeks went by; I thought she was avoiding me. I tried to work out what I might have done to annoy her; her silence couldn't be about the flask of green tea at the airport, could it? Eventually, I jumped on a plane. I went to my mother's house and found it up for sale. My lack of ability to speak Serbian meant that making enquiries was confusing and complicated. Initially I thought she'd done a bunk; finally decided I just wasn't fit to be in Dottie's life in any way, shape or form and so run away from me. Eventually, the accident was explained to me. A neighbour had taken charge of the funeral arrangements. I was handed an urn of their combined ashes and a lot of sorrowful looks.

The fury burnt through me with the heat of an incinerator.

When I was a child, my mother used to tell me the story of the Magic Porridge Pot. It was about a poor, hungry woman who needed to feed her family. She wished this so vehemently that her desire came true. She acquired a magic pot that produced porridge continuously. But it got out of control. The porridge overflowed out of the pot, off the table, out of the door, up the street, until it seemed the entire town was in danger of drowning in it. I think it was supposed to be a funny story. My hate was like that. It got out of control. It became overwhelming.

Hate ran through my body, poured out of me in every thought and feeling I had, in the things I said when I bothered to speak to people, which wasn't often; hate pulsed through all my chilly, contained actions. After I lost my mother and Dottie, I had to continue to work, but the role I played with all my clients was a cold, cruel mistress. I didn't accept any clients who expected a chat. I just couldn't find it in me to be pleasant, not even fake pleasant. I was so lonely, brittle, broken. And still the hate kept growing. Self-loathing wasn't enough. The vastness of the regret, pain and sorrow was simply too big to be contained within me. I looked for someone else to hate.

Shaun Beaufoy was the obvious choice; the man who had backed me into a corner was responsible for all the choices I'd had to make. He was ultimately responsible for my losses. I turned all my pain and shone it on him; a nuclear ray – no warmth, just destruction. I really had nothing left other than that damned trait of mine – longing. I simply craved something different then, no longer channelling my ambition into my career or my child. Instead, I had a new goal, a new life aspiration.

I wanted to destroy Shaun Beaufoy. Make him pay. Ruin him.

I wanted to kill him.

I am glad he is dead. I'd kill him all over again if I were given the chance. From the moment he turned up at the chateau, I knew that at best, only one of us was getting out alive.

I'm a winner.

# 51

# *Dora*

It's peculiar meeting my future mother-in-law, Catherine, at a dinner to plan her husband's memorial service, especially when you consider that I was once the dead man's lover and that he cheated on her with me. Of course, she doesn't know this. Evan does, though, which is awkward, but not as awkward as the fact that I killed the man whose memorial we are planning. I find it's best not to dwell. It's a good thing my past career placed me in a number of peculiar situations; ignoring potential embarrassment, latent shame or regret is a transferable skill, it seems. I can drink pre-dinner cocktails, make small talk about the deliciousness of the canapés and discuss flower arrangements for the service without any obvious mortification.

There isn't much of a body to bury, no lungs full of water, no flesh at all. Evan and I did a thorough cover-up. A decent job of being ruthless. That's something. Really, at this stage, it's everything. The memorial service has taken a month to organise. We have spent most of the past four weeks dealing with the administration of death, which in this case goes beyond responding to sympathy letters. Following the initial

356

statements we made to the French authorities, there has been a lot of talk with lawyers, who have dealt with more officials and insurers. However, it seems that Evan was right: everything is going to be OK.

I'm going to get away with murder.

Evan returned to work almost immediately. 'It's what Dad would have wanted,' he said bravely, and no one can argue with that. Least of all me. Shaun's words ring in my head. 'Properly channelled, that focus he's shown might turn towards something worthwhile. If not distracted, he can help build the family company, continue to grow it.'

The memorial is a big affair, with an extensive guest list. Not only is the order of service printed on stiff cream card, but also a seating plan. Initially I was uncertain where I would land on the plan, but Catherine was kind and insisted, 'You're family, darling. Of course you'll sit in the front pew with us.' I guess it's a good thing that Shaun doesn't have a grave; he'd be spinning in it.

Whilst Evan doesn't feel the need to share with his mother my relationship with her husband (thank God), when Catherine enquires what I do for a living, he isn't shy about telling her, 'She was an escort, Mum, until very recently.'

Catherine doesn't miss a beat. 'Did you meet through work?' she asks with a broad, interested smile. I think she'd have asked the same question if he'd said I was a management consultant or a marketing director.

Still, I rush to reassure her with a lie. 'No, just at a regular party.' It's one thing knowing your daughter-in-law is a sex worker; it's another thinking your son might have used those services. 'I'm not in that line of work now,' I add, thinking it might be something else that she'll be relieved to hear. 'Well, not directly. I'm looking to work with a charity that supports victims of modern slavery. Trafficked women, you know?'

I expect her to recoil a little, or perhaps turn an impenetrable cold shoulder my way, but she smiles and nods. 'Well, that sounds admirable. We all have a past, Dora,' she says, patting my hand. 'The lucky ones have a future. I'm just glad that you've been here for Evan at this awful time. He worshipped his father, you know.'

'Yes, I do know.'

She leads me away from Evan towards the drinks cabinet, where she begins to prepare a round of gin and tonics. She adds in a gentle tone, 'Evan seems to be taking his father's death extraordinarily well, especially if you consider the particularly awful circumstances.' She shudders involuntarily. 'I wish I could have saved him from going through that. It must have been horrific. Well, for you both, of course. But for Evan, watching the house burn, his father ...' She trails off; it's too ghastly. I nod. She smiles, a tired but wan smile that suggests she thinks I don't quite understand what she's saying. 'When you are a mother, all you want to do is protect them, you see. Even though he's a grown man. It's silly really.' I nod again. I do understand, but there's nothing I can say. She forces her smile to broaden, and sighs, 'Well, anyway, he's coping far better than I might have expected, and I believe that must be down to you. Welcome to the family, darling.'

And just like that, I have a family again.

A number of important people have had to move key meetings, rearrange travel plans and cancel lunches in the best restaurants in order to attend the memorial service; politicians,

CEOs, dignitaries from overseas, even a distant cousin of the Queen all want to pay their respects. This leads me to believe that the great and the good are either incredibly foolish, and have no idea as to the real nature of Shaun Beaufoy's dealings, or they are also corrupt and therefore dizzy with excitement that their particular secrets are dying with him. I don't know, and I'm not in a place to cast stones. I watch as they file into the cathedral, an endless trail of serious and sombre faces: men in dark suits, black ties; women in hats, and shoes with sensible one-and-a-half-inch heels. I notice that it doesn't take them long after they have settled into their pews to start animatedly chatting among themselves; the solemnity has slipped, replaced by something that looks a lot like cheerful networking. It's a habit of mine; my eyes switch from one face to the next to see if I recognise a client. If I do, will they recognise me?

I'm wearing a black Chanel haute couture dress for Shaun's service; it cost the equivalent of six months' mortgage payments. Evan bought it for me, said it was ideal. My shoes are not at all sensible; the heels are four inches high. My hat is wide-brimmed, people have to duck under it to get close to me. They don't, generally; they keep their distance, and it's the way I like it. I note that Catherine is dressed equally dramatically. Also Chanel, a black suit with gold buttons the size of plates, accessorised with pencil-thin stilettos and red nails; there's even a tiny veil on the brim of her hat. The whole nine yards. She catches me staring at her nails and seems to read my mind. She whispers to me, 'He'd have wanted me to be a glamorous widow. That over a grieving one, possibly.'

'He certainly knew the importance of appearances,' pipes up Catherine's mother. A woman in her eighties; tanned, tiny and taut. Diplomatically, Catherine doesn't respond directly to the comment, which seems barbed, but instead remarks, 'Aren't the lilies glorious, Mum?'

Catherine cries at the service. Or rather, she elegantly sheds a few tears, which she catches in an immaculate lace-trimmed white cotton handkerchief. Evan's sister, Harriet, sobs hysterically. She's a dangerously thin young woman and I think she is going to collapse under the weight of her grief. She clings to Evan, who behaves stoically; everyone comments on it.

Following the memorial service, a select one hundred guests have been invited to a private reception at Claridge's. And it is there, amongst the gentle tinkling of teaspoons against fine bone-china teacups and the low hum of posh voices commenting on the decent wine, that I finally manage to get some alone time with Evan. 'How are you doing?' I ask.

'I'm just glad to get it over with.'

'Of course.'

'All those readings, the affirmations of his greatness.' He shakes his head with disbelief; maybe something as strong as disgust. 'He tortured you,' he snaps angrily. I glance around warily. This isn't the place to discuss it.

'It was his memorial service,' I point out.

'So no one could stand up and say that he was trying to murder you.'

'Exactly, and it would hardly be the wisest point for *us* to make.' I squeeze his arm and look him in the eye, silently pleading for him to let it go. He nods, tightly, understanding me, and takes a swig of whisky. I realise it's pointless suggesting tea.

'Do you want to leave?' I offer. 'We've done our bit, spoken to a lot of people.'

'Can we just slip away?'

'Yes, of course. It's overwhelming here. You go and hail a cab. I'll just find your mother, tell her we're taking off. I'll meet you outside.'

I spot Catherine talking to a group of men and women around her own age. I gather they are friends rather than business associates when I notice that a woman in the group is openly weeping. I feel a flare of frustration on Catherine's behalf. This woman ought to keep a check on her grief; it isn't fair to expect Catherine to absorb that on top of her own. I'm unsurprised that I feel a wave of protectiveness towards Evan's mother. Over these past few weeks, she's shown me personally only kindness and exhibited generally nothing other than grace. I've grown to care for her. I've also noted that she has a commendable honed astuteness that I've come to admire. Funny, because years ago, when I thought of her as nothing other than Shaun's wife, I assumed she had to be a bit pathetic or dull-witted at worst; long-suffering and passive at best. She is none of those things. She appears to be the sort of woman who knows what's what. I wonder how she endured being married to Shaun all those years. I can only assume he was incredibly cunning and deceitful around her; she can't have been aware of any of his reprehensible practices. She just isn't the type to accept immoral and illegal goings-on. I guess it's possible to be astute and trusting at the same time.

As I approach the group, I hear what the weeping woman is saying. I gasp at her insensitivity, her selfish blunder. 'I just can't stop thinking about the pain he must have felt at the end. I mean, burning to death, that's the worst, isn't it. That's my nightmare.' Her eyes are red raw and swollen. I briefly wonder if she slept with Shaun. When she was younger, maybe; I can't imagine him entertaining a mistress his own age once he hit forty. I haven't got time to think through my theory, as my attention is on Catherine. How is she going to react to this woman's horrible, tactless comment?

She impresses me by remaining calm. 'Yes, it is shocking.' She shakes her head and adds, 'The surprising thing is, I always thought it would be water that got him, not fire.'

I freeze. 'Water, why?' asks the husband of the weeping woman.

'Because he couldn't swim.'

It's as though everything in the room has suddenly been dimmed and turned to mute. Catherine's words, by contrast, pound in my head and chest.

'Couldn't he?' The man looks surprised, possibly even a little contemptuous. Men like these are extremely competitive with one another, even after death. 'I thought he was quite the action man. Always had him down as such.' Evan thought Shaun could swim too. His father had obviously lied to him about his abilities. Some sort of macho posturing? Bemused, the man continues to bluster. 'I thought everybody could swim nowadays.' I don't know why he's going on about it. It's hardly relevant to any of the mourners at the service, or to Catherine, whether Shaun could or could not swim.

But it is relevant to me.

There is a gap in the conversation and I find myself filling it. 'Not everybody can swim. I can't,' I volunteer. 'And nor can Evan,' I add.

'Oh no, Dora, you've got that wrong,' says Catherine, turning to me with a patient smile. 'Evan is a brilliant swimmer. He

362

swam for his school and at national competitions. The library is stuffed to the rafters with his trophies. Are you all right, darling? You look very pale.'

'Oh, I just came to tell you that Evan is taking me home. I shouldn't have worn these shoes. I need to take them off. I need to lie down, actually.'

'Of course.' She bobs under the brim of my hat and kisses my cheek. 'Let's catch up tomorrow, Darling.'

I turn away from the group and head swiftly towards the large wood-panelled doors. I need to get out of the room. It's cloying, suffocating. I need fresh air. As I move away, I over-hear Catherine saying to the group, 'I wouldn't be surprised if those lovebirds make an announcement soon. Ever since I met Dora, I haven't been able to put my finger on it, but she seems a little off, you know. Lethargic, peaky. And then it dawned on me!' She laughs. 'I think I might be about to be made a grandmother.' The group break into a round of positive, approving murmurs. 'You know, it would be a blessing. There's nothing like a birth to help ease grief.'

# 52

# *Dora*

Outside, it is raining. It has been a poor June, the sunshine
unreliable, the showers ferocious. The pavements are always
dark with puddles; people keep dressing incorrectly and ending
up looking cold and irritated. Evan has successfully hailed a cab
and is waiting with the door open, his suit collar turned up in
an attempt to stop rain trickling down his back. Despite the
rain, and the fact that the meter is running, there's no sense of
impatience emanating from him. When he claps eyes on me,
his face seems to relax; it lights up.

*I* light him up. I breathe in that fact. I own it.

I had thought that Evan was unable to help his father and
had decided to protect me from the consequences of Shaun's
death. Now I see that his love runs deeper, it is more ferocious
and extreme.

He didn't simply protect me from the consequences of his
father's death.

He protected me from his father.

'All OK?' he asks. His voice is slightly creased with the

telltale signs of stress that only those remarkably close to him might detect. I wonder when, or if, the stress will ever fade.

'Yes.' I force myself to smile, a broad ear-to-ear smile, as this man deserves. This man, who will do anything for me. Who *has* done everything for me. I am valued beyond my wildest hopes.

'What did my mum say about us leaving early?'

'She thinks I'm pregnant.'

His eyes widen; panic and excitement flood through him and shine out of him. 'Are you?'

'No, thank God. Imagine if I were. It might be Jonathan's, or Giles's.' His face collapses, remembering. I don't want him to linger there. Evan and I, well, we're imperfect. Obviously. We are intense and damaged, we have done terrible things and we are not being honest with one another, not completely. And we possibly – probably – never will be. The reality is, I can't tell him I had a daughter who died. He can't tell me he let his father die. It's too much to lay on each other. The guilt I feel about Dottie is all-pervasive; can a parent ever forgive herself for letting go of her child? A child who then was lost completely? Often, I am sitting in a chair, at a table or my dressing table, and I feel her slip down my body as she did in the launderette all those years ago. The imprint of that moment, carved into my heart, replays constantly as though it happened yesterday, and every day since. Then I gave her away to someone whose grip was even weaker. And although I didn't know it was going to be so, my daughter died as a result. I didn't keep her safe. Can I ever forgive myself for that? Would Evan be able to?

He thinks I'm better than I am. And maybe, just maybe, because he thinks it, I can be. Now, and in the future. Because despite our vulnerabilities, our mistakes, our faults and failures, this feels right. Isn't everyone entitled to a second chance? What did Catherine say to me? Everyone has a past; the lucky ones have a future. I was supposed to be Dottie's harbour; I swore I would be. Always. But I wasn't. I failed. I would give anything in the world for her to be alive, but there's nothing I can trade to get that wish. So I have to forgive myself. I owe that to the man who traded his father for me.

I look up at Evan, doused in rain, and I want to make him happy. I want to be happy too. 'Although there's nothing to stop us from trying now,' I add, carefully. 'Your mother thinks a birth eases grief.'

'And what do you think?' I can hear the hope in his voice. He's trying to suppress it. He doesn't want to pressurise me.

Something seeps through my body. I take a moment to identify it. For years I've been taut with ambition, fear, shame, grief, revenge. An insidiousness of some form or other has been a persistent presence for so long. Now I feel my shoulders move away from my ears, my stomach unknot. I feel a sense of calm flood through my veins. Peace.

I trust him, completely. I'm not sure I've ever trusted anyone completely before.

'I'd like it. I'm ready,' I tell him with a shy grin. 'Let's go home and make babies.'

'What are we waiting for then? Get in the cab.'

If he could have told the cabbie not to spare the horses, I think he would have.

# EPILOGUE

# *Andjela*

Andjela walks into the kitchen and breathes in deeply. It smells sweet; the scent of the birthday cake that she made this morning is still lingering. It fills her lungs and her heart, working in much the same way as relaxing aromatherapy diffusers work on yogis. Lifting her, stretching her, filling her with a sense of well-being. The kitchen is light, airy, one of her favourite places in the house. Probably in the world, since her home is her world. Andjela doesn't crave travel or novelty; she never has. She is what is generally described as a home bird, happiest with a fridge full of good food, a sideboard heaving with photos of joyful occasions, and an overflowing toy cupboard, which whilst barely opened nowadays – because her daughter prefers consoles and skateboards – was once often visited. She always bakes a cake on her daughter's birthday. They ice it together and eat it while it's still warm, with large glasses of milk.

This idyllic scenario was one Andjela imagined a hundred times before she became a mother. She also imagined building sandcastles on the beach, eating picnics on a blanket under a tree in the park, reading bedtime stories, and her daughter declaring 'I love you' as she dropped into her lap and demanded cuddles. All these scenarios have played out, many times. However, Andjela did not imagine the moments when her daughter would refuse to eat, spat food out on the floor, woke screaming from nightmares, slammed doors, yelled 'I hate you'; scenarios that have also occurred with regularity too. All part of parenting, just perhaps not the part they advertise.

Today's birthday celebration was a mixed bag. Dottie loved her presents: Apple earbuds, two new tops and some jeans from Zara. She said thank you, unprompted and with huge and obvious excitement. The cake was also a success, light, fluffy, tasty. Plus, they honed the plans for Saturday's sleepover, when Dottie will have five friends coming over; they will watch a movie and giggle to the early hours. Andjela has agreed on popcorn and painting toenails but vetoed full makeovers. However, birthdays are always charged with emotions and expectations – all high, some unrealistic. Birthdays of adoptive children have an extra layer of complexity because questions arise into everyone's consciousness that on other occasions are perhaps left dormant.

Dottie is now upstairs playing on her PlayStation, a rare midweek treat because it's her special day. Dušan is sitting at the breakfast bar, reading the morning paper, even though it is now 7 p.m. Andjela often wonders why he bothers; by the time he finds time to read the paper, the news is old. She sometimes suggests he watches the news on TV instead, but Dušan maintains that if he reads a paper and curates the news himself, he is better able to discern what is really going on in the world, rather than just receiving what they decide to feed you, what they want you to believe. Andjela admires her husband's independent thinking, although she wonders how it sits alongside his intractability about the level of opacity he advocates with Dottie.

'Dottie asked about her birth family again today,' she announces without preamble. Dušan lowers his newspaper, looks over his reading glasses. This gesture makes him look older than forty-two. Or maybe it is the mention of Dottie's birth mother that makes him look older; weary, defensive.

'Did she?'

'Yes.'

'Well, it's her birthday, it makes her curious.'

'Yes, and she will become increasingly so.'

'Not necessarily. Tomorrow she will forget about it again.'

Andjela feels the chill wind of his uncharacteristic coldness. Dušan is at heart a kind, sympathetic, open man, except when it comes to Dottie's birth mother. A subject that scares him, that he can't process. 'I don't think so,' she comments gently. 'We should tell her what we know.'

Dušan sighs, takes off his glasses and rubs his eyes with the heels of his hands. 'Do you want a glass of wine?' Without waiting for a response, he moves towards the fridge, retrieves the bottle of rosé they opened the night before and starts to pour it into a couple of elegant glasses.

Andjela waits until they have gently knocked their glasses together. 'Cheers.' She knows Dušan will return to the topic rather than ignore it, because he respects her enough to address all her concerns. Throughout their seventeen years of marriage – punctuated with fertility tests, rounds of failed IVF, and interviews at adoption agencies – they have had their share of difficult conversations.

'What good will that do? We've already told her everything about the woman who was her mother before us. A woman who died tragically. That was a lot for a child to take in. Does it need to get any more complex?'

'Yes, but Radmila was an adoptive mother, like I am. It's not fair allowing Dottie to believe she was her real mother. Dottie should know about her birth mother, and her birth father too. Today she asked if he was alive when she was born. She asked how Radmila had her so late in life. I think she has guessed we are not telling her everything we know. These questions are getting complicated.'

'Poor Radmila,' says Dušan with a sympathetic sigh. 'After her husband's death, she must have adopted Dottie thinking she had a whole new lease of life in front of her. Only to find out a few years later that she had breast cancer.'

Andjela and Dušan both know this is a tragedy, but they also know that if the tragedy hadn't happened, they wouldn't have Dottie, their longed-for child, their much-loved daughter. It is impossible to articulate such a thing. Too passionate, dangerous and truthful, too selfish and unfair. The closest they can ever go to expressing the fact that Radmila's tragedy was their blessing is Andjela carefully commenting, 'Still, at least the diagnosis gave her time to prepare the adoption. Imagine if she'd died in that car crash without the paperwork being under way; we might not have got Dottie.'

'Dottie might not have had anyone. She might have ended up going into the care system and becoming just another statistic,' adds Dušan, shaking his head, saddened by the thought. 'All I can think is thank God Dottie wasn't in the car with Radmila when the crash happened.'

Andjela shivers. That is too much. Horrendous. 'Oh Dušan, shut up. Don't even say it. It's unbearable to think about.'

'Exactly my point. Dottie's early life was very traumatic. She's had a lot to process already. Why do you want to rake up even more drama?'

'I don't, not really,' Andjela admits.

'What can we tell her about her birth mother that is at all helpful anyway? We don't have a name or contact details. All we know is that she was a teenage prostitute.' Andjela winces. She doesn't like thinking about the profession of her sweet daughter's birth mother. 'That's why Radmila's notes said that when she died, under no circumstances must the birth mother be considered as a suitable mother for Dottie, even if she did stake a claim. Which, notably, she did not.' Dušan pauses, and then adds, 'Maybe she is dead herself.'

Andjela gasps. 'Why would you say that?'

'Oh, I don't know. Someone in her line of work. Drugs or violence might have got her.' He shrugs. He's not a callous man, but he finds that he is always defensive when this matter is brought to the table. 'If she is alive, she most likely thinks of her teen pregnancy as nothing but a mistake. If she thinks of it at all. She's probably put the whole matter right out of her mind. I can't imagine her giving her baby a second thought after she gave her up.'

'I don't think it will have been that simple.' Andjela sometimes hates the careless birth mother for giving up her baby; she must indeed be a monster. Other times, she loves the teenager almost as much as she loves Dottie, for the exact same act. It is confusing.

'Dottie already grieves for Radmila; why tell her about

a birth mother who didn't want her? It just gives her another dollop of pain.' Dušan has repeated this argument over and over. He has no intention of wavering. 'And we would have to tell her that we have lied to her up until now by letting her believe Radmila is her birth mother.'

'Well, only for her own good, to protect her.'

'If you believe that, why would you change your mind now? There's no room for inconsistency with parenting.'

Andjela sips her wine. It's dry and fruity. She can feel it taking effect already, and her belief that they ought to tell Dottie the truth about her birth mother begins to recede a little. Dušan is right, why introduce a problem? 'Do you remember when she first arrived with us, and she talked about having a big sister? What if she ever turned up out of the blue?'

'But the authorities said Dottie was mistaken. Radmila's notes didn't mention a sister. No one is going to turn up out of the blue.' Dušan tries to remain patient, but he wishes his wife wouldn't do this. She has a tendency towards catastrophising. He supposes it's the years of disappointments. 'Dottie must have got confused. She was only six years old. Let's just have a lovely evening, should we? It's her birthday. A day of celebration. Why rake over old ground? Let sleeping dogs lie, I say. We're her parents, Andjela, and we're a happy family. That's enough, isn't it? That's everything.'

The conversation is brought to a close at that moment, because Dottie suddenly bursts into the kitchen. She's rosy-cheeked and excited. She starts to prattle the news that she's just received an email from school confirming that she's been picked for the netball A squad, and she will play this Saturday. Excited, she asks for another slice of cake; she wonders if her mum has time to style her hair into a French plait; she hugs both her parents, skipping between them with easy confidence. Andjela cuts a generous slice of cake and tells her to go and find a hairbrush. Dušan puts on some music; he selects Dottie's favourite playlist and dares to nod his head, shake his hips a little. Dottie squeals and declares he's embarrassing, 'Don't do that on Saturday when my friends are here!' she says, laughing hard so that her thin body shakes with the fun of the thought. The room hums with the very real sense that Dušan is absolutely right: they are indeed every inch a happy family.

# Acknowledgements

So, if you read my novels regularly you will know that my thank yous and acknowledgements have a tendency to be a bit long-winded! Fair to say, if I were collecting an Oscar, they would be playing music and bustling me off the stage. However, bear with because I do think it's really important to say thank you in life.

I want to start with saying thank you to Kate Mills, my utterly fabulous editor and publisher. Kate, you are a joy to work with. You are always so positive and proactive; you combine tenacity and creativity. I am incredibly fortunate to have you. The same goes for Lisa Milton. How wonderful to have such a force for good at the top and centre of HQ. It is a total pleasure working with you both and it has been from the get-go.

Thank you, Charlie Redmayne, for being such an engaged, motivating and, frankly, brilliant fun CEO.

I'm so delighted to be working with an incredible team. I am thoroughly grateful for, and appreciative of, the talent and commitment of every single person involved in this book's existence.

I know you all work with passion, perception and professionalism. Thank you all very much, Anna Derkacz, George Green, Harriet Williams, Angela Thomson, Sophie Calder, Joe Thomas, Joanna Rose, Vicki Watson, Rebecca Jamieson, Becca Joyce, Rebecca Fortuin, Darren Shoffren, Kelly Webster, Angie Dobbs, Halema Begum, Sophie Waeland, Agnes Rigou, Aisling Smyth, Emily Yolland, Kate Oakley, Anna Sikorska and Laura Meyer.

Thank you to my agents Jonny Geller, Viola Hayden, Ciara Finan and all the team at Curtis Brown for your continued support. I know you are always cheering for me and have been doing so for over twenty years, which is so wonderful.

I want to send massive thanks across the seas to the brilliant teams who publish my books worldwide. You really are making my dreams come true. Thank you, Sue Brockhoff, Adam Van Rooijen, Natika Palka, Loriana Sacilotto, Margaret Marbury, Nicole Brebner, Leo McDonald, Lia Ferrone, Rebecca Silver, Carina Nunstedt, Celine Hamilton, Pauline Riccius, Anna Hoffmann, Eugene Ashton, Olinka Nell and Rahul Dixit. There are many other publishing teams, who I have yet to meet, but I am so grateful that incredible professionals across the globe are giving my books their love and attention. It's so ridiculously exciting. Thank you.

Thank you to all my readers, bloggers, reviewers, retailers, librarians and fellow authors, who have supported me throughout my career. You will see at the front of my novel that I have dedicated this particular book to my readers, because without readers, where would I be?

Thank you to my mum, dad, sister, nieces, nephew and other family and friends, who are always so supportive and proud.

Finally, but I think most importantly ... save the best for

last ... thank you to Jimmy and Conrad. Obviously, I'm not the most conventional wife and mother on Earth. I realise you are both constantly accommodating that fact. I hope you know I'm devoted and adore you both. I hope we can agree that living with my peculiarities, passions and penchant for saying literally every thought that ever enters my head aloud is, on balance, worthwhile! I love you both.

ONE PLACE. MANY STORIES

Bold, innovative and
empowering publishing.

FOLLOW US ON:

@HQStories

# ONE LAST SECRET

## ADELE PARKS

ONE PLACE. MANY STORIES

HQ
An imprint of HarperCollins*Publishers* Ltd
1 London Bridge Street
London SE1 9GF

www.harpercollins.co.uk

HarperCollins*Publishers*
1st Floor, Watermarque Building, Ringsend Road
Dublin 4, Ireland

This edition 2022

1

First published in Great Britain by
HQ, an imprint of HarperCollins*Publishers* Ltd 2022

Copyright © Adele Parks 2022

Adele Parks asserts the moral right to be
identified as the author of this work.
A catalogue record for this book is
available from the British Library.

ISBN:
HB: 9780008395636
TPB: 9780008395643

**MIX**
Paper from
responsible sources
**FSC™ C007454**